BABY JESUS PAWN SHOP

LUCIA ORTH

BABY JESUS
PAWN SHOP

Fic
Orth, L.

THE PERMANENT PRESS
Sag Harbor, NY 11963

Credits

The quotation from F. Sionil José's book, *The Pretenders*, is used with the kind permission of F. Sionil (Frankie) José, Solidaridad Publishing House, Manila, Philippines, Copyright 1962, Sixth edition, 1987.

For information, address:
　The Permanent Press
　4170 Noyac Road
　Sag Harbor, NY 11963
　www.thepermanentpress.com

Library of Congress Cataloging-in-Publication Data

　Orth, Lucia
　　Baby Jesus pawnshop / Lucia Orth.
　　　p. cm.
　　ISBN-13: 978-1-57962-170-4 (hardcover : alk. paper)
　　ISBN-10: 1-57962-170-8 (hardcover : alk. paper)
　　　1. Americans—Philippines—Fiction. 2. Dissenters—
　　Philippines—Fiction. 3. Insurgency—Philippines—Fiction.
　　4. Philippines—History—1946–1986—Fiction. 5. Manila
　　(Philippines)—Fiction. 6. Political fiction. I. Title. II. Title: Baby
　　Jesus pawn shop.

　PS3615.R78B33 2008
　813'.6—dc22　　　　　　　　　　　　　　2008012283

Printed in the United States of America.

Author's Note

For certain information essential to this story, my thanks to Maria Paz Ramos Paano. Also I express my gratitude to Fred and Machrina Mesch for their friendship and hospitality in Manila, and special thanks to Machrina's mother, for her afternoons of stories. There are so many others to thank in Manila, but I wish to make special mention of my colleagues at In Touch Foundation, my students at De La Salle University, and Frankie José, who, when I spoke to him at his bookstore regarding writing about the characters in this book, said, "Stay for lunch."

To Judy Bauer, Laura Moriarty, Mary O'Connell, and Mary Wharff—thank you for the great times we have, sharing our work with each other.

For other essential support I am so grateful to Marla Adkins-Heljeson and Rebecca Curtis. Most special thanks go also to Stephanie Von Hirschberg, and Martin and Judith Shepard, who made this book possible.

Finally, I thank my husband, John, for his constant encouragement in my work and his mutual sense of adventure as we travel.

Acknowledgments

Works Consulted

Although I lived in Manila for many years, I relied for some points of historical information on Stanley Karnow's excellent book, *In Our Image, America's Empire In The Philippines* (Ballantine Books, 1990, first published by Random House, 1989).

Other books consulted include *The Marcos Dynasty*, by Sterling Seagrave (Harper & Row, 1988); *Revolution in the Philippines*, by Fred Poole and Max Vanzi (McGraw-Hill, 1984); *People Power*, edited by Monina Allarey Mercado (James B. Reuter, S.J. Foundation, Manila, Philippines, 1986); and *Some Are Smarter Than Others, The History of Marcos' Crony Capitalism*, Ricardo Manapat (Aletheia Publications, N.Y., 1991).

For information on hybrid rice and stem borers, I consulted two very helpful books: *Field Problems of Tropical Rice*, a field manual (International Rice Research Institute, Laguna, Philippines, 1983); and *World Bibliography of Rice Stem Borers, 1794-1990*, by Z.R. Khan, J.A. Litsinger, A.T. Barrion, F.F.D. Villanueva, N.J. Fernandez, and L.D. Taylo (International Rice Research Institute, 1991).

For the meditations and discussions on theology, I turned to works by William Sloane Coffin, especially *Credo* (Westminster John Knox Press, 2004), and the many books by Walter Wink.

The Bayan Ko

This song was written in 1928 and was originally a nationalistic protest against American colonialism. In the 1960's, it became a symbol of the radical student movement. The song was banned at the beginning of martial law in 1972. I first heard the song after Benigno Aquino was assassinated in August of 1983.

The original Tagalog lyrics are by José Corazon de Jesus, and melody by Constancio de Guzman.

CONTENTS

We all want to forget something, and so we create stories.

— AKIRO KUROSAWA

Forgetting: absolute solace and absolute injustice.

— MILAN KUNDERA

PROLOGUE

The carabao are known for their gentleness, especially with children. They are docile, long-suffering, although they will strike back if provoked. Doming's animal would kneel to let his sisters climb on its back, and on fiesta days they would decorate its flat broad head and wide horns with sampagita flowers and shiny paper and lead it carefully by a halter, making wide turns to avoid its hooves. The infinitely patient beast would seem to stare at them with those all-knowing orbs and sigh. But then one night their priest, Father Rex, an Irish Jesuit, came to their house and warned the family that the military were in their barrio looking for labor organizers, and urged Doming's father to hide.

So his father hid in the grove where their old carabao pastured at night. Doming's mother heard the creature's bellows a few hours later. The soldiers first put out the creature's eyes. Then they put the man under the beast so that in its mad trampling it crushed him. He lived one more day. That was the end of the family's only time of happiness.

Father Rex was taken the same night. By special order from Manila he was transferred to the north, to Ilocos Norte, Marcos country. There were no strikes in Ilocos, no labor organizing.

Doming was the other one they hunted, but because he was preparing for an exam so that he could enter the seminary at Dumaguete City, he was not at home that night. He was instead at the mission and the military, although they were looking, did not find him. They wanted him because he'd also worked with Father Rex, organizing the sugar laborers to ask for better pay. President Marcos had declared labor organizing illegal in the sugar industries.

That night at the mission, unaware of disaster, Doming studied. He had one candle left, which he put into a coconut shell. There was a wind, a moaning in the trees, that more than once blew out the candle. Later he'd realized it was the sound of death coming. But he paid no attention. He studied all night, telling himself, just a few more weeks and you will be free of this place. When he came home in the morning, his mother looked at him as if he'd come back from the grave, and prayed thanks to Father Rex's god and her Tiboli gods on whom she still relied. They had no money for a funeral and no priest now. There would be no money unless he provided it.

Two days later he butchered the carabao to put it out of its dark misery. The tormented wandering beast was good to no one except for its meat. It would never pull or haul or follow a furrow again. He could sense its self-control, even as it stood yielding. It could read his thoughts. He sharpened a long-handled knife on a turning stone, and then he spoke soft words in the giant ear, not looking at the gouged-out eyes. He reached for the folds of throat and felt the one that pounded like his own heart and plunged the curved blade in, turning his hand to open the ancient channel of blood and sinew and heavy chest. The animal dropped to one knee, then the other. A sound like a promise of a river came from it and a low as if confiding to Doming some secret knowledge. Perhaps the carabao dreamed of untasted fields, newly green each morning. One giant horn settled sideways on the ground, the broad head sloping, and its haunches fell and shuddered like a tremor passing under the earth.

Doming's widowed mother sold most of the carcass and gave Doming the money for a ferry ticket to Manila. He would not eat its stewed meat, although his mother urged, but his younger brother and sisters ate with solid hungry hearts their livelihood, their companion.

This was the first time he craved revenge, and it tasted in his mouth like bitter bread with too much yeast. To avenge his father's death, the torture of man and beast, he burned a cane field before he fled. This would not seem like such a terrible thing, such a simple act by a peasant, but after martial law, Marcos had declared such actions by the opposition or rebelling laborers to be a subversive act, and hence, a crime against the state. It was the purposely contemptuous, youthful act of one who was unyielding, unafraid.

The field burned greedily. The flames sounded to him like a thousand hands clapping. The burned raw cane smelled like *leche flan*. Grasshoppers and birds flew up. Lizards crawled out dragging their bellies.

Everyone knew who'd done it. Now he had two offenses.

He fled to Manila. He took the ferry. Even its name held promise, *La Suerte Galera*, The Sweet Line. He would find work, send money for their support.

On the ferry an older but well-dressed woman had touched his sex, and despite himself he'd responded, too surprised by her urgency. By the time the ferry arrived, he was still seventeen but no longer a virgin, several times no longer. He pulled out of her, but she held his hips to her. That's past me now, she said.

He couldn't remember her face, but he still carried the address she gave him.

A few days after he arrived in the city he noticed a blind carabao in Quiapo market, going round and round, turning a stone to power some machine, and he said to him, *Brother.*

The animal was tormented by horseflies and the unrelenting sun. A carabao was not like an ox, it was a water buffalo. It could handle the paddies or fields all day and its massive hooves would not rot, but don't ask the thing to tread upon city streets in the blasting sun, to labor in circles.

Part I
The Cockfight

Manila, Early June, 1982

In the early morning market newly caught milkfish swam circles in a tub. On one counter a majestic lapu-lapu fish, the size of a small child, lay on ice with its gills flaring. A fish vendor scooped up a live catfish from another tub and knocked it in the head with the handle of her cleaver, just hard enough to stun it. Rue's desire to buy anything vanished.

"Always have them do it this way for you, so it will stay fresh longer," Baby Varcegno said to Rue. Baby, Rue's landlord, opened the white umbrella she always carried. The vendor and Baby gossiped. The woman fingered the amulets she wore on her wrist and around her neck as they spoke. Her teeth were stained red from betel juice. She pointed out which stall had the fresh asparagus from the cool mountains of Baguio, and which sold the swordfish caught only this morning. She was Baby's *suki*, her personal vendor.

"I'm one of her most important customers," Baby explained to Rue. "You come to her, and she'll make you a good deal. I've told her if the police ever bother her again, asking for more bribes, she should mention Raymonde's name, because he has connections."

Baby's earrings flashed. She claimed she didn't wear her best rings and jewelry here in Baclaran Market. You can get better prices if they see you're not full of *palabas*, showiness, she told Rue. Baby's light skin and dimples and a smile that curved her lips impishly made her name fitting. She was in her mid-forties, about ten years older than Rue.

It was Baclaran Market Day. Each Wednesday this parish celebrated mass and market, and drew farmers from the south. The streets and alleys around the Redemptorist Church filled with vendors. Although it was early morning, the sun was piercing at this time of year. The wooden stalls around the churchyard, overhung with yellow canvas, offered the market's only shade.

This was the market. *Lechon*, whole roasted pigs with rust-colored shiny skin stretched tight, mouths open with teeth showing, eyes half-closed as if squinting, savory-smelling strips cut away. Frantic live chickens and others just butchered, wild birds smuggled from Indonesia or Papua New Guinea, mynah birds from the cathedral in the town of Taal, trained parrots that spoke with an Australian accent, rare orchids illegally harvested from the island of Palawan, whole stalls with rosaries, potions, holy water, rainbow-colored miracle oils in vials, Santo Niños set out like garrisons—hundreds of newly made Baby Jesus statues in a row, life-sized down to creche-sized, one group wearing swaddling clothes, another the shorts and straw hat of a fisherman, another the woven loincloth of ethnic northern tribes, others wearing royal blue felt robes and gold paper crowns. But all the figures stared out at her from an identical placid face, eyes benign, light blue, and framed with horsehair lashes.

Each Santo Niño repeated what seemed to Rue an empty-handed gesture. She'd seen mothers make this same gesture of upturned empty hands to their children, *Walána*, no more, or a shopkeeper in the market, turning his hands out, would say, *Walána*, out of stock, Ma'am.

"*Trepang, trepang,*" a vendor said to her, pointing to his sea-cucumbers. She had learned early on that she could easily pass for Filipina, for the tall, finer boned, luminous skinned mestiza, on the streets and in the markets. Especially

18

when she wore sunglasses like here in the market, the vendors would automatically speak to her in Tagalog, but when she answered back more hesitantly, they would double their prices in English. Somehow she didn't mind.

It's the price we pay for being here, some of the other foreign women said; we're constantly cheated, they complained to each other.

I cannot let you be cheated, Baby, her Filipina landlord, had said to her when she insisted on this outing. I will make sure you are getting the best bargains, Baby said.

A beggar without forearms sat on a piece of cardboard on the hot pavement. He held a cup wedged under his arm and gestured at Rue with wild eyes. He had running sores on the stumps.

"They do that—gouge them out regularly to keep them fresh, just to provoke sympathy," Baby warned.

Rue reached into the pocket of her light skirt and dropped a few coins into his cup.

"You shouldn't encourage them," Baby said. But nonetheless, she also gave the man coins and said, "Patawarin pô" to him. *Forgive me.* Rue knew the words, the traditional response to beggars. Forgive us, all the rich.

Baby began her haggling for orchids she would bind with wire onto the trunks of new papaya trees in her garden.

Rue walked on toward the church. Just outside its iron gates, women sold necklaces made of sampagita flowers. They crowded each other, pushing forward. A few had gone there to sell and had some success, but now there were too many and none of them could make enough money.

The sampagita necklaces were made by threading the waxy greenish-white flowers, the size and shape of honeybees, into intricately knotted designs. Twenty women beckoned her. They wore their wares around their necks, held bunches in their hands, and hung more from their wrists and fore-arms. They called in sing-song high-pitched voices.

A lush fragrance rose from the hundreds of necklaces.

"How much?" Rue said to a girl.

But the girl shrugged. Their way of not saying, to get an offer.

"*Magkano?*" Rue insisted then. How much. She knew the Tagalog words for marketing.

The girl said, in English, "It's up to you, Ma'am."

But when Rue took a five-peso note from her pocket, the standard price, the girl begged, "Ten, Ma'am, ten please."

Then other sampagita vendors came nearer, like magpies fighting over the same crust. Eight, eight pesos only, Ma'am. Two for fourteen pesos only, one of the young girls called, pushed forward by her mother. Rue gave the ten-peso note to the first girl. She put the necklace over her head and felt the coolness on the back of her neck, jasmined with its perfume.

She passed through the open iron gates and into the church yard where massive acacia trees spread their shade. Along the portico of the old church, a thin woman held a tiny dull-eyed baby in one arm. The woman squatted on the grayed marble, under the open archway that led inside, holding a charred tin can. When Rue neared her, the woman jangled the can's few coins and placed the can directly in her path. They regarded each other.

Rue's first thought was that this woman was too old for the child to be hers, but as she watched the woman drew out her breast from her blouse and offered a puckered nipple to the infant. Her breast was flat and withered. The child fussed and nuzzled, but refused to take the nipple in its mouth.

"The baby is for sale, Ma'am."

She turned to the girlish voice behind her. She felt her heart trip. Had someone read her thoughts?

"Who are you?" she asked a thin girl who might be in her teens.

"I am the eldest and there are too many of us, Ma'am. She is my mother's ninth child, and the littlest one is not yet two years," the girl continued in school English.

Her words sounded well-rehearsed. The girl glanced around, she seemed about to bolt. The old woman was too businesslike—nodding and pulling back a blanket to show the child's tiny feet, its clenched but unblemished ashen legs—a vendor showing her sea-cucumbers.

"And look, Ma'am, she is very white, like you," the girl said.

The child looked the unhealthy color of raw gray dough.

"How much? *Magkano?*" Rue asked.

"Thirteen hundred pesos, only, Ma'am," said the girl, her eyes narrowing, as if she were afraid Rue would try to bargain. The woman ignored them now, straightened the baby's clothes.

Less than ninety dollars.

"This is your own child, isn't it," Rue said, lowering her voice. She saw the girl's heavy breasts under the loose-fitting housedress.

The girl glanced at the woman on the portico nearby.

Her mother? More likely her handler. Girls fled to Manila from the provinces and couldn't find jobs. The housemaids were the lucky ones.

"I need money to take care of her medicine, and they won't advance it, Ma'am," she said. "A few pesos to spare? Ma'am, if I don't have money she might die, I'd rather give her away."

Another beggar's ploy? Should she be so foolish, so trusting? It must be another scam. Baby had warned her— beggars will say anything to make their quota. A woman with the syndicate will rent a baby to carry in the rush-hour streets and, not being the mother, will shrewdly pinch the child to make it wail more pitifully while she stands with her tin can tapping at a car's dark windows.

So, say she paid this girl, and then she could take the infant anywhere else, to a hospital, or to the orphanage in Makati that Baby had mentioned.

"Maria Fe, *tena*," the old woman commanded, scooping her hand under in the digging motion that meant *Come here*.

"Please, Ma'am."

So Rue made her choice, and took from her skirt pocket a fifty-peso note. A little more than two dollars. The hard-eyed girl snatched it.

"I'll get the rest, I have more in my car," Rue said. "Just wait here for me, *sige*? Wait. Do you understand? I can do something for you." She hurried. Once she looked back, and the girl was still watching her.

She reached the car, which was parked along Roxas Boulevard near the fish market, about a block away. Baby was nowhere in sight. The car doors were unlocked, bags unguarded. Where was Doming, her husband's usual driver?— his job was to stay with the car, this was the driver's duty when in the markets.

She denied the absurdity of what she was doing. Who would want another sick child here? A beggar nearby pleaded, Ma'am, Ma'am. An old woman who'd spotted her came and stood next to the car. She was holding a wooden box of boiled peanuts and watermelon seeds, and offering the ever present sweepstakes tickets, urging her, "Take a chance, Ma'am, today is your lucky day."

And why not—act, live.

But she'd never heard of a winner.

So she hesitated. This would be a mistake from start to finish, her logical side muttered. But with ninety dollars, fifty even, she could change a child's fate, perhaps. There are only a million more like this one, Trace, her husband, would say. Do you think the authorities or hospitals want another unclaimed child?

She would take the infant, she decided, to the best hospital, Makati Medical, in the business district. Well-to-do Western-trained Filipino doctors worked there.

She wanted goodness for once, not swift and irrefutable logic; she wanted to intervene and stop some suffering before it happened. All it would take was a meager amount of money, some transaction.

To save the child from a life of misery was all she wanted, she told herself, not to take her home, not seeing already a black-haired girl eagerly holding up a hand at school. This infant already possessed the demeanor of a wrinkled old woman, without any expectation in her eyes.

She took the crisp U.S. embassy envelope of bills, soft, almost weightless Filipino fifty-peso notes, from the woven market bag she'd left in the car (beggars won't pester you if they see you don't carry a fat wallet, Baby would say). She ran to the churchyard and through the crowd of sampagita flower girls that surrounded her again. The woman was gone, the baby, the girl. Perhaps she'd feared Rue was getting the police.

She stood there, feeling foolish, foolish yet bereft.

Rue pushed the folded envelope deep into her skirt pocket. She walked around the outside portico of the church and stepped into its shade. Hundreds waited for the ten o'clock Wednesday mass. Inside one archway wrought iron shelves held thousands of squat burning candles, wax dripping like steady tears onto the floor. From a distance they were almost a single flame. The breeze blew across them and Rue smelled the wax burning. Filipinos crowded around the candles lighting new ones, finding a place for their own. As quickly as these were lit the breeze would blow some out, spread the flame to others.

She walked toward the back of the church. Sparrows flew in and out, intent on building their nests. The lines of the vaulted ceiling arched up, a vast glorious space above her. She watched the crowds for the woman and child amid hundreds of black-haired worshipers. Two lines of women, on their knees, proceeded down the main aisle in front of her. Each Wednesday the Kneelers moved slowly down the main aisle, some fanning themselves with woven abaca fans from the market. When they finally reached the altar, their knees would be black from the dirt of the old marble and the diesel soot that settled on everything. These women had worn a groove in the stone slabs, over the years, in this path of oblation. Their petitions to the Virgin, whispered in this open-air vault, breathed like the wind off the bay.

One old woman made little progress as she crept along. She gripped a jeweled rosary. She was a pale mestiza, well-dressed in dull black silk, and very thin. A young maid in a light blue uniform, also on her knees, followed the old woman and fanned her with a carved sandalwood fan. They moved only a few feet and then stopped so the old woman could rest. She stopped again, steadying herself with her hand against one of the ornate Corinthian columns, and her maid fanned her more rapidly. The pulse in her turtle-like neck beat, the cords of her neck were taut with effort. Others moved slowly past them down the aisle.

The kneeling women believed that if they prayed like this at this Church of Baclaran for nine consecutive Wednesdays they would get what they prayed for, the wish of Baclaran. Things lost, broken, desired. What did they wish for? Endurance? Some sign from God, some sign they'd not been overlooked? Or was it faith, courage of spirit, rising up like sap, some vital juice, through the bones, their knobby knees, from these marble stones they crept upon?

She saw the priest in a brown vestment emerge from a small arched door at the front of the church like a drone from a hive. The Kneelers continued their slow procession and murmurs as the parade of priest and altar boys and uplifted crosses went down the aisle around them. She stood in the back of the church. A sea of black hair faced the high pulpit. The priest read the scripture, first in Tagalog, then in English, and then spoke only in English about giving up the craving for material things.

Lines formed for communion. Sodden notes poured from a reedy voiced pipe-organ somewhere above her. Gray sparrows chirped. She watched again for the old woman and the girl with the baby.

Then she left, going out on the far side of the church that bordered the walls of an old barrio. From beyond the wall she heard a woman's voice calling musically, inflections of names up and down a scale of syllables, as if calling her children for lunch. What would it be like to live there, on a lane beneath the shade of the massive tamarind trees, to have a family and call, it's time for lunch, to live in a wooden house in the shade of a churchyard, with Manila Bay sending its breezes from across the boulevard, and call your children to the rice and fish you'd made for them?

It would seem such an easy thing, she thought, for someone like her to have an ordinary life, a happy marriage, a happy home with children, something anyone could obtain. You could buy love, hope, happiness here, even life. Foreigners came to buy new kidneys and have operations at the exclusive Kidney Center that Imelda had built only for the rich. They could cheat death. But Baby's husband Raymonde had once boasted that he could arrange even the death of another for a few thousand pesos. In the orphanages and on the streets, they sold children. In the brothels they sold love. In the market outside the church, they sold health, life, charms to ward off sickness, multi-colored holy waters and amulets for protection. In the churches, they sold forgiveness and redemption, the promise of a new order in a new world.

In Manila, it seemed, you could buy anything. And for those who had no money, who had something they would give up, there were the pawn shops. You could trade.

Here in the churchyard the sun's heat on her was like noon on a white star. Bitter smoke drifted toward her and the smell of cooking came with it, garlic and the ripe dead odor of the sun-dried fish that the poor savored.

The sign at the lane said, "This property owned by Baclaran Redemptorist Church of Our Savior, a public road. All are free to Pass Here." She wandered through the maze of alleys and market stalls, past lepers and blind beggars and ragged bird-like children, a raging madman, the wild white cockatiels that whooped and called, live placid hens and bleating ducks waiting for the butcher. She stepped around piles of rotting fruit and human waste and fish entrails surrounded by storms of flies. She walked on and on, turning right and then left, trying by intuition and her good sense of direction to retrace her steps.

She was lost.

A rooster crowed.

At an opening between the buildings another sign pointed to the Chapel of Our Lady of The Abandoned. A name that could be in a dream, a name she imagined Trace laughing at—claiming it to be a symptom of Filipinos' chronic sense of the dramatic. She turned toward the place, along a ten-foot-wide sunlit passage formed between the old barn-like wooden and stucco buildings with their high latticed windows. In each lattice was a white capiz shell, so flat and thin as to be almost translucent, what they'd used for glass in the days of the Spanish. The lane was deserted. Only a carabao stood by, hitched to a wooden cart. She passed the massive animal slowly, as if trespassing, not wanting to startle the thing. She heard its breathing, smelled the sweet hide's reek like moldy green grass. It looked at her expectantly.

She tried a door that was set in a deep opening between the stone and stucco and of course, she thought, locked. What did she expect to find in this place? Say perhaps a high lofted ceiling with those translucent windows that let in soft seashell light, like underwater, a place where spirits waited to comfort. Perhaps even the restless spirit of her father, or of any unsettled soul. Or was this the place where souls were summoned, like players just offstage ready for their call, to fulfill the wishes of the Kneelers of Baclaran? She put her hand flat to the door, as if feeling for a heart-beat. It felt like the barn door from the place of her youth, roughly grained, deeply set.

What, what, she breathed in a mumble. As if some part of her was struggling to get out too.

"Ma'am," Doming said.

She startled, and turned to face him. He was several feet away from her.

"Ma'am," he said, "Mrs. Varcegno is waiting for you, she's fussing."

"How did you find me?"

"I don't know, but you must come now. Mrs. Varcegno, she's in the sun and the car's very hot and she's complaining."

"I went back to the car and you weren't even there, no wonder it's gotten hot inside," she said to him, wanting to put him on the defensive. She felt exposed, his finding her here like a lost madwoman. Drivers were supposed to stay with the car, open the doors to cool it.

She saw him twist his mouth and work his jaw on the soft skin inside his cheek. He was her husband Trace's driver, but Baby had insisted that they couldn't possibly find a place to park on market day and Trace was out of town anyway. Rue had noticed Doming's set jaw when Baby spoke to him so imperiously, and she knew this work of shopping and waiting was beneath him, was for old men. He regarded her now, behind her sunglasses, but said nothing.

How had he found her? This place was beyond the gaudy wild birds and orchids for sale, the stalls of expired antibiotics sold by the piece and smuggled canned goods with dirty labels. The carabao, grayed muzzle, waiting patiently at the cart nearby, looked at them and raised its flat head. Doming picked up the water bucket nearby and poured some water over the shiny black hide and thick neck.

"They cannot sweat," he said. "They always need to find shade or a mudhole."

She watched, dazed from the sun. The carabao stretched toward her with its nostrils. She reached and felt the warm hide, put her hand on the carabao's broad burning forehead.

Something shifted in Doming; she could recognize but not name it. He slapped the carabao hard on the shoulder blade and knocked away a horsefly with a flip of his index finger.

"Mrs. Varcegno's bellyaching to your husband will cost me my job—or more—if we don't get there," he said. He turned and left her, hands in his jean pockets, not looking back.

So she followed him, through the maze of alleys and market stalls. The musky civet smell of the carabao still on her hands reminded her of sweetly decayed silage in a limestone barn, of black earth, purple sky. She heard the slightly protesting murmur of throaty pigeons above them. In looking back she would think, this is how it must have begun, a vinegary uneasiness between them.

June 20, 1982.

Of course he would not vote in the election for president tomorrow. He had no Name, officially, and no Permanent Place of Residence. He carried a fake I.D. he bought one Sunday morning at the corner of Taft and Aquinaldo Streets. Plus the election was rigged to begin with, he told himself. There was no real decision to be made. At many election sites, the boxes of ballots would be exchanged with identical boxes with all the ballots inside already marked for Marcos and his party hacks and sycophants.

If we organized we could have one of our own people stay with the ballot box, he'd urged his neighbors, squatters in his own barrio in Cavite. But who could be the one? Who was brave enough, who could leave their job, or their daily scrounging for a meal for children, for water? Peasants in the countryside, squatters in the city, go under one by one. The government wants us worried about daily bread, survival, rather than organizing as a group of laborers or barrio voters, Doming had said to his neighbors a few nights before. The powers that be *want* you to feel helpless.

29

Ah, so you're an Organizer, one said, watch out, Marcos has his spies in each barrio, you will be reported.

Or perhaps by speaking up, this is your preparation for your own campaign as barrio captain, another said.

By the end of this night, it would seem as if his whole life had been a preparation only for one decision—could he will himself to arrange his enemy's execution, even for revenge?

Around nine in the evening, Doming drove Trace and Rue Caldwell home from a reception at the U.S. ambassador's residence in the city, in North Forbes Park.

He was glad when he turned south, heading out of the city toward Ayera, to take them home. They didn't speak to him. After two years with him, Trace could almost forget Doming was there.

They talked freely in front of him, continuing some argument or conversation from the reception.

"I'm just synthesizing information, it's not like I'm making the policy," Trace said to her. "Emotions running amok like they have here make fatalists, make fanatics," he said. He reached over, took her hand.

"But is there ever simply information? Is there ever any fact or piece of information or landscape that's not affected by the eyes and imagination of the one who's seeing it?" she said.

"Imagination? I'd call it anticipating the worst, and planning for it, for any contingency," he said. "We have to keep our interests one step ahead of that."

"You mean President Reagan's interests, the NSC interests," she said.

Doming turned off the highway and inched the car along in line at the toll booth. He paid a few pesos. The toll went not to the government but to the concrete-crony who'd gotten the contract to build it. Even so, the crony had added dirt for cement. The highway's overpasses were crumbling.

"I know better than to ask you to compromise, but if there's any problem, any problem at all in the next few days, stay at home, don't go to work," Trace said.

"What sorts of problems are you expecting?"

"It's his first election since sixty-eight, Marcos is nervous, there's a level-five alert, anything could happen. The returns will be coming in for days."

"Is that the embassy's official line of the day, anything could happen?" Rue said.

"That's everyone's line. Carter McCall said tonight that Marcos is already ordering some villages in Mindanao to be emptied, the military putting them in tents alongside the highway, for refusing to register to vote," he said. "If the results look clean enough, Reagan and the State Department are planning to send Bush for the festivities next week."

"What festivities?" Rue said.

"The Inauguration is in ten days, he's not waiting around," Trace said. "We'll need to be there," he added.

"Will the vote count even be finished by then?"

"Unofficially? It's finished now, Sweetheart."

After a few moments Doming heard the click of Trace's briefcase opening. Then the reading light in the back window came on. Trace always had work with him in the car, sometimes left the briefcase in the car. Doming had taken advantage of that to look at what was there, cables and other briefings.

Nothing Trace said surprised Doming. The election would be over before it began. Everyone knew that when Marcos' slavish national assembly, a motley group of recycled toadies, changed the Constitution only a few months ago so that Ninoy Aquino, in exile in Boston, would be exactly four months too young to run, it was over. The old politico who'd run as the opponent was paid by Marcos, and, it was rumored, Marcos had sworn to his pre-election safety and then a comfortable retirement.

In the days preceding the election there'd been nightly noise barrages, car horns and jeepney horns, pots and pans, church bells, all for *Ninoy, Ninoy.* Ninoy Aquino, the opposition leader who'd been exiled to the United States by Marcos after seven years and seven months in solitary confinement at Fort Bonifacio. To spite the people in their noise barrages, Marcos had ordered a curfew, ordered some church bells soldered, like tongues. Other bells were roped to silence.

But of course, the president learned of plans to boycott the election to embarrass him. His announcement interrupted the Maja Blanca Variety Show on government television. Looking out at the people from behind his desk at Malacañang, he announced that it was the people's obligation to vote, that it was a sin not to vote, although the good Cardinal Jaime Sin demurred when asked.

Ten minutes later, they were at the Ayera house.

"See you tomorrow, Doming, seven sharp," Trace said.

Trace Caldwell, forty-four, tall, light hair thinning, well-educated. Doming had once overheard him reason with Ambassador Lange about *the integrity of compromise. The whole-ness of our part-ness*, Doming had silently translated the words from Latin. An absurd meaning, Doming thought, wondering if the man really fooled himself with these rationalizations. Words could be like bleach to sanitize reality, to hide behind, to obscure the truth. And the truth here? The military, the growing paramilitary, and all their weapons were paid for by the U.S., and were used to keep any dissent in check.

So now, the growing New People's Army movement, the political protesters, the explosions and fires going off at night in the financial district of Manila, all were directed at the U.S. as well as Marcos. President Marcos had publicly warned the U.S. that political opposition to him would threaten their military bases unless he was given enough money and leeway to rout them. And the ambassador's job was to hold onto the bases, hold them at any cost. Clarke Air Base and Subic Naval Base, and various "listening posts" such as at Cubi Point, were gateways to China and Southeast Asia, to U.S. strategic interests in the whole Eastern hemisphere, even Iran, Trace and the ambassador would say. This was what mattered. This was the deal—we'll call you a democracy if you'll let us keep the bases, we won't ask about torture if you'll open another free-trading zone. The Host Country, as he'd heard Trace call the Philippines, and Doming pictured the bases like parasites, perverse organisms feeding on their hosts.

Peace and Order, Trace called his work. Counter-insurgency. Doming had looked up the word, insurgent. *Resistance.* The very word Father Rex urged on Doming. Resist. To counter resistance, to neutralize or oppose resistance, with force.

He waited in the car until they went inside the front gate. Neither of them wanted him jumping out and opening doors for them, unless they had guests with them. He parked the car in the driveway along the side of the house, turned off the engine, put the key in its place under the seat, and got out.

He walked the few kilometers back to the security gate of Ayera Village. He passed through the employee's gate, showing his driver's license to a guard who made a mark in his book to prove Doming had left for the night. No employee or servant could come or go without showing his I.D.

Doming fingered the folded copy of one of Trace's embassy cables in his pocket. He would deliver it tonight. This material, as before, he would pass on to his best friend Sonny, who'd urged Doming to learn whatever he could, when Doming went to work for Trace, a Counter-insurgency Specialist.

Trace conducted a constant winnowing for leads to find and root out any opposition, especially the NPA, New People's Army. Peace and Order, Long-term Security Assistance. All benign words in themselves, Doming thought. Like tranquility. But in the last few years, Marcos' chief of secret police became the chairman of the central bank. U.S. military aid increased to seven hundred million dollars.

And like Trace, Doming also became a gleaner of information. Trace Caldwell was not the first intelligence officer he'd driven for. Doming saw the allure of their work, the pleasure, the power of secrecy. To be constantly watching and evaluating, not fully participating, was a way for a man to not have to engage in life. He felt he was in a position to know.

Along Azapote Road he caught a jeepney on its ten o'clock run, going further south, away from the city. They passed along the flat plains at the south end of the lake, Laguna de Bay. Behind him, ten miles north across the water, the dirty air over the city gave the night sky a greenish cast. The Meralco power plant plumed smoke.

He was meeting Abbe, his cousin, and Sonny, at the Los Baños cockfight arena.

Jeepneys and cars were parked in the fields surrounding it. The eight-sided structure was made of massive wooden beams, and the roof of planked wood. The cries of vendors selling snacks, "*Baluuut, baluuut*," rang out, mixed with the cry of the crowds inside.

Doming spotted his cousin, Abbe Villa Hermosa, standing just outside, holding onto a leather cord attached to his latest fighter. The bird strutted around like some Don, full of himself. Abbe was telling those around him of his scheme to breed the bird, a champion, sell the offspring, so of course he was looking for just the right combination— physical power, speed of movement, courage, and the killer instinct—in a gamecock. He claimed to know how to tell when a particular bird began to be willing to fight.

"I have a fine breeder hen at home that I just brought back from the provinces," one man said to Abbe. "I call her Pampanga, Mother of Champions."

"Bring your hen to my place then, the pawn shop, and we'll have a wedding," Abbe said. "The children can bring a bit of net for the hen's veil, we'll sing, and Masarap will crow at the top of his lungs while she worries, the way hens do, as if she is already the wife, scolding him."

"Placating him," another said.

"Asking him for money," Abbe said.

"Bossing him," the hen's owner said.

"We'll all be the sponsors," Doming said. The rich always lined up all their compadres and local politicians at weddings or baptisms as sponsors, solidifying their allegiances, their entanglement in Marcos' tentacles.

"Why do you call your fighter Masarap?" Pampanga's owner said.

"Masarap? *Tasty?* To put fear into him—if he is a coward and does not fight well, the children will eye him hungrily and beg my wife to cook him," bragged Abbe, full of *palabas*, full of San Miguels, likely, to be so brash before the match was even set, Doming thought. This was Masarap's fourth match in two months. He'd won or gotten draws in the others.

Abbe spoiled the bird like a favorite child. He would wake up early on cockfight-days to give his current bird a massage to relax it, blow cigar smoke in its face to soothe it, before giving it a practice session and exercise. He bred the bird. Bred him, but not too often, Abbe bragged. He is a ladies' man, but we must keep his strength, he'd tell his boy Paco.

"I presented him, and she accepted," he would say formally, of Masarap's prowess with the hens. He was devoted to each most recent gaming bird. He kept thinking this bird would be the one to make him grow prosperous. He'd saved the money to buy the pawn shop, but it was not doing well enough.

At almost forty, Abbe seemed already old to Doming, who was twenty-eight. He was tall and lean like Doming, but stringy-muscled. He was smart, but he couldn't read. Doming had taught Abbe's two children reading for his room and board, when he'd first come to Manila. The eldest, who would have been fifteen now, had died of meningitis. The younger, Paco, now twelve, learned to read at four years old. This success made Doming want to teach more. Paco's little sister Linay was six, and now there was a new baby girl, not even a year old. Angel, the mother, was only thirty. Miraculously, they had survived and almost thrived and Abbe still loved her after fifteen years. She came out of the garbaged hills of Smoky Mountain, from Tondo, Abbe would say of his wife, but her skin was softer than the finely ground rice powder of the rich, her hair like rain on my face, and the fine down on her legs and between them as delicate and cool as new corn silk.

"Tito Doming, it's time for Masarap," Paco called to them now. He was at the age boys began to attend these fights.

Doming and Paco went into the arena and sat down. Abbe's match was being set up, as orchestrated as the Holy Communion on high holy days that Doming had helped Father Rex with at home. The man who ran the fights, the mañanari, chose a blade from his collection, a *tari* the right length and curve for Abbe's bird. Abbe nodded. The mañanari tied the glinting spur onto Masarap with a leather lacing. It seemed to Doming that some birds, like some men, keened for this moment, when they possessed a weapon. But for now, until the fight was ready, the man placed a leather sheath back over the razor-sharp *tari*.

Abbe carried the bird into the arena, cradling it on his forearm, and placed it face to face with its foe. The two men each held his own bird back, to within a hand's length of the other, to gall them into readiness to fight. The two restrained birds struck with their beak, the neck feathers ruched and ruffled out, taut necks straining.

The crowd began making their bets, their low murmurs sizing the combatants up, appraising the bird's leg scales, plumage, sharpness of eye, tautness of its *palong*, comb. Some meeting place between his heart and his gut, said Abbe, this is where the betting man decides. After this deliberation they called out their bets to one of three men, known in their profession as "Kristos," who wore bright gold barong shirts. Each Kristo stood in the center front of one of the tiers of seats. Using hand signals, his arms raised the entire time like the ascending Christ, his "Kristo" pose, the Kristo could remember what every bet was. He would preside over the exchange of money at the end of each match. Only once had Doming seen a stupid man try to renege on what was promised.

Doming heard the sounds of betting from the stands grow louder and louder, to almost one human shout. Like the tower of Babel all the languages of man came pouring out, and only the Kristos could keep track of them all. Without a show of money the Kristos acknowledged the bets, and the crowd began to roar louder and louder as the Kristos' hands moved faster and faster, taking and acknowledging each bet. To Doming, the Kristos were the true stars. The birds' roles were over in a matter of seconds.

"If you don't look closely, you can miss it all," Father Rex had said to him the first time Doming had seen a cockfight.

On the wooden floor, strewn with bloody sawdust, the two birds' beaks cracked together. But in response to some commotion near the main entry to the arena, the Kristo halted.

General Ess, wearing mirrored sunglasses in the half-light of the cockfight pit, strode in with his entourage.

The manager rushed to them with bottles of beer, led them to seats across the arena from where Doming sat. One of Ess' men carried what even Doming, who knew little of the specializations of the fighting birds, recognized as a Red Hulsey rooster.

"The best, it's imported," the man in front of Doming observed, flaunting his expertise.

"They say *The Sir* is imported from Arkansas with a professional handler, flew in on the president's own plane; he will be the maker of a dynasty," he continued.

Ess settled into his seat and signaled the match to go on. Raymonde de Varcegno was with him. Looking at them, Doming thought of the butcher-birds, their hooked bills, the way they impale live prey on thorns, barbwire, or sharp fencing, as if by instinct causing suffering. General Ess had ordered the Philippine Constabulary troops into Hinigaran eleven years ago, against the sugar workers. Now Doming regularly drove Trace Caldwell and Raymonde de Varcegno to meet Ess and his entourage at one of the coffee shops in five-star hotels in Makati. Raymonde de Varcegno—Baby's husband. Doming had already enraged him once, seeming to shame him when the man was falling-down drunk in front of Trace, and Raymonde had cursed at him with pure venom.

The match preliminaries resumed. Fresh sawdust was scattered over the old, broken feathers brushed aside. Then Abbe and his opponent loosened the pouches over each bird's razored spur. At a signal so subtle you could almost miss it, they tossed their birds toward the center of the ring. The feathers and wings lifted up, hanging motionless. For a moment all noise stopped and the crowd listened for the slit of the razor. Then, one bird was spurting blood almost before they came to the ground, and in an instant, *kisáp-matá*, it was done. Abbe's bird Masarap fell into the dust. The crowd roared. *Itó na, itó na*, some cried. The other bird stood on top, upon the losing bird's neck.

"*Itó na, itó na*," the crowd of men and boys shouted more loudly. *It is, it is.*

Sic transit gloria mundi, Father Rex had said to him the first time Doming saw a fight like this. Thus passes glory from this world.

"You can see a man's soul, whether he is rich or a peasant, when he is in the cockfight galerias, my boy," Father

Rex had said. It was true. Some souls were gallant, but at the same time relished brutality, and being part of the mob.

"And when can you see a woman's soul," Doming asked Father Rex, at age fifteen wanting to know more of the secrets between men and women.

"That has never been my privilege, I can only imagine," Father Rex had said, smiling at Doming's forthright way of questioning him, words Doming would never have used at home. Father Rex. What possibilities the man had seen in his prize pupil, and, in the end, his only pupil.

The match was over, Masarap done for. If he were a superstitious man he would take this defeat as a bad omen, but Doming was not. Abbe would alleviate his disappointment with drink and drugs, he knew. But there was more action required. To be declared winner, the victorious bird had to acknowledge its victory by pecking at the defeated one. If the winning bird refused this ritual, it would be a draw. But the victor the crowd called Mad Dog pecked, and the crowd's roar became a howl. The men stood, and Doming saw their faces distorted with passion, with contempt, all for a goddamned bird.

Until the end this formal etiquette prevailed, which the Spanish loved, and the Filipinos emulated their worst traits, Father Rex explained to him. Behind this was some men's enjoyment of and complicity with savagery, of cruelty, the priest had said.

Abbe disappeared into the crowd, chastened by his loss. He carried the limp bird, holding it out away from him, this bird that had spent its days cradled on Abbe's left forearm, its head tucked into the space between Abbe's elbow and ribs. The healers had special quarters underneath the stands. They could sometimes work miracles on injured game birds, for a price.

In moments two new birds were presented, their accomplishments called out to the gamblers. Doming and Paco left the arena, going down the wooden steps worn smooth and through the opening nearest them to the arena's underside. They waited amid the forest of old *narra* beams the diameter of three men lashed together, made from ancient trees harvested from the slopes of Mount Makiling. These girders had borne the hopes and regrets of gamblers, who'd pawned their futures for a moment of glory, for the past sixty years.

"Paco, boy, where have you been? Bring water for Masarap and come with me," Abbe called. Paco scrambled to their jeepney.

Doming heard the shouts of bets for the next fight rising up from the arena.

A Kristo walked up and stayed near him, but Doming didn't recognize this Kristo from the matches just played.

The Kristo held out his pack of cigarettes to Doming, but he shook his head and moved several paces away, trusting his instinct for danger. Breeding hens in a nearby bamboo crate made their worrying noises as they picked over the rinds of breadfruit a vendor had tossed.

"Stay a while, Doming," the Kristo said.

Doming looked him straight in the face.

"How do you know me?" Doming challenged. The first fear was that this was someone from Negros who recognized him as the one who'd fled, and made it a point to ask who he was, learn his new name. There was cash offered for him in Bacolod City. The hacienda landlord had a long memory.

"Your compadre Sonny told me which one you are," the Kristo said. He held his palms up, placating.

41

His hands looked soft and fine to Doming. These were not the hands of a working man. He was perhaps in his early thirties, eyes quick and knowing.

"I have an offer for you. Six thousand pesos if you deliver Raymonde Varcegno to us for the Sparrows—assassins. We ask that you let us know when he is with your employer. Triple that if General Ess is with them."

This was Sonny, always wanting revenge. Sonny was the most educated man he knew well, after Father Rex.

"Eighteen thousand pesos," the Kristo said, "about one thousand dollars U.S. In fact, we could make it in dollars."

Doming knew the price on his own capture offered in Bacolod City military police headquarters was five hundred pesos, but that amount had been set before the peso had lost much of its value.

"I'm not interested," Doming said.

"We're being very generous," the man said.

"What makes you think I could arrange this?"

"When General Ess or Ray Varcegno and your employer are together, in some public place, the coffee shop of a five-star hotel, or one of the *toro* nightclubs in Mabini, you just let us know," he said. "We've been watching. We would be nearby. And we'd have our Sparrows ready." Sparrows were two-man teams who'd ride motorcycles, pulling up on each side of a car or jeep. They went after those responsible for picking up and torturing "subversives," and they were effective. Like the sparrows diving for their food, it was said, if the first one misses, the other does not. Anyone who did not go along, who offered any opposition to Marcos—university professors, priests, nuns, students, laborers—was labeled the opposition and considered fair game as a subversive.

Sonny had friends from his student days among the Sparrows' commanders.

"Think about it, we would be careful of you."

"Who are you exactly?" Doming said.

"My friends call me Alejo," he said.

Doming recognized the name. A friend of Sonny's who'd given up an academic position at the University of the Philippines teaching literature to go underground. Sonny had said of him to Doming, a poet is like a subversive.

At that moment, Alejo took out a rag from his pocket, wiped his face with the black and white woven cloth. The same odd pattern that the knife-sharpener wore tied around his head, the one who always worked under the tamarind tree on the road in front of the Caldwell's house. It occurred to Doming that nothing this man would do or say would be without purpose. Then he realized he was thinking like Trace Caldwell would, looking for connections where none existed.

"The thing is," Alejo said, smiling in the half-apologetic way of one bringing bad news, "we're watching the American. If you won't help us, we can't be so careful. If our target is in the car, anyone would be fair game, if they got caught in the cross-fire—your employer, his wife, even you. This is fair warning."

Doming considered the offer, the threat. He knew the embassy gossip about the American defense attaché and his Filipino counterpart being set up by a sewing woman who came once a week to the American's fine Dasmarinas house. In the end she was picked up and given over to General Ess. She was forced to eat one of her son's ears. The boy was freed as a warning, his mother's body found *salvaged*, a new word that had somehow come to mean a body's being dumped after torture. It was said that cattle prods were used on her vagina and breasts. The officer responsible was a compadre of Raymonde; they had trained together at an American-run police security academy in Taiwan.

"You know, Ess will do anything to take power now that Marcos is dying, and Varcegno is his front man. We'll be ridding the world of vermin—to say nothing of revenge for all those who've already disappeared," Alejo said.

"Ess and Raymonde are sitting in there right now, go get them," Doming said to the Kristo.

"With bodyguards everywhere. Too many would be hurt. The white priest said you would equivocate, that never once did you see black and white. You're closest to them of anyone we can get to. Don't you know Ess' potential for treachery? When Marcos dies, he'll prop up Imelda to front for him. And Raymonde will be rewarded—get back his family's mortgaged plantations in Cotabato."

Cotabato, in Mindanao. Land of the frontier. Land of bananas and pineapple. Cattle ranches. The province of Mindanao where Raymonde and Trace regularly traveled to, Doming thought.

Doming said, "The white priest, you say?" Perhaps Alejo did indeed mean Father Rex.

"In Mindanao, that's where he is. Why do you hesitate? You are the one who knows when they're with your employer at some fancy hotel bar or coffee shop, and you know they're not so much on guard then," Alejo urged.

When Doming didn't reply, Alejo sneered, "Aren't you almost Sonny's younger brother? What have you become, the foreigners' *tutu*, lapdog?"

"I've passed along the cables that I could get for you, copied them for Sonny, isn't that enough? That doesn't mean I'd set up my employer like that." Doming had copied these cables by hand when he waited for Trace. Trace had missed nothing, he'd leave the briefcase in the car with Doming when he went into lunch or to a motel.

"We're not after the American, we can keep him out of the way, but if you don't do this we can't be so careful; the Sparrows will be after the car, even if their women are with them," he said.

A roar went up, another match had been played out. Someone nearby hissed at the Kristo.

"You must decide soon," he said. "We'll be waiting, get word to us through him." And he pointed with his chin, pursing his lips, toward a row of jeepneys. A motorcycle was parked there. Doming recognized the *hasaán* man, the knife-sharpener who worked his trade riding a bicycle around Ayera. The Kristo Alejo cut between the rows of jeepneys and got on the back, and the two sped away.

Doming saw that Abbe was already in the jeepney he'd rented for the night. He slumped over in the battered driver's seat.

Doming got in the front seat with him, and he smelled the sharp medicine-like odor of *shabu-shabu*, the drug of poor men, a high that took away all sorrow. This was also sold at the healer's.

"I'll drive," Doming said. Sonny and Paco moved Abbe over the seat to the jeepney floor behind them, between the two benches that faced each other, and Paco held him. Abbe mumbled and cursed the bird he'd left behind, that he'd flung into the *camia* bushes nearby. Sometimes the butchered gaming birds were taken home for a special meal, but Abbe did not have the heart.

Everything he tried to do ended in failure, Abbe muttered.

"What do you expect, *kuya*, you expect too much," Doming said to him.

45

"Do you know what they want from me?" Doming said, turning to Sonny. He gunned the jeepney engine hard and it sputtered.

Sonny had saved him when he came to the city and Doming tried to show this *kuya*, older brother, the proper respect and gratitude. Doming's cousin Abbe was the one who took him in, in 1972, not questioning this unknown young cousin from the south, but it was Sonny who had the contacts and found out how to get Doming his new name. And Doming's survival meant a brand new I.D. for his first job—driving a jeepney. This is how it began for many, a spider's thread spun out from the provinces to the city.

Marcos' imposed curfew was still in force in those days. After eleven at night, all drivers were stopped and I.D.'s checked throughout the city. Though they could be bribed, Doming couldn't afford to attract the attention of young ambitious military police. His name did not appear in the Central Registry, he had no past.

So Doming tallied again what he owed Sonny, this brother of his heart, a deep debt of gratitude that could not be repaid, *utang na loob*.

He'd begun passing on copies of cables, anything that looked interesting, that he would read when Trace left his briefcase with him, but now this was too much to ask. The jeepney engine strained into second gear.

"Why are you such a reluctant participant?" Sonny said. "These are our enemies, murderers of innocents, they deserve justice."

"I won't be a part of executions," Doming began.

"So you also will tell us to turn the other cheek, like the priests who support Marcos, who want us quiet, passive?" Sonny argued. "And now our bishops also say be passive, wait for your reward in heaven. For me? Never. For you, all

46

that learning, wasted. It's turned you irresolute, *waláng-hiya*, without shame," Sonny said.

Doming nudged the jeepney onto the highway north toward Manila. "I've given you the cables," he said.

"You don't care about anything except your own survival, sleeping and eating," Sonny began.

"Eating and sleeping, in that order," Doming said, taking up the argument.

"It's a chance to do something that really matters. What do you have to lose? Your heart has become like the mango seed, flat and stringy," Sonny said.

"You're judging him too harshly," Abbe said, slurring.

"No, perhaps Sonny's right," Doming said. "Revenge gives life its only meaning for some. For the rest, eating and sleeping is all Marcos wants us to care about. Malnourished people have short memories. Marcos knows this; those who have to worry about their own survival makes neighbor against neighbor, tribe against tribe; if we are against each other we can't resist him.

"So, whether we eat and sleep, he wins, or whether we go hungry and tired, he wins, as long as we are against each other and thinking only of revenge," Doming concluded. Sonny loved to debate, and Doming enjoyed arguing both sides, leaving Sonny in the middle.

"I don't believe you," Sonny said to Doming, continuing the argument. "Should we be passive and not strike back? That's not good enough for any man to live on, where is the good in that, where is hope, wanting only sleep and food, no more life than that of an ox?" Sonny said. "I want revenge, I'm out of cheeks to turn."

Doming said, "That's just it, I've told you, you misunderstand—the book of Matthew says specifically, if a man strike you on the right cheek, then offer the other. A blow, you see, by the right hand between equal men would hit the *left* cheek. Only a backhand slap would hit the right. This was a story about how slaves could resist being humiliated by a master. It's not about accepting or even repaying violence, not an eye for an eye.

"His listeners saw this offer was impossible—their master's left hand could only be used for unclean tasks. Under their laws, if the rich used the left hand for anything else, it was shameful, they were fined. Look, I try to slap you backhand on your left cheek, with my right hand, the only hand I can use," Doming said. He made the awkward gesture, turning his right palm outward for a backhand slap. The jeepney veered slightly.

Sonny held up his left hand, attempted to backhand Doming.

"See? It can't be done without looking ridiculous. You have to turn your arm so. His audience, the poor, the slaves, *got* it—meet your master's force with ridicule, their teacher was saying. They would resist being treated as sub-human with humor, with shaming the shamer, offering him the opportunity only to use his unclean hand. It took away their masters' power over their own dignity. It wasn't about simply countering violence with violence or with inaction."

"So we should imagine Marcos might make a new law that we can't use our left leg, our left eye," Sonny said.

"Our left ball, also?" Abbe asked.

"To turn the other cheek means—I deny you the power to humiliate me, to treat me unjustly—for we are equal human beings," Doming said.

"I know, your old priest, sent to pacify us by the foreigners, to make us be good servants, but to what end? So we can get to heaven, on pride? On dignity? On humor?

The priests call for nonviolence when they mean tranquility, leaving the status quo," Sonny said.

"You *should* have been a priest, all your studies for nothing, only to make you too hesitant to join us, Doming. What is the good in all this?" Sonny added, raising his voice.

They passed two wagons pulled by the white oxen, the special oxen that pulled wagons piled high with woven goods for the city. They'd be there and settled by daylight.

Doming considered Sonny's question seriously. What was the good? He drove past the spewing power plant that burned soft coal and made sulfurous dark clouds over the lake. They passed a broken-down blue bus also headed north toward the cankerous city. A train bound for the south, the Bicutan Express, rumbled past on tracks that ran near the highway, where shacks skirted its edges. He'd seen those who lived there yank their children off the tracks where they played just outside their doorways when the train warning—bits of broken glass hung from strings like a wind chime—would begin to clink together and soon the ground would shake violently. Doming noticed the shadows riding on top of a few cars, hitching a free ride.

"Where's the good? What if it's gone?" asked Paco, who'd been listening and waiting for an answer.

Doming tipped his chin up toward the warehouse they passed—Bicutan Food Terminal Junction Station, the sign said. "Perhaps that's the place where the good is hoarded and dries out. Marcos stole that from the people, too, locked it up in a warehouse where it dries up like old *casavas*." Sweet potatoes.

So that people will never band together or trust each other—Marcos, the insatiable belly, has feasted on the people's memory, imagination, urge to kindness, till there is none left. These have dried up, too, he thought.

"So we can grow more," Paco asked.

"Of course, Paco, we just need the cuttings," Doming said.

Sonny laughed. They would smooth things over between them for now.

The wind blew in.

Doming heard Sonny suck in his breath over his loose false teeth as an open army jeep drew up next to their jeepney and slowed to match their speed.

This is what torture had done to a man like Sonny, Doming thought. It made Sonny numb except to violence, indifferent to everything but revenge and justice. He had led some student group years before, when martial law was in force, and was picked up at Mendiola Bridge in the protests there. They have names and they're still looking, he said. Why wouldn't they? Ess' National Intelligence grows to fifteen thousand strong, the Presidential Security Command is another fifteen thousand. Each barangay now has its youthful informants, the *Kawals*.

Sonny had ugly false teeth and an inflamed anus, a fissured opening that still bled each morning. It was only by chance, he told Doming once, that some of us returned and some didn't, depending on what the general had for lunch, whether his cook fixed his favorite dish, whether there was salty *balut* from his favorite vendor, whether his young *querida,* mistress, had been peevish with him the night before.

Perhaps people and nations lurch along according to fate, and say fate is made by what the general had for lunch and whether his bowels moved that morning, Sonny always said. And Sonny's own fate had become entwined with Marcos' and Ess' like a helix. Do it to him again, the general had said, as several of Ess' goons made the blood flow down Sonny's backside and onto the pants at his knees. They'd sucked the marrow out of him in 1969.

But the army jeep next to them was driven by Raymonde's driver Delgado, who was alone. He wore army-style mirrored sunglasses like Raymonde's. Doming wouldn't look directly at him, just like he wouldn't have looked a wild dog in the eye. He saw that Delgado remained impassive and unsmiling. Raymonde's sweet-guava smoothness with Trace Caldwell, his cunning, couldn't be trusted. And he didn't trust Delgado's false toadying and thug-like attentiveness to Raymonde.

The jeep sped away.

"But will your God hold anyone accountable?" Sonny asked. "Will he take my revenge for me?"

Just after the 1969 elections, crowds of students stormed along the Pasig River, crossed the bridge and rammed a truck through the gates of Malacañang, and hundreds ended up beaten and arrested. Homemade bombs went off around the city. Martial law was declared on September 21, 1971, and lasted eleven years. Political opponents were rounded up that night, Ninoy Aquino the prize. Sonny was with them. The Philippine Constabulary, the army's civil order branch, held the students in a sealed-off section of their headquarters in Camp Crame.

And after that night the small stone bridge, Mendiola, which led over the Pasig River to the palace in the heart of the city, was closed forever and guarded by the Presidential Security Forces who were now under General Ess' command. The city's snarled traffic was perpetually rerouted away from the crossing, which was closed with barbed wire and concrete blocks. No one knew why. The *tsismis* flew.

Then the city discovered its own secret, Imelda's fortuneteller's prediction—if the crowds of protesters ever again passed over the Mendiola Bridge, the reign of Marcos would be over. Marcos and especially Imelda believed it. And their reality became the city's as well, and the bridge had been blocked off for these past eleven years.

Doming and Sonny would talk about all this, many nights when they sat on the back porch of Abbe's place, on a dirty canal leading to the Pasig River, while Sonny worked his false teeth like an old man. In 1970, Sonny had been one of the "Ten Outstanding Young Men of the Philippines," TOY Men, his senior year at the University of the Philippines. He had job offers from Coca Cola, Del Monte. "And that's what they wanted, TOY Filipinos," Sonny had said, "little men in ties and starched shirts and fine jackets made in Hong Kong who would represent their company." Now Sonny owned a bar.

"You've let them make you what you abhor, *Kuya*," Doming countered now, "a mirror to their violence."

Sonny would have his revenge, Doming decided, no matter what, that's what he lived for. It was now his woman, his vocation, his yoke.

"Do you know, Sonny, that the yokes for carabao are specially carved to fit each particular beast, and you are carving yours?"

"But now you are offered a way to repay your father's death, your family's suffering," Sonny said.

"He was my stepfather."

"All the more reason, if he raised you as his own."

Agere contra, Father Rex often urged Doming. Fight your inclinations, my son. The inclinations to lash out, to repay violence with violence.

But Doming wasn't sure if in his hesitation he was a coward, afraid of doing what they asked, or a good man, tempted, or simply made of anger, clay baked and hardened to stone. And God?

God must be blind, what had He noticed on this dead star, Sonny often argued.

It was true, Doming thought. General Ess had the heart of a viper. Raymonde de Varcegno was his toad. It would be as simple as getting rid of a *suyod*, a head louse, which had attached itself too deeply to be tolerated any longer. No one mourned for such vermin.

"I agree, Sonny, for you, you need revenge, you know no other language," Doming said.

"They taught it to me," Sonny said. If Sonny did not stay angry, he would weep.

"And I'm telling you, Father Rex taught me another," Doming said.

"If it happened to you, to your child, you would know," Sonny said.

"That's why I would never have a child, I couldn't bear that, just as your father could not," Doming said.

"And your stepfather?" Sonny asked.

"When he told me to leave, at the end before he died, he said, Boy—never come back here. I still don't know if he meant it as a blessing or a curse."

"Sons should avenge their fathers," Sonny said.

But Doming was afraid of wanting revenge, wanting anything too much, like Sonny. What was a man, desiring not even desire, or sex or other pleasure, but the yoke of revenge, nothing else?

Doming delivered Abbe and Sonny and Paco to the pawn shop in the city. Abbe's rooms were behind it, Sonny lived nearby. He left the jeepney with its owner along EDSA

Boulevard. Then he took another jeepney, a public one with a set route, toward home, through the asshole of Cuneta Street, and then south, out of the city along the coast road to the hook of Cavite, where he lived. If he'd become a priest, as Father Rex had planned, he'd be getting up now for early mass, reading. But instead, he would go home, cook rice, think of nothing.

Cavite, an historic place, where Emilio Aquinaldo had lived. His house was still standing there like a shrine to the 1896 Revolution against Spain. Aquinaldo, who was later captured by the Americans and held at home in Cavite like a monkey in captivity for fifty years until he died, converted to all things American. He'd had the first bowling alley in the country installed in his fine house. He was not a prisoner at the end, of course, just a worn-out old man. When Doming passed the house, sometimes, he would look at the grand empty space and say *Brother–Aquinaldo.*

When Emilio Aquinaldo died in 1964, Marcos himself was the one who led the funeral delegation.

Now Imelda had resettled thousands here, in Cavite, far from where they could find work. There was talk of a Free Trade Zone to follow. Imelda, Minister of Human Settlements, had them carted out of the city barrios on garbage trucks with their pieces of galvanized metal and wood and cardboard, the boxes they lived in. She needed their land for another building project. Imelda's edifice complex, Sonny called it.

"Isn't this your stop?" the jeepney driver called back to him. Cavite, *the hook*, for the shape of land that jutted out into Manila Bay like the sharp curve of a *balisong* knife.

Election Day, June 21, 1982.

The old cook Celia made every special dish for her American employers. Two years with them now, after a total of fifty years with Baby de Varcegno's parents and then Baby herself. She would make fresh *lumpia, saopao,* spicy *adobo,* and delight in their gluttony, as if that would make them happy, fertile, full of love. She brought their *pan de sal* and morning tea to the lanai at five-thirty each weekday morning. Her hands, holding this morning's tray, were as brown and wrinkled as cured tobacco leaves.

"They say the First Lady is growing scales on her skin, scales like the *banak* fish," Celia said, brushing at crumbs on the tablecloth.

"That's market gossip, Celia," Rue said. She poured canned Carnation milk into her tea and sniffed at it.

"It's fresh, Ma'am," Celia said, annoyed, but she picked up the pitcher of milk and fanned her hand over it to bring its smell to her. "Imelda will turn into a fish and swim away down the Pasig River, this is what my priest says."

A wailing cry came from the field beyond the house, another feral cat caught in a trap. Celia crossed herself. On this, the Election Day for Marcos, she wanted some sign, something to rely on that the Marcos dynasty would not last another one thousand years.

"This they say at my church, Ma'am," Celia said, "this is the story I've heard—Madame's fortunetellers say her scales are a curse from the *encontodos* in the waters of San Juanico. The new bridge she built there disturbs them. The only way she can cure herself is to offer children to the waters there. Her perfect skin, her pride, white and soft as your *pan de sal* roll, no more. She has even been to see our Cardinal Jaime Sin and he could not help her.

"And Ma'am, they say street children are disappearing in Manila. One morning a load of children gets on a ferry, and the next morning that ferry returns with coconuts," Celia continued. She waited, but it seemed this too-rational young woman would not believe the stories Celia heard each week before mass and in the markets.

Sometimes Celia missed how Baby Varcegno would listen to the stories Celia told, the gossip, the *tsismis*. Baby, her former employer, her child almost. After all, Celia was her *yaya* from the day Baby was born. She missed how the grown-up Baby would come home slightly drunk from a Nationalista Party event and, like a performing child again, act out for Celia each Blue Lady's part in Mrs. Marcos' pageants and extravaganzas, the simpering and fawning, and then Imelda's haughty lording it over them, these women who years ago had been rude to her when she'd turned up in Manila, a socially incompetent but beautiful girl from the Visayan south, a niece from the poverty-stricken branch of the clan of an important politician. Celia knew the story the way any girl knows a Cinderella story. The moment Marcos met young Meldie, the girl was having an ice cream at the National Assembly canteen while she waited to deliver some food for her uncle's dinner. She was wearing a house dress and old shoes, but at that moment, Marcos saw his future, his way to the palace, which he coveted. Young Imelda's distant family connections were what he needed as an Ilocos Norte Senator to gain a national following, and he talked her into marriage two weeks later. And she'd done it, married—the little fool, the crafty witch. She sang for his rallies and was rumored to have seduced an election official in 1962. But Marcos' doting mother took a dislike to Imelda, and his mistress, his *querida*, with whom he already had two children, made fun of young Imelda's naive provincial tastes.

Now Celia wanted proof of her priest's prediction, proof that the First Lady was indeed turning into a fish and would soon simply swim away from Malacañang Palace, down the Pasig River and into the sea. Celia waited, picking brown leaves from the potted ferns and bamboo palms that stood in the shaded arches of the lanai, waited to take the tray away. She sometimes worried that this boyish American woman had too little flesh. Worms? Parasites? Too much work in the heat at the Rice Institute?

"Why don't you sit down with me, Celia," Rue said at last. Celia, pleased, worked her false teeth into a comfortable place and sat. Rue moved the tea tray toward her, offering an extra cup. Sometimes early in these mornings Rue invited Celia to sit with her, drink some tea, something Baby had not done in Celia's years with her. Celia had never once sat on a chair in one of Baby's, or even of Baby's mother's, fine houses—only in her own room or kitchen. So, finally she'd been able to slowly sit back and rest her hands on the rolled arms of the old rattan chair on the cool lanai. For a moment she felt proprietary. She was sixty-four. Her sister Mary, who still worked for Baby, was five years older.

Fifty-two years before, in the year 1930, Baby's father rescued Celia, then twelve years old, and her sister Mary, then seventeen, from their home in his hemp factory in San Juan, Manila. He heard the sounds of an overseer having his way with the older girl one night while their father worked as a night watchman, and took pity. The two sisters joined the staff of eleven household helpers, a cook, three yayas, labanderas, maids, sewing girls, gardeners, drivers. Eight years later, the surprise youngest girl, Baby, was born, and Celia poured out her love on her. Baby—Rosita Navitidad de Varcegno. Celia was the one who buried Baby's afterbirth under a tree in the garden of the house in San Juan, in an iron pot, for luck.

But when Trace Caldwell and his wife Rue rented the house from Baby and Raymonde de Varcegno, Celia learned she would go to them with the house. Baby had insisted Celia's cooking would be perfect for them, perhaps wanting, after a lifetime of Celia as her *yaya* and then her cook, to be rid of her. But Celia knew also that Raymonde despised her, because she knew his secrets. She knew he was not a good man.

"*Batang tupa*, Raymonde called Baby at first, *my baby lamb*," Celia had said to Rue, shaking her head, "and after he eats lamb, he belches." She'd looked forward to being rid of Raymonde and his compadre General Ess. But now, instead, Trace Caldwell was a compadre of Raymonde's and tight as a tick with General Ess. Trace had never invited the General to his home. If he did, Celia would have spit in the General's food, put ant poison in his *bagoóng* sauce.

To Celia it seemed that Baby and Raymonde, and now Rue and Trace, were like windows. It was not difficult to look at them and know their most private concerns. Celia had to be far away and nearby at the same time. She knew their footsteps on the floor above her room, and heard even their sighs in sleep and could tell a good dream from a bad one.

"Are you going to vote tomorrow, Celia?" Mr. Caldwell, Sir, as she called him, had asked her yesterday morning.

Thirteen different voter certificates had arrived in the mail at their house in the last few weeks, names she'd never heard of. Flying voters, as they were called, would go from barrio to barrio today using falsely registered names to vote for Marcos.

"No, Sir, the lines in Ayera will be long, but I'm sure somewhere in Batangas someone will be casting a ballot in my name, Sir, and the name of my sister and maybe even our departed mother's name," she answered her employer.

He laughed.

That pleased her.

She knew he didn't care for her to take any interest in politics. In the provinces and countryside, there'd been calls for an election boycott by the opposition. Here in Manila, it was rumored, the generals were arranging a landslide for Marcos. What would one old woman's vote against him mean? What would banging her pots and pans in protest, like the women in the city, mean?

She'd heard on Radio Veritas that Ninoy Aquino was being watched in Boston by a few Filipinos specially assigned to the Philippine embassy. He was the only person Marcos feared, some claimed. Besides Imelda, others added.

Celia gathered the dishes onto the tray and took them to the kitchen. Once her morning chores were done, Celia would take all day cooking, chopping fresh garlic, cutting some bitter leafy greens, then mixing in ground pork and green onion cut fine, cutting into the green-rinded *kala-mansis* and squeezing the acidic juice out of them, adding pungent local soy sauce. Then separating the delicate *lumpia* wrappers, made of rice flour, and expertly wrapping some of the mixture in each, and cooking the dough with its filling in hot oil, serving with a tangy red sauce, the kitchen full of smells that brought in flies that Celia banged at with her fly swatter made of a stick and lengths of leather.

But now, her radio show was starting, a morning and evening soap opera, *Kisáp-Matá, In the Blink of an Eye*. The opening theme song, Spanish guitar, carried through the house on the wind and out the open windows through the coconut palms, to the swaying bougainvillea. She swished down the long hall overlooking the garden to the master bedroom. Parish bells from the Sisters of Mercy nearby were tolling. Seven in the morning.

She heard the laundry girl singing to herself below the bedroom window, on the side of the house where she did the wash in large plastic laundry tubs. Celia called to her from the open window, *Labandera*—Easy, *na*. The girl in her zeal scrubbed mercilessly, disintegrating anything delicate. Celia herself would have to do Trace's fine cotton shirts he'd ordered from the American ambassador's tailor in Hong Kong.

She quickly made the bed, shook the pillows, and tucked the white mosquito net under the mattress. On her new employers' first night in the house, the rainy season's first monsoon winds came. A wind from the east, so strong it whipped the sheets off the bed. An impetuous wind, this *maragsang hangin*, Celia had thought then, an impetuous wind is blowing here. And she watched them for its symptoms.

From beyond the garden wall bordering the lanai, Rue heard a man's voice, shrill and high pitched. He called, *Ha-saaán, ha-saaán*. Soon the grinding sound began, like a scraping of bone. What does that man want? Rue had asked Celia, the first time she heard him, more than a year before. The sound chilled her. He cries, *Sharpen, Sharpen*. It's for the knives, Ma'am, Celia had told her.

The hasaán man, the sharpening man, as he was known, was calling here in the neighborhood, along the road outside the house again this morning.

They'd rented a fine house from Baby and Raymonde de Varcegno, as a favor to Raymonde, who needed the money.

Rue was certain Baby's husband Raymonde encouraged Baby to see Rue regularly to maintain the family ties. The two couples' friendship was made of formality, based on the ties between Raymonde and Trace, ties of obligation. And Rue knew the crucial ties between *compadres* were the connections that made things run here, that made confidences flow like energy through a wire.

Their house in Ayera Village was built of stone and adobe with a tile roof and overhanging eaves to keep out the midday glare and monsoon rains. A dark red tile walk led to the wide front steps and a shaded doorway, where *kalamansi* trees grew in clay pots. Spanish friars had used these pots for wine, traded the wine to the Chinese merchants for their green celadon porcelains. Everywhere pink and white bougainvilleas and red flame bushes and *kalachuchi* trees grew and blossomed. The house stood alone in a field along a broad avenue in what had once been rice paddies and mango groves, twelve miles south of Manila. The entire village was being developed by a Marcos-supported industrialist who was their neighbor. He'd bought up the land just before martial law began, and built his own house and stables for the horses for his polo team.

The field grass was just beginning to green now as the rainy season began. The ancient mango trees were left from orchards planted when the Spanish still ruled, the seeds brought by ship from Mexico. Beyond the mango trees stood the west wall of the village compound, a wall of stone and block around the entire ten-mile square. A few hundred of the former rice farmers who'd leased the land for generations had been paid well to build the wall for Don Ayera in thirty-nine days.

Sometimes at the end of the day, the worst of the heat over, Rue would walk up the road to the wall. She'd climb up the branches of a *pili* tree that grew next to it. Pieces of broken glass were set in concrete along the wall's top, dark brown necks of beer bottles, clear glass with edges like blue veins. Above the glass, shimmering razor wire curled between the metal posts. But in the distance, she saw the fields and coconut palms and a few newly settled squatter areas that continued several miles down to Manila Bay, damson lavender on the horizon. The setting sun was as orange as the flesh of a ripe papaya. The tunneled island of rock, Corregidor, made a shadow in the distant water of the bay's entrance. Sometimes it seemed to her that life itself had leaped over the wall and gone on there.

Rue left the lanai and passed through the garden to the garage. The garden was a botanist's paradise—arching bougainvillea bushes, papaya trees lining the drive, banana trees growing up to the second floor bedroom windows along the back wall of the garden. They were sweet plump gloria bananas, a vice of Baby's, Celia had confided to her. Rue asked her about every unknown plant. That, Ma'am, is the dragon tree, the *pandan* tree, the *camia* bush, the sorrowless tree, Celia would answer. Along the front drive, the gardener began his work before the morning heat rose up. He kept the grass clipped low with long bladed scissors. To Rue the sound of the blades clipping was like the biting tick of a clock.

Rue backed her old black Toyota up the drive, past the gardener, and out onto the road. The car had been a taxi cab in Tokyo in its past life, its yellow paint visible inside the doors.

At the street, the knife-sharpener nodded at her, smiling. Like many laborers, he wore a long piece of cloth wrapped around his head and neck. His was black and white, the rough weaving like a pattern of white skulls on a black background. The dark wiry man, spider-like, pedaled his bicycle in place. The front wheel turned a smooth stone attached to the bike with a belt made out of a piece of inner tube. Sparks flew out from the stone like shooting stars and hissed onto the cracked pavement. A small cosmos was being formed. A maid from a house down the road carried kitchen knives, a gardener stood there with his clippers.

A half-dozen feral cats scattered from an open garbage pail. They were being trapped, these pitiful cats with the pinched faces and always misshapen tails. Marcos' Minister for the Environment had offered fifty pesos for each carcass as part of his new campaign—Save The Songbirds. The yowls of wild cats fighting over the garbage scraps had been in her dream last night—she'd just given birth, but to a kitten with a crooked tail, and so the doctors sawed off its tail and the newborn cried. Stop, she was calling, but they ignored her. Stop, I'll take him like that, and then she came awake. She heard the cries of a feral cat caught in a trap, making a sound like a baby's crying. The breeze carried the smell of early morning cooking fires and moved the white mosquito net around her like a ghost.

Rue turned the car down Acacia Boulevard. Here, each house was garish, over-proportioned, with manicured front gardens, aping Spain or China or Hollywood in the way that only Filipino culture could. That's what Raymonde had said when he first showed them his own house. He was Spanish, *mestizo*. He claimed Baby had designed their house too tastefully, that was why no Filipino would rent it from them. But she wondered why he was shunned by many. Sometimes Baby seemed like his deluxe spy.

She drove south into the flat countryside where the broken edge of Taal Volcano rose in the distance. Ten thousand years ago it had loomed up twenty-five thousand feet, and now just the base of the cone remained, a cone holding a lake, wide enough that all of Manila could stew in there. This was how Doming had once described it to her.

"The foreigners in Manila are like the scum of a simmering *nilaga*, stew; they understand nothing of what's going on beneath them," he'd added.

Now near the shores of the lake, divers had found ancient underwater towns, a small church. Poisonous sea snakes that live only in salt water swam in and out of the broken bell tower twenty feet below the lake's surface. The ground here sloped slightly upward, so gently you wouldn't notice it at first. The base of the long-ago volcano, Taal, began here, several miles from its rim. It fooled you, you didn't notice that everything was already on a slight slant. Then you realized you were climbing into the sky. You reached a ridge. There in front of you the vast basin of Taal Volcano Lake opened from horizon to horizon—the empty space left when a volcano vanished in an instant. Ifugao natives building their rice terraces two hundred miles to the north thousands of years before had seen the perfect cone and its smoke, and worshiped it. What must they have felt, she wondered, when their god vanished on a morning like this.

All that remained, in the Taal Lake's center, was a small stone island and on that island a blue lake with yellow sulphur fumes that bubbled over a few times a century—a lake within a volcano on a lake within a volcano, the people there described it.

She turned east, away from Taal, toward where she worked in Los Baños. She was lucky to have a real job. She could do her work and research and get paid in dollars. The Rice Institute, less than an hour south of their house, was renowned as the leading center for the green revolution in Asia—higher rice yields, strains resistant to disease, fine hybrids, but strains that were still vulnerable to the stem borer moths she studied. This is what she'd come for, the Green Revolution.

She was here. The Rice Institute.

IMPERIALIST CONTROL
OF THE RICE SEED IS
STARVING CONTROL OF OUR FATE.

The hand-lettered banner had been tacked up in protest outside the gates, hung from the wire fence.

She pulled on her loose canvas shorts and light sleeveless shirt and left the changing rooms. Women who dressed this way in public were stared at. Filipinas were very modest, would not even wear sleeveless blouses which would show their shoulders when they were in the markets, and so she'd learned to change clothes at work.

She would spend some of each day in the screen houses, enclosed plots of rice, about two hundred by one hundred feet, covered by double-screening, heavy wire for support, and fine-mesh screen, so that the moths or other insects cultivated there couldn't escape. Each screen-house assigned to her produced a different rice variety. She studied the resistance of various hybrids of rice to the stem borer larvae.

She settled into her lab, a whitewashed block building with open windows. Sok, her helper, brought in the moth larvae he'd already gathered that morning. He was an old man the size of a child, dwarf-like, with a terribly hunched back.

"I'm late, Ma'am, just a few more minutes," he called. "The lines for voting were very long."

"Did you vote, then?"

"They said we must, so my son and I, we took ballots but did not mark anything; many in Los Baños did this," he laughed. "He can make us cast a ballot in the box, but he cannot make us mark it."

"Here they are for you, Ma'am," Sok said now. He'd carefully gathered some of the orange larvae, as fine as silk threads, in his cupped palm and carried them into her lab. With a piece of rice stalk, Rue placed a few of the larvae on a slide, put it under the lens. She would measure the mandibles of each stage of the larvae development. She compared the size of the larvae mandibles in each of several hybrid rice varieties, how much resistance each rice variety could make, to wear down the jaws. It had come to her one day in a flash—go after their bite.

Her research focused on the Yellow Stem Borer moth, *Scirpophaga incertulas*, YSB in the field manuals, the cause of more damage to tropical rice than all other insects combined. The straw-colored female moth flies into the paddy at night and lays its eggs on the rice tiller, or stem. Then in a few days the newly hatched larvae bore into the stem to feast on the soft growth there, severing the stalk's vascular system before it can flower and produce the grain.

So, as the larvae would feed within, the tiller would stay green on the outside. But when she broke them open, these stalks in the infested rice paddies, the inside would be brown. Deadheart, the field manuals called it.

The Institute is funded by a bunch of chemical companies, Doming had once said to her. The stem borer moths don't seem to notice, she'd said, irritated. *But do you know that the farmers can live with some loss of crops if they don't have to buy expensive hybrid seeds and fertilizers?* he continued. I'm trying to re-integrate the wild rice back into the supply, to resist the stem-borers, she said. *But I bet they won't pay you for that,* he said, *there's no money in it for them.* I do research, she'd argued, research, I get paid for thinking. *Sure, but they don't have to use your ideas if it only saves money for the farmers,* he countered.

Why did she bother to argue, why did he discredit her work? But the truth was she was getting less certain of the politics of the Institute and didn't want to debate. Corporate Rice, they call it, he'd said. Green Revolution for green U.S. dollars.

About ten-thirty, she and Sok stopped work for morning merienda. Each day he offered her some of the brewed tea he brought to work, and they would sit and look out at the mountains and talk. He'd been surprised that any rich woman would drive a car herself, would put on old clothes and crawl around day after day in the screened rice paddies, he revealed to her after months of working together.

On the window ledge mud wasps worked. In the distance, in an open rice paddy, a pair of white egrets lifted their wings in the same beat. Beyond, she could see the hilltops near Taal, where the landscape's outline against the sky had changed in recent days. As if a bite were missing. You foreigners understand nothing, nothing, Doming had said.

"What's going on up there?" she asked Sok, pointing with her chin. She'd learned not to use her finger to point, ever. To us, that's like a dog, Celia would say, lifting one hand like a pointer, and dog was among the rudest words a Filipino could be called.

"Finally they have gone too far," he said, "when the First Lady's workers began tearing into the highest of the hills surrounding the Taal Volcano Lake." Imelda planned a summer palace, taking advantage of the view and cool breezes. There they would build the Marcos Museum. But Sok said that the *hilots* in the hills near there had warned that the spirits in Taal now churned. Taal would awaken his brother volcano north of Manila, a volcano so old, dormant for six hundred years, that no one even remembered its name. Pinatubo. Pinatubo was there before Magellan, there before the Chinese, and the Spanish and the Americans, there when Taal, its brother, exploded and changed the landscape forever. "As if even the land will become outraged and kill off parts of itself," he said. "They say fish will fall from the sky, dust will fall like snow and cover Manila.

"The healers warn that not even the First Lady can overcome the powers of these hills, powers the *hilots* near there use for good."

Sok had told her once, while they shared tea, "Ma'am, there are healers in these mountains near Taal and the Rice Institute. They cure disease by operating with their hands, a miracle, opening the skin of neck or thigh or belly, anywhere, reaching in and removing the center, so that the soul of the disease is captured. Then the body begins to repair the damage."

She'd met a visiting doctor from Columbia University who'd shown the American Club the slides he'd taken while witnessing a *hilot* at work, a healer. In the dark ballroom of the Peninsula Hotel, Rue saw pictures of the healer pushing the skin and reaching in. She saw pieces of dry gray basalt, red sand, bits of melted bubbled metal like pieces of meteor, clear glass worn smooth, sharp aqua coral, rusty flat iron nails, all from cures this man had personally witnessed and photographed. The aqua coral, from a weeping uterus, the *hilot* had claimed. The bubbled metal, pain in the lungs, perhaps TB. The iron nails—in children, malnutrition, in adults, wasting of the bones. The glass worn smooth, melancholy of the arteries, slow internal bleeding. Dry gray basalt, dust in the blood, she remembered.

What would a healer find in Trace and in her? How would his hands feel?

Late in the afternoon, she drove home. But few people were out on the streets. The day's voting was finished. By dark, the names of those in the barrios who'd cast blank ballots in protest would be known.

Saturday afternoon, two days later, was the day of the annual picnic for the "domestic employees" of the American embassy's personnel, and these employees' children—*Domestic Employees Appreciation Day*. This was a yearly event in June, always a week or two before the nationally celebrated *U.S. and Philippines Friendship Day*. The picnic had in the past been held under the giant acacia trees on the embassy grounds, but this year there were security concerns, so the Manila Zoo had been reserved. Today the zoo was closed to all but the Americans and the Filipinos who work for them. They were to bring their families for an afternoon fiesta.

"Perhaps you could bring your cousin Angel and her children," Celia suggested to Doming, since Celia and Lleoni, the young maid, had no children to bring. At last year's picnic the other cooks had a houseful of foreign children to look after, and so Celia had gotten Trace Caldwell's approval now. Celia wanted children to take care of, too.

So Doming drove them—Celia, Lleoni, Angel, Paco, Linay, and the baby. The zoo was just off Quirino Avenue, not far from the Coconut Palace and Cultural Center that

Imelda had built on the reclaimed land along the bay. Rue drove her old car there from work and met them.

Everything was free, provided by the embassy. Cotton candy shaped into pink and blue and white clouds or birds or flying fish, by the special vendor hired by the embassy. The warm sweet-burning sugar brought back to Doming the smell of the cane field burning.

He was curious to see Rue with the children.

Inside the zoo gates, an old Chinese vendor took long blades of bright greenish-yellow palms and wove and folded them into shapes four or five inches long. In his skilled fingers they became grasshoppers, dragonflies, frogs, curling snakes. He attached each to a long piece of palm-leaf spine so that as the children held the other end the creatures appeared to fly or creep or hop. They looked almost real.

"What is this in English?" Paco asked, pointing to one. Its long antennae, as long as its body, were also made of a palm-leaf spine.

"A praying mantis, that one is called in English," Rue said to him.

"Why that," the two children asked her, and she folded her hands together and bowed her head slightly, raised her eyebrows as if looking to take a bite of one them. They giggled and began to be less nervous. They were paupers compared to the other children here and they sensed that.

"My grandfather made these as a boy, brought the skill with him from Fujian Province," the Chinese man said to them. Paco took his apart and wove it back together again.

They found a table. There would be games and prizes, animal tricks.

Angel told Rue and Celia that she worked at the candy factory in the San Juan section of the city, near Cardinal Sin's palace.

"I took the afternoon off, but I brought you some free samples, Ma'am," Angel said to them.

Doming saw she carried her best handbag. From it she took some factory-made expensive *povlerone* candies of rice flour, tied in colorful wrappers. Rice flour and instant milk were cooked dry and combined with butter and green fried crispy rice and poured into molds.

He knew that Angel was shy with Rue and Celia, because her English was not good, but she was so proud of her children she would not let them come without her.

But something very strange happened that almost spoiled the afternoon for them. Soon after everyone arrived, about two o'clock, one American woman sent her driver to the market for a chicken. She'd announced she would give the children some demonstration of feeding time, but then the person in charge at the zoo told her she must bring her own supplies, there was not much food.

Doming saw cages that were unpainted, stark, like prisons, rats crawling along the cobblestoned floors. The animals seemed half-starved. Public money for them was gone, pilfered. In one cage a mangy foul-smelling lion chewed on green grass, as old Filipina servants stood in front of the cage and made the sign of the cross over themselves and took leaves from the *balete* tree that grew there that they would use for medicine.

Soon the woman's driver came back. The man carried a fine rooster, a fighting gamecock, there were no hens, Ma'am, the man lied. It was clear that he hated to give the bird up, the woman had given him way too much cash and he spent it all on this fine bird. It was clear he expected her to say, well of course, we can't sacrifice such a fine bird to the crocodiles. But she didn't know its worth. She didn't know he'd just bought it from his friend in the market, perhaps a bird he'd coveted for some time, at a good price.

So the American woman, a heavy woman who wore a dress of silky black with large white dots, one placed unfortunately over the center of her breast, took the rooster by its tied feet. Then she called, in a patronizing, false high voice, "Watch, children," and before all of them, Americans and Filipinos and the exotic mixes that diplomatic families become, she tossed it with both hands out over an iron-fenced muddy pool. For an instant, the bird hung there, wings beating like wind. Then darkness rose up—there was a snap, and without another sound the bird was gone.

Linay gasped and cried out.

Doming hated the woman.

Silence, the rippled water smoothing, languid mud again, and all was still, uncannily silent except for the sound of the children's scared breathing.

The swiftness, the doom, the silence that followed, shook everyone gathered there, except the woman who gave up the bird. The crowd that had gathered to watch her dispersed. Doming and Celia, Angel and the baby, and Paco and Linay and Rue returned to one of the plastic-covered tables and sat down.

Finally Linay said, "*Buwaya*, the saltwater crocodile." The one that now came in her worst dreams, that she was afraid might one night emerge from the dirty canal just behind her house.

Doming murmured some words from the Mass for the Dead, made the sign of the cross toward the murky pool, and Paco and Linay glanced at him in alarm, and then they saw he was playing with them, but they didn't smile. Celia coaxed them to eat, and got American soft drinks, plates of the embassy club's catered food for them—hotdogs, potato chips, cookies, apples.

But there was more to their fear, Doming knew. That damn woman. Paco and Linay had never been around foreigners. Now what a thing it was for them to see the foreigner sacrifice such a fine bird, because of one thing they knew for sure—such a bird was worth much more than either of them would be in the city's markets.

But perhaps Rue sensed this as well, the woman's stupidity and waste, the horror she caused in the children. Perhaps she hated her too, he thought. He waited for some sign that she was not an unwitting conniver in this show.

The zoo was actually such a sad place here, he thought. Even the lion, giraffes, mangy wolves, suffered from Marcos' and Imelda's greed, from the Americans' arrogance that they could fix the world to their liking because they had the money to do it.

"She is greedy," Paco said. "Remember, Titó Doming, you told me how the Tiboli god of things that grow met a hunter in the woods, returning from a morning hunt with all he could carry. Share with me some of your food, I'm hungry, but the hunter refused, saying, It's mine, mine. So the god turned him into a frog, and that's why all the frogs today say only one word, *Akin, akin*, mine, mine."

"Like Marcos and Imelda," Doming said. He pulled a large paper napkin around his shoulders like Imelda's fine woven wraps, pursed his lips. "Mine, mine," he said, in a froggy tone.

Linay smiled.

But Celia said sharply, "Doming, where did you learn that story?"

"From my mother, Pô," he said simply.

73

She chewed a piece of red betel in her mouth, a treat for today. She was strangely quiet, grouchy.

"We didn't offend your politics, *Manang*?" he asked.

She shook her head.

"Indigestion, *impatso*," she said.

"Perhaps the bad lady will put a bad spell on us," Linay said.

Rue took the silver-colored embassy salt shaker from the tray in front of them. She shook a bit of salt into Linay's paper cup of bubbling American-bottled pop, direct from the embassy commissary.

"I will make you a potion," Rue said in all seriousness to Linay, "so the crocodiles will never come near you, and neither will *she*." Rue lifted her chin in the Filipino way and pointed contemptuously to the fat, sweating American woman in the black dress with the white spots.

Then, in the next moment, she looked at him and he looked back and they each saw compassion, authenticity, and curiosity tempered by long solitude, some understanding passing between them.

He refused to consider that he might already love her. He thought only that he had judged her too harshly, that she was not like the other foreigners, yet.

Rue spoke slowly to Paco and Linay. "Here is your safe charm from that woman—Beware the Jabber-walker, with spotted chest, red claws that test, beware her jabber words and sorry bird, and the jabber beast into which she'll turn."

Doming saw that Linay was still alarmed, her eyes big and quiet, but she believed. She adjusted the light blue headband she always wore, pushing her long hair out of her face. Then she sniffed at the glass of salty soda, took a drink, and swallowed thoughtfully.

"Imagine, in my country if that woman threw anything to animals in the zoo she'd be in trouble," Rue said.

But Linay said, "I heard in your country they throw black children to the crocodiles."

"Psssht, *tahimik!*" Celia interrupted, hushing Linay.

"This Jabber-walker, what does it turn into?" Paco said politely, always the diplomat.

Rue looked away, pained, Doming thought. Then she began, "It has the head and jaws of a crocodile, the claws of a vulture, the poison of a toad, and the body—"

"The body of a huge rat," Doming said, finishing. "I will never, never let them get you, Linay." He hugged her hard and Paco relaxed.

Doming pictured them playing happily in the shallows off Abbe's mother's place in Negros, visiting their *lola*. They had never met her.

"Ito ba ay matamís?" Are they sweet? Doming asked, pretending to gnaw at Linay, who laughed now.

Of course, Sir.

That was the end of the Employee's Appreciation Day.

In the next day's news, when a Filipino journalist was declared missing in southern Mindanao, Malacañang Palace announced that after inquiries were made it was learned that he had likely been eaten by crocodiles.

That next night Doming was at Abbe's place.

In the preceding weeks Doming's cousin Abbe had put together some of the explosives going off in Makati in the middle of the night. He worked in the back of his pawn shop and gave them to fast young men who'd set them off when the fancy buildings in the financial district were empty, and then flee.

Abbe had bought the pawn shop by scrimping for twenty years, working as a jeepney driver to save money to begin a business. It had taken him five years just to save enough to marry. But then when he bought the shop, he found that all his profits were going to bribe inspectors, to bribe the Metro-Com, to contribute for gifts to the barangay captain (who had ambitions), and to low-ranking bleary-eyed officials in the mayor's office. He'd had to bribe the fellow at the electric company to overlook the illegal electrical hookup the shop-owner before him had made. When Abbe objected, things got more difficult.

"You have to have some connection to do anything," he'd complain to Doming. "In this country there are eleven words for bribe, and I know all of them."

In his disgust and disappointment with his entrepreneurial skills, and because Sonny was his friend and neighbor and had connections with the opposition, Abbe had offered his place for some in the urban arm of the New People's Army. He'd begun helping Sonny assemble explosives for them. He was good with his hands.

These months of opposition-sponsored bombings in Manila, outside state-run and crony businesses, had embarrassed and infuriated the president. Less investment, less tourism, more concern among the Makati financial district American Chamber of Commerce that perhaps Marcos was losing his edge, it was said.

"I want to go tonight," Abbe said to Doming. "You can drive me around. We want to try this new bunch of timing devices."

"You're not as fast as the young men who set them off," Doming said, worried Abbe would take such a chance himself.

"I want to see how good these new fuses work," Abbe urged. "Come on, we can't just roll over for Marcos like dogs."

Despite his hesitation, Doming agreed to make a quick run to the fine avenues of Makati. It was a form of resistance that was disruptive but not aimed at killing. Plus the foreign press always reported the night-time explosions in the financial district. Daniel Gold, a journalist Sonny knew, had shown Abbe the articles he had written for the *Christian Science Monitor.*

"Someone like Gold can urge you to be reckless, but he can fly out of here with his passport and escape," Doming said. "It's dangerous enough assembling them, without you being the one to set them off, Abbe," Doming added.

"This must be the greatest city on earth. Do you remember when you first saw the city and told me that?" Abbe called to him as he drove Abbe's jeepney. Abbe was jovial now that he had prevailed and was working with these newly delivered fuses in the back of the jeepney. Doming had not spoken again.

"You never let me forget, I was green as a new coconut," Doming said.

That was eleven years ago, he thought, and now Abbe and his friends were ripping the city up, week after week, with their explosives; they would rip into every power station and water works and every bank, if that would loosen Marcos' grip.

Doming drove the jeepney toward the valley of the tall buildings in the financial district of Makati. He drove down Tejeron Street, along Pasong Tamo, over the little bridge toward Makati Medical Center and then onto Ayala Avenue. He heard the familiar hiss, and the first device went off near Rustans, a department store owned by a crony. He turned around in front of the Inter-Con, and went north up Makati Avenue, flying past the statue of Gabriela, the nation's heroine.

The next went off too quickly, just after Abbe tossed it. He slowed in front of Mandragon House, an office building. A window shattered, the boom echoed off the buildings. Doming felt the jeepney's metal sides vibrate. Leaves from the perfectly clipped tamarind trees floated down. The letters S and U from the Sugarmen's Trust Bank sign fell. Several children came out of their shelter, an abandoned storm pipe that sat in the vacant lot across the street. They cheered, *Mulî*, again. They demanded *Lalô, lalô*. More, more, as if the explosions and breaking glass were part of the celebration just for them.

"Very close, be careful," Doming said from the driver's seat.

"Little Brother, this is like clucking your tongue compared to the bigger ones I've put together," Abbe said.

"This is the last one," Abbe said. The moment his left hand brought the cigarette lighter near, a blue light exploded in his hand.

Doming quickly turned to look. Abbe's face bore a peculiar surprised expression Doming would always remember. His left hand, torn open up to the wrist, hung in pieces. His face and shirt shone with bits of mucused muscle and blood, white splinters of his fingers and knuckles. Blood began to seep slowly from the wound.

A smell of burnt flesh hung in the air. Doming's white t-shirt was flecked with tiny bits of red, seeping and spreading into the cloth.

"What have I done, what have I done?" Abbe's voice, full of regret, called out.

"*Kuya*, hold on, hold on." Doming drove a few blocks farther north and pulled into a dark driveway beyond Buendia Avenue, off Burgos Street. He stole a shirt hanging on a window sill, to wrap around the wound. Press it down hard, he urged Abbe, relieved only that the blood was dark. Doming drove along back streets with Abbe on the seat next to him. He made no protests, but Doming heard him dry-retch.

"You have to be placid as a hen," Doming urged him. "Be very still, we'll get help."

Doming readied himself to take on the officious front-window clerks at the hospital, the doctors who acted as if they were serving time in hell to be in the midst of them. He wished Sonny were with him now. Sonny could put on airs of the rich, revealing his upbringing. But Sonny was at work this night.

He decided to take Abbe to the charity clinic near Santo Tomas and hold the money to use for medicines, or bribes. When they passed a public jeepney full of passengers on their way home from the election day's celebrations, old women looked over at Abbe, stared at the darkening t-shirt, and made *tsk* sounds with their tongues.

Doming tried to map out a plan—he would need money soon to pay for Abbe's medicines. He would not ask for a salary advance. He never had; he would not ask them for anything.

In the clinic there were other accidents—eyes and scalps burned, eyebrows singed, wounds from fights or knifings. They sat in a green hallway in the two-story building, an ugly shade of green, the color of official business, of charity.

"Why can't someone look at him? He's in pain," Doming said to each uniformed nurse who walked down the corridor where people lined up waiting on each side.

But Abbe had no national I.D. with him and this was holding things up. "Where is it?" Doming scolded him.

Abbe said, "You were not to know, but I gave it to Sonny. He threw his in the river. Mine is the one he carries now, I'll get another copy."

"For God's sake, why didn't you tell me?" Doming said.

"Because Sonny was afraid they would torture it out of you."

"He trusts me so little?"

"No, we wanted to protect you from knowing."

The doctor on duty finally came out of one room, with an on-the-toes walk as if he didn't want to soil his shoes. Doctor Edmond Deldrano, Doming learned, was on assignment from Makati Hospital, had offered to fill in for his son-in-law, a young doctor who was on his honeymoon in the States. Deldrano doctored the rich Filipinos and foreigners, their sore throats, their allergies and asthmas. You're very fortunate, the nurse told Doming. Dr. Deldrano is very well trained.

I'm exhausted, this work is for young doctors, Doming heard Dr. Deldrano complain. The faces are indistinguishable, the burns, the wounds, the knifings—like a visit to hell.

After a while a young nurse came out of one room. She gave Abbe a shot just below his elbow, for reducing pain, she said, and began to clean the wound. Doming waited in the corridor as Abbe was taken into an examination room.

The nurse came out in a few minutes and said to Doming, "They'll cut it off at his wrist. With this wound the doctor says the hand can't be saved."

Doming watched from outside the door, looking in through a cloudy window. They didn't put Abbe to sleep, but someone gave him more shots to numb it all. Abbe looked terrified but remained quiet.

"Why don't they put him to sleep?" Doming asked a passing nurse, pointing to where Abbe lay. He was also afraid Abbe might be asked questions and be too groggy to consider before he spoke.

"We have no more beds for when he wakes up," she said.

There was something just short of fury in Doming—at them, at Abbe, at himself. If he paid any more attention to that, to the stomping in his brain, his heart pounding in a mad beat, he wouldn't be able to think for both of them.

"It's a wound from fireworks, you say?" this older nurse said now.

"Yes," he said, cautious.

"It was strong, then. More like explosives."

"They were the fireworks from Chinatown, some big ones."

There was a good chance that the clinic staff or the doctor might report this injury to the police—they'd get a good reward for turning in what the government called urban terrorists. There was a bounty now for troublemakers, as Defense Minister Enrile had called them. Like Imelda's campaign for flies and cockroaches, one peso each, and fifty pesos each for feral cats. Now there was a bounty offered to informers by the city vigilantes, El Diablo Crimebusters. A new kind of citizen police, authorized to dispense justice immediately. Priests, nuns, students, labor leaders, farmers in the markets, journalists, even jeepney drivers, disappeared, or were found "salvaged," killed and left in the countryside, dumped along the roads. The vigilantes paid well for tips. The thing is, Sonny had always said, they must turn us against each other, brother against brother.

When Doming looked in from the hall, it was still just Dr. Deldrano with his bloody coat and the nurse. A boy, seemingly oblivious to the gore, wiped the floor with a mop. The smell of the solution seeped up from under the door and made Doming's eyes burn. He watched the doctor cut with a saw, like the butcher in the market, and then stitch with a shiny curved needle. He stitched expertly, unthinkingly.

The cots were full when he finished, so a nurse and Doming led Abbe to a wooden pew in the chapel to lie down. Abbe slept a while, then opened his eyes. He looked at Doming, looked at his bandaged stub. Doming decided to let him speak first, to wait with him. Finally, Abbe sat up. Realizing where he was, he eased himself down from the wooden bench onto the kneeler, grasping the pew in front of him with his one hand.

"At least it's not Angel or one of the children," Abbe said, finally, addressing a space above the chapel's altar. "But if the pawn shop doesn't make it, and it seems it will not, how can I drive and shift a jeepney, make change, with only one hand?" he demanded.

Doming was not even sure Abbe was talking to him.

Getting no answer, or not the one he hoped, Abbe bowed his head on the pew in front of him and began banging his forehead against it. Each time Doming restrained him, he banged harder. Again, again, ten times, twenty. Not fast, but it seemed to Doming like Abbe was pounding nails into hard *narra*, stopping to see that the nail was straight, pounding again. Like nails into a coffin, nails into a smashed soul.

The nurse came in, looked, and then left. She returned and gave Abbe another shot, this time in his good arm.

"This may ease the pain, but he might talk out of his head, too," she said. "Poor man."

A while later, Abbe began again. He talked to the statue of the Virgin above him. Doming saw that her feet had been rubbed smooth by the petitioners.

"It's true what they say," Abbe said, "even when the limb is gone, you feel the pain of it, I feel my hand, a fly is crawling across the knuckles."

"Shh," Doming said, rocking him. "The nurse told us it would go away in a few days."

"In the place my thumb is, it itches as if black sugar ants crawled there," Abbe said.

"Rub it," he said, holding out the bandaged stump. So Doming pretended to take the thumb and rub the ants off.

"It's the memory of all my hand has felt," Abbe said.

Angel's breasts when she was new to him, he talked of that. She came out of Tondo but her black hair was silk. And when we couple I put one hand where she likes and one hand at her breast, and my mouth on hers so she won't cry out and what will she do with a one-handed man. I will disgust her.

Doming tried not to listen, but envied this intimacy between a man and a woman. He hated being reminded of a time when he thought he could get what he wanted. When he'd come to Manila, he wanted to be educated, he wanted to learn every language in the world, to find and need one woman.

But now he sat with Abbe, whose lost hand would cost him everything. He considered the foolish bad luck of the poor, the way disaster sits waiting for them like a shiny housefly rubbing its forelegs together. Even children knew that for the poor, disaster, fate, *bahala na*, whatever name you gave it, could rise up like the saltwater crocodile and grab you in its jaws in an instant.

They heard the roosters. He wished he had Sonny there to talk to, argue the night away.

It was 4:30 a.m. In two hours Doming had to be at work, at the Caldwell's house outside the city.

He shook his head. He was being foolhardy, his mind racing, the cost of a night with no rest, the cost of hearing Abbe already anticipating his Angel's beauty withheld.

He got more medicine and took Abbe home. When they got back to Abbe's place, Angel began to shriek the moment she saw Abbe with his arm held in a sling made of a torn pillowcase, an arm missing a hand. It was terror Doming heard. Fear of future want.

"Quiet, you must be quiet, or the neighbors will want to know what has happened," Doming warned her.

Two days later, a Friday evening, Rue sat alone in the back seat of Trace's dark blue embassy Cressida. Doming drove. She was on her way to Intermuros, the oldest part of the city. It was just north of the embassy and along the Pasig River. She was to meet her friend Anne Larkin.

At a light, a boy with his legs bent under him like broken twigs pushed himself across the street in front of the car. He rode on a four-wheeled dolly, a square piece of board with four coasters nailed on. He stayed to the side of the street—the sidewalks were too crumbled—and pushed himself alongside the rush-hour buses and jeepneys there.

"Is it true their legs are broken on purpose, when they're born?" she asked Doming.

She watched his eyes in the mirror, for an answer. He didn't even glance at the child.

"Yes, there's a man near Quiapo market under the bridge who will crush legs, for a fee."

Before she could ask why, he went on.

"They think that the child will always be able to beg, so pitiful, so at least he'll never go hungry," he said.

Her questions vexed him sometimes, she knew.

"But why do that, damage them? They could still beg," she persisted. Able-bodied ragged children were constantly knocking on the car's dark windows when she was in the city, along Pasay Road near Baby's house. Then they would laugh and run to buy Magnolia ice cream from a street vendor when she gave them money, while she was still looking, chagrined at first at being duped for change but now used to it.

"You can only be in a begging syndicate if you're like that, already damaged," he said.

Like another of Baby's warnings—don't be overly sympathetic to the cripples and beggars, they're professionals. Rue was no longer amazed that she was just supposed to accept this.

It is a pity, alas, *Sayang*, Baby had said.

Doming drove. He turned up the air conditioner, the air humid with coming rain.

Trace was on another trip with U.S. military advisors and their Filipino counterparts. He'd left for Mindanao on Thursday morning and told her they would return on Saturday.

Rue hadn't understood Trace's work until she'd been to a series of embassy dinner parties where each detail of Philippine *tsismis*, or gossip, was analyzed. She hadn't realized the meaning of Trace's real work. *Counter-insurgency specialist* was his title.

His work consumed him. Peace and order, he described it.

But peace and order for a country had seemed theoretical, dinner party conversations when they were in Washington, and this work was not. What he did was real, even if she didn't quite know the substance. Peace and order—a euphemism for tranquility at any cost. He refused to discuss it now.

Preserving domestic peace and order, Trace had explained to her before she'd agreed to move to Manila with him, that's what I'll be doing there. That had sounded so noble, so much the way she thought of him, in the early days. It didn't occur to her that he might not be doing good.

We just can't let the opposition take out Marcos, he said. If Marcos goes, then the U.S. bases go, and our access to the country goes, and that affects the balance of power in this whole part of the world.

It began to rain, the first rain in months. This was the beginning of the rainy season, the monsoons. There were three seasons, she'd come to see after two years here. A temperate dry season, a hot dry season, and then a hotter monsoon season, June through October. So now the rain came each afternoon, a steady pouring. The monsoon season was made of these muggy days when it clouded up during the afternoon and rained during the evening rush hour, washing the vinegary smell of spoiled garbage, human excrement, and the reek of decay. The rains settled the bus and jeepney exhaust that hung over these streets, where luxury cars, belching buses, gaudily decorated jeepneys and pedicabs, and even oxen carts traveled as if in a slow caravan.

She'd met some well-traveled foreigners, who'd spent their lives in third-world capitals, and they said this ripeness was the same smell everywhere, you got used to it. It was the smell with which most of the world lived. She marveled that it had grown so familiar to her.

"What time are you to be there, Ma'am?" Doming asked.

"About six, you can leave the car there with me and be done for the day," she said. Her car, the old taxi, was in the shop in Makati.

Doming took some back streets to cut due west toward Intermuros. Along one sidestreet she was sure she'd not been on before, he lifted his chin, gesturing to a shop near the curb.

"My cousin's shop up ahead," he said.

Baby Jesus Pawn Shop, she read from the wooden sign above the shop window. No streetlights worked there, but wires were strung like haphazard laundry lines from the utility poles. Run-down dark shops and shabby metal roofed houses lined the narrow street. No tourists would visit this shop, and no foreigners would pass through this street unless they were lost. It was not on the way to anywhere.

In the shop window lit by a yellow bulb, she saw the finest things no one had returned to collect, now for sale— Chinese porcelain dishes, curved *balisong* knives, antique tribal jewelry made of woven abaca and colored beads and mother of pearl. In the center of these stood an almost life-sized *Santos* of the baby Jesus with open hands spread.

It seemed to her this *Santos* made the same gesture as the vendor in the markets—*Walana*, no more. No more grace? No more hope?

Who had pawned that icon? Rue imagined a woman her age, taking from her house this wooden idol, admired or coveted by many, wrapping it in a new dish towel and carrying it to this pawn shop where there was a market for such figures. A wooden white-faced blue-eyed icon. What was she willing to give up, to get something she needed more.

"Do most people come back, to reclaim what they've traded?" she asked Doming.

"Not here, so much. By the time they come here, to my cousin's shop, they're desperate—he does his business in re-sales, mostly."

"And the *Santos?*"

"That he won't trade."

Antique *Santos* figures of the babe were valued almost superstitiously, although now even the crudest-made primitives brought decent money from collectors. But most were hoarded and passed down through families and prayed to in their little shrines built into the walls of the most humble shacks. To give up a family *Santos* was to give up your heritage, your beliefs, your sense that here was an image of a kind and loving being who determined your fate in life and after death.

They reached Intermuros, the historic Spanish fort and city. On one of her first days in the city Rue went there as a tourist. She'd seen a small horse pulling a brightly painted *calesa,* two-wheeled cart. The high wooden wheels were decorated with paper flowers for tourist rides. The horse was foaming at the mouth in the heat. This is one of Imelda's most successful projects, restoring these ruins, the tour guide had said.

The car passed through the stone gates and into the old walled city of Intermuros. The rain poured down as she felt the car bumping over cobblestones. When she'd first seen the cobblestoned streets in Intermuros, the worn round stones had looked like a path of half-buried geodes.

Her father had died when she was a child, and she'd placed half of a broken geode in his casket, to go with him. They'd found many over the years, hunting for the gray domes half buried along stream-banks in northeastern Iowa, in their own limestone hills.

The geode was a hollow rock about the size and shape of his two hands rounded together. She expertly split the stone with the rock hammer and pointed chisel he'd given her. Then she breathed in the air from eons ago, looked at the dark crystals lining the hollow core, now exposed. There was some miracle to her in letting the air out, and exposing to light a place hidden for a million years, the now-open geode. It had opened like the round earth itself being cleaved. For her with his death, the earth itself had broken open and lay in two halves.

He'd died, she'd reasoned, from emotion, feeling too much, and so she'd held back, some exile of the heart. Perhaps she'd held herself from not loving anyone, again, too much, and from craving the love of another who would love her with his whole heart. This was the great mistake in her life.

Intermuros, *within the walls*, Doming silently translated. The place where Rizal was imprisoned by the Spanish, where before the Spanish had discovered them a Malay chief had made his fort. For centuries, races had mixed here and fought their battles. He smiled to himself at the irony—he'd learned his history and languages from Father Rex, and now that knowledge was useless, but it was where his mind always took him as he did his routine tasks, driving, waiting, driving, waiting. These ancient city walls stood twenty feet high and five feet thick and within them was a more impenetrable prison, a dungeon along the Pasig River, where Doctor José Rizal lived his last days before the Spanish executed him.

Doming had gone there on one of his first days in the city, when he didn't even have the price of admission. We are a nation without a soul, José Rizal had written from his cell in Santo Tomas prison there. We cannot let the Spanish continue to divide us as a people, Rizal had urged.

The car bumped over cobblestones and narrow streets, past the St. Augustin church, well-lit restaurants, and newly opened antique shops for the tourists.

"Café Adriatico, Ma'am?" he said.

"Yes," she said.

She'd told him she was meeting Anne Larkin there, one of the few foreigners among their friends that Doming liked. Several times he'd driven the two women. Anne practiced her Tagalog on him and had been the one who encouraged Rue to learn the language. But Rue butchered it, sometimes. *Pusà* for *pusò*. Wily cat for heart. Saying *kita*, with the wrong accent, so she meant earnings, rather than *kitá*, you and I. Once she said *iwasák*, to destroy, when she meant *iwanan*, to entrust. It was like hearing music you thought you knew being sung off-key, he thought.

It had at first surprised him that English speakers knew so few languages but their own. His own knowledge he'd taken for granted at first.

"We're just about there," he said.

Then he noticed Trace walking toward them on the sidewalk just ahead, on Rue's side of the car. A young woman walked close to him, a Filipina. Trace had one arm around her, and held his big black umbrella over them with the other, partially blocking Doming's view of them. She wore a flowered dress. He recognized her, and knew—the heart-shaped face, tiny nose, lots of make-up, child-sized hands, small feet in high heels though she still didn't reach Trace's shoulder. Melinda, an architect, well-connected to the powers that be. In a moment she and Trace were next to them. Doming kept looking straight ahead, hoping Rue hadn't seen them. Trace's attention was on the short woman next to him. They were almost past.

Doming glanced back in the mirror.

She said nothing. Just a sharp breath in—she recognized him. She turned to look at her husband. It was to Doming as if ten thousand miles separated the husband and wife. They were not connected. He should have sensed her presence. As she had sensed his. The couple had already turned, up a cobbled walk at a sign for a well-known tourist restaurant and inn.

"Stop," Rue said. But she didn't even wait, she started to open the door.

He reached into the back seat and grabbed at her, catching her arm. He'd slammed on the brakes.

"Let me go," she said, indignant, pulling away.

But he tightened his grip. "It's not a good idea," he said.

"How do you know, you don't know anything," she said, pounding on his hand that held her arm.

The car horns behind them were screaming like there was some urgent business everyone else must get to.

He would not let her go. To what end.

"Go on, then, drive," she said.

The rain on the old narrow street, reflecting the headlights and shop lights, made the street seem streaked with pieces of light, something he must drive over carefully, like broken glass.

She sat back on the seat, leaned her head against the back, eyes closed.

"You've seen him with her before," Rue finally said.

He decided that Trace hadn't seen them.

"Tell me, answer," she demanded.

He wondered whose wrath was worse, whether Trace would think Doming had set him up to get caught. Trace was so ready to look for the undercurrent of connections even when they weren't there. This place made men like him do that.

"Yes, I've seen her, more than once," he finally said. *I'm General Ess' niece*, the young woman had loftily informed Doming the first time she rode in the car with Trace, *niece* being a loose term for a perhaps more distant family relation. He saw she was also too ambitious and a little vain and that she was unknowing bait, offered by Ess to trap Trace, ensnare him in vanity. Trace would be a fool to use her to get into General Ess' circle, to some inner circle of what was real here, some solid piece of intelligence.

Melinda had spoken to Doming at first in English and he'd purposely replied in halting English back, as if he'd misunderstood. She'd disregarded his presence after that and talked freely to Trace, and Doming had learned much as he'd listened. After weeks, it was clear the foolish girl was in love with Trace. Perhaps she was his reward for some diplomatic favor, because he was always about work and not love—meetings with Filipinos for lunch and drinks and dinners, the constant winnowing for information, connections, something real amid all the *tsismis*.

And perhaps Rue Caldwell didn't suspect the several times now he'd driven her husband and this woman to a particular one of the "love motels" near Cuneta Avenue at lunchtime. *He's gone tropo*, it was said of foreign men who succumbed to Manila's temptations, as if it were a hot weather disease he'd caught. But rich Filipinos would always run around on their wives, that's expected, a sign of machismo and success, to afford two households. He was surprised Trace had lasted as long as he had. *Querida*, the mistresses were called. Filipina wives grew up expecting it. He'd heard the old saying, "It doesn't matter if you do not love me, as long as you do not shame me." For the rich, as long as she had the official title of wife and was well provided for and had many children, she seemed not to care.

But Rue, did she care? Tragedy to the rich Filipina is the extra weight she carries on her belly and in the fleshy hump on the back of her neck, her children marrying a non-Catholic. But what was tragedy to this woman? Why had she married this man? Celia had told Doming once that perhaps most Westerners think they marry for love, but underneath, it is the same—they want a home, security, children, stability. Baby married for what she thought was love, Celia always said, and how much better it would have been for her if her father had arranged something.

So now he drove, without asking her whether to go on to the cafe. The car made slow progress in the narrow street of Intermuros.

She didn't cry, she didn't say anything. He glanced back. What most struck him was her solitude. Filipina women always had someone with them, a sister, a friend, a child, a maid.

Dank water filled the deep curbs along the streets. Traffic barely moved. The sky opened up with more heavy rain.

"He's not in Mindanao, did he even go?" Rue said.

"I'm certain they were in Mindanao, Ma'am, I took him and others to Villamor Air Base yesterday, but sometimes they come back a day early, on General Ess' own military plane, it's just a few hours away, you know," Doming said, keeping his voice neutral. The day before he'd watched the plane tear over Taal on the horizon. He'd felt a part of their complicity, as he did now, not telling her more.

Here was Café Adriatico. Rain-streaked windows reflected a golden candle-lit elegance. Doming pulled to the curb, stopped.

"You're as bad as they are," Rue said to him, her voice hateful, as if she heard his thoughts and agreed.

He felt accused. As bad as them, Ess and Raymonde and Trace. As disloyal to goodness?

Trace had a way of jutting his jaw, slung forward slightly. She'd noticed that profile. He'd tossed his head, flipped his hair back, a boyish nervous habit with his thinning light hair. When Rue looked back, she'd seen Trace's arm around her, his umbrella over them. The delicately built young woman was like a china doll wearing a silky dress the colors of polished gemstones—emerald, turquoise, coral.

There was something missing between Trace and herself, for how long, she wondered—some correct formality had come between them since she'd arrived and they'd begun living out their home-life in front of Celia and Lleoni. She'd become aware that he did not love her. He'd married her because he admired her, perhaps, her intellect, her lack of the sort of flightiness his first wife possessed. They married because she'd become pregnant with his child, and though she miscarried a few days before the wedding, he'd insisted they press on. Had those been his words? Press on. He was ten years older and already had a child with an ex-wife. On her very first day with Trace, sailing off Annapolis, she concentrated on missing the boom. He said he liked the way her long legs looked on his boat. The one time the boom caught her had made her ears ring.

Now he complained when she wore heels that made her as tall as he was. She felt his eye went first to whatever was lacking. He'd never told her she was beautiful. Once, within the first year of their wedding at the Cosmo Club in D.C., after she'd miscarried for the second time, she'd spent an hour getting ready for some important event at which he would speak. The shoes make you too tall, was all he said. These were the shoes the maid Lleoni now would try on when Rue was out.

He was smoothly arrogant. Is there anything he doesn't do well, one of the wives at an embassy gathering had asked Rue. She wasn't sure at first if the woman was joking, or asking if he was good in bed. But this woman was older, married to a hard-working, earnest and impossibly tongue-tied economics officer. Rue saw her looking at Trace with total admiration, and at Rue herself with envy.

"We're here, Ma'am," Doming said.

"Wait for me, don't leave," she said.

She felt with surprise that the rain was warm on her. She hadn't realized she was so cold in the car's air conditioning.

My boys, Anne Larkin would say to Rue, my boys, talking about them like a song. She adored them and talked about them constantly. Rue envied her. Anne's two grown sons were in school in England and Canada. They visited twice a year. Her first marriage had broken up in Pakistan, where she'd met David, her husband now, also a Canadian. We were all in Pakistan, when David and I met again, Anne had told Rue, and fortunately David didn't find the local women appealing to him. That was always the way she told it, making light of the fact they'd crossed and re-crossed paths for years in various international posts.

Her short hair framed doe-ish eyes. She was Canadian, Scandinavian descent, in her mid-forties, large, beautifully boned.

They sat in high-backed rattan chairs at a small marble-topped table. A waiter brought them clear soda flavored with *kalamansi*, the small local limes.

They'd first met one day at the Rice Institute, in one of the screen houses there, just after Rue had arrived in the country. Anne was taking pictures for a journalist who was writing an article about the Rice Institute for *Asia Week*. Anne had lived in Manila five years already. Later the two women had traveled together, north to Sagada, and south to Cotabato and the Tiboli region. Never complain, Anne often said. Think of this as home, not someplace to just tolerate, as some foreign women do.

"I'm sorry but I can't stay, after all," Rue said after they'd talked a few minutes.

Their tall glasses were in white crocheted holders, but water still collected around them in the moist air. Rue drew her index finger through the beaded water on the marble tabletop.

Anne had invited Daniel Gold, a friend of her brother's in Vancouver, to join them.

"But he'll be here soon, and he only has an hour or so. He's just in town for a few days this time. I want you to meet him. He's a journalist, his wife's family's close friends of Ninoy's."

Rue blurted out in a rush—I saw Trace, near here, with a young woman, he's supposed to be in Mindanao.

"So I can't stay," she said, after she'd told the details. She made marks with the water on the table, lines of canals as if some maze were being worked on.

"Someday it will be ancient history," Anne said. "This happens to almost everyone here."

"To you?"

"No."

"How did you know, what decided it for you, when you left your first husband?" Rue asked.

"When I realized I was constantly daydreaming about what I'd wear to his funeral," Anne said. "Seriously, go to my house tonight if you want, if you don't want to be alone at home. Dorrie will let you in, I'll just be an hour or so here."

Anne's helper, Dorrie, in her prissy starched uniform, the woman's nosey eyes on her, her saccharine ways.

"Thanks, maybe I will," Rue said.

But they both knew that meant no.

They stood and Anne kissed her on each cheek. Rue still had not grown used to this, the European way of women kissing when they met and parted, but she liked Anne's true affection for her.

"Should I drive to the house?" Doming asked her, as soon as she returned to the waiting car.

"No, not yet, just drive." She didn't want to face the house alone. Lleoni and Celia would have watered the front garden before the rain, washed the walk and drive and gutters, swept them with their short-handled brooms made of twigs. They would gossip with the other maids from houses across the fields who'd come out from behind the walls when the day cooled, *yayas* hired for the children, holding a child by the hand or pushing a stroller. At home she would sit on the lanai, have a drink, watch the bougainvillea blossoms drop one by one, certain in the knowledge that Lleoni or the pool boy would sweep them out by early morning.

The car made slow progress south from Intermuros. They were approaching Mabini, a street of sex clubs and bars. She'd been there only a few times when she toured the city as a newcomer.

Carter McCall, Trace's embassy colleague, had offered to give her the tour—the real Asia. Carter's reputation as an unmarried ex-pat was already well-known after his three years in Manila. How he could go walking down the streets of Mabini showing a newcomer around and the girls in many bars would call to him by name. How he'd begun a friendship with a young ambitious bargirl named Rennie, and now that she ran a place owned by a German he would still go back to visit her and anything he wanted was on the house. How he sheltered a former colleague's old girlfriend and that man's child in an apartment near his, and made sure she got the money she waited for from Australia each month, not telling her the money and gifts sometimes came from him instead of the man who'd not forgotten her entirely but had moved on and said his time in Manila seemed to be disappearing into the far distant past. Everyone fooled each other and lied about it, even from the best of motives.

Carter claimed to know the best places to go for sushi, or to hear the best music in nearby Ermita, or to see the most beautiful whore in Mabini at one of the private Japanese clubs. He volunteered to show Rue all the sights just after she arrived in the city. She could see how he and Trace would complement each other. Both were men who always got what they wanted, through hard work, charm, or compromise.

Carter would say of the women, this month it's legs, or ankles, or lips; she'd seen him once escort two women, one in a black frothy dress, the other dressed identically but in white, one on each arm, at some function. They were cousins from some well-known family—this was all she remembered. A young Filipina from a good family was sometimes not allowed to go out with a man without a companion or chaperone along.

It occurred to her that the woman she'd seen earlier might have been one of them.

That look on Trace's face tonight—she remembered that look when she'd first met him—roguish, charming, certain. They'd sat at an outside table on a rooftop restaurant near Dupont Circle on a balmy Washington evening.

Pogi, Handsome, the Filipina secretaries at the embassy had nicknamed Trace, she'd learned when she arrived in Manila six weeks after he had. But something had changed him during this time, something had shifted.

Here was Carter's Mabini. The neon lights over the bars flashed. Signs said *FIREHOUSE, BLUE HAWAII, TOMATO CLUB, NEW BANGKOK, LIVE SEX!, MACHO TOROS!!* Doors were propped open, and stray shards of light escaped as a mirrored ball revolved like a moon over the bar counter. Inside one bar two thin girls danced, grinding slowly on a counter. The car moved through the slow wake of cars and crowds. American music mixed with the rain and constant blare of horns, "Born in the USA," and "One Night in Bangkok." Everything was glazed with wet color, the cracked neon green sidewalks, the red taillights, white headlights, the hot pinks and cool blues of flashing signs. Brown frothy sewerage spilled from a broken pipe.

Then one of several girls standing outside a bar came to their car and lifted her tight knit shirt and pressed her bare breasts against the front passenger window, her small nipples the brown-rose color of figs. She was very young and lovely.

"Meester, meester," she called, high sweet voice almost like a song. Rue saw that her eyes were half-focused, the pupils pinpoints. The girl seemed to be looking at herself in the dark window glass that would reflect her face like a mirror.

"Mister, two hundred pesos only meester, for you, only for you." Her eyes half-closed. "For you," she sang again.

Doming reached over and opened the window a few inches and shouted at her, a question perhaps, something Rue didn't understand. The girl answered, *hindi*, no, and she lowered her shirt and backed away while others called over and moved their pelvises suggestively.

"I'll drive to your house now?" Doming said.

"No, not there, not yet, I need a drink, someplace where I won't see anyone else I know." She wondered if the Filipino waiters at the Embassy Club dining room had been especially solicitous toward her lately, if they knew, if Trace had been with a woman there too.

Doming didn't answer for a while.

"Beyond San Juan, in Pasig, my cousin and I go to a place there, my friend Sonny runs it, they have some food," he said.

Of course, he'd had no dinner. She'd completely forgotten. She was supposed to have let him go when she went in the cafe. Perhaps he was delicately reminding her—all the household help guidebooks counseled that Filipino employees get agitated and anxious if you keep them working without eating. Wouldn't anyone, she'd thought. But it was stressed, that it was a cultural taboo to have employees work like beasts without regular snacks, morning and afternoon *merienda* times especially. They'll get frenzied and have even more trouble concentrating, the guidebooks cautioned.

"I'm sorry, Doming, you haven't eaten," she began, annoyed with herself.

"Ma'am, you said you want a drink, but you'd better eat too," he said, in a neutral tone as if talking to a stranger's child, but she could tell he was provoked at her patronizing him. "I'll take you there because it—it's a decent place."

He turned toward Edsa Boulevard, the main thoroughfare north toward Pasig. A large sign in yellow and red letters just beyond the bridge for the Pasig River said, *Jesus Saves.* Graffiti scrawled below these words said, *Jesus + Laurie.*

Huge garishly painted billboards along the road, crudely lettered, advertised local movies. *Gia Colomba Goes Bold*, the young actress pictured there. Bold. One of the worst things Filipinos could call a woman, to willingly show her breasts, to be willing in sex. They passed Toronto Massage Parlor and Disco, where gray sheets flapped drying on clothes lines strung on the rooftop.

Sonny's place was on a bluff, facing northeast toward the hills of Antipolo. Doming parked the car on a side street and nodded at one of the ragged boys who beseeched him—Watch your car, Sir? Watch car? they asked. Unless he agreed, they would steal the hubcaps before he came out again.

Rue followed Doming through a covered entryway overflowing with bougainvillea growing in rusty metal cans. *Ihaw-ihaw*, the sign said, Beerhouse with Barbecue. She smelled *lechon*, roasted pig, spitting and crackling on the grill off the back patio. Fans in the corners of the room blew the warm pungent air. Music played, Freddie Aguilar singing "Magdalena." The place was still almost empty.

The bartender raised his eyebrows, acknowledging Doming, and said something quickly in Tagalog. She heard *mestiza?*

They sat at a table near the back of the room, which opened onto a patio with a tile floor that was being used as a dance floor by only one couple. Yellow light bulbs hung on cords strung around the room. She smelled the sharp incense of mosquito coils. Dengue, breakbone fever, was rampant as this rainy season began. She knew the female tiger mosquito, that hunted only at night, carried the disease.

Doming got San Miguel beers and a plate of thinly sliced green mango. She did what Doming did—spread a purplish paste of salty cured shrimp eggs, *bagoóng*, that smelled decayed but tasted right with the greenness of mango.

"An acquired taste, *bagoóng*," Doming said.

She found she was hungry.

Groups came in, couples sat at small iron tables. Slow music played, people danced. All were Filipinos.

She heard some Tagalog words in a refrain, sounding in English like *not old, not old, not old*.

"Doming, I'd like another drink, maybe something stronger." She pointed to the bar where she saw a Jack Daniels bottle.

"It's just a local mix they put in re-used bottles, the stuff burns like acid," he said. He went to the bar, got two more beers.

No one paid much attention to them.

She saw that the bartender, Doming's friend, greeted everyone, seemed to know everyone.

"What did he say to you when we came in?" she asked.

"Ah, you don't want to know, that's Sonny, always giving me a hard time anyway," Doming said.

She waited, more curious. "It was about me, *mestiza* I heard, what could possibly bother me now?"

He shrugged, annoyed. She saw she was the pushy American.

"You want to know? All right, what he said exactly—
Is the *mestiza* buying you tonight or are you buying her?"
Doming said.

"You mean he thinks you're paying *me*?"

"Well, is that any worse than if you paid me, in that
way?" he countered.

He spoke like she had, in low tones, mimicking an
American accent.

"Actually, I have it right—he was joking that you're
paying *me* for my time, like rich *mestizas* used to," Doming
said.

"That's disgusting."

"That's the unembellished fact," he said, seeming to
goad her.

"What fact, tell me," she said. She folded her arms, sat
back, making a demand she knew she had no right to.

He stretched his legs out in front of him, expansively,
stretched his arms up, taking his time. More people were
coming in. He glanced at the door. Then he began.

"At the Polo Club in Makati, some old rich Filipino
women have for years employed various young men who
go dancing with them, once or twice a week, to be their
escorts at the club. When I began driving for a Chinese-
Filipino family, a friend of Mrs. Wo's asked her if I was available to be her escort."

"The woman just saw you and said he's the one?" Rue
said.

"More or less. I was twenty-three then, that's young for
a dance partner. But some of these ladies take their older
escorts all around with them, even to family gatherings,
and call them their attorneys, though no one is fooled. You
know, most Filipinas don't like to be alone. So she gave me
money to buy a new *barong*, new black shoes, black pants. I

went to the gate of the Polo Club in Makati and gave the guard my name. He let me in and I walked up the drive and waited in the entry of the club as she told me.

"It was a paradise. Clear water flowed in the artificial fountain and two-story waterfall, making soothing noises. The ceilings were high enough for indoor banana trees and palms that never bloomed. Even the birds, blue parrots and one white cockatiel like the two you once had, were in a giant aviary. They had a boy whose only task was to feed and clean them, although they screamed for their freedom.

"Each of us stood waiting, and when each lady's car drove up her escort would go out, open the door, give our arm, and in we'd go. There was live music, a band, sometimes an early hour of dancing lessons, and we just danced, danced with our lady."

"And they paid you?" she said, surly.

"Three hundred pesos for an evening. These women are old and rich, it was almost a competition between them. Sometimes they'd pay just to have someone play mahjong with them at the club. They were lonely. It still goes on."

She couldn't imagine Doming doing this. He had too much dignity.

"But it was like trying to lead a carabao around, dancing with them. Some ladies picked out their special songs, Barbra Striesand was their favorite, and they would be the one to start the dancing, waltz, salsa, traditional."

"It sounds like a show-dog on a leash," Rue said. She remembered then, too late, *Dog, Dogeater*, in Filipino, the most derisive term, less than human.

"I'm sorry, I'm sorry, I meant—you're too . . ."

She felt horrible. She wanted to say, *too good*, but she didn't know him. Only that he had great dignity, pride, and reserve.

"What—you think she paid for sex? She's someone's *lola*, for god's sake," he said.

He worked his jaw, chewing the soft flesh inside his mouth. Anger made his eyes go flat.

"Do you think I didn't feel like a fool?" he asked, his voice low and harsh. "Do you think I'm so simple? Is that enough story? My primitive ways? I needed money to send home."

He picked up his beer, drank it down, looked down at his worn knit shirt and jeans, shook his head. "Don't ask me anything else," he said.

"You're too touchy, too proud," she said. "Just because you must have seemed so ridiculous to yourself. You told me this to make me disgusted with you," she said.

"And look how easy that is," he said. He cursed her under his breath, *asong babae*.

She felt him watching her, a look so untenable she would never forget it, intelligent challenging eyes, brown and gold, guarded, and elegant cheekbones, like a Mongolian, with not much beard or hair on his face, and a high forehead. His nose had a small arch as if once broken. He was tall for a Filipino, as tall as she was, five to ten years younger. She wouldn't have noticed him in the market or on the street.

There was a kind of Filipino man whose Malay blood would cause him to go amok, it was said, who after bearing some indignity or humiliation for so long would suddenly lash out, violent. Like the carabao, they said, he is patient, intelligent, and long-suffering, and then suddenly brutal, raging, unslaked.

Doming was not meek. Trace had threatened to fire him once for what Trace could only call the look in his eye. He didn't smile much. But he was cool-headed, Trace said, he'd trust him in an emergency, meaning if the car were ambushed. It had happened to others, a JUSMAG officer who was aiding the Philippine military, killed near Subic Bay before Trace had arrived in the country, a Japanese banker kidnapped and held by the NPA, New People's Army.

"Let's go," he said. "I have to be somewhere, I must take you home," he said. "You are stupid about our ways."

"I was just trying to imagine what it would be like for you, I was trying to be sympathetic."

"I don't need kindness—a lonely old woman with no family."

She felt her cheeks grow hot, as if slapped, her eyes teared.

"That's very cruel to call me."

"I mean the old woman." He enunciated each word as if she were a child.

"She loved to dance with her heavy feet," he said. In his chair, Doming clunked his feet on the floor. "I felt sorry for her, okay, *sige*?"

"And so do you feel sorry for me?" she asked.

"No, but I'm sorry that you don't grasp the complicity you are a part of here, what your husband does, your self-delusion that you are not involved, your sense of detachment from the injustice, your country's—" He looked past her, toward the entrance.

"Dance with me," he demanded. He stood up suddenly and pulled her up, led her to the outdoor dance floor lit by yellow bulbs. He put his arm around her waist, took her hand.

"Tell me, what are they doing, the three who just came in?"

She saw the bartender opening beers for three men. They wore the light khaki-colored uniforms of the Philippine

National Constabulary, cloth the exact color of mud termites. They wore the knee-high black shiny boots, and the mirrored sunglasses of the PNC. Sonny stood cracking his knuckles, unsmiling as they talked and drank their beers.

"Drinking, and talking to your friend," she said.

One stood looking around the room, his feet spread, belly out. The man raised his eyebrows at her appraisingly. She looked away.

Doming held her tighter.

The music, Freddie Aguilar, the refrain, *Ikáw, ikáw.* You, you. She understood this.

In about five minutes the men left, each one carrying several beers. They'd helped themselves from the cooler while Sonny appeared to ignore them. She whispered to Doming, "They left," but still, the two danced. She wanted to say, you're a good dancer, but considered even this would provoke him.

Sonny came out to the patio when the song ended, to where they stood. He spoke quickly to Doming in Tagalog. She strained to understand him. He had odd teeth, too big for his mouth, somehow. But he, too, had a handsome face, his hair already with gray in it.

Doming interrupted him. "This is Sonny, and this is the wife of my employer," Doming said, in a low voice, as if ashamed of her.

Sonny's face froze, his mouth snarled words. She made out—*Espiyá*, spy? And *Walâ dini, walâ dini.* Get out, get out.

He stalked away.

"Time to go," Doming said.

She followed him. "What kind of trouble are you in?" she asked.

"Only what you are bringing me by being here. Sonny used to be a student leader, in the old days. He doesn't like Americans."

She knew the Constabulary was picking up anyone these days, any university student, demonstrator, journalist, anyone who'd made trouble.

They went toward the door.

They were standing in the bougainvillea-covered archway.

"Why did you bring me to this place, then, if he dislikes Americans?"

"I didn't know where else to go to suit you. I'm not dressed for the bar of a five-star hotel; if they'd just looked at my shoes they wouldn't have let me in." He was angry. She saw it shamed him, to have to explain this.

A foreigner, a heavy-set man with a dark beard, was coming in. They moved aside. She looked down, afraid it might be someone who knew her. Then she watched him go to the bar and greet Sonny, who brought him a beer and then sat down with him.

"Who is that?" she asked.

"A friend of Sonny's, Daniel Gold."

"Anne knows him—what's he doing here?"

"He's a journalist, he was a visiting teacher of Sonny's at the university, then he met the Filipina who would become his wife and stayed for a few years until Marcos seized her family's properties," Doming said.

The night smelled of that mix of heavy blossoms from a frangipani tree, smoke from fires all over the city, tires burning, green leaves burning, charcoal for cooking, mixed with the diesel fumes of an army jeep that was parked just up the road with its engine running. She saw an orange glow from a cigarette like a firefly, dark men in light uniforms.

It was nine o'clock. Sirens were going off all over the city.

At the car Doming gave some change to the boys who'd watched it for him. One opened the front door for her. She opened the back one to ride in her accustomed place, which provoked a chattering speculation from them.

"What does Sonny have to do with Daniel Gold?" she said.

"It's just Sonny, reliving his days of glory, when he was with the protesters, telling him his old stories," he said.

She heard a lie.

She studied Doming's hands, there on the steering wheel. His hands, large palms, long fingers, beautiful hands but with straight white scars over the knuckles. What are those from, she'd asked him once. From the cane, its leaves are sharp, he'd said, shortly. It was like Chinese calligraphy carved there, an undecipherable past.

Can you hear light, he wondered. A high-pitched screaming, an electric howl, seemed to come out of the streetlights in the city. He drove with his window open. He sped past the Intercontinental Hotel, taking her home, heading out of the city toward Ayera. He had to get back to Sonny's. He had cables to pass on to him tonight. But he wanted nothing to do with Gold.

"They're looking for me, there's a new list," Sonny had worried earlier this week.

At her house, he pulled up in front. She got out.

He watched her cross in front of the lights along the walk, looking at her legs through the long gauzy skirt she wore. She went to the front door. He parked the car in the driveway along the side of the house. No lights came on. Perhaps he was too hard on her.

He had watched her and sometimes admired her. How she looked closely and admired the minutiae, the particulars of nature, the small changes in the daily being of plants and animals. Within the first week in the country she'd rescued two filthy, half-dead cockatiels from the Divisoria market, and she'd coaxed them back to vitality. He'd seen her in the garden, holding the white birds with her under the outdoor shower beside the pool. She wore a black swimming suit. The grateful birds nuzzled and nipped at her. But she'd given them away after six months as a gift to her friend Anne when they were restored to health. He'd tried to talk her into keeping them, offering to build a bigger cage.

They need someone with them, and I'm gone all day, she'd explained to him.

Besides, Celia had muttered, Sir doesn't like their shrieking and carrying on when they see her or even hear her voice. Too carried away.

But he felt she lived in complicity with all that was indecent and unjust here.

She was naive and curious as a child. She would ask questions about everything. She wanted to know the name of every new tree, every plant. She'd look at the hot grill of the car to see what insects were embedded there. But before his grudging humiliated answers silenced her, she'd asked too many questions—Why did you come to Manila? Why did you not go on to school? What did you want to be when you were a child, what was your ambition, Doming?

There it was. To be a man meant one must have ambition. That was Trace Caldwell.

The kitchen was dark. A lamp came on. Rue stood there. Sometimes he watched them in the kitchen at night, after he'd brought Trace home. There was nothing the maids didn't know about them, even how often they slept together, for the laundry girl would gossip even about that while she had her *merienda* of coffee and *suman* in the maids' own small kitchen off the garage, where Celia also made delicious food for Doming. Celia scolded the laundry girl, but it was always this way—as if they, Trace and Rue, Sir and Ma'am, lived their lives on a stage. Doming, like Celia, considered that he was beginning to know things about them that he didn't even realize he knew. They saw Trace no longer had affection for her. He was a man consumed by his ambition for control, for power.

Rich or poor, men and women could make each other unhappy in many ways, Doming considered. Trace, tan, always in a starched shirt and a jacket, and never agitated. A cultivated calmness.

It was two in the morning when Doming walked from the jeepney stop to his house in Cavite. His house showed a sparseness that was made not only of poverty but also the desire to be left undisturbed. He had secrets and he wanted no more questions. Only the children came inside.

He lived not far from the bay, about twelve kilometers west of the Caldwells. He'd rented a clay brick house, with a tile roof, from the guards who were paid to protect the property of an absentee owner. The owner had built a furniture factory and housing for workers and then was forced to flee and sell off his interests to a Marcos crony, after he'd complained too often about kickbacks and corruption.

Now the factory stood empty. The few dozen houses had also been empty until a year ago when Doming and a few others from a squatters' barrio nearby had approached the guards and offered bribes for access to the ghost-like factory-village. Now the guards themselves were the land-lords and came round each week and collected their fee. If any inspector comes, they warned, run, or we'll arrest you for trespassing. We'll dump your possessions over the wall and into the river, everything that you don't carry, they warned.

Doming made his way through the barrio, down the path to the river. He crossed over a small bridge of bamboo and wooden slats, then climbed up the steep bank to a block wall, topped by glass, and went into the factory com-pound through the broken metal gate.

Few drivers lived with their employers, or they'd be on duty any hour of the day. There was no privacy, no solitude. He'd lived briefly with the Chinese he'd driven for, Mr. Wo, and found he couldn't save money as the man charged him extra for food, and the sari-sari stores in the neighborhood gouged servants with their prices.

At least it wasn't as bad as the city, as Abbe's place, where the sweet hopeless stench of human waste assaulted you, where you could hear the heaves and moans of the men and women from the crowded barrio, who'd paid for half an hour alone in someone's room, where nothing could disguise the sound of the neighbor beating his wife or the persistent howls of a mangy dog pegged to a rope. Here Doming heard the wind swishing the coconut palms like a woman's skirt, clicking the hollow bamboo stems.

They like to live close together, crowded in, they can't stand to be alone, that's their nature. That's what they said of the Filipinos. But that was not the nature of a rich Filipino, Doming thought. The rich Filipino has his space, his privacy, his room for breakfast and his *salas* for entertaining, his lanai, garden, air-conditioned bedroom, and rooms for the children, a closet for his clothes, for his handmade shirts and embroidered barongs.

He found something to eat. He sat at his table, an old hinged door he'd gotten from a fine house that was being remodeled. Stacked chicken cages formed its legs. He lit a kerosene lantern. Things were scattered by the wind. Papers, receipts. Drawings he'd scratched into the dust.

He moved some of the white canvases he'd stretched. He'd begun buying wood and canvas and rice powder in the market, stretching the canvas onto frames and preparing the canvas for painting. He sold these for good profit. Father Rex had taught him how to prepare canvases by painting on five layers of thin white rice paste. Now the art shop owner in Makati had asked him to copy drawings of Ikat figures, or peasant landscapes, onto some of the canvases.

"Just draw the outlines," the art store owner had said, "like these paint-by-number kits." The shop owner sold them to weekend painters who'd hang them in their *salas* and claim the work as their own original, which it was, in a way. We Filipinos are the world's greatest copiers, after all, the man said. And it felt good to Doming, when he was restless at home, to make something with his hands, the stretched canvas frames. The shop owner gave him calendar samples of original art or tribal prints.

"Just lightly print in the name of the color in the correct space; I'll double your payment for the kits," he told Doming.

At first Doming would follow the lines of a painting by Juan Luna, from a postcard the shop owner gave him, and know only that he could draw and draw but had learned nothing of color and light and never would. But several times when he was drawing those lines a feeling overtook him. He'd immersed himself in the place, the canvas, and time passed without his knowing it. Hence several canvases, large and small, were propped against the wall with drawings completed, but he was unwilling to part with them until he was more desperate for money. It was as if, in stirring the rice paste that he painted on in thin coats to make a base for paint, he'd see in the white viscous mixture some scene from home. Then, if he stared long enough at the drying layers of paste, lines would form there.

He was hungry. He'd been too proud to act ravenous in front of Rue at the bar much earlier. He scooped more of the fried rice he'd made early that morning on a cook-stove he shared with one neighbor, and mixed it with greens.

The next morning he found a note, stuck into the slats between the gate.

Hintayín mo kamí. Mag-abáng.

Wait for us. We are watching, the note said.

It was signed by Alejo, Sonny's friend, the Kristo at the cockfight.

Celia opened the windows in the kitchen, checked the rice.

"Steamy rice means bad weather is coming," Celia said to Rue. Rue sat at the marble-topped kitchen island in the grand kitchen, a room that Baby would never enter. The smell of browning adobo had drawn her.

Celia stood over the stove. She was making her sister Mary's favorite dish, chicken and pork adobo. She measured out kalamansi juice and soy sauce into the browning garlic, watching her level hand pour. She added peppercorns. Her kitchen, the second smaller kitchen off the garage, the "dirty kitchen," as it was called, where the maids cooked their own foods, smelled strongly of the milkfish she was drying. Rue complained the smell was like a wet dog. It was the only food Celia had found that Rue would absolutely not eat. But Mary craved it and Celia would find a way to deliver these treats for her older sister. Mary, dried and shriveled as an old hyacinth bean, still worked for Baby and Raymonde, but she was sick, very sick. Celia asked Rue for an advance to pay for her medicine and Rue gave it to her, but asked, isn't Baby paying for this? That was generally expected of the Filipinos whose help worked for them for a lifetime. But Raymonde was cheap, he wouldn't agree and Baby was afraid to cross him. Mary had heart failure, the expensive doctor at Makati Medical had told Baby.

Celia shook her head. There was more on her mind than money—a few days before the young maid Lleoni had announced to Celia that she was leaving soon, to get married. She hadn't yet met the man, she admitted.

Lleoni, who was nineteen, had found a foreign man through the Filipina Bride Guide. She was meeting him at the Regent Hotel tonight. Celia was very worried about this.

"Lleoni isn't very smart," Celia said to Rue. "Lleoni's not clever."

Celia blamed Lleoni's impetuous decision to leave their household on an incident a few weeks before. Celia had discovered Lleoni in the big kitchen, with the white plastic garbage pail in front of her.

"*Buksán*, Open," Lleoni was saying in Tagalog, then in English, Open.

"What are you doing, girl?" Celia said to her.

"Why does it open for you and Ma'am and not for me?" Lleoni asked plaintively.

Celia didn't understand. She walked to where Lleoni stood and put her foot as usual on the little pedal tucked into the bottom of the rectangular plastic garbage pail. It was a western one that Rue had bought at the Embassy compound's store. The hinged lid popped up.

"There," Celia said.

"How did you do that, what do you say?" said Lleoni.

Understanding then, Celia had laughed with pity, and told Rue, who'd come into the kitchen, what had happened.

"She thinks we're like witches, Ma'am, that we know the magic words." Celia suspected that's when Lleoni had made up her mind to leave. She'd lost face but still didn't know why.

Celia saw that Lleoni still didn't get it and resisted the temptation to say some wild incantation as she opened the lid. So she stooped down, her knees splayed out and arms between them, like an old woman planting rice seedlings, and gestured to the girl to join her. She put Lleoni's hand on the little pedal set back under the edge of the can.

"Like this. *Ganyán ang gawín mo riyán*," Celia said, gently, "Do it like that."

Then the pretty girl had hung her head in shame, her long hair she was so vain about falling across her knees to the floor. Celia had perhaps shamed her, not meaning to, but *hiya*, face, it was all-important. And perhaps being talked to so kindly, like the child she still was, made her miss her own *lola* who'd helped raise her in Samar.

What else had prompted Lleoni, Celia considered—it was the time Raymonde had visited the house and acted smitten with her, complimented and cajoled her and gave her a crisp fifty-peso note, said her fingers were too fine for the rough mending Celia asked of her. Lleoni didn't know his history with housemaids.

So it was probably then, Celia suspected, that Lleoni had made up her mind that she needed these things, garbage pails she couldn't understand, a nice house, and money she could send home to support her family in the provinces. She'd answered an ad to appear at a look-over to meet foreign men. *MEET FOREIGN MEN, FOR MARRIAGE.* She'd meet one and she would leave.

"She will go to a fancy hotel to meet him, Ma'am," Celia said to Rue, turning over to her the responsibility for this girl in her charge.

It's true, Celia always said, that a pretty Filipina with a toss of her head and a lift of her chin could convey total sensuousness and cool disinterest. Many professed to find the Western man quite unappealing. Even Lleoni had said that of the slack-skinned blue-eyed Western men with eyes like dead fish, and she'd shuddered. But these women, like Lleoni, were desperate to get out of the country. Old men would arrive in Manila on package tours, men who'd chosen several girls' pictures in marriage catalogues that go out overseas.

Celia walked across the highly polished red kitchen tiles to the plastic garbage can to drop some chicken bones in. The lid popped open for her like a hungry mouth.

From the long windows Rue saw Lleoni, her long hair shiny as a blackberry, sashaying back from her shopping trip to the market. She held a Chinese paper umbrella over her head, against the sun. A boy from the neighbor's house carried some of her packages. The attention and discounts she received from the vendors always pleased her. Lleoni had confided to them that an Australian man was writing to her. He'd seen her picture in a guidebook to Filipina brides.

She worked hard and conscientiously for Celia. Every other day Lleoni washed the Mexican tile in the downstairs wide halls and then polished the *narra* wood in the upstairs floors with the oils from a dried half-coconut. Rue knew the girl tried on her expensive shoes when she straightened Rue's bath and dressing room. Rue would find them slightly askew, the high-heeled ones. But the girl's feet must have been like child's feet in them, clomping around. Perhaps Lleoni looked at herself in the full-length mirror Baby had installed as the house was built for her, perhaps she pushed her hair up like Rue wore hers when she went out, stuck one hip out with her hand on it.

Rue considered what she could do for Lleoni.

Every few weeks she had noticed these old men, pink-skinned foreigners who looked oddly peeled, wearing formal barong shirts, outside the hotels along the bay. They'd be with their child-brides, outside the Regent or Hyatt near the Embassy Club—these girls from the provinces who didn't even know how to use the toilets there. She had sometimes noticed the dusty footprints on the toilet seats in the Embassy Club where these young women from the provinces, unaccustomed to the marble and porcelain luxury, simply climbed up and squatted. And this is what Lleoni would trade for—clean water and perfect Western bathrooms.

"They marry them and then they go to the U.S. and they are never warm again," Celia said.

Rue imagined Lleoni going to the U.S. or Germany with some older man, shivering from the temperatures, inside and out. She would be like a hired slave and prostitute in one, but send money back to her family each month until he tired of her. She would be dauntless, and foolish. It took a strength of will to take this leap, a self-willfulness Rue recognized and understood.

"It's up to you, Ma'am, what to do, what to do," Celia worried. She swatted at a fly in her kitchen with the rawhide stripped fly-swatter.

Rue remembered Mrs. Ashmar, the deputy chief of mission's wife, had once warned, "The Filipina is the most feminine, delicate, womanly, ruthless of all the women in the world. She wants to shop in the embassy commissary, all those imported goods, she wants to go to America and shop at Walmart." But this was Lleoni, wanting to shop at Walmart, to buy gifts to send by UPO to her family in the provinces, gifts of canned hams and instant coffee and money, finally enough money. That was the compromise, that was the deal.

Children, security, plastic gadgets, a house, a home. Rue walked through the kitchen and *sala*, out into the wide front hallway. On Baby's antique altar table in the front hall stood three of the tall Indonesian puppets Trace had brought back from a trip, their long moveable arms, elbows out like wings, flat palmed hands in angular gestures, carved heads facing each other in profile. He always brought back beautiful things, expensive, tasteful, relentlessly bargained for, as if even in the market his negotiating and diplomatic skills must win out. Diplomacy, the cult of commerce, her friend Anne Larkin had joked when Trace told his foreign "shopping" stories.

Sometimes Rue thought she would not have survived the first six months here if she hadn't met Anne. If Anne hadn't come to the Rice Institute on one of Rue's first days there, they might never have met. New arrivals, Anne always said, it takes at least a year before they stop asking you for advice about the maids and shopping and stop complaining about everything. Some never stop. Never complain here, was Anne's first and then constant advice to Rue. No matter how bad it gets.

Wives arrive with the word *DEPENDENT* stamped on their visas, Anne had explained. Accompanying spouses, they were called in embassy jargon. Like appendages, hanging on, like decorations, not essential. Wives do their charity work, they play mahjong each week at the embassy club, moving the pieces around with a clacking sound like old bones, their hands and perfect nails a sign of the privilege, their pampering. Scandinavian women, they say, become committed to tennis and golf. Other Europeans sail. The Australians snorkel and sunbathe. The British women, as if coming back home to India and Ceylon, develop a high tolerance for mid-day sherry and gin and tonic during their card clubs. The Americans go to dressmakers and shop, and replicate the baseball leagues and lessons for their children. The horror stories—bridge clubs, tennis, cocktail parties, embassy women club meetings and subcommittee meetings, steering committees for this or that charitable endeavor, the yearly ball at the Army Navy club that took weeks of organizing, the proms and fifties parties organized by women's groups with little to do but plan, elaborately and endlessly.

"So," Anne concluded, "they told me when I arrived in Pakistan, you can play golf, you can decorate your house, in some countries you can have an affair. Fortunately, David and I found each other in the midst of it all.

"And a few women just go mad. The heat, the dirt, the way you have to avert your eyes if you want to survive. They imagine home as perfect. But then they go home. The best is to feel that this *is* home," she said.

But say there's a kind of power that women, especially, find when they live as foreigners in countries where labor is cheap and obliging. Perhaps there is something potent in this sip of power, so that once tasted it must be swallowed, even by those who thought they would spit it out.

Anne had helped Rue find Lleoni.

"A maid from another embassy family came to our door and offered to work for us," Rue said to Anne.

"The first rule—never take another expatriate woman's maid directly from her," Anne had cautioned, only half-joking. "It's like taking her husband. Go to Trinity Episcopal Church and ask for their Servants Registry."

And so almost two years ago they'd made the trip to the church at the edge of Forbes Park where Anne lived. It was a Tuesday morning. Potential house-maids and *yayas* and cooks and drivers were already in lines stretching down the drive. It would take all day just for those already waiting in line to have their applications processed. Rue and Anne found Lleoni. Lleoni had placed herself with Rue, and now, Rue thought, Lleoni was looking for a better deal. She would place herself with a Western husband, the great commodity here.

It was a few days after she saw Trace on the streets of Intermuros. The night before Rue dreamed she and Trace were eating off broken white plates.

In Ayera, the new morning smelled like green smoke from the fires of laborers who were building a new house for the Minister of Tourism. They would cook their rice over open fires, live in the unfinished building, its white stucco walls and blue tile roof glaring in the light, its windows still dark gaping holes. The rising house across the field would cut off her view of the mountains in Laguna.

"Don't cut down any more banana trees," Rue told the gardener, when she saw him in the driveway. He was dragging a newly cut banana tree by its trunk. The frayed green leaves hissed along the stone driveway. She'd watched it flower, the pinkish-red blooms turning into dark pods and then into gloria bananas the size of a man's fingers. Then the leaves became tattered fringe.

"But Ma'am, the tree bears only once and then it must be cut down to grow again, that is the way," he said, shaking his head in despair, thwarted from doing the job he knew. He'd taken his newly sharpened *balisong* knife, a curved sickle, and hacked the green stalked tree down from the stand. Rue loved how the trees' new-green leaves unfurled like banners, knocked against the bedroom screens at night with some urgent unknown news, and then became wildly fringed when the monsoon winds began to shred them. To her their beauty alone was worth preserving. She was angered to see them cut and tossed away. To waste beauty like that.

The gardener tossed the hacked pieces of the only tree he would cut that day into the field outside the walled garden. Juice dripped from the green cored trunk. Dragonflies and mudwasps were already buzzing around the pithy heart. Rue noticed the neighbor's two plump domestic cats sitting on the top of the garden wall. They hunted from there for lizards in the tall grass below. She'd seen the female return with the shed tail of a lizard still twitching in her jaws.

Celia flicked at the cats with a dishtowel. "They're after my hummingbird, Ma'am," she said. "Shoo." Celia complained that she saw these lazy cats ignore field mice, that they were afraid of the rats, but they'd wait all day under the *kalamansi* trees for the hummingbird to visit the sweet white flowers. She hummed to herself, something familiar to Rue.

"Where did you learn that?" Rue asked, remembering words from an old song, *Daisy, Daisy, give me your answer, do.*

"My *lola*, Ma'am, who learned it from the American soldiers who were here when she was a girl, after the war with Spain. During the big war with the Japanese, when I was a girl, the soldiers did not sing for us, no one sang," Celia said.

Why is it that you and Sir don't bear children, Ma'am? Celia had asked one morning more than a year before, when she'd been with them for only a few months. It was an acceptable question, in a place where children were valued like gold, cementing allegiances between families, godparents, and godchildren. To Celia, Baby's older brothers and sisters, and then Baby's own daughters, were proof of her own fortune and good standing with God.

"I had a mis-, a mis-carriage, Celia," Rue began.

"What is *amiss,* Ma'am?" Celia said.

Rue looked in her Tagalog phrase book. *Miscarriage: not the way it should be, out of order, mali, wrong. Miscarriage: a failure to reach its destination.* Rue searched for words. Sometimes it seemed Celia pretended to understand less, especially when she wanted to know more.

Sometimes, the doctor in Washington had said to her, trying to console her, these things just aren't right from the start. Where did these things start? She and Trace had been married seven years. Now his fourteen-year-old daughter lived in London with his first wife.

Rue had a total of three miscarriages and an ectopic pregnancy; the first miscarriage happened just days before they married.

"Ectopic, Ma'am?"

"The egg in the wrong place, you can die from it," Rue said.

"But you didn't, I'm glad, Ma'am," Celia said.

There is a house near Makati, a clean place, Baby told her, where they take abandoned babies for sale, and where a broker buys fine ones on commission. I'm going there, I want you to take me, so that Raymonde doesn't find out where it is.

A few weeks before Baby had discovered that Raymonde was keeping a *querida*, a young mistress, and with her had a baby boy. Baby only had the three girls with him. The *querida* had come to the house in San Lorenzo and demanded money from Baby. Raymonde was quite taken with the boy. So now, Baby told Rue, she would get a fine boy herself. Baby had asked General Ess to be a sponsor at the christening and Ess had agreed and that sealed it for Raymonde.

Rue thought she might find the baby from Baclaran market. She'd dreamed about the child. She would leave money, do something. Anything could be possible in this place where children were sold like *lechon* in the market.

Doming drove them to the place, which was between Makati and Pasig in a rundown section of the commercial area not far from Makati Medical Center. Baby did not want Raymonde's driver to know where the child had come from. Boarding houses and small shops lined the street.

Rue went in first, through an open front door of a house that had only a number, no sign. She was curious.

Doming and Baby followed her. One long room took up the first floor, and light poured in the back through bar-covered windows. The only decoration was a Marcos calendar on the wall with some names scrawled on various days of the month. The calendar picture showed Imelda and Marcos as Greek gods, Imelda in a sea foam shell like Aphrodite. The only desk was vacant. There were no files, no papers out.

A middle-aged woman in a housedress hurried down a stairway. She carried a box of powdered milk. The woman's lips pursed tight as a clam shell when she saw the two women.

But she spoke to Doming first. "Who are you, an attorney? A journalist?"

"*Hindî*, no, I am a driver," he said.

The woman laughed in relief, and ignored him after this.

"So much trouble lately with the government," she said, fawning over the two women in a high whining voice like the vendors in the market. "Trouble because they threaten to close me down, because the big-wigs want their cut," she said. "We have the best clients, too, the ones who can pay."

"Your prices seem high," Baby said.

"You can't imagine the expenses I have already," the woman said.

She settled Baby at the desk, produced folded papers from her pocket. These would result in an original birth certificate, as if the child were born to her. "I know the judge," the woman said.

Rue heard wailing. She walked toward the bottom of the narrow wooden staircase, heard the sound again.

"Payments to the local police, to the barangay captain, to the mayor's office. But tell me what I can do for you," the woman said, catching up with Rue, taking hold of her arm.

"I saw a baby at Baclaran Church, I heard you're one who buys them," Rue said.

"Ma'am, you don't understand properly," said the proprietress, defensive. "I pay for services only."

"I see," Rue said. She started up the stairs. The landing was dark and smelled of urine. Doming followed her up the stairs, the woman hurrying behind them.

She saw that the entire second floor consisted of bedrooms and a bathroom. In each small room six narrow slatted wooden cribs were pushed together in the center, leaving just a space to walk around the outside. There were two or three infants in each crib. Two girls were dressing and changing the babies, propping up bottles on rolled-up diapers, shooing off flies. They went from crib to crib. Light glared in from unscreened upstairs windows and played off the walls, painted light green, shiny enamel on rough plaster, the color of shallow sea water.

"There's nothing for them to look at, no stuffed animals, nothing hanging up," Rue said. It was a far worse place than Baby had led her to believe.

The woman frowned. "No, anyway, they're not here long enough for that," she said.

At one crib, Rue stopped and looked down into the face of a wide-awake girl. "Look at those beautiful sloe eyes," she said. The child's eyes were perfect dark curves, as if painted with Chinese ink. She was beautiful.

"This one," said the guide with some pride, "was born just a few weeks ago on one of the half sunken ships in the bay. Squatters live there now." She made *tsk* sounds. "Imagine, this out of that squalor, rats everywhere, my girl said. We paid a lot for her, she is a beauty, her mother only seventeen. I've had a Chinese do her charts, they are very auspicious. Today a German sea merchant, Captain Hegar and his Filipina wife, are coming for her. All the arrangements are made. They have paid me twenty-two hundred cash in U.S. dollars. But let me show you this jewel over here."

They followed her to the next room.

A little girl perhaps eighteen months old sat alone in a wooden pen on the floor. "Her name is Bernadette, Ma'am."

Bernadette, with sad anxious eyes, only looked toward them when she heard her name. Bernadette, it's time for lunch, Rue imagined herself calling.

"You see how white she is, we have never let her go in the sun," the woman bragged. "And she already feeds herself, so little trouble."

The sound of laughter, children playing in the rank canal that ran along the back and splashing themselves in the stagnant water, came in to them.

"But she does not yet speak," the woman said. A harsh smile almost disguised her anger. "I even had the doctor in to look at her and there is nothing wrong. She has had all her vaccines and I would not charge for those." She sighed dramatically.

Rue ran her hand along the wood of the playpen, felt the roughness.

"If someone does not take her soon, I will have to trade her," she said to Rue, with feigned regret.

"You're trading on her sympathy," Doming said to the woman.

He turned to her, his head lowered.

"Rue," he whispered, "you can walk down any side-street in Mabini and see the children there, they are the same, offered for the sex trade."

It occurred to her that he'd never said her name before.

"Tell Mrs. Varcegno you need to leave," he said.

She knew about the Mabini children. She recognized the owner's smooth sales pitch, saw her lashless appraising eyes, reptilian. Perhaps the woman calculated the price she could charge for a rich foreigner's anguish.

But Rue couldn't stop herself—she scooped up Bernadette and held her.

She felt the child pull her small arms and legs close in, like a bird in its nest, her little neck hunched into itself like an old woman's. The warm dark head rested tensely under her own chin, against her neck, as if the child tried the place out like it was a covered roof. Under the roof of her chin, it was her own heart beating hard. Rue put the toddler down. In an instant the girl scrambled away and climbed to the top of the iron grillwork of the tall windows. She looped her leg to hold her and watched them.

"That's her favorite spot, she's strong, nah?" the proprietress said apologetically.

Doming coaxed the child down, first holding out his arms to her high perch, then turning round with his arms out, offering her a twirling ride.

The girl came down, they twirled, then her owner, for that is what she seemed to Rue, put her back in her pen.

Downstairs, Baby had received her child. He was about six months old. The woman wasn't sure. He has no astrological charts done, so you can make up an auspicious birthdate for him, the woman told Baby.

A girl, a helper, put him down on the wooden table. He squawled and turned red. The proprietress undid his diaper, and showed his parts were all in order. He wet on her, and the woman shrieked for the helper to return. The girl cleaned him gently, cooing low and kissing his damp hair. Rue felt the girl was reluctant to give him up. She wanted to reassure her that the boy would be in a good place, but would he? She wondered whether Raymonde would have anything to do with the boy.

Baby efficiently gathered her new boy up from the young helper who'd changed him. She'd brought a finely woven white blanket, hand embroidered. The child screamed for the girl.

"Perhaps he protests to go with you, Ma'am," Doming said. "Hear his great lungs."

"Nonsense, he will love me, he will be a prince," Baby said. She handed the woman a thick envelope. Then she turned with her treasure and Rue heard the taps of her high heels across the floor.

"They are sweet, Ma'am, so sweet, come back next week and I will have the one for you," the woman said to Rue, in a voice smooth as leche flan.

Rue was surprised by her own sharp envy. She felt her breasts stir, her hands want to reach out for Baby's new boy.

"Perhaps the one for you is already gone, Ma'am, I got rid of her yesterday," the woman said to her, wanting to do business, sensing a willing customer. "There will be new ones next week, I will make you a good price. I will make you very happy. Don't you want to be happy?"

"They are sweet, Ma'am, so sweet," she called after Rue.

They settled Baby into the car. She was beaming with relief and happiness. "Raymonde will love you, your papa," she cooed to the squalling six-month-old like a sleek-feathered mynah.

"I wonder, Ma'am, if he will take to the boy so well as you do," Doming said. This was Rue's worry as well. She tried to imagine Trace welcoming such a child. She could not.

"You are so sweet," Baby continued, ignoring him.

Ito ba ay matamís? Rue thought—Are they sweet? That was a market phrase Doming had taught her.

Baby proudly carried the boy, her prize, inside the house in San Lorenzo. She'd already hired a *yaya*, who was waiting at home.

In Ayera, at Christmas, Rue had driven past live nativity scenes, live scenes with real Marys and real babies, posed in front of the mansions. At Christmas rich people paid squatters to portray the holy family and the shepherds. It cost more to rent the sheep, Doming had told her.

"There was a young woman in Baclaran market with a baby for sale," she'd told Doming.

"There's also a sign in the Ayera market, Ma'am, baby for sale," Doming said, purposely not answering. "We pass it every day."

"You cannot save them all yourself," he added.

But why not even one, she thought.

The only person Rue told of her visit to the orphanage was a colleague at the Rice Institute, Doctora Gloria Magnasan. In the early afternoon that same day, the two women had lunch in the Institute's small cafeteria. Rue ate the worker's rice with some unknown but tasty kind of stewed fish with greens. *Kangkong* greens, they're called, Dr. Magnasan said. It grows at Lake Laguna, this is peasants' food but it's tasty.

Doctora Gloria Magnasan was one of the few Filipina-nationals at the Rice Institute, a senior scientist who worked in plant ecology. She had four children, two boys and two girls, and it was clear she considered herself the most fortunate of women. Her round Chinese-looking face beamed with intelligence.

"You should not have gone to that place, that vile woman," Dr. Magnasan said to Rue. "One of our maids is expecting. She is not married yet. I told her I'd help her— perhaps this is the one for you."

The cafeteria was almost empty. Few of the Filipino laborers had come to work. All the jeepneys and public buses were being used to transport demonstrators to a pro-government rally.

Later that afternoon, Sok and Rue worked in the screen house. Only Sok seemed to know how to cut into the stalks of infested rice to extract the small larvae without damaging them. Rue lay on her stomach, peering closely at the rice stems, looking for signs of damage to the plants, for some sign that the rice that had silica added was resisting the larvae infestation. The air was close. At first Sok had not wanted her to crawl around in the heat and liquid air of the rice paddies, new rice growing inside the screen houses. It was like being in a vast cage, the sun and rain coming in at will but the screen so fine that the moths could not get out.

While they were working, a young man came in. He was a big boy, not a dwarf-size man, but he looked like Sok without the hump.

"This is my son," Sok said. Then he said something to the boy, who smiled at her. She assumed he knew no English.

But when she spoke to him in Tagalog, Good afternoon, he looked at her and pointed at his mouth. He opened it so wide she could see some blackened teeth.

"He can't speak, since birth, Ma'am," Sok said, his voice a mix of sadness and apology to her.

"Why is he here? You've never brought him before."

"Like I say, Ma'am, there's trouble now, some military police looking for those who didn't vote, or who cast blank ballots. All the ballots were marked to identify each one of us, we didn't know," he said.

"Then have him stay here, in my lab," she said.

"Even tonight?"

"Of course."

"They say the trouble will be over, once Marcos is officially sworn in as president," Sok said.

"Do you believe that?"

"No, Ma'am," he grinned. "But he promises not to devalue the peso again."

Sok had confided to her that the cost of these hybrid rice seeds was more than many farmers could afford, with all the imported fertilizers and pesticides that had to be added.

She had focused her research on the effects of the stem borer larvae on a local wild rice strain, an heirloom variety—seeds she discovered were not even being stored properly. She shared these with Sok, who took some seedlings home to his own small paddy. The wild rice was proving more resistant to the larvae, just as the old local farmers suggested it would. This was the way against the larvae, not organophosphates, not genetic re-breeding to higher levels of poison. But there were no profits to be made in this by the multi-national companies who supported the Rice Institute.

She and Sok had discovered that these discarded strains in some cases were more impervious to the larvae of stem borer moths. Why? They had more silica in their cell wall—especially wild rice in paddies along the edges of old volcanoes.

With silica their cell walls hardened just enough to wear down the mandibles of the hungry larvae more rapidly, so that fewer and fewer larvae would consume enough at each stage of maturity. And silica was simply slag, the volcanic ash. The ash came down like blossoms, the ash hardened and made earth. The ash became silica and the wild rice absorbed it and wore down the mandibles of the yellow stem borer larvae. The wild rice kept its green heart. Since no amount of the expensive poisons would kill all of the moth larvae, she and Sok could try to strengthen the experimental rice stems against the larvae, by spreading the ash from old volcanoes, from the center of the earth. The larvae would gnaw and gnaw and wear out their jaws on cooled ash from old volcanoes.

Perhaps the Green Revolution might be over. The idea of hybrid rice had seemed modern and progressive in the nineteen-sixties, but here was the end of progress. Progress gave way to new companies wanting to have the exclusive patents on the most basic food and way of life, the cycle of rice planting and harvesting.

They would own it all.

The Green Revolution was now all about profits, not about feeding the hungry. If a hybrid rice crop failed like it had in 1969, there were no backups. Soon multi-nationals would own all the seeds, and thus all the farmers, she thought.

Meanwhile, in the provinces, children's deaths from hunger were officially reported as meningitis, Doming had told her.

When she drove home that afternoon farmers were still in their rice paddies or tending pineapple fields along Lake Laguna. Once in the northern rice terraces, Rue had watched an old woman working all morning bent over at

133

her work, without stopping. She'd reach into a woven basket for each tender shoot of rice to plant in the terraced paddy. At the end of the day, Rue saw the same woman walking along the road, going home, bent over in that same position.

Home in Ayera. She stretched out on a bamboo lounge chair on the lanai. A gecko's bird-like screech roused her. She looked for it, and spotted the liver-colored lizard stalking a spider on the post nearby her. Dark-pink bougainvillea, growing skyward, spread wildly over the trellis and arced out over the eaves and pool and dropped their petals one by one. Broad-leafed white lilies, bamboo palms on yellow stalks, wild ferns, in pots around the edges of the lanai, thanks to Celia. She tended them all.

"Ma'am," Celia said from the lanai doorway that led to the front hall.

"Celia?" She'd given up reminding Celia to call her Rue.

"I'll make you and Sir some fresh *lumpia* tomorrow," she said.

"Good," Rue said. "But I'm not sure if Trace will be here if the election returns are still coming in."

"So I'll bring you some dinner now, Ma'am?" This was what Celia really wanted.

"I'm not very hungry, Celia," Rue said.

This garden was the reason she'd agreed to rent the house, far south of the city. Sapphire-blue hummingbirds worked on the flame flowers. Tiny bright-green frogs the size of a man's thumbnail leapt across the lanai and stuck gummily to the adobe walls or hid on the inside of the guest-room toilet. Snails the size of her fist left silver trails on the stone walls of the garden. These were jewels to her— some new discovery each day.

In the fields around the house she'd seen giant stag bee-tles with huge hooked horns, a pair of males interlocked in battle, one of them held in the air by the grasping jaws of the other. She found rhinoceros beetles, with their single sharp curved sword, heavy wing covers opened, ready for flight. Celia brought her a loosely woven dim sum basket, wanting to stick a pin to hold one armor-plated beetle in the basket for a collection for Rue. Absolutely not, Rue said, appalled at her and then sorry because it perhaps was the only time she'd spoken harshly to Celia, and Celia was shamed.

Then one blissful morning an atlas moth had appeared in the bamboo palm. The largest moth variety in the world, the size of her hands held in front of her, its body the size of her thumbs overlapping. She'd searched for it on her trips north to the town of Banawe in the northern *Cordilleras*, where rice was grown on the terraced mountains.

Finally, in her own garden—the background of the moth's wings was brown, the color of the drying tobacco leaves she'd seen in the market. But in the center of each wing was an eye of iridescent blue and purple, the size of a silver peso. Translucent white bands ran from the blue, in a membrane as fine as bougainvillea blossoms. She'd seen drawers full of preserved atlas moths and prehistoric looking beetles in her work in the entomology lab at the Smithsonian Natural History Museum and Johns Hopkins. But it was splendid, splendid, here in this garden. I am here, she thought. This is what she'd come for. She'd felt pulled to this place far away as if by gravity.

Trace's work for the National Security Council had actually brought them here and she'd been glad, out here in the countryside. But Trace, more and more consumed by his work, wouldn't tell her much. She hadn't asked him about the woman she'd seen. She knew. He would say it was part of his work. It's part of the macho culture here, Anne had said. Trace had worked for the government in El Salvador and Guatemala for several years with his first wife and their daughter. It was part of the macho culture there, too.

She examined her face in the mirror surface of a lit aquarium where angel fish floated. She turned her head side to side, lifted her chin. Looking at herself as if underwater. He never tells you you're beautiful? Anne asked her about Trace. Of course not, she said. She couldn't imagine him saying that to her.

The opportunity for them to go to Manila had presented itself just as she'd begun to think of separating. She was as alone with him as without. Travel, a change of scenery, we can begin again, he'd said. But he'd begun again without her. She had come to love the place, the country. That was what was new.

Like her father who taught her, she was a naturalist at heart. This tropical abundance captivated her. It was as if she, too, had been bred for it. There were one million to one hundred million insects still to be discovered. Like the stars, still to be counted, configured, named.

Her father named her for the herb of grace, *Rue graveolens*. He grew pears and peaches and apples in his orchards along the northeast Iowa bluffs. While still a young man, he bred a new variety of pear, crossing a Fortuna and a Gaume with a Bergamot and a Pequod, making a prized variety, mellow with fine aroma and excellent texture. He taught her the name and habit of every living thing, and everywhere there were small universes to learn.

Dead by his own hand, as the vicar put it in his eulogy.

His right hand, he is dead by his right hand, she thought. But his left hand, she wondered, had it been praying half a prayer? A silent twelve-year-old, she'd taken comfort then in her certainty that the worst thing that could happen already had.

"Michael McGlebe, son of the earth," her father's friend, the Episcopal vicar said at the end of his graveside service, "you are home." Those were all the words she heard the vicar say. It was over. Michael McGlebe, botanist, reader, midnight thinker, drinker. She hoped the earth would hold him, quiet him, that God was compassionate. And guiltily, as if she could never atone for it, feeling as if she were abandoning him now as much as he abandoned her, she left him in the cemetery near three ancient red cedars that stood with bowed branches over the grave like mourners forever there. A cardinal's call seemed to say, *Hurry home, hurry home.*

Later that afternoon at their house just outside town, Rue's mother sat among the mourners, iced in her grief and guilt as if caught by a hard spring frost. She was a leafless silvered tree. Rue watched a galaxy of parlor dust spin in the canted light from the wavy-glassed windows. When she could escape she fled outside to breathe. The worst thing in the world had happened, everywhere blossoms fell as new green began, everywhere common things were still shining, and the wind soughed through the branches, moving them gently back and forth.

Rue didn't know why it had happened. She was certain only that it was not intellect that killed him—he'd died of emotion, feeling too much. Something welled up in him like the river in the spring and a levee gave way. He was gone. She was damaged. She couldn't atone for it.

She had thought no despair could be worse. But say she'd been wrong. Say always living an ordered life, always choosing an accumulation of facts and security, trusting intellect rather than ever risking the rim of desire and longing, this absence might also be called despair.

In college she'd rediscovered field biology and botany and so she'd survived like the greening soft core of tropical rice stem hardened by adding ash, by adding the residue of catastrophe. Like a limpet she fastened onto the sureness of things that could be objectified, known, and measured. But here in Manila, in her rice paddies, even her research and biology itself was not neutral, was not simply a thing of bliss. The bottom line was high profits, high yields for some, hunger for others.

"Good food will cure almost any ailment," Celia said. She put a woven tray with a white plate of fresh mango and pineapple before Rue. "Eat, eat," she said. She'd cut each half-mango and turned it inside out so that the orange flesh looked like a flower, and added some of her own precious fragrant rice, steamed in green bamboo, in a celadon porcelain bowl.

"Sir must be staying in the city," Celia said, as if trying to guess and name what Rue was thinking. There was a sort of courtesy Celia observed, following the Filipino custom of smooth relations, *pakikisama*.

"Did Mrs. de Varcegno get her baby this morning, Ma'am?"

"Yes, a big boy."

"You'll feel better, Ma'am, when you get a child from the orphanage like Baby does. And just think, my sister Mary gets to be there with him, a boy for once."

"Trace would never agree to it."

"Does he think so little of Filipinos then?"

"He doesn't want a child that might be damaged," she said. And he worries about all the money he has to pay for his daughter in London.

"What makes a child damaged?" Celia asked.

"I'm not exactly sure—it can be in the genes or can be something that happens later, in childhood. But it's not something you see right away, like a scar. My father shot himself, Celia, when I was a child. Does that make me damaged?"

Celia drew back, crossed herself. "Oh Ma'am, yes it does, the judge might not even agree to an adoption here in those circumstances," Celia said, taken aback, a horrified look on her face. "That is rare here, we know God, life is too hard and precious to just throw away. I will pray for his eternal soul. To give up on life is the greatest sin. You will not see his soul in heaven, you must miss him for eternity."

She hurried out.

It grew dark with the sudden darkness of the tropics, no long dusks, a mass of violet and ochre and scarlet flung out from the western horizon. The frogs began, in the newly formed ponds from the first rains, thousands calling, a chorus drowning out any more conversation on the lanai. Celia would be saying her evening prayers in her room. Then her radio show would be on.

In a corner of the dark lanai, Rue took off her sweaty work clothes and slipped in the pool, tunneled into the reflections of the sky. She would swim almost every night for half an hour in the small pool, back and forth. The garden gate clanged. A mangy cat sat on the garden wall after feasting on fish bones in the garbage. White blossoms fell into the pool water, drifting down around her like slowly falling stars, white ash from the hot glowing night sky. Embers of stars.

Months ago, at a pool outside the Peninsula Hotel in Makati, while waiting for a meeting, she'd watched an early morning swimmer. The man got out and was rinsing off in the outdoor shower. He was wearing jeans cut off, standing with his back to her, his skin the color of clear diluted tea as the water ran over it, a beautiful body. He turned the shower off and stood there in the sun, drying himself, lean broad back, solid thighs. Each atom seemed to resonate, the glossy turquoise of the water, inky greenness of shaded leaves, his skin. Then he turned around and oh, god, it was Doming.

Later in the car, she questioned him coolly.

I've done it before, people think I'm the pool boy or lifeguard, he said.

Why? You know it's private, only for the guests.

We haven't been able to get water for several days at my place. It's difficult during the dry season. Water is harder to get. We can buy it by the can, or wait in line at a faucet to carry it.

She'd remembered the U.S. Embassy Women's Club project to get a new water tap put in at the squatters' area near the Embassy Seafront Club, how unsuccessful it had been. When the new tap first began to run one morning the line grew and grew, women standing in line for hours with every pot they could find, so certain the supply would run out. By the end of the day the water had run constantly, the fine dust turned to a bog, thick mud that made sucking sounds, children grabbing tin cans and pouring the free, clear water over their heads like it was silver. But a few local people, who had always made money by hauling and selling water to these sixteen thousand squatters, were resentful. This charity would ruin their business. So during the night they pulled the new water pipe out.

In their blind do-goodness, the American clubwomen's quick solution had been thwarted. There were inextricable tentacles that pulled the city under, pulled anyone trying to climb out, that kept its secrets.

Why did she expect him to live any differently than the thousands of other people she passed every day, hidden along the railroad tracks, inches from the train that traveled along the south superhighway, or openly along the roads, a few feet from the wheels of jeepneys, rusted-out trucks, ancient buses, pedicabs and carabao carts, and dark windowed luxury cars that traveled the Azapote Road, or the thousands who were settling along the Bay around the reclaimed land for Imelda's cultural center, the ones who lived in the old merchant boats half sunk in the Bay?

It may have been that until then she hadn't even seen him as a man.

After about twenty minutes, she climbed out of the pool and took her cotton robe from a group that hung from hooks on a nearby post at the edge of the lanai. She shook it to make sure there were no lizards or insects hiding in its folds, and pulled it around her. A gecko hidden nearby chirped rhythmically. Seven times. She found herself counting.

Celia had left a screened cover over the tray of supper on the table. Rue scraped the spoon on the inside of the mango skin, pressed the fork tines into the large mango seed, picked it up and ate from its edge the sweetest part that couldn't be cut away from the large flat seed at its center.

Celia came out to the lanai.

"Ma'am?" she said, to the darkness.

"I'm still out here, Celia," Rue said. "Don't wait for me, I'll take my dishes in when I'm finished, it tastes good."

"I'll lock the front door now?"

"Thank you, Celia."

Rue heard the bolt turn. Baby and Raymonde had never given them keys to the house. I don't know where the keys are, Baby had said vaguely. Besides, not to worry, the house is never empty, there's always a girl here to answer the bell at the gate. The long sliding doors that led to the lanai squealed as Celia pulled them together. She and Trace were like paying guests.

She realized she was chewing on the edge of the mango seed, digging her teeth in and running them along the sweet edge.

Even without a key to her house, this was home. Manila. We don't have to own a house, the land, the country, to cleave to it, she thought.

The world itself is a holy place, like a vast cathedral, her father had often said, when they were in the orchards working. Light poured in though the arch-like branches above them. But then the orchard trees were no longer pruned, peach borers thrived in the trunks and nymphs feasted on the veiny leaves and thistle and wild onion and red cedar grew up between the old trees.

That child is damaged goods, she overheard a lady at church say. A few days later the first phone call came for him, from someone who didn't know. The owner of a bookstore in Boston was calling about some obscure book on English horticulture her father had ordered. The voice asking if her father was there sounded profound and biblical in its Brahman King James accent.

He's—not home yet, she lied. She found she was not able to bring herself to say the word, *dead*. Feeling accused, guilt-ridden, she hung up. It had sounded like God. Looking for him, she thought.

"Ma'am?"
"Yes, Celia?"

Celia stood in the garden near the moonflower vines with their flowers that bloomed only one night; she'd come out quietly through the kitchen door.

"God does not overlook us. He will not leave us comfortless," Celia said.

"Thank you, Celia."

"Goodnight, Ma'am."

Celia plucked one of the lustrous white orbs to take to her room.

Rue folded her arms on the table, put her face down. She cried. Bereft, the word came to her. She was not used to being touched by kind words and she felt her grief, at many things, break open. And finally, she began to feel forgiven.

An envelope stuck out through the slats of the green gate that led to a common kitchen area between his house and the neighbor's. For a moment as Doming reached for it, he thought it might be a message from Sonny's friends again. But the limp gray paper was a telegram from his home province, and he didn't open it. At his door, he heard noise inside, but the room was empty; only a swift flitted, disturbed from her rest.

Doming put the telegram down. He got something to eat and he sat at his table. Finally he reached for the telegram. He'd waited as long as he could. No telegram from the provinces ever bore good news. They were too expensive and too rare. He opened it, took out the gray paper of PLDT, Philippine Long Distance Telephone company.

MARIA FE, something about Maria Fe, his youngest sister. She was five years old when he had left home. He had trouble reading the words. The ink had bled. Tagalog language? No,

Ilongo, from his province in Negros, he could not remember how long it had been since he'd seen it written.

MARIA FE IS DISAPPEARED-COME HOME-AND-OR-SEND MONEY. GABI. Fear broke over him, a wave. The meaning, *disappeared*, suggested the NPA or military had taken her. But what would his brother's wife Gabi know? She had the most schooling, that's why she had written the telegram. It was risky to go back. He wondered if he were being set up, if somehow this was a trap. If anyone were looking for him to come to Negros, they'd know he might come home now. An opposition barrio captain had been ambushed when he'd visited his mother's grave on the traditional fortieth day after her death. This week was the one-year anniversary of his mother's death, a date always marked by families.

Maria Fe is Disappeared.

When she was delivered from his mother, the child was blue and dying. His mother, a beautiful Tiboli tribal woman who'd come to Negros from the south island of Mindanao, had walked around like an old woman while she carried this sixth child, her fifth with this husband. She was thirty-five years old. After the birth Father Rex had been called and, having a look, said, we must baptize the child quickly, before the soul departs and she is condemned.

Doming said to him, "You mean this God who you say knows us so well, if this piece of blood and bone goes without the magic words you say over it, he'll send her down to hell to await Marcos and Ess and General Reloza? What of the other ones born today in the fields, buried there, who can't afford a baptism? Will he send *them* to hell? If that's so, I give my baptism back!"

"What did you say?" Father Rex had said. Doming was his prize student. Father Rex stood holding the clean linen and a paten of holy water.

"I give heaven back to you, I renounce it, I'd rather be with the baby," Doming said.

His mother raised up from where she was lying on a cot and reached to slap him. He was the eldest, her favorite, the son of Mindanao. She'd left her Tiboli hills for the lowlands and met his father, and then her family shunned her and arranged to send her away. That was all Doming knew.

"He's sick, he's sick, Father," she cried.

"I'm right, God is savage," Doming insisted.

"He's still a child, God won't hold him accountable, don't worry," Father Rex said. He held her hand back from Doming.

And he'd looked at Doming and nodded. "Your heart is good, but don't torment your mother like this. Your mother will be okay," he said. He was a man made of kindness.

"Your boldness is noble, it gives her something to live for," Father Rex added, in a softer tone.

The women in the barrio began a collective wail, praying for the sick child, who remained as pale blue-gray as the moon.

"Doming has brought the family bad luck with all his questions of God and the missionaries," said a newly devout convert to the Protestant radio station from Bacolod. She stood at the door of their house, with other neighbors, watching. Whenever the priest came to a house, others knew it meant birth, or death.

"This boy, who can talk in so many languages, it's unnatural, he'll bring you bad luck," the Protestant woman always said about Doming. His mother was not from this place and the woman never liked her or her children. "Some kind of devil has him, a child who can speak so many ways."

He remembered hearing the tinny Protestant radio station's holy words, sent out past Mount Kanlaon, sent out with requests for money, down the spine of Negros Island. A chain of volcanoes rises in its center like a central nerve, dividing Negros Occidental Province on their side, Sugarland, from Negros Oriental on the eastern side of the island. Like a body divided against itself, he thought, we in the west speak the language of the Panay Islanders, Ilongo, while those on the eastern side speak Visayan, the language of the Cebuanos and the rich city of Cebu. My right hand and left hand don't even know each other, my two ears hear different words, my eyes look in opposite directions, the island says. The protestant missionaries tell us repent and be saved, crying Jesus, Jesus. The Catholic priests say confess, confess all your sins, observe all the sacraments, eat flesh and drink blood, feast on the innocent.

Yet after the feast, when their god belches, it is like the sound of the cane mills, rumbling, pouring out hot foul air from his belly, from the earth.

When he impetuously renounced his baptism, his mother scolded. "What if all you teach him takes him away from us?" she complained to the priest.

But Father Rex did teach him more.

Limbus infantum, Doming learned, was the region that exists on the border of hell as the abode of unbaptized infants. So he would go there with them. It was also the place of *limbus patrum*, the place for the just, for those who had died before Christ's coming. That sounded like a fine place. Doming looked at his dictionary, a gift from Father Rex, his prized possession. *Limbus*, the ridge which borders the crater of a volcano. He would live on this crater's edge willingly, to be with the just, not with those who could buy their way into heaven.

But then Father Rex was gone, taken by the military and exiled, sent back to Ireland, some said, sent to a labor camp on Mindanao, others said, sent to Ilocos Norte, the officials said. A typhoon's wind had blown away the piece of paper Father Rex had once given him, the address of his people in Ireland. What is the name for the wind that does that, Doming wondered.

He sat at his table, the telegram still in front of him. Moths sacrificed themselves in the kerosene flame. Doming took another drink of the sugar-cane brew he'd bought in the Cavite market. How could he go back to Negros, that crippled place, and to what end? He was the eldest, he had obligations, and he was being summoned. He drank more, too much, and felt his heart full.

He decided that he must go back to Negros for his sister. He would go to the stone masons in Quiapo market before he left and buy a marble plaque for his mother's burial place, carry it with him, to be engraved once he got home. He would not even risk carrying her name with him back to Negros, much less his own. He'd saved some money. He would look for his sister, but what would she look like now, at sixteen? Thousands of girls were now going to the bases at Clarke and Subic, even Okinawa, hoping to become entertainers but ending up as prostitutes. She was foolish, to leave without coming to Manila to him. He put his head down on his crossed arms, his head cradled.

He awoke a few hours later. Roosters proclaimed the morning matins. The smell of heat mixed with the rotten smell of dried milkfish, *bangús*, his neighbors were already preparing for sale in the market. His whole body ached. Rags were wound around his heart and in his chest from the rot-gut alcohol. Once upon a time he had prided himself on his lack of vices, his clean living, as Father Rex called it, and his studiousness. But his first thoughts now were not of his sister, as they should have been, but of Rue.

He was aroused, he had dreamed he was dancing with her at Sonny's bar, under the yellow light, his hands pulling her hips close, to some slow beat.

Later that morning he attended mass, considered going to confession, penitent, obtaining absolution. He changed his mind—the mass homily was on the sin of lust, the obscene force of desire. To an assembly of old women, pious young, weepy old men, a belching organ that sobs its notes, the priest talks about the sin of lust, of coveting another. Teach us guilt, shame, regret, the law, he thought. In a country made of struggle, where a few possess wealth beyond measure, in a place where even when the earth itself is without a name and the names of the hills lost to time, still the poor will endure, and the priest speaks to us of a man and a woman desiring each other, comforting, yearning?

But this is an easier sin to name than hypocrisy, the government's will to power, the urge for violence and revenge, he thought. This is a sin easier to name than corruption, injustice. It is safer for the priest to speak of coveting lust rather than the country's reality, so no statement would be reported, so that no military jeep would arrive at the chapel to take him away.

He left, having found no answer, no comfort. How difficult it would be to be a priest and speak the truth, to covet truth. But perhaps the truth was also that he coveted her.

At six-thirty the next morning Doming appeared at the Caldwell's house as usual. He would ask Trace Caldwell for five days unpaid leave, to return the day after the inauguration. Celia told him Trace was in the shower, so he asked for

Rue. She came to the garage off the maids' kitchen, because he would not go in the main part of the house. That was not done, usually, and he didn't want to seem too familiar with them.

"Of course, you must go then, if your family is calling for you. Will your friend Sonny go as well?" she said, sounding suspicious.

"No, Ma'am, it is a family matter," he said.

"Will you come back?" she said.

He was sure that she didn't believe him, where he was going.

"Of course," he said.

"Look, here is the telegram from my family, calling me home."

"I can't read that," she said.

Celia had overheard them from her kitchen.

"Really, Ma'am, when family calls here, it is an obligation," Celia called.

Celia invited him to her kitchen to have a bite. He'd told her once before that he'd not been home in a long time. Now she gave him a sweet *suman*, a brown sugar and sticky rice snack, charcoaled in a green banana leaf.

"It would only be some bad news to take you home so quickly," she said as he ate.

When he did not answer, Celia asked, "Did someone die?"

"This is to see my mother's grave, the one-year anniversary, I'll be back to work the day after the inauguration," he said.

"*Mabuhay*," Celia said, as he prepared to leave. *Live*, it meant, literally, a formal word for greeting hello and good-by and good trip. "I'll try to fix it for you with Sir, I'll remind him how these family obligations work."

"*Salamat Pô*," he said to Celia, and took her hand and touched it to his forehead, in the way of a young person leaving a beloved older relative.

Before he went to the ferry harbor along the north port, he went to Abbe's house to leave money for some medicines.

"My hand is healing, I can try working some," Abbe announced, putting on a brave front when Doming told them he must leave for a while, and why.

Paco begged to go with Doming. Abbe, surprisingly, agreed. It was as dangerous for them here in Manila, Abbe reasoned. And he wanted Paco, of whom he was so proud, to finally meet his *lola*, Abbe's own mother. She and Doming's stepfather had been cousins. She and Doming's mother had become as close as sisters for a time.

Sonny came in, just home from working overnight in his bar.

They consulted him, and even he agreed.

"You can't tell anyone what place we've gone to," Doming warned Abbe.

"And I have favor to ask," Sonny said. "Perhaps you could be the courier for a small package from Bacolod, only the size of a suitcase. Timing devices and fuses would be hidden in with fancy needlework from the Sisters there."

Doming felt his throat close in, as if he forgot how to swallow.

"I'll arrange for a priest in Bacolod to have it ready for you only when you are already waiting for the ferry back here to Manila. It may be some benefit to you as well, for you to help us this way," Sonny suggested.

"I don't want to transport weapons," Doming began.

"They're not for killing, they're for protesting, for embarrassing Marcos. More big booms and broken windows at night when the financial district is empty. Only resistance, *na*?" Sonny countered.

"What about Abbe? He could have been killed," Doming said.

"It's worth it, if I'd been quicker—these explosives would not hurt a fly," Abbe said.

Doming considered.

"I promise, they're only for delivery," Abbe said

"But Abbe, what about Paco with me?" Doming asked.

Doming didn't like the idea. What if we're stopped, he worried.

"Just don't travel with Paco on the ferry coming home, *sige*? You won't have the package until then. He can buy his own ticket and food, he'll be an experienced traveler by then," Abbe said. "Perhaps, soon, Paco may be a courier for us as well."

"Please," Paco begged him, "I will be good, I will be brave, and I won't be any trouble."

"These explosions are no more to Marcos than the bites of mosquitos," Doming argued.

"But even mosquitos can drive a beast to distraction— and besides, my friends would be in your debt for the time being," Sonny said. He did not say the name Alejo.

What good could come of this? Perhaps this favor for Sonny's friends, who were still expecting him to lead them to Raymonde, would satisfy them for a while, Doming thought.

For months these bombs had been exploding late at night, outside state-run banks and businesses. But one night just outside Rustan's Department Store, owned by a friend of Imelda's, a planted bomb had killed an American woman.

That had not been their intention, but it had gotten a lot of international press. Between these explosions aimed at business, and fires in earlier months in the oppositionists' Light a Fire movement, tourism and business were way down. This was all a plan to strike at Marcos' dictatorship, embarrass him in the international press. A guerilla campaign to topple him eventually, to discredit his power before the people. This had been Abbe's mission the night he was hurt. Generally, Sonny provided his expertise—the runners, the young men, the contacts. Their cause was just, they used what they could get their hands on, a David versus Goliath.

So Doming agreed.

The way that evil prevails is when the good man does nothing, Father Rex had said to Doming, more than once. Sin can be described as the absence of something, as an abiding silence in action or word, Doming thought.

Sonny was the one who accompanied Doming and Paco to the South Port. No family would allow a member to leave on a journey without being seen off, and Sonny was clearly honored that Abbe had asked him to take his part in this.

"Look, Paco," Sonny said, indicating a massive gray-black structure that rose like a megalith from reclaimed land along Manila Bay.

"Imelda's film temple, one and a half billion pesos it cost us," Sonny said.

A black box enclosing a central courtyard, on a site larger than the polo field in Ayera, rose from the swampy land on a series of gray marble steps, and squatted on thick columns that ran around the façade. Doming had heard the rumors—two hundred laborers accidentally buried under fast-drying cement one November night seven months ago now. The roof collapsed as they slept on their job-site. But construction continued the next morning, unabated. Bodies half-buried were sawed off, in Imelda's rush to host an international film festival.

The ferry made a long piercing whistle.

"*Mabuhay,*" Sonny said to him.

"*Kuya,* I will not let you down," Doming began. The stones of the city are paved on the backs of the poor, he thought. He felt in his gut the desire to strike back against the black box and all the lives it was built on and the billions of pesos wasted. Anger rose in his throat. He could not speak more. We do not let evil dictate the terms of our opposition, the priest had taught him.

To Rue it seemed Raymonde de Varcegno cultivated his friendship with Trace like an orchid gardener, constantly tending the air around it with boasts and flattery.

A few days later, on a Sunday afternoon, she and Trace watched Raymonde play polo for the Ayera team, against the American team from Clarke Air Base. This had been planned for weeks. Raymonde loved an audience, and he played on Ess' team. Originally, Forbes and the other polo clubs had been for foreigners only, but when the war ended well-to-do Filipinos were allowed to join. Now, their teams imported ringers, young Argentineans, Brazilians, or retired Spanish players just past their prime, with impressive handicaps.

She was shaded by flat-branched acacia trees, old trees twice as broad as they were high. The flags of league members flapped on silver poles. It was a perfect day, clear air. In the distance, she heard children shouting in the pool with its *nipa*-hut snack bars, attended by their *yayas*. Farther, a rotund Filipino hacked balls from a golf course tee, and beyond him she saw the green outline of Mount Makiling to the southeast.

There was a break in the match. Then each player changed horses, their polo ponies. Each had several to use during the match, wearing out one after the other. Each horse had a groom or two, young boys barefoot or in rubber thongs, currying, washing the sweat off, warming up the horses by riding bareback back and forth behind the bleachers. The fresh ponies each player had waiting on the sides watched with flanks trembling, as if eagerly rehearsing the run, and each was soothed by his own boy.

Raymonde had insisted for weeks that they must see this match. It seemed his opportunity to show his skills.

Raymonde waved, strutting around in his white knit shirt and jodhpurs, stomach and haunches tight, black boots shining. He was in his element, among the rich and pampered of his youth, though now he couldn't afford it at all.

He loved an audience.

She heard the sharp crack of a long-handled mallet hitting the bone-colored wooden ball to begin the second chukker. She felt the ground rumble beneath her with the pounding of the fine-boned fast ponies down the field.

In the end, Raymonde scored the winning goal. General Ess' hired Brazilian fed Raymonde an easy shot. He rode his black pony, its front legs high stepping, down the side of the field. He stopped where she sat.

He invited them to his house in San Lorenzo later that evening. He insisted.

At Raymonde's, the old servant Mary, Celia's sister, hurried out of the house. She unlocked the barred security gate. Celia had accompanied them, and brought Mary her favorite snack, *suman.*

Rue and Raymonde sat together alone on the lanai of the Varcegno's small house in the Makati housing compound called San Lorenzo. Baby showed Trace her newly decorated *sala*, or sitting room, and the new son's room.

"She decorates as if we are primitive tribals," Raymonde said to Rue, of Baby's unerring eye for using fine old things, antique Vigan clay jars and handwoven blankets from Iloilo. Baby worked to make it fine and gracious like her Ayera house. But Raymonde favored the highly polished Spanish colonial reproductions.

Raymonde drank San Miguel beer steadily. He'd already repeated his old stories about his days in the U.S., at Fort Benning in Georgia, the School of the Americas, then paramilitary training at a camp in Texas, and with the Philippine Rangers, and complaints about the furniture factory he ran in Mindanao (now with labor problems), making bamboo and rattan furniture for export only, and his plantations. The first time she met him he told of a former business partner who'd threatened his life. Rue always wondered what Raymonde had done to him first. He was not someone to have as an enemy.

"Now without the regular military training, I have a gut on the front of me," he said, and patted his beer belly. "But everywhere else, I'm okay," he said. He had a strong feral body. He held his arms slightly flexed and away from him, like an over-muscled boxer.

"When did you leave the military?" Rue said.

"Who said I left? I never really quit the Rambo Rangers. Some work for me now. We have useful contacts with Dole and Del Monte in Mindanao, taking out any trouble-making labor organizers," he said. He peeled pistachio nuts and ate them as he talked, tossing the shells onto the ground off the lanai.

Rambo soldiers, Raymonde called the Scout Rangers. At the Rice Institute one evening she and Sok saw soldiers in khaki and camouflage, sunglasses and headbands. One wore a t-shirt with writing in English—I may not go down in history, but I will go down on your little sister. They lounged in a roofless jeep. Those are AK-47s they carry, Ma'am, Sok told her. How do you know, she asked. He smiled and said, the New People's Army carry those from soldiers they ambush.

Raymonde continued, "In fact, the head of one company flew in from Hawaii. In Mindanao there's a price on him from NPA and former local landowners—he asked me for my own bodyguard, for his protection. What, you don't believe it?" Raymonde laughed, showing white small teeth, an almost feminine mouth it was so perfect.

Trace and Baby joined them.

Baby sent Celia, who waited on them in place of her sister, to get the baby. Bring the photo albums also, she said.

Mary was ailing.

"Heart failure," whispered Baby, as though Celia should not know. "Her lungs fill up with the fluids."

Baby had bragged to Rue, even though this boy of six months has only just come from the orphanage, with his knobby little penis, he is becoming like a bantam emperor, pounding his perfect fists, shrieking when his demands are not answered at once, eating his imported baby food with gusto, as if born to her and not to an unknown peasant.

The newly-hired *yaya* brought in the baby boy, paraded him around like a little Caesar.

Raymonde must have gotten in deep trouble with Baby, Rue thought, for he was all smiles about the darling infant. But she noticed with a pang that he seemed genuinely smitten with the boy, referring to himself as Papa, holding out his arms. When he noticed that Trace looked on with no interest, Raymonde ordered the girl to take the baby away.

Celia brought the album of the child's homecoming, and official picture. But she also brought the old album of Baby and Raymonde's wedding.

"Ray talked me into marriage when my father thought I was far too young," Baby began, turning the pages for Rue, "but Ray negotiated with my father and he finally relented."

Rue knew from Celia all the old de Varcegno stories, how Raymonde had coaxed Baby into marriage when Celia also thought Baby was too young and Raymonde not the right man. "Even then Raymonde was rumored to be having an affair with an older married woman, Peaches Gonzalez, the whore of the Manila Polo Club. Raymonde turned on his charm for Baby, but I warned her," Celia had said, "don't you marry this *mestizo* for his house, his family, his money, rather than love. The woman who does this is also a kind of whore."

While she told this to Rue, Celia had beat at the camote in the kitchen, bent over, pounding the leaves. She'd stretched and tried to straighten her bent shoulders.

It was 1958, Celia continued, not long after President Magsaysay had been killed in that plane crash. I was Baby's *yaya* and I was with her, visiting at her married sister's on the de Varcegno family plantation. Baby was stretched out on a bamboo lounge chair, near the pool, playing with a fan, a carved antique fan with cloth made of pounded banana leaves, pica cloth, with lacy cut-outs. She'd seen her sister's friends use their fans at lunch at a Chinese hotel there. She learned from them how to close the fan by tapping it against a finely manicured hand for emphasis, then snap her hand holding the fan outward, to make the fan fly open. She'd hold it near her neck, her chin lifted high and arrogant.

She threw out the woven fan from the market that I'd bought for her and was playing with this fan. She'd put a bit of coconut oil on the workings to make them move smoothly. She held her head like these women had, women ten years older and a thousand years more experienced, and it was in this attitude that Raymonde first saw her, the first time they'd met since her sister married his brother, when Baby was just twelve years old.

But Baby did not see the surprise on his face, the narrow way he looked at her displaying herself on that chaise like a newly caught fish laid out in the market, Celia said.

"It all seemed like a game to Baby," she said, bitterly. "The girl was once intelligent. I told her mother that she should go to a good school, that she needed someone to teach her more than how to be a deluxe servant. And her father's friends raised their eyebrows and pursed their lips at each other, over their *balut* and beers, when she purposely walked by their card tables, swaying her sapling hips.

"But by the time she was twenty-three only, they had three girls. Now they are grown and have left her. She knows Raymonde will stray, all men here want sons, Ma'am, many sons. Did you know Mary said it cost her ten thousand pesos from that baby broker? So, there will be a christening at Forbes Cathedral, we will cook for a week, all the best dishes, and General Ess will be one of the sponsors this time," Celia said.

"And your daughter and her husband are living in the States?" Rue asked Baby. She closed the wedding album.

"Yes, her husband is reporting on the Movement for a Free Philippines, some leftist communists there in Boston, where Ninoy Aquino is. Next he'll go to Georgia for military training."

"Hush, Baby," Raymonde shouted.

She saw Trace snap to attention.

"What is this he's hearing about Aquino?" Trace asked.

Raymonde sighed. "Ninoy? He was just like the rest of us, what happened to him? So preachy, so honorable now that he's safe in Boston and stirring up trouble with his journalist friends and the American-journalist husband of his sister. He's from an old family, always political, you can bet he'll try to come back and run for president," Raymonde said to Trace.

"But the key for us is to find a successor who has Marcos' friendliness to the U.S. bases here, to the business community, someone without the heavyhandedness," Trace said. "How well do you know Minister Enrile?"

"If Ninoy comes back it will turn the world here upside down," Raymonde said. "The U.S. would lose its bases, of course," he warned. "He's changed, I knew him for years, but what's got into him?"

"Seven years of solitary confinement, and no woman?" Baby said, baiting Raymonde.

"That woman talks too much," he said.

"Now, let me tell you how it really was between me and Baby," Raymonde said, continuing his own story.

159

Baby took Rue's hand—"Don't believe him," she said.

Raymonde had told it to them his way already, the first night Rue met him. She'd gone with Trace to the de Varcegno's house he wanted to rent.

"In those days I'd just returned from Spain," Raymonde began, "and I brought with me a beautiful saddle for polo. Baby was visiting at my family's house. Her older sister had married my older brother and I hadn't seen her since she was perhaps twelve years old. I brought out the new saddle and showed it to Baby and her sister. But how will it look on Peaches? my brother asked. Peaches Gonzalez, he meant, my sweetheart up in Manila. Baby, that's what her family calls her but Rosita is her name and she was eighteen and innocent I assumed; Baby giggled so much that she put her fan to her face and tears came out the corners of her eyes. I thought perhaps she cried from jealousy already."

"Raymonde!" Baby interrupted the story then. "I was ashamed for you, and I had a fiancé already. Peaches Gonzalez was the whore of the Manila Polo Club, that's what my sister called her. You were the one who wanted me. My fiancé was German—and rich."

"But he was Protestant, hah!" Raymonde shouted, as if that settled the question.

"I should have married him—and you are the one who now makes me to be jealous. If you minded your family business more and spent less time with General Ess and his massage parlors and politics we wouldn't be having to rent my house to them." She indicated Rue and Trace by lifting her fine petulant chin. She wasn't used to arguing with Raymonde in English and he had the advantage, Rue suspected.

It was true then. Baby gave up her beautiful garden and privacy in Ayera because Raymonde needed money, and

Trace wanted Raymonde to be in his debt. But what could Trace get from him, Rue wondered.

"Since my father died, it is my own business interest, no one else's," Raymonde said to her. Then he added something in Tagalog.

"You have run a good business into the ground, squandered most of your inheritance," Baby said. She left them on the lanai and fled to the old sisters, Mary and Celia, in their kitchen.

Much later that night, Rue saw that Raymonde's stories were all told. Raymonde appeared very drunk and Trace slightly from at least appearing to keep up with him. Rue went to look for Celia. She found her curled up in bed with her arm over Mary. She imagined the two old sisters slept now like they did as girls, first on piles of hemp in the rope factory and then in the garage of Baby's father's house.

Raymonde walked with them through the front garden and down the dark driveway. The capiz lantern Baby had hung from the tamarind tree made a small moon. There were no stars, the city's sky was too polluted, it was like looking up at the inside of an iron pot.

Trace had left their car parked in the street. One of Raymonde's guards, wearing camouflage fatigues, stood outside the gate.

"Where's your driver, night off?" Raymonde said.

Rue heard the belligerence, the disapproval.

It was the drinking perhaps, or more simply that he'd disliked Doming from the first moment they met, when Doming hadn't shown proper respect.

"He left for a vacation," Trace said.

"Back to some hovel in the provinces that he crawled out of?"

"He took unpaid leave, some emergency," Trace said.

"Same difference, some sick auntie right, and they need money? You can't let them walk all over you like that. Did he ask for a loan, an advance in pay?" Raymonde quizzed Trace.

"Did he?" Trace turned to Rue.

"Yes."

She'd advanced him fifty dollars, in U.S. currency which she used at the embassy commissary, after Celia asked her. This was all she had that morning.

"I told you he's a scumbag, he's taking advantage of you," Raymonde said to Trace. "Get rid of him."

Trace, circumspect, said nothing.

"You need someone like my man, Delgado. He'd lick the dust off my chair if I told him to," Raymonde said.

Raymonde's own driver, Delgado, another former military man, crooned songs as he drove and was always asking for handouts, trying to seduce the young labanderas in the neighborhood, Celia said. Someday he will rebel, someday he will see Raymonde is not a god, she'd said. Always obsequious, smiling and fawning for Raymonde. If a hired man did not behave so, it got him Raymonde's attention and resentment.

Trace drove. He had indeed been annoyed when she told him Doming would leave for four or five days. There were monsoon rains starting, and not a parking place in the city, Trace had complained to her.

They turned south on the highway toward Ayera.

Celia sat in the back seat alone, being chauffeured.

"Like I'm the fine Ma'am sitting back here all alone," she said, smoothing her best skirt.

Trace turned slightly and saluted her like the security guards at the embassy did for him each morning.

"Raymonde never liked Doming," Celia said. "From that first night they met."

"I suspect he simply has some goon he'd like to place with me as a driver," Trace said. "Probably nothing personal against Doming. But Raymonde says he would never trust a smart servant."

"Which is why he never trusted me," Celia said.

"Perhaps instead he has a new cook in mind for us, Celia?" he said, teasing her.

"Raymonde does not like me, but he knows my cooking is the very best, Sir!" Celia said. She sat up straight.

"We would never let you go, Celia," Rue said, soothing her. "I don't think Raymonde likes me much, either," she said, trying to change the subject.

"He's just not used to women working, except as servants and laborers," Trace said.

"Perhaps he just doesn't like women who are smarter than he is," Rue said.

"But that's every one of us, Ma'am," Celia said.

"Celia!" Trace said, scolding. But he laughed.

Celia in the backseat, pleased perhaps with her joke, with Rue's reassurance of her place with them, hummed. It was the "Bayan Ko" song of the opposition and Radio Veritas. Rue realized Trace didn't recognize it, but she turned and raised her eyebrows at Celia.

Celia simply raised her eyebrows back at her, and made a face innocent as a child's.

Rue remembered the first time Raymonde had met Doming. It was the night she'd visited their fine house in Ayera that first time. Trace wanted her agreement to rent the house. From the first moment in the garden, Rue felt certain she could live there. But from the first moment with

Raymonde she disliked him. He seemed ruled by his concern for money and pleasure.

The two couples had toured the house. In the master bedroom the east windows looked out into banana trees, and beyond the trees was a field of tall grass, then the acacia-lined avenue, and on the horizon the tiny lights on the hills and mountains beyond Laguna de Bay strung like necklaces. A slender curved mango moon, the color and form of one of Baby de Varcegno's perfect nails, tilted on the horizon.

At the end of that first evening, Raymonde, drunk from bottle after bottle of San Miguel, as if he had a thirst that could not be quenched, hung on to Trace at the door of their Ayera house, calling him *compadre*, leaning on Trace as he and Rue walked down the wide paved walk to the car. Raymonde was so clearly relieved that Rue had agreed to rent his house, with the standard one year's rent in advance. His immediate money problems were solved. Labor problems in my plantations and factories in Mindinao, he'd said vaguely.

At the car Trace had eased himself away from Raymonde and got into the back seat. Doming had waited with the car, and held the door. Raymonde staggered and Doming tried to grab hold of his arm as Raymonde fell against him.

He'd slapped Doming, said something to him in haughty Spanish, and Doming answered back in Spanish, more perfect Castilian Spanish.

Then Raymonde had reared up tall, saying, Don't touch me, "*Nóli me tangere,*" almost as if he were frightened.

But Doming continued to hold him under his arm as Raymonde swayed.

"Let go of me, you dog," Raymonde said, and slapped him square in the face with the flat of his hand.

"You can't even walk, you're so drunk," Doming spat back at him.

"Don't speak to me in Spanish like you're someone," Raymonde said. "Where did a louse, a *kuto*, like you learn to speak Spanish like some *Don*?"

"*Hindot ka*," Doming said, switching to Tagalog, Fuck you, then. He let go.

Raymonde fell hard against the car. Unable to stand then, he let loose a string of curses that contradicted the European bonhomme he'd displayed all evening. Raymonde hadn't let this anger slip out again in front of her, in the two years she'd known him.

"You're a nigger, *baluga*, a bastard, your sister is a whore, *puta*," Raymonde spat.

Trace was already between them.

"Back off," he said to Doming, and to Rue's astonishment he apologized to Raymonde.

Baby and Celia came from the front door where they stood. They took Raymonde inside with them. Two weeks later Trace and Rue moved into the fine Ayera house, and Raymonde never mentioned Doming again, until tonight.

Celia was snoring lightly in the back seat.

They drove through the Ayera market. They passed a man sleeping in one of the market stalls, on an empty counter under the still-burning bulb. The smell of vinegary garbage came into the car.

"What's Raymonde working on, with former military men, why is his son-in-law spying on Aquino?" she whispered to Trace.

"He's hired a lot of private security guards, private militia. I don't know what General Ess has on him, exactly, but he's in deep."

"Baby knows what kind of a man he is," Rue said. "She's afraid of him, I think."

"Well, she's smart enough not to antagonize him, smart enough to know much of what he does means nothing."

"What means nothing?" Rue said.

"There's a lot of stuff I can't tell you, not now," Trace said.

She usually didn't ask, but she pressed on. "What are you doing, in Mindanao?" she said.

"It's not worth discussing; we need a new military base there, out of harm's way," he said.

The one time she'd flown over the province of South Cotabato on Mindanao, when she and Anne were on a trip, the hills below were bare red dirt, stripped clean. Villages were fortresses, the local people sullen, and they had two armed guards in the jeepney that took them through the South Cotabato valley and up into the hills to a Tiboli mission where Anne took pictures of antique textiles. When they soaked in a lake, leeches had fastened onto their legs within a few minutes. Neither woman screamed or carried on, as one helped the other remove them; and that trip to the jungled lakes of the Tiboli in southern Mindinao had cemented their friendship. A tribal elder had collected the stubby earthworm-like leeches they'd plucked, putting the things in a jar.

Not to eat? Anne had asked, worried.

He'd didn't try to hide his wonder at their ignorance. To clean the wounds of a young man who'd refused to join the military training for the government's Civilian Home Defense Forces, he answered.

Rue remembered the Tiboli hills in Mindanao as one of the few blessed places in the country the Spanish had never conquered, that the foreign mining or fruit companies hadn't penetrated. There was nothing to buy, no fawning over tourists, just a culture that had lived for a thousand years. The men rode fine-boned horses with hand-cast brass bells woven into their manes. The women in their finery wore girdled belts of bells on their hips and the sounds of fine bells came up through the early morning mist to the houses, each of which stood alone on the top of a hill. Rue thought for the first time that if she had lived before this would have been the place. She recognized the rhythm.

It was said about Mindanao that the number of Moro—Muslim—civilians killed after martial law probably numbered in the hundreds of thousands. At least half of the two and a half million not killed had become refugees. No one paid much attention, since it was far from Manila, and besides, they weren't Catholic down there.

They passed the pink-stucco Ayera Cathedral, lit up in the dark. To her it appeared to be floating. Then the car-lights showed a line of five Filipinos, an old man, two women, two children, trudging single file along the dark road.

They were almost home. She could see the guarded security gates of the Ayera Village. After that they were safe, Trace always said. Royal palms lined the main street. She saw him relax as the two security guards waved them in.

"What are you worried about?" she asked.

"The whole country," he said.

"You could quit, you could leave," she said. "You get all the dirty work to do."

"Don't be ridiculous, after this they'll owe me, there's an attractive spot with the NSC, and besides, you love the goddamn place."

"Yes." She heard Celia snore, but she thought Celia was awake, listening.

"Trace, what will happen to us? What are you really working on here?" she asked. She tried to determine when things had changed between them. His face these days had a curiously dead expression, the face of one of the carved Indonesian puppets in their front hall. God of deception.

"It's just business as usual," he said.

They were home.

At dawn the next morning, Monday, Celia heard Rue, she guessed, up very early indeed. She heard the door to the porch off the lanai slide open. Celia fastened the buttons up the front of her light-yellow maid's uniform. She combed her hair, more gray than black now, smoothed it into a twist, and clipped it with an old clip of Baby's. Her room was not in the basement, where she'd lived before, in a room next to the sewing girls, but instead she lived now in one of the children's rooms just over the kitchen. Baby had been appalled Rue had moved her and Lleoni to this room. It's big and light, with a nice view, and we certainly don't need it, Rue explained to Baby.

Celia and Lleoni had set up high shelves between them. It was the first time in her life Celia had a room to herself, had privacy. She found she liked it. She could be alone. But this was the first time she and Mary were apart. She was afraid for Mary; perhaps this was what had made Mary's heart ill, being alone without her. But Celia didn't want to go back to live in a house with Raymonde. That would kill her.

Celia hurried out into the wide hall and down the mahogany stairs. But it was Trace she found standing on the lanai.

"My head aches," Trace groaned. "Do we have something for it?"

"Yes, Sir," she said.

Celia first got coffee for him. His reddish hair was combed back, still wet from a shower. A perfectly starched and ironed white shirt, thanks to me, Celia thought.

"A hangover, that never used to happen," he said.

"I've heard the San Miguel has embalming fluid in it, some chemical to preserve it longer, and that causes it, Sir," she said.

She left him sitting on the lanai. Then the *hasaán* man, the knife-sharpener, began, the high calling, *Ha-saaan, hasaaan,* the scraping of stone against metal. He was outside the garden wall, under the tamarind tree along the road. The sound started and stopped as he worked.

"Celia, would you chase that man off?" Trace called to her. "Why is he always near our house? The sound makes me crazy."

Celia crossed the lawn. Nearby, the gardener began his work, cutting back the flame bushes that were almost finished blooming. She went to the front garden wall, stood on her toes to see over.

"Pssst," she said. She tapped on the wall with the stick-broom and waited for him to look.

She considered her words. She liked him, she'd seen Lleoni laughing with him, and she didn't want to offend him. He'd been coming around for several months.

"Pssssst," she said to get his attention.

"*Magandáng umaga, Pô,*" he said, politely. Good morning.

"You must leave, our Sir doesn't feel well."

But the man surprised her. He said, "Ah, too bad. *Manang,* when might the owner come round here again?"

"You mean Don Raymonde de Varcegno?" she said, drawing her neck up haughtily like Baby, rolling her *R's* like Raymonde did.

"I have something that belongs to him. When can I return it, when will he come?" he said politely. He spoke in the humble tones of a flatterer, she thought.

All her instincts told her he was from the opposition, not evil, but dangerous.

"*Su,* Shoo," Celia said to him. "He wouldn't want anything from you, what do you want of us, anyway?" She pursed her mouth at him, showing her displeasure at his forwardness. Perhaps he only wanted to borrow money. She wished Lleoni were here so she could ask her what she knew, but Lleoni had not returned from her engagement at the hotel two nights before, not even for a change of clothes.

Celia went to the kitchen to make tea. She hadn't slept well.

When Celia was Lleoni's age she'd once been bothered by a friend of Baby's father. Mary had intervened, but then Mary had borne the brunt of the man's displeasure. Celia prayed Lleoni would not be pregnant, like Mary had been. What a business that.

Celia went to the lanai, gathered the things there. Rue had not come down for breakfast. The grinding sound stopped for the morning. In the kitchen, she washed the cups and looked out from the long row of open windows. She could see far north toward the city. Dirty sky the color of her dish water marked its place. She watched a hummingbird harass the gardener. The bird darted searching for its orange flame flower. The gardener was intent on cutting them back.

She remembered the headache medicine for Trace and she felt like the whole household depended on her sometimes. She relished being so essential, so valued. She went to the lanai and saw him frowning, at work already, probably writing another cable to send away to the States, written words poured into the telephone. She still didn't understand this.

His mind chokes his heart, she thought, imagining the wooded vine that grows up the fig tree.

Before Trace left for work, at about seven-thirty that same morning, the *hasaán* man had put away his sharpening stone.

No one noticed that as Trace drove through Ayera Village the man followed the car at a distance on his bicycle. The man stopped just inside the guarded village gates and spoke with another man who sat straddling a motorcycle there. They saw Trace's car turn east, along Azapote Road, past the pink Ayera Cathedral.

A few days before, Trace and Carter McCall, his colleague, had joined General Al Haig in a private meeting with Marcos, just after the election was declared over. Haig promised that the Reagan administration would assist Mr. Marcos in fighting terrorism. They would begin prosecuting and passing on names of U.S.-based Filipino activists. Covert surveillance reports on Filipino dissidents would now be regularly passed on to the Philippine Constabulary. Department of State reports on Filipino subversives would first cross Trace's desk, and then be shared with Marcos and his generals. An FBI raid in San Francisco six months before, at the Psinakis home, an anti-Marcos family, in December of 1981, had yielded a coded list of underground operatives thought to be in Manila.

This morning, a week after the election, Trace read the list at his desk in his office overlooking Manila Bay. The

171

names would be delivered to Ess and the first computer in the country, supplied by an AID grant, would be used to consolidate this with Ess' own lists of subversives. Some had already been picked up, Ess reported to Trace, and sent on to one of the re-education camps. The foremost among these was Camp September Twenty First Movement in Los Baños, named for the martial law date.

They were closing in on a name on the list—Sonny Dominguez. He was a past student leader and had contacts with foreign journalists. They had reports on where to find him.

Another name on the list was for a young man wanted in Negros, for labor organizing. But his name no longer existed. It had lain for eleven years at the bottom of the Philippine Sea, wrapped in a bag weighted with a stone. He had a new name, Doming Aquinaldo.

PART II
Inauguration—The Prophecy of Bridges

Doming came from near the town of Hinigaran. His stepfather's people worked the cane fields on the hacienda there for many years. His mother came from the south, the island of Mindanao, Tiboli people of South Cotabato, with a priest who brought her to the Visayan island of Negros when she was twenty and Doming was a toddler.

My people have no word for sin, she often teased Father Rex in the confession box. The only word for *trespass* means to disrespect our Tiboli tradition.

And in that, she had transgressed, she had left and gone to work for lowlanders. And she'd paid dearly. She'd become pregnant with this baby boy and given birth. When Doming was already walking, she'd left and come to Negros in an arranged marriage. With Doming's stepfather she had five more children. This was all Doming knew.

Katiyakán, Assurance, was the name of the ferry that carried him and Paco now. But someone had scrawled the word WALÁNG in front of the name, so it became *Without Assurance.* The ferry carried him back to Negros, to Sugarland, during the week between the election and Marcos' inauguration. Because the stolen election was finished, many government troops stationed in Negros got holiday leave, so he was counting on travel being safer than at anytime since he had left eleven years before.

From the harbor the two travelers took a public jeepney south. When it reached the town of Banilad, they waited at the market intersection for the last link of the journey. Doming began to feel edgy. His name and picture would be posted with the Constabulary here. He looked around, and recognized the church. It faced the market square and was the northernmost of several parishes Father Rex had regularly visited.

Stay here, Paco, he said. He crossed the square, tried the door. It was unlocked, but there was no priest, no rows of seats. Benches were being used as beds, the remains of a fire smoked under the center tower. In a wooden cupboard, he found one of Father Rex's old brown robes. He took off his own shirt, folded it in a bundle, and put on the robe. It fit. When he went out, he pulled the robe's hood low over his face. Paco looked on in amusement.

They waited for the last jeepney ride.

A barrio official approached and told him there had been a death here during the night. The local priest has vanished. "You are traveling through?" he asked.

"Yes, to return the boy to his family," Doming said.

"Will you say the mass—she was an old woman, my grandfather's sister."

To avoid suspicion, Doming agreed. The old words came easily. When he was a boy, he helped Father Rex with the mass so many times.

When he sang the *Our Father* in Ilongo, his old language, the women wept, the daughters and granddaughters, for their *manang*, their auntie. He did not feel like a fraud. God is the fraud, he thought. Like other rulers, sometimes He gave them just enough hope and fear to keep His people from rebelling.

Doming was just using the priest's robes to pass through, to keep anyone else from dying because of his mistakes.

So he did the mass for the old woman, grown old like the mighty pandan tree that thrives in swampy soil. She was born, they told him, in 1898, when Aquinaldo declared the first Filipino republic. She survived the Japanese, but now was gone on the first day of Marcos' next one thousand years.

What do we owe you, the family asked him when the mass was ended and the food eaten.

He remembered how the well-to-do would pay for some special intention or blessing. Father Rex would never refuse the expiation offering of the rich, thinking perhaps of all he could do with the windfall. Anything new would be blessed—fishing boats, tricycle taxis, houses, granaries, factories. *Kyrie eleison. Christe eleison. Requiem aeternam dona eis, Domine, et lux perpetua luceat eis.*

When the old woman's family asked what they could give him for his service, he said, "A ride the last few kilometers, to the south, along the coastal road, for me and the boy." The family found a place for them on the back of an old cane truck.

Paco slept. The truck passed through a forest of green. Everything was green. Trees with trunks five feet thick, tamarind, ebony, cedar, banyan. Thick groves of bamboo, jungle vines as thick as his wrist, with dark leaves like faces growing over him. Then a view of the sea, fired a cobalt blue he'd almost forgotten, a few *banka* boats bobbing there like children's toys, the sun burning white above. It was the fix of light he saw in his dreams, uncreated light, everything in the foreground. He leaned back on the hardened sugar that the old cane had wept, and looked up at the sky. He would recognize home when the sky turned brown from the cane factory and the ground rumbled with the sound of the mill and the air smelled like black sugar ash.

When he was a boy, Father Rex read month-old newspapers from Ireland and England, and listened to the radio—

Baby See, Doming heard him say, for BBC. At first he thought it was an Irish nickname for the Christ child, that a part of the Father's all-seeing God was always out there somewhere on the wind at night. Then the priest explained how the sound came from England, land of Arthur and Lancelot, the stories Doming read from his books. He imagined it bounding the seas at night, striding on long legs over the Alps crossed by Hannibal and over the deserts of the Arabian nights, riding upon the storms, wading the South China Sea to Palawan, finally falling into Negros.

Doming and Paco walked from where the truck dropped them a half-kilometer from the town.

It was all as before—the clinic with children everywhere, mothers who waited for the once-a-week health worker. The children who still sucked and sucked on raw sugar cane as if it were their mother's teat. A little boy begged from an older sister, he called her *ah-te*, sister. She held a tiny baby; the brother asked for milk from her breasts. Doming watched while she fed him, one arm around him, one balancing the infant, her full round breast the only beautiful thing to be seen here.

A young soldier approached as they walked toward town. Doming motioned for Paco to be quiet.

"Father, I want to confess. My last confession was more than one year ago. The priests here have left," the young soldier said.

"I cannot do that," Doming said.

He was a boy almost. "Father, please, they bring us here from Ilocos Norte, we don't know the people. I was the one who dug the pits, for the bodies of the cane workers."

Paco listened attentively.

"I will put a cross near the place, and bless it," Doming said. "What you've told me is sufficient. Now you must choose. Walk away, if you have to. Your heart is good, my son."

And here Doming stopped—those were the words with which Father Rex had constantly reassured him.

"They call it an ammunition dump and store trucks there," the young man said.

Doming made the sign of the cross. "Go in peace, God has heard you, you must find a new place."

He did not say, Your sins are forgiven. He did not have the authority.

"Paco, let's find your grandmother," Doming said.

Doming remembered the house. He sent Paco forward, alone, and watched him go through the shabby gate and surprise the old woman with gray cataracts. She was sitting under a guava tree and spitting betel juice. She was Abbe's mother.

"Say nothing yet except that I'm your teacher from your school in Manila. I'll check on you late tonight," Doming had told him. The woman would know not to ask too many questions.

So then, to the river, past the mill, toward his own house. The Sugarland of western Negros knows only two seasons, the milling season and the off-season. This would be the milling season, a bog wet with grease and syrup. The cane must be milled within hours of harvest to preserve its sweetness. Doming found the stone gate of the sugar plantation shut, the mill quiet. Old friends who would now be cutting and loading cane had left for work at a new and bigger mill near Iloilo, because cutting was all they knew. But there was an over-supply of sugar, it was said, and prices had collapsed.

He was a ghost by the time he got to his house. Dusty brown chickens pecked in the dirt, fighting over some weevil. A low fence of crossed poles marked the garden, which seemed to grow children, children everywhere. His old guava tree was grown large.

He called from the gate. First a child—his niece?—came running out. She called a bigger girl, and then came his sister-in-law. They ushered their guest inside. They didn't know him at first. He was a stranger. In a way, he was relieved. It was the priest's brown robe, and his eleven years had aged him.

His brother Eduardo was the first to recognize him.

"*Kuya, Kuya,*" his brother Eduardo said. Older brother, the same word of affection and respect he used for Abbe and Sonny. Eduardo brought out *tuba*, cheap alcohol made from fermented sugar cane. Doming drank with him. The neighbors tried to come in the door, of course. There was no such thing as privacy.

"Not now, the priest is the cousin of my wife, he must rest," Eduardo explained to them.

Eduardo's wife Gabi soon was whispering to Doming, as if he really were her confessor, that Eduardo spent too much time with his *barkada*, his group of friends. They play billiards on the outdoor table at the beer-house, bet on cockfights, she said. Talk to him, she urged.

But his brother Eduardo, his half-brother, looked beaten down.

His wife complained to Doming, "See, this is why you must come home and lead the family now, you're the eldest, you can help him find work. You're not bad-looking, you would find a good wife." She leaned toward him provocatively.

No one mentioned Maria Fe until he asked. "What have you heard?" Doming said, when the evening came.

"They come recruiting for the bars in Olangapo and Manila," Eduardo said, "or more likely, I think, she has gone to the mountains with the New People's Army, with a young man."

"*Bahala Na*," Gabi said, shrugging her shoulders, Let it go, it's fate. "She was a hard to handle girl, she cut her hair like a boy's and ran off with a man from the next barrio. They are in the NPA and that brings our entire family under suspicion," Gabi complained.

"And she stole your mother's keepsakes, and her necklace," Gabi added.

The hens scratched in the dry dust around the house where Doming sat outside until late that night. How their lives had turned out, how differently than he'd imagined or hoped.

A rooster crowed, again, and he remembered Father Rex would say, "Like Saint Pedro, you are, the rock."

Around ten o'clock that same evening he walked to the cemetery behind the church, ran his hand along the coping stone of a whitewashed alabaster tomb. The dead were above ground, in crypts. The rich may get an entire room, a marble mausoleum, covered houses that the whole surviving family can fit into when they come to celebrate All Soul's night. The poor get stacked up on top of each other, put into an outdoor wall of rough cement.

But the orange-blossomed frangipani trees were grand. He recognized the *camia* bushes along the path with their spiky leaves and sweet white flowers. His mother would boil the *camia* stems to make medicines for her family and the neighbors. But she never fit in well—she became a proud beautiful Tiboli when she wore her jewelry and hair ornaments for fiestas.

He walked in the dark toward the village square. Two soldiers lounged in hammocks, asleep under a canvas awning. Armalites rested at their sides. They were part of a detachment of the Seventh Infantry battalion.

The square of the village looked the same, the Tongco Family Store with its Cola signs where everything was sold on credit and promises. A *calesa* cart, with a single driver and a couple in the back, went round the square. A wedding celebration, perhaps, the cart with its wooden wheels painted bright yellow, decorated with pink and white tissue paper blossoms. The reigns were woven with garlands of *sampagita* flowers.

He passed by a row of dark storefronts, wooden buildings with peeling paint. One old man who made sandals from old tires and strips of carabao hide, a man he remembered as young and strong and who made his first good pair of shoes when he was a boy, sat in one doorway. The man squatted on thin corded haunches, with his hands resting on his little pot belly as if that were his only treasure.

After the last strike the bodies of seven cane workers had been found buried in a fallow cane field. Twenty others were missing. This was what the young soldier had confessed to, bodies in an ammo dump.

Doming reached the place and found women, mothers and wives, digging carefully with short-handled spades and with wooden spoons. Their light from a torch flared up and down with the breeze, making large shadows that moved against the trees where he stood watching. They scooped methodically. Like good farmers, they could have been planting lima beans in season. He'd forgotten the night here. Thousands of stars sprung from an indigo sky.

The women were here because Paco had told his grandmother what he knew. One of her nieces was married to a man who'd disappeared with the others the month before. So now the women worked silently. A few soldiers watched. One took mock-aim with his M-16.

"Father, pray for us," the women called to him. They paused.

From memory, he recited:

> *Comfort us in Exile, O Father,*
> *though the fig trees do not blossom,*
> *nor fruit be on the vines,*
> *the produce of the olive fail*
> *and the fields yield no food*
> *the flock be cut off from the fold*
> *and there be no herd in the stalls*
> *yet I will rejoice in the Lord.*

The women crossed themselves, and resumed their work.

"There is still a price on you, I've learned," Eduardo said when Doming came in very late.

"And will you turn me in?" Doming said.

"No, but Gabi suggested someone might, there's gossip about who you are," Eduardo warned.

Doming decided to leave the next day, and leave a telegram for Maria Fe in care of the post office in each town on the way north to the ferry.

But later that night Paco and his grandmother appeared. Doming wasn't sleeping, he had no mosquito net, and he awakened feeling a cockroach crawling across his shoulder, its antennae tapping a path. He heard the knock.

Paco led his grandmother by the hand. Even in the half-light he looked subdued and ashamed.

"They want him," the gray-eyed woman said urgently.

"Who, *Manang*?"

"They want the boy who told where the workers are buried."

"Then we'll leave now," he said, thinking aloud.

"And Father," the grandmother added to Doming, though he wore no robe, "I told them it was you who knew about the cane workers, and told, not the boy. Forgive me."

"So you still have your quick wits about you," Doming said. "That was the right thing to do."

Paco said nothing. He's like I was, Doming thought. His forthrightness can bring down disaster.

"Do you want to come back someday, Paco?" he asked.

The boy burst into tears, and threw his arms around the old woman's neck. "*Lola*," he said.

She apologized, she had no food left to send with them, she'd fed the boy everything she had. Doming had not had an opportunity to talk to her privately, but Paco had painted a glowing picture of Manila for her.

"Someday I will come there to see my boy, Abbe," she said.

Doming left almost all the money he brought, giving it to Eduardo to distribute among the family. Outside the barrio, Doming had Paco climb into a laundry bag he'd carried as a pack on this trip. He would carry Paco in it. He walked out into the night with the pack over his back as if it were a light load, a priest, alone. He wore again the old cassock of Father Rex. He could feel the boy's shaking in rhythmic sobs that settled into occasional catching of breath.

"Now that you are calm, Paco, listen carefully."

The bag grew still.

"If I put this bag down behind a tree, say, or in a ditch, you are not to move until morning, no matter what you hear, do you understand?" Doming asked, keeping his voice neutral.

"Yes, Tító," Paco said.

And to Doming it seemed it was the coarse brown cassock he wore that would carry him north toward Bacolod until morning.

When he grew sleepy after many kilometers had passed, they sang. They sang quietly, first the words of the "Bayan Ko," then Doming sang the old Tiboli songs of his mother. They sang to bring the new day into being, Doming thought.

Paco had met distant cousins and saw the place his father Abbe had talked about all his life. But Paco also heard the gunshots at night and heard the stories of older boys who claimed they would soon join the NPA. Doming was proud of Paco and hadn't regretted letting him go along, until now. Still, the boy was made of good fiber, he reminded him. You know your lessons. I teach you like Father Rex taught me. But this was bad judgment, Paco, and we'll speak some more of it when we get back.

"But it was the truth," Paco countered.

Truth will overcome the lie. This was Father Rex's faith.

"But your speaking out changes nothing there, for those women," Doming began.

"They know the truth now, about their sons," Paco said. "It changes everything for me—I wanted to kill them, the soldiers who were watching them digging. Then I thought of the one soldier who confessed to you, how his speaking saved him in a way."

Doming stopped. Does it take a bag on my back to tell me things I once carried in my own heart, he wondered.

In life it is not the criminal that provokes the most hate, but the honest man who is not afraid to speak the truth. We cannot keep silent against injustice. That is why the Spanish never wanted Filipinos educated, to keep them silent and ignorant, clan set against clan.

"You're right, violence creates more of the very thing it seeks to destroy," Doming finally said.

What have I learned, Doming wondered, what am I teaching him? To counter evil with passivity, to run? But there is no neutral ground to run to. He felt capable of doing anything to protect Paco, to keep him from danger, to keep him from becoming a young man furious only with his own lack of dignity and impotence, furious enough to finally give into that nemesis, the goddess of revenge.

He'd noticed Paco had been careful around these boys of Negros who had no schooling, careful not to show off his learning. He thought Paco was simply a too tender-hearted boy who could not resist telling one who grieved where her husband was buried.

We must not keep silent to save ourselves. This is who he'd been with Father Rex. Despair, or cynicism, had muted him for all these years.

They traveled off the road, north to Bacolad, and spent the next night there. Paco bought his own food now, and he watched Doming to know when to stay close to him and when to be strangers. The next morning Paco waited at the ferry while Doming went to the priest's house to get the package for Abbe.

"Yes, Maria Fe came here," the priest said simply.

"Was she a courier for you also?" Doming asked him.

"You know I couldn't tell you that," he said. "But know that she is a dauntless girl. There was a military lieutenant here who had his eye on her each time she came into town.

She had a sweetheart, one of the local boys who joined the NPA. They left here together. Leaving was safer for her than staying."

And so Doming took the chance, gave the man his address in Manila—his house in Cavite.

"If she comes back here, tell her to come to my place," he said to the priest. He carried away the package of embroidered goods, tightly packed. He still wore the brown cassock of his old teacher. Perhaps this, the cassock itself, was what he'd returned to Negros for, this last time.

"It's a mission project," Doming explained to the ferry's captain, when he carried on a cardboard package wrapped in brown tape, a package the size of a small suitcase. The hand-embroidered goods from the mission in Bacolod were sold to foreigners for a good price, and covered four dozen timing devices.

Manila! They say that at sunrise on the morning of Inauguration Day, June 21, church bells began to sound all over the city, all over the island of Luzon, all over all the islands of the Visayas and Mindanao. The people would say the bells dinged and donged of their own accord, even the bells that had been ordered roped to silence in the protests during election week, shook with the urge and effort to sound the same two syllables. Those who heard say the bells were calling *Ni-noy, Ni-noy*.

Around that time, too, a ferry entered the mouth of Manila Bay. It was a fine morning. The passengers had traveled all night from the southern island of Negros, but not one was coming to share in Marcos' inauguration festival that morning.

Doming stood at the railing. The rising sun pierced the jagged edge of eastern sky like tin, outlining Luzon's silver spine.

He wore the cassock with its hood pulled up to cover his head and he wore sandals made of carabao hide he'd gotten from the generous priest in Bacolad. A distant sound came to him from the land, a sound like a thousand dogs barking. The ferry rose and fell in a steady motion as if the creature on whose back it rode breathed expectantly beneath it.

Some first-class passengers began to push toward the bow where they soon would disembark. The ferry's deck sloped more and more. Soon the ferry captain shouted over the loudspeaker to move away, move away, or we'll tip. That made everyone else rush upstairs from the dark hold.

A young woman in tight jeans and a bright green shirt now stood near Doming. As the boat shifted, her hands clenched the rusted railing.

"I cannot swim," she said to him. She'd told the other passengers she'd been in Bacolod to visit her family and bring them money she made in Manila. She claimed to be a housemaid, but he saw that her hands were well cared for and her long fingernails gleamed with silver polish. Those around her knew what she was—a very young woman for sale—one of Negros' top exports now that sugar had failed. He thought again of Maria Fe.

The ferry lurched again in the choppy water as they passed Corregidor Island. Each year some ferry boats sank. Provincial officials were bribed to take on too much cargo or too many passengers. The passengers could not banish this fear from their thoughts. A few months before two hundred and forty had perished off Samar Island when an overloaded ferry headed for Manila went down. In Manila, the families stood at the North Harbor for two days waiting for some word. Then the reports came—sharks feeding on bodies.

Now each time the ferry pitched in the turbulent waters entering Manila Bay's narrow mouth, this young woman cried out.

"Pray for us, Father," she begged.

He hesitated.

He felt the passengers crowded there look at him, asking each other why he did not begin, wasn't that his job. *A priest who will not pray?* And so finally he began. He prayed in Tagalog, the pious words coming easily, "Father, protect this woman and those who travel with her, from all the dangers of the deep, from dangers of the road, from sharks and poisonous rays, from evils seen and unseen." He chose the ornamented language that the superstitious would approve. But when he glanced at the young woman she was no longer listening with her eyes closed. She was looking toward the distant harbor already coming into view. The climbing sun reflected off the galvanized metal roofs of shanties along the north port as if the city were made of gold.

He paused.

Perhaps she thought as long as his words flowed, they would hold evil and danger at a distance. Perhaps she thought that if the boat tipped now she would find herself held up by holy hands and floating like a *banca* boat.

Paco, clad only in shorts and rubber flip-flop sandals, came hurrying to Doming and tugged on his sleeve. Doming held up his hand, priest-like, to quiet him and bent over to him.

"I'm sick, seasick, Tító," the Paco whispered.

Doming pulled the brown hood more fully over his face.

"Go to the side, Paco, and let it go," he said.

189

He continued with a variation on the traditional prayer calling for a blessing of the First Lady and the Pope. Marcos had only converted to Catholicism as a grown man, he didn't have to be included.

"Protect our First Lady from the water buffalos, that they may not gather to plot in herds of three or more under her Crimebusters' Emergency Act; protect her from the dogs that call out their morning propaganda against the First Lady in code. Bless her efforts to contain the sparrows from illegally squatting on the property of Malacañang, that she may resettle them outside the city and bring us all to bliss."

The ferry passed the abandoned freighters half sunk in the shallow waters nearer the docks. He saw the fires from a cookstove on the deck, where squatters lived.

"Finally, Our Father, if it is meant to be, that our First Lady turns into one of these blessed, your cold-blooded creatures, a *lapu-lapu*, say, let her live a long cold-blooded queen of the fish life, and gain the wisdom of the *lapu-lapu*, so that when we meet her dead-blue-fish-eyes in the Baclaran market, we will say, ah, here is a first lady of *lapus*, a queen of *lapu-lapu*, ring the bells in the markets of Baclaran Church and steam her with ginger and *kalamansi* juice and crown her with *kangong* greens and *gabi* leaves and serve her with coconut rice and *leche flan*. Let us drink San Miguel and toast her as the first mayor of Lapu-Lapu City." A few half-toothed old men smiled. A too-pious matron exclaimed, *Dios!*

He heard the young woman's laughter. Others near them covered their mouths. He said some words in Latin and made the sign of the cross. He was pleased that automatically, those nearest him, their arms already holding their ragged bundles and cardboard boxes, struggled to do the same. Some carried the traditional gifts, *pasalubong,* of one who returned to their family from a trip. And now Doming carried a gift of sorts for Sonny from the priest in the town of Bacolod—timing devices and fuses smuggled into the country from Jogjakarta.

The ferry's bow again slipped dangerously toward the water as it neared the south harbor dock and people with their bundles moved forward. *MANILA!* the loudspeaker screamed now as their ferry butted the rotting wood of the dock.

The last time he'd arrived here was eleven years ago. His mother had sent dried *bangus* fish and rice that would last the trip. She'd even sent some of the meat from their slaughtered carabao, but when he'd discovered that package he'd thrown it overboard. The first few nights in the city he slept in Rizal Park in the Luneta, under the statue of José Rizal. He was amazed at the rich people passing by during the day on Roxas Boulevard. Only the bishop at home had dressed so well. On the second night a well-dressed man offered to buy Doming *balut*—duck eggs—and beer and rice from a street vendor. He was so hungry by then.

"I'm not *bakla* myself," he said to Doming, "but these foreigners, even some of the American military men, they'll pay for a young man's company." The bones of the *balut*, duckling embryo, crunched in the man's mouth. Doming drank the beer, greedily wolfed down fried rice.

"I'm seeking good-looking young men who want to work for easy money," he said. "You get new clothes, you'll work for me. You can read their faces like dogs, these Western men. Just give them a little of what they want, and they will want to show you how rich they are. The rest is up to you," he said. It would be good money, he said.

But Doming carried his salvation, the name of a jeepney driver, his distant cousin, Abbe Villa Hermosa. "My boy Abbe is in Tondo with a wife, that's all I know," she'd told him, Paco's *lola*.

After several days of inquiries he found Abbe living with his wife Angel's family. They were squatters, garbage scavengers, but already Abbe had found other work and took him in without question. Doming could have made up any story. All night Abbe would drive a jeepney route from Divisoria Market to Baclaran, and he took Doming along. That was when Doming first saw the hotels, the colors of the city along Manila Bay at night, the movie theaters and churches, the huge markets, busy day and night.

"This must be the greatest city on earth," he said to Abbe when Abbe first let him go along on the jeepney route, learning it, always careful of the curfew time because martial law was in effect. He'd hoped that he could study during the day and drive a jeepney at night and send money home.

"Think that if you want, little brother," Abbe said, using the term for the first time. "This is the only city we'll ever see, so of course it must be the grandest, believe it."

But the idea of it now made him anguished for the boy he'd been then. Running from the militia, all his family's savings to buy the ferry ticket, leaving behind a burned cane field and his father dead.

The greatest city on earth, Doming had thought. This cesspit, whore, queen madame Manila.

Now, this city, on the morning of Marcos' first inauguration in eleven years, was being sold at a discount. Anything could be bought, or anyone. That was the price of survival, of *balut* and beer. Eleven years had passed, Doming considered, and he had nothing to show for them, despite his ambition. The ferry tied up to the dock's rotting wooden piers. Across the city bells again began to ring. This was the auspicious time Marcos had prescribed. At the south port, the deep bells from Quiapo Church sighed mournful gongs over the greasy waters. The inauguration day's festivities were beginning. Doming thought of the man of dark brown wood inside Quiapo Church, the life-sized figure of the Black Nazarene, stained a dark tea-brown the color of Doming's skin, the healer of Quiapo who was taken out only once a year, the ninth day of January, and paraded through the streets for miracle cures, who stood bolted, hands clenched, the other three hundred and sixty-four days.

"Go on ahead of me to the Luneta Plaza, Paco," Doming said.

Paco was waiting, no longer pale.

"Refill your stomach and meet me along the plaza near where the *kalachuchi* trees grow, there'll be some shade for you to rest," he told him. The boy was tired from the trip. He'd slept little in the last few days until the rocking of the boat had lulled him.

Waves knocked dully against the docks, carrying coconut shells and trash. The inauguration fiesta, with free food and drinks, was beginning on the Luneta Plaza, south of the docks, past Manila Bay Yacht Club, past the grand Manila Hotel. Doming didn't want to have Paco near him when he reclaimed the package he'd carried on the trip. Sometimes a government official was on hand to inspect for illegal imports and take his bribe.

And this was how the one known as Doming Aquinaldo arrived in Manila for the second time in his life, how he came to be unloading a package from the "Mission of Mary and

Martha, Bacolod" from a newly arrived ferry at the south port on the morning of inauguration. The ferry master turned his head away, looking out at the bay.

"We've been lucky, Father," he said now to Doming. "Just a few weeks ago a ferry tipped, five hundred lost."

"That one wasn't in the news," Doming said.

"No, the ferry was overloaded. They say there were many children on it, many," the man added.

A low thunder rumbled and became a deafening roar above him. Five jets and their shadows passed just meters above them, from north to south, over the Luneta Plaza, and then banking west over the bay. By what seemed no will of his own, he dropped to his knees, as did those around him, feeling the waves of hot breath in their wake. Marcos, it seemed, could make them do what even God could not, to kneel before him. Doming got to his feet, and picked up the package labeled "Fine Embroidered Children's Clothing and Table Napkins—Export Only."

The ferry captain spit into the brown water.

Tonight Doming and Abbe would make the delivery. His younger brother's parting words returned to him—"You and I? We will endure, *Kuya*. Don't you remember what our father would say? A drowning man will grab onto anything, even the blade of a knife."

Gulls screamed above Rue. Dirty pigeons patrolled the aisles of the inauguration grandstand, waiting for the scraps. The morning air around her was already a steamy mixture of street food and the sewage-fouled sea and diesel fuel that leaked from half-sunken ships and abandoned freighters in

Manila Bay with their bent and toppled cranes that to her looked like a field of brontosaurus, grazing.

It was 6:30 a.m.

Manila. The morning blast. Then the heat at noon making all the vegetation grow limp, and these days the late afternoon rains when the sky tore open and the water poured through the gray leveed clouds, and everything green, green. The whole countryside blooming itself into quick decay. The way the vegetation gives way to melting rot. The way the monsoon rain comes without warning— no thunderstorms, no lightning, just a sudden heavy pouring out of stillness, God's water pitcher tipping over. The rain-drops pound the ground like small fists.

Rue took another sip of the slightly chilled cham-pagne from the souvenir crystal glass. Marcos had ordered one for each foreign guest. From the diplomatic section in the Quirino Grandstand she could see across Luneta Plaza. From all parts of Manila, a city already so hot in the June monsoon season that it seemed to cook in its own juices, the people arrived. They poured from the blue Metro buses and took their ten pesos in payment for their presence.

For his first inauguration in twelve years, Marcos' Minister of Information and the generals assured him of a turnout of one million. If they rounded up only half of the squatters in the city of six million they would succeed. Meanwhile, the cronies and diplomats arrived by car and assembled in the Quirino Grandstand.

She hated these official embassy events, these vast orches-trated productions, but Trace had insisted. It'll be a show, trust me, he'd said. Her work got her out of many of these performances. She felt her bare shoulders absorb the sun's heat as if she were made of stone. Trace wore his formal morning clothes. He looked elegant. Wear something white and cool, he'd told her.

"Will Marcos make it through this term?" the Australian ambassador, who stood a few rows behind them, called to Trace.

"We'll be lucky if he lasts through the morning," Trace said.

There were rumors that a second operation, to replace a kidney, had failed. Marcos' grown son, the son of his long-time mistress who lived in Greenhills, Manila, had donated this one.

Waiters hovered around them with trays of drinks and food, skewered meats, melting pastries. She reached for a delicious-smelling *satay*.

"I wouldn't, the embassy doctor calls it hepatitis on a stick," Trace warned.

She drew her hand back.

The Luneta Plaza in front of her was bordered on the south by the old American Army Navy Club, which led to the park-like grounds of the American Embassy. On the north side of the plaza stood the grand lady—the Manila Hotel with its blinding white façade, MacArthur's head-quarters after retaking Manila, and now home to most of the visiting international journalists. In between the bowl of these buildings was the plaza, vast enough to hold the crowd of one million Marcos' generals had promised.

The paid crowds waited. At seven o'clock the church bells would ring for seven minutes. Seven was Marcos' lucky number, this was the reason for the oddly timed ceremony.

Seven. So it was no accident, it was said, that during martial law he'd held Ninoy Aquino in solitary confinement at Fort Bonifacio for exactly seven years and seven months. Ninoy's crime—he was considered the likely successor if free elections were ever held. And this date, the twenty-first of the month, a multiple of seven, was a day Marcos had chosen for other big events in the past.

Nothing was ever left to chance, it was said of Marcos. Now the people had been called to assemble, and were paid to make believe.

It was chaos before martial law here, Rue heard many long-time Americans in Manila repeat to each other, as if to rationalize their silence in those days, *we needed it.* They would not hold themselves accountable for what went on in Fort Bonifacio, just up McKinley Road from their fine mansions in Dasmarinas and Forbes Park.

When half the opposition party was killed in the Plaza Miranda bombing on August 21st of 1971, Marcos blamed subversives, and one month later, on September 21st, he declared martial law. In two days, six hundred opposition legislators, newspaper owners, radio personalities, and journalists had been rounded up and were being held in military camps, Senator Ninoy Aquino the prize. But the president of the local American Chamber of Commerce announced that he was "very bullish" on martial law.

That same week Rudolfo Ess was promoted to head Marcos' new personal security force, ten thousand strong. Cold blooded and dim-witted, it was said, he'd risen slowly through the ranks at first, small-time smuggling and black market profits he shared with the president. He'd started as a bodyguard when Marcos was just a congressman from the northern province of Ilocos Norte. He headed a goon squad as martial law began, rounding up twenty-thousand lesser known "subversives" from the opposition.

Now she watched General Ess making his way toward them. He climbed crab-like up the whitewashed grandstand steps. Raymonde and Baby were with him. He had short arms and legs and a barreled torso that stretched the front of his white short-sleeved dress uniform. She'd seen Trace amuse his staff at the embassy, mocking General Ess. Trace described the general as a toad, and did a wonderful imitation of him—"I judge de woman by de ankle," Trace would begin, hunching over and puffing himself up.

"I guess this day belongs as much to General Ess as to Marcos," she said to Trace now, nudging him and indicating the general's approach. At home she'd glanced at Trace's cables reporting whole villages in Mindanao, where the majority did not vote, being forced into roadside hamlets, young men being forced to swear their allegiance to Marcos and join the Civilian Home Defense Forces.

"Tell him that, it's just what he'd want to hear." He straightened his shoulders.

"I didn't mean it as a compliment," she said. She searched in her bag for her sunglasses and put them on. You work with vermin, he'd said once. No, you do, she'd snapped back.

The General's hair shone, wet-black and slickly parted. He carried his visored military hat tucked under his arm. A thick square of medals glimmered above the chest pocket of his cruise-ship captain's jacket.

HRS—The High Ranking Sadist—was his nickname.

She'd met him once, he'd been playing polo with Raymonde. She'd seen him bumping along like a sack of potatoes on the fine-boned mare.

Trace introduced Rue to him again. Ess' skin around his sunglasses was pitted like a peach seed. She felt his pudgy cool hands. How did you learn to be cruel? The very first time you saw someone in the palace's dreaded Black Room, did you watch? Did you feel a moment of compassion? When an electric probe was handed to you, and you began, did you hesitate? Some days do you look at your hands and wonder if they are separate beings from the hand that takes the wafer at mass, that strokes your nieces and nephews and god-children? All these questions she wanted to ask him.

Raymonde had told them Ess was paying for the education of all those nieces and nephews and then would set them up in business.

But Trace's hands, too, were almost the hands of a stranger, now. They were well manicured by the embassy's on-site manicurist, but tanned and rope-burned. Sometimes after work he sailed in the bay, certain the boat would not tip, and it didn't.

"Ah, Madame," Ess said, kissing her hand. "Your husband nebber mention he was married to a Filipina, you are *mestiza*?"

"No, General, American." she said. She smelled the generous splashes of expensive aftershave, citrus and musk.

"Den what province, what state, California?"

"Iowa."

"Ah, Ohio, like thee ribber." She saw Trace's warning look and didn't correct the man.

"How come a woman as beautiful as you, you are here and we never meet?" He smiled what he must have thought his most charming. He'd been too drunk to remember their first meeting at the Ayera Polo Club after he fell off that mare, and now he attempted the upper class manners, a *mestizo's delicidaza*. Trace's and Raymonde's polished manners fit much better into the highest diplomatic circles of Manila that Ess coveted, yet from which he remained excluded.

"Or perhaps this is your number two, Tray-cee-boo?" The General laughed with his lips together and chest puffed. Trace raised his eyebrows in mock amusement, a gesture she'd seen the ambassador use to good effect as well. But she knew Trace detested this diminutive nickname for him.

She felt in surprise Trace's arm close around her shoulders as if to say, pay no attention, as if this were all a play or vast production.

Ambassador Edward Lange joined them, shook hands all around.

"My work keeps me away, General, the Rice Institute south of the city," she said in her most gracious tone.

"You must be care-pul then, the New People's Army," he stopped, cleared his throat of phlegm, nodded to Raymonde, "the NPA is ambushing our troops there near Mount Banahaw. The whole area is dangerous for women."

Laborers at the Institute called the NPA the Nice People's Army.

"You know, we did meet, General, at the Ayera Polo Club after a match, I remember you well," Rue said.

Trace's arm tightened almost imperceptibly. She recognized even Ambassador Lange's vague look of alarm and she found she enjoyed the men's momentary discomfort. Everything seemed about "face" with them, not substance. She might say something to shift the delicate balance of power and jousting with the General, this man whose confidences and complicity were so essential to the embassy, while his penchant for intrepid young men and torture was disregarded. Pity the man his coarseness, she imagined Trace might say, but for god's sake don't cause him to lose face here. But here, we are the savages, she thought, our cool logic—rational savagery.

In that gap of a second Raymonde asked the General about the campaign in Mindinao, where he and Trace had met General Reloza a few weeks before.

"In two weeks, we'll have half a million Moros in re-settlement camps, very expensive," Ess said, mournfully.

Ed Lange withdrew, silent. The Silver Fox, Lange was called by the Filipina secretaries at the American Embassy, for the silver hair he was so vain about. The ambassador complained that Ess was always speaking of empty pockets, waiting for the Americans to fill them.

She took another long warm sip of the champagne the waiters kept refilling.

She saw Ess' eyes were like the dry brown dung in the market lanes, dull and hardened. Once he could have been a well-fed peasant sitting in front of his little house in the provinces. She sensed there was nothing left inside, some part had fled and left an empty shell. It could happen to anyone—to Trace, to her.

"Look, Sir's children are arriving," Ess said.

Sir, Ess called him. He spoke of Marcos like a hired man would have, his Sir. Ess pointed with his lips in a street vendor's typical gesture, pushing them out to point where he would have them look—toward a long line of black limousines and armed guards on motorcycles. The crowds parted. Bong Bong, the son, and his two sisters were emerging from one car. The son wore a gleaming uniform like a young prince, the daughters in *terno* style, puffed-sleeved gowns of fragile stiff *pinyá* cloth, hand loomed from the fibers of the pineapple plant, clear gossamer gathered high at the shoulders like small wings on sphinx moths.

"Where'd you get the San Miguels, General," Raymonde asked Ess. "There's only champagne in these rich seats."

"Come with me, gentlemen," he said, "we're giving them away along the plaza. We ordered a million bottles of San Miguel and a million bottles of New Society pop, one for each man, woman, and child here on the plaza today."

Some other urgent state secret waiting to be revealed by Ess, for the transaction fee, she thought. They would make their exchange in private.

"My niece is asking me to send you her greetings today," she heard Ess say to Trace as the men left her.

"Which niece is that, General?" Trace said. "You seem to have so many."

"My favorite," Ess said. "You know, Melinda, she is dark as a plum and just as sweet." He laughed with his grunting close-mouthed cough. She watched them walk down the steps and toward some booths on the plaza. Like a great market there, but everything free, a million-person village fiesta.

She remembered the gossip, the *tsismis*, that Ess' other job was keeping a constant supply of young women available for the endless diplomatic receptions, dinners, and discos and fashion shows where only swimsuits and finely embroidered negligees were modeled.

Trace greeted a couple in the diplomatic crowd. She recognized Cindy Ashmar, and her husband, the Deputy Chief of the embassy, the second in command after the ambassador. Trace was one of the few staff members who reported directly to the ambassador. Mrs. Ashmar tried to take new spouses under her wing as they arrived. It's a pity you have to work, she'd said to Rue, you'll miss our Embassy women's club meetings and outings. Some wives become real experts on the culture here.

It seemed so grim to her—like an overseas Junior League, all the wives were captive members of the club, and Mrs. Ashmar was president. Mrs. Ashmar had orange hair and startled-looking eyes as if she were perpetually frightened. Her chin had poured into her neck, until she'd had it lifted at Makati Medical. She fought to become thin, like the willowy Filipinas. "It's not that we've grown larger here. It's just that our husbands' brains have shrunk," she often would say to other wives.

They're like cats in heat, Cindy Ashmar had once said about her servants, the underpaid sewing girl who'd happily run off with the gardener. I let my helpers go and hire new ones every six months so I don't get caught up in their dramas, she advised newcomers.

Rue heard a distant rumble begin, and in moments it built to a shrieking roar. The million on the plaza looked up. Five jets flew over, coming from the east over the city toward them, banking over the bay, turning the hot air into mirrored ripples.

"Those are our Tiger-twos, military aid," the new defense attaché a few rows in front of her shouted.

When Trace and Raymonde returned, Carter McCall, also from the embassy, was with them. Raymonde was talking rapidly, in a thicker accent than he generally used. It meant he'd had several drinks in quick succession.

"Trace, who is Melinda?" she asked, interrupting them. She'd saved this question for ten days.

Her husband's eyes widened.

"A girlfriend of Carter's, isn't that right?" Trace said.

"Oh, yeah, she was," Carter said.

"Does she work in Mabini?" Rue asked.

"Mabini? Of course not, she's choice, she's a—"

"A girlfriend of Carter's, a fash-oohne designer," Raymonde said, drawing out the words expansively.

She hated all three of them.

With hardly a pause, Raymonde continued, "I still have my people in Boston, watching Ninoy. If he moves at all, they'll be waiting."

"It's our first line of defense," Carter said.

"Well, I'd bet on Senator Enrile as a successor," Trace said. "He has a brilliant legal mind and beautiful wife—That goes a long way here, the same combination FM once had."

"Enrile may have the cash, and his own military support, but they say he has the heart of an accountant, not a leader," Carter said.

She watched the crowd growing, the performers assembled in a roped-off area of the plaza—a dozen priests, a children's choir, then one thousand solemn men and boys in gold choir robes, and finally native dancers holding their gonged instruments and bamboo poles on their shoulders. It would be part circus and part church.

"It's all so dibbi-cult, who is to be dee king," Raymonde teased in an accent like General Ess' heavy Ilocano.

"And the Ilocanos like Ess are the very worst to deal with, Raymonde," Trace said.

"But at least you know what you're getting in the Filipino mongrel mix," said Raymonde. "The arrogance of three hundred years of Spanish priests, the laziness of the half-breed Malays here, the ruthlessness of the Chinese in them." He was proud of his Spanish blood. He opened a large blue and white golf umbrella, careful to stay out of the sun so his skin didn't turn dark.

"So we've just got to sit back and not try to make things happen too fast," Carter continued.

"Yes, sit back," Raymonde said, "And you know, it's the same blood combination that makes our women so compelling, Carter—the haughty coolness of the Spanish Madonna, the whoring beauty of the Malay, the intelligence of the Chinese."

"Is it really worth it, Ray?" Carter said.

"For the business or the pleasure?" Raymonde shot back.

Then they turned back to business as the ambassador took his seat again.

Carter said, "Ed, we're getting inquiries from some congressional staffers about the election, and Marcos cutting out Ninoy. Also journalists—and they're all friends of Ninoy's of course, and even his brother-in-law's a reporter there."

"It's always been this way," the ambassador assured them. "I was here in sixty-six, an early assignment. The U.S. AID officer here then—his previous assignment had been organizing the South Vietnamese police into a paramilitary force for urban counter-insurgency programs. Know where he went when he left here? Iran, the Savak. Not to worry."

Rue took another sip of her drink.

In the background the steady hollow beat of waves against the seawall, knocking at it with water-logged coconuts, seemed the only thing that Marcos and Imelda and the American embassy could not control or orchestrate. Military music played, shrill brass that glittered on the plaza before her. The sun burned its way into the morning sky. Her eyes hurt from the brightness.

Soon a message was hand-delivered to Ambassador Lange—The First Lady was running late and the festivities would be delayed until exactly 7:21 a.m. The crowd below them was growing restless.

Within fifteen minutes, a line of limousines following police motorcycles with sirens blaring drove straight onto the plaza. Rue watched Imelda and her entourage of Blue Ladies emerge. Imelda's hair was piled so that she would tower over the president as they stood together. As usual, she wore a long silk scarf draped over her left shoulder. In her high-heeled shoes, she walked the last two hundred meters toward the podium, where the president sat on his gold throne, waiting. She must know the crowd of squatters watched her, transfixed.

Now, only *Ninoy, Ninoy* was left.

Rue heard voices in the crowd calling out his name, as if they could summon him.

Imelda blew a kiss in their direction and Ambassador Lange seemed to summon a boyish blush. The ambassador and Imelda were already friendly—he sang duets with her at Malacañang Palace and she'd had her photograph taken with him holding a white silk-fringed umbrella for her on a "goodwill trip" to her hometown of Tacloban, on the southern island of Samar.

With mincing steps the First Lady, governor of Metro Manila, Minister of Human Settlements, approached the dais and climbed the wooden steps to where the President waited for her, aware of all eyes on her. Imelda's bare arms and shoulders looked as soft and fair as *pan de sal*.

The bells rang.

They would ring for seven minutes.

Imelda took her seat on a smaller throne next to the president.

It was said that the president had given up his favorite foods. Anything but the blandest food brought on the symptoms of his disease, his lupus. *Wolfbite*, the people called it, or *Noli me Tangere, Touch Me Not*, because of the red spots that would appear on the skin of some lupus sufferers. If he ate or drank now he'd piss all over himself before the morning was over. Kidneys shrinking and turning to granite, then the rest. Who could pity such a man, Rue wondered.

Then she sensed more than felt the shift. The earth fell away from beneath her feet, and Trace reached out to steady them both.

Her drink spilled on him.

"My God, did you feel that?" Trace said.

Now the earth shook and a sound like a sharp groan came from the mud below them.

She imagined being shaken into that foul sea. The ground would tilt and then they would slip down and off the edge and into the murky waters.

The crystal glasses on trays made a gentle high ringing like wind-chimes.

The crowd went silent, also waiting. The silty earth here under the plaza briefly trembled, like the hide of a gnawed-at beast, trying to shake off its tormenter. Then it was over.

It's okay, people around her said. Here above the mud along the bay, in the embassy, we feel these slight earth-quakes more.

"Not to worry," Ambassador Lange announced to his special guests. "Around here, it happens all the time."

Doming moved through the crowds of people who were all intent on making the most from this national holiday that they could. Free San Miguel beer, free food. The bussed-in crowds were drawn further onto the plaza by the over-whelming smell of all the free foods Marcos had ordered, dishes he savored, but could no longer eat because of his bad kidneys. Savory *siapo*, pork dumplings, greasy chicken *adobo* stewed in garlic and vinegar and *kalamansi* juice, and also *suman*, sweet sticky rice wrapped in young banana leaves and steamed over coals and served with amber sugar crystals from the sugar plantations in Negros. All these smells beckoned and enticed.

The women and children drank juicy New Society pop, and collected *pasalubongs*, take-home gifts—Marcos and Imelda calendars and New Society coloring books with waxy crayons. Men who'd been lured with a free day's wage and free beer grew restless. Fights broke out between neighbors. New Society pop went warm and flat, waxy crayons keeled over in the heat. A small earthquake made the reclaimed land shake like *buko gulaman*, green coconut gelatin.

Doming heard the church bells ringing.

He looked and looked for Paco but could not find him.

He looked toward the grandstand, the diplomatic section, certain that she was there.

He heard people in the crowd whisper *Ninoy, Ninoy*. He has sent word he will come home. But the other rumor was that Ninoy Aquino had good reason to stay out of the country. Imelda had warned him once already. *We can't control what might happen if you risk coming back*, she'd said publicly when she summoned him from Boston to meet her at the hotel she'd just bought in New York City.

Since 1975 Imelda had served as appointed governor of Metro Manila. When the president got too ill to rule, General Ess would back her, the people said. There was no vice president to worry about. The opposition had no money, no voice. The president had taken the radio stations, shut down newspapers, met with an editor in the Black

Room of Malacañang when he wouldn't shut up despite all their warnings. Marcos had shut down seven English daily newspaper, three Filipino daily newspapers, seven English weekly magazines, four Chinese daily newspapers, seven television stations, sixty community newspapers, and two hundred and ninety-two radio stations.

Only Ninoy was left. And the noble old Senator Tanada.

Doming saw Imelda get out of her car.

The climbing sun shone on her unrelentingly and her powder was melting. "Send a boy for an umbrella," someone behind her said. Her umbrella, her umbrella, he heard the words passed on. She'd left it in the limo.

He watched her walk, well balanced on her very high heels. She walked toward the dais where the president and his entourage were seated. Aware of all eyes on her, holding her head regally high on her still-beautiful long neck. Perhaps she considered again with pleasure her fortuneteller's widely known prediction that the next president of the country would be a woman.

She came so close to him he heard her dress of hand-woven *pinyá* cloth rustling shamelessly.

She was a woman who was sure she still looked beautiful from a certain distance.

As she passed the Quirino Grandstand, she blew a kiss in her honored guests' direction. Ambassador Lange bowed slightly.

On his gilt pedestal Ferdinand Marcos beamed.

To Doming, the president seemed to look past Imelda, out over the crowds still gathering behind the barricades along the Boulevard, where the people feasted on the foods he'd ordered. He looked like a very old god, sitting on his gold throne, a gift from the President of Bahrain. He looked like God's father.

The First Lady came to the microphone. I love you all, she said, in Tagalog, then in English. A slow wave with her right hand pitched slightly forward, a blessing, a benediction.

Imelda sang, she warbled. The loudspeakers near Doming crackled with static. She sang a Filipino love song, "Because of You." The crowds around Doming hooted with laughter, until security guards in civilian clothes rushed to silence them. Doming looked around for Paco. He offered a vendor five pesos to keep his package behind the counter. Doming, worried, began searching through the crowds for the boy.

The Madwoman of Malacañang, Rue remembered, a foreign journalist had labeled Imelda Marcos. Imelda came to a microphone on the dais.

A love song for my president, she said.

Rue noticed something flash, the sun reflected off Imelda's upper arm like diamonds there. A flash again, a turn of light—the First Lady is growing silver scales like the *banak* fish, Celia had said.

Then children from the Quezon City Children's Home came onto the plaza, climbed up the steps to the large wooden dais. First they danced the traditional Filipino *Tinikling*, the heron dance, between sets of bamboo poles that adults dressed as "natives" held near the ground and clapped together. Then they danced the *Singkil* to the sound of Muslim gongs and wooden flutes and bamboo poles clapped in five-beat rhythm. Graceful, slender, solid bodies, faces lit up with the joy of performance. The girls held their long skirts with one hand and swished gracefully, and the boys danced with their shoulders stiff, in light barong shirts and dark pants.

"They're beautiful children," Rue said to Baby. Baby smiled proudly as if each one was her own.

"How is your boy?"

"We're planning the christening for New Year's, when my daughters will be home," Baby said.

Rue pushed her hair back from her face, pieces that had come loose from the pins that held it in a twist. She felt a trail of sweat run down her chest from her clavicle.

It was time. Time fixed by the place of the sun and the moon and his birth date and this date, set to the moment by the Chinese astrologer who lived in the palace.

"Mr. President, we love your adherence to democracy," Vice President Bush began his short speech.

In front of her, Ambassador Lange groaned, clutched his heart. The young aide with him scrambled for a walkie-talkie.

"What is he saying? Was he not briefed?" the ambassador inquired peevishly. The journalists would repeat Vice President Bush's words of praise for Mister Marcos' democratic process in newspapers around the world.

A Supreme Court justice swore Marcos in. No bigger than a monkey, someone behind her said of the justice, who was pigmy-like in his whiskers and dragging robes. Loudspeakers carried the richly accented voice of Ferdinand Emmanuel Edralin Marcos, who would faithfully defend the constitution. His voice was strong, from where did he summon that old reserve of musical voice, she wondered.

It was known that years before he'd amazed his law school professors with his ability to memorize entire sections of the legal code. He could recite the Constitution backwards. He had a photographic memory, it was said, or was it just the palace fortunetellers and spies? He was omnipotent. Just look at how he would always learn what was going on behind his back.

Even from where they sat, perhaps one hundred feet from the president, Rue saw that after he used his best effort to project his rich voice to the people he now looked pale and exhausted. He leaned on Minister Enrile as they walked down the steps of the dais together.

"Let's go, FM's headed for the boat," Ambassador Lange said to his entourage. He smoothed his silvered hair. Trace once told her he'd never seen the man sweat. Now they would all go on to Malacañang Palace for the reception.

"At least we don't have to follow him up that river," Trace said to her.

Marcos, superstitiously repeating his success of 1965, would travel by barge up the Pasig River to the palace for the elaborate reception. The Pasig was the stream of time in Marcos' history—he and Imelda had cruised up it, Kennedy-like, after his first inauguration in 1965. They'd been a young, attractive, dynamic couple who held every promise. Now the Pasig, which flowed from Laguna de Bay through the city and emptied into Manila Bay, was the most polluted river in the world. A sewer, a cesspit, a river of shit, she'd heard Trace call it. The Pasig smelled so, it was said, that Marcos boarded up all the windows of Malacañang Palace, so the smell didn't come drifting in over state dinners.

At the north end of the plaza thousands of white doves flew up, released from cages below a two-story papier-mâché bust of Marcos, a replica of the one being created on a mountainside near Baguio, gray cement and scaffolding like an iron mask. "The birds are up, Sir, the birds are up." The words came from the microphone at the dais, someone trying to get the president's attention to the sight above them.

For the recessional, a choir of one thousand men and boys thundered words of Handel's "Hallelujah Chorus." They sang the music Marcos himself had requested for the recessional:

> *King of Kings, and Lord of Lords;*
> *King of Kings, and Lords of Lords,*
> *And he shall rule the earth, shall rule the earth,*
> *And he shall reign for ever and ever,*
> *for ever and ever.*

Rue heard the familiar tune from the *Messiah*. Hot liquid brass like lava, and tympani like a deep volcanic rumble— *Forever and ever.* The diplomats joined the recessional.

Rue, with Trace, Raymonde, and Baby, made her way down the crowded steps of the grandstand. She felt slightly groggy from the champagne. She craved the shade on the far side of the plaza around the Army Navy Club, but the diplomats were kept apart from the plaza crowds by ropes and guards.

"Trace, I don't want to go to the reception," she said.

"I don't mind, but why not go? Brunch for seven hundred— the ice carvings alone are rumored to cost a hundred thousand pesos.

"I'll take your car to work, I need to be there to do some measurements, before noon." She knew her exactness in her work pleased him. So measure-able.

"Work?" Raymonde asked. "Everything's closed today."

"Not at the Rice Institute," she said.

"The moths don't know it's inauguration day?" Trace said. "They were supposed to be here in the moth delegation."

"Did they vote? I'm sure they got their ballots," Raymonde said.

"If she's not going, I'm not," Baby announced. "Rue can drop me off on her way out of town," she added.

Rue heard a half-demand, like she was a servant herself, but Baby knew no other way. She was relieved the morning was over and she followed Baby across the Plaza, into the crowds who'd stay until the food and entertainment ended. No one approached the elegant women, both wearing white.

"Watch out for pick-pockets," Baby warned. She'd paused at a booth to see what food they had, and was turning her diamond rings in toward her palms.

"*Ubus-kaya*, Mr. Marcos has for us today, eat all you can because he cannot, we eat the feast for him," a man in a food stall said to Rue when she paused there. He handed her a still warm green-wrapped *suman*, sweet sticky rice in banana leaf roasted over coals.

"*Salamat*, thank you," she said.

She turned back the charcoaled banana leaf and ate a few bites, standing next to his stall.

"This expensive undertaking without sparing the costs. Today, we are all *waláng-mayroón*, poor men who live like the rich," he said.

She and Baby walked on. Savory aromas came from the booths of fatty roast lechon that dripped over glowing coals.

Rue could blend in with Baby, even though she was taller. She had learned to move like Baby was moving now, not with the business or haste of a tourist, nor the languidness of an available woman, nor with the self-importance of a Filipina socialite, but like Baby. Baby had unconsciously learned that walk through a crowd, like a maid in the market, from

Celia, who had been more like her mother at the beginning. Rue was certain Baby had no idea of the resemblance—unobtrusive, straight-backed, not looking around.

On the Plaza behind them, the men and boys' choir finished the entire eight-minute chorus and now began again. They would sing until the president was out of earshot. But then above the music, above the crowd, one boy soprano's perfect voice arced over the plaza, the old folk song colliding with the coronation.

The boy sang the "Bayan Ko," My Country, the nationalist folk song Marcos had banned because it pierced him like an arrow. A few women in shapeless house-dresses danced to it, hearing the melody like a whisper, like a breath, inside the *Messiah* chorus:

> *and he shall reign for ever and ever, and ever and ever . . .*
> *(Birds that freely claim the skies to fly)*
> *Forever and ever and ever and ever and ever . . .*
> *(When imprisoned mourn, protest, and cry)*
> *Forever—King of Kings, and Lord of Lords,*
> *(How much deeper will a land most fair)*
> *He shall reign forever and ever and ever!*
> *(Yearn to break the chains of sad despair.)*

One small song offered like a bird on the wing, like the white bird named *Ninoy* that the people whispered even now.

> *(How much deeper will a land most fair)*
> *He shall reign forever and ever and ever!*
> *(Yearn to break the chains of sad despair.)*
> *Forever and ever—*
> *(Philippines my heart's sole burning fire,*
> *All that I desire—To see you rise—forever, Free!)*

Each time Rue heard the "Bayan Ko" melody, it seemed the most beautiful tune she'd ever heard. Yearning, haunting, and yet undaunted. She heard it sometimes played like a waltz, or a lullaby, it could be sung as a Gloria. And now, like some counterpoint to the procession before her, it was a green promise of hope.

She and Baby almost involuntarily walked closer to where the song was coming from, pulled toward the clear voice. But then in the middle of the refrain the singing stopped. Outside the barricades around the plaza, about fifty feet away from where she stood, two men in the khaki uniforms of the Presidential Security Command pulled a dark boy, skinny arms and legs whirling at them, from among the pruned branches of a tightly clipped *kalachuchi* tree. He fought them, scratched and kicked, but then a khaki uniformed arm raised up.

The crowds moved away like water parting. The presence of evil was something they recognized. They'd prayed to God and he hadn't answered, and here was the Lord of Lord's paid crony swooping down. A military helicopter hovered, thumping the air over them for a few moments and Rue saw a preying pterosaur, the mandibles open. It flew on. No one made a sound of protest for the boy. They'd gotten him on his feet to hustle him off.

She saw a priest intervene and hurry over to speak to the soldiers. He put his hands together at his mouth in a plea of leniency. They let go of the boy. It was Paco—she'd met him one day at the zoo. She pressed forward. The priest took hold of him and gripped his shoulder tightly, pushing him down to his knees to apologize. The shaking boy took each soldier's hand to his bowed head in the way a Filipino would do to an elder and mumbled his words of repentance.

The priest turned away to leave and she saw it was Doming. She felt a start of recognition, then a surge of gladness to see he'd come back.

He looked right at her from under the brown hood of the cassock he wore, but he gave no sign he knew her. Disdain and complete indifference—that hooded look when eyes go flat and dull, a face like quicksand, registering all, but revealing nothing.

"That's your driver, nah?" Baby said, pointing his direction with her chin, her hands full of food, when they reunited.

"No, of course not," Rue said. She aimed for a calm tone, matter-of-fact. What was he doing here like this? Her curiosity mixed with fear for him. She watched him and saw him walk to a food stall and take up a brown-wrapped package from the vendor there.

She and Baby went on to Trace's car, parked in the shade of towering acacias on the embassy grounds. Doming had once said to her, this place is not a place for too many questions. This place, the city, the country, Doming had said to her, was like some hearts—a question too many, too much light shining on dark places, too much discontent, was hazardous. Hazardous. "You know *azar*, don't you, Ma'am?—in Spanish, an unlucky throw of the dice." She sensed his pride in mastering the languages he learned from the old priest, but it was knowledge that must be useless to him now, she thought, except for the way his mind always dug into the root of a word, as if words could protect him.

In the distance the choir continued. She imagined a tenor who was known throughout the city for his gift prayed to God to forgive him this song. His people had survived the Spanish, the Japanese, floods, drought, plagues that killed the rice, bouts of malaria, and they would survive Marcos.

Nearby, at the south port along the bay, the bells from Quiapo Church sent their gongs thrumming over the bay. To the south, the heaviest bells at Baclaran Church cut the air and reverberated in the market stalls, shaking the circling fish and the live birds and the Virgin Marys in their tents of clear plastic and white snow. Farther south, in Ayera, Celia heard the nearby bells in the Sisters of Mercy Parish and Asylum and crossed herself.

Rue drove Trace's car out through the open gates of the embassy grounds, the Marine guards there expressionless behind dark sunglasses. It was as if the embassy compound were part of a different country, so cool, clean, and fortified from the rest of the city. The guards closed the high gates behind her. They would look in the trunk and under the hood of each incoming car for possible explosives.

Beyond the compound walls, along the boulevard, a few young men with towels over their heads and faces, the way construction workers covered themselves against the dust and heat, carried signs, *DOWN WITH THE U.S.—MARCOS DICTATORSHIP*. Some of them would wear under their shirt the yellow t-shirts that read *Metro Aide*, the uniform of street sweepers, and have a street-sweeper's broom made of sticks hidden nearby. If the Constabulary came, they would run and in seconds be sweeping the palm-lined walk along the seawall.

In front of the embassy, outside its gates, she saw the people already standing in line waiting for the consular office to open tomorrow. Since this was a holiday they were already in line for the larger crowds that would come tomorrow. These were not the visa applicants. Instead each night, the same people would take their place in line, sell their place in the line, and each morning go to sleep under the palms near the bay, that night again holding a place that might lead to the promised land. They would make enough to live on for the day.

She turned south along Roxas Boulevard, then cut through Cuneta and its clusters of "love motels."

Edsa Boulevard, the main street to Baby's house, was hung with gray acrid fumes from blue diesel buses and jeepneys. Signs overhead proclaimed—*CELEBRATE THE YEAR OF THE MARIAN FAMILY; THE FAMILY THAT PRAYS TOGETHER STAYS TOGETHER, BY YOUR MAKATI ROTARY CLUB.*

"Baby, why hasn't Celia had a bank account all these years? She had to borrow money from me to pay for Mary's medicine," Rue asked.

"The poor, they have never learned to save," said Baby, snapping her new fan.

"I'll repay her sometime," Baby said after a while.

Neither of them said anything more until they were almost at Baby's house. They passed a billboard, *SOCIALITE DRIVING SCHOOL.*

"How did you learn to drive?" Baby asked her.

"In the States we learn when we're young, everyone does," she said. What a knot Baby lived in. She didn't even know how to drive. She was never taught. Like Celia said, every time the girl Baby tried to grow wings they got lopped off. Now she was so used to being taken care of that she had no sense of any but her own needs. Like Imelda. Pah, Celia once said, a sound of breath blowing out, I wanted to teach her how to sew, but her father wouldn't let her learn how to thread a needle.

Baby rang the front gate bell at her house again and again till Mary came out and pushed open the gate as usual. It seemed much too heavy for her now.

"I was washing Sir's dogs, Ma'am," she said to Baby.

Ray's dogs were kept in an air-conditioned kennel.

"They behave for you, Mary, better than for Ray," Baby said. Raymonde kept big black dogs that looked to Rue like a cross between large Labradors and wolfhounds.

Rue worried Mary did not look well after the morning's work. Picking the ticks off the dogs was a weekly job for her, especially during the rainy season, when the things seemed to multiply daily and become engorged to the size of her fingertips. She would put them into a glass jar with kerosene at the bottom. Mary was afraid Baby would fire her if she didn't earn her keep, Celia had said.

Baby began to go inside with Mary, but then said, "Wait, I've lost an earring."

Rue looked on the car floor and then under the seat. She saw the earring there and reached for it.

"Raymonde gave me that, it's very precious to me," Baby said. It was a single dark blue sapphire stone mounted in hammered silver, splendidly crafted. Rue had heard the stories about how Raymonde gave Baby jewels. When she and Trace had first come to their house, that first night, and agreed to rent it, Baby had taken Rue into her large dressing room and bath and shown her the secret place she hid her jewels. Not even Celia or Mary knows about this, she'd said. Pah, we know, Celia said, when Rue had shown her the inset case that fit under the bottom drawer of Baby's dressing room. Why would she hide them from us, Celia said. The jewels told their story, each fight or indiscretion paid for by Raymonde. Now Celia claimed to have found termites in the dressing room and used smoke from coconut blossoms to suffocate them.

Rue drove out of the city.

The night before she first arrived in Manila, the worst typhoon in one hundred years struck. Manila Bay had breached the seawall and waves leapt at the American embassy and five-star hotels and abandoned storefronts along Roxas Avenue. Leaves and palm fronds ripped from the trees. When she'd walked out of the airport alone, after her flight, it was ninety-five degrees under an aluminum gray night sky, and though the typhoon's floods had rinsed the fetid canals there was still the smell of quickly ripening fruits in the market, under the canvas-sheltered stands. Her taxi had crept through grid-locked traffic. Street vendors peered in at her through the darkened windows.

Within a week she and Trace had attended a small palace reception for upper-ranking diplomats. The president pointed out a small gold-framed document in his receiving room. He wants you to read this, his foreign minister said.

She heard the president's labored breath like little grunts as each of the two dozen guests took a turn at the elaborately framed five-by-eight inch piece of paper—an old telegram, dated the first night of martial law, the same night the thousands were rounded up. Sixty-seven thousand finally.

SEPTEMBER 21, 1971
SIR: THE AMERICAN CHAMBER OF COMMERCE WISHES YOU EVERY SUCCESS IN YOUR ENDEAVORS TO RESTORE PEACE AND ORDER, BUSINESS CONFIDENCE, ECONOMIC GROWTH AND THE WELL BEING OF THE FILIPINO PEOPLE AND NATION. WE ASSURE YOU OF

OUR CONFIDENCE AND COOPERATION IN ACHIEVING
THESE OBJECTIVES. WE ARE COMMUNICATING THESE
FEELINGS TO OUR ASSOCIATES AND AFFILIATES IN THE
UNITED STATES.

She felt a dread, unnameable, that by not objecting, following life lived on an iron track, she was also a part of the farce and the horror and just as responsible for the misery as General Ess, Raymonde, Ambassador Lange—and Trace.

How could she explain to anyone what was happening between them? It wasn't just a woman. Rather, the country, his part in it, the business of military aid and turning a blind eye to its use. Her instinct that she couldn't just go along with what he had become here. That if she yielded a part of her would be lost forever. But if she left him now, she would lose her place here. And it was the place that somehow held her.

The road into the Rice Institute was closed. More nonvoters were being rounded up and put into vans, and the highway was blocked by military trucks. She turned around and drove back toward Ayera, cutting through the local market area.

A few dozen boys blocked the main square, and they pounded their fists on car hoods, beat on the hot metal of cars caught in their wake. They had white towels wrapped around their heads so only their eyes showed, like the streetsweepers or construction workers, who would mix their cement by hand for the mansions they built in Ayera.

The blue diplomatic license plates on her car attracted their attention and they circled the car. She rolled down the car window, she wanted them to see she was alone. Several boys began jumping on the car's front and back fenders, rocking her. She took off her sunglasses. The late morning's white heat took all the color out of everything. The trees in the square looked black and loury.

"White lady, what are you doing here in our place?" one boy who looked about twelve called.

Four boys still rocked her car's front and back fenders. Some cars squeezed by on one side. Other boys turned to a car there, a gold Mercedes whose driver kept his hand solidly on the horn. Jeepney passengers got out and began to walk toward the market.

"Aren't you afraid of us?" another boy shouted through the half-open window.

"No, *hindî*," she said. But weren't they afraid of the military police, like Sok was?

"What are you doing here?" the first boy said. He kept pulling up the towel around his face, like a young Lawrence of Arabia. He wore navy blue shorts that were too short for him, and a yellow sleeveless t-shirt that showed a boy's muscles.

"I work at the Rice Institute," she said, glancing toward the south, at Mount Makiling. She was careful to never point, never gesture with her fingers pointed up to beckon. It was what you would do with a dog.

"What, you clean and cook for them?" he said.

"I'm a biologist."

"My father says the rice you make there will make us sick someday," he said.

The truth was the farmers complained about the need for imported chemicals and fertilizers. The truth was that their heritage rice varieties were not even being preserved.

"Do you go to school?" she asked. She imagined taking him to her lab, showing him the view through the microscope, of a drop of water from the rice paddy, or a drop of blood, the whole world there.

"My father works in the fish pens of Lake Laguna, I fix the holes in the pens, under the water. I'm the smallest so I don't get caught by the nets."

"Your English is so good," she said.

"But I don't go to school anymore—I work. Today, traffic police. That will be five pesos, my *tong*," he said, making bold fun of the traffic police who would make a temporary hand-lettered sign—*NO LEFT TURN*—and stop motorists who violated it, accepting a bribe for not writing a ticket.

The boy squared his bony shoulders and stuck his chest out. He held out a curled palm like a small brown cup. She reached for the coin box she kept and picked out some for him, purposely coming up twenty centavos short.

"And will they let me pass then?" she said. Other boys harassed the honking Mercedes like so many thin-legged mosquitoes.

He looked at what was there in his palm for a few moments. She saw he couldn't open his withered hand, the hand he shook back and forth to her now, a hassled bureaucrat.

"Short, this bribe is short," he barked.

"Here you are," she said, pleased, and gave him what she owed, two more thin ten-centavo coins, worth less than a nickel.

The boy mosquitoes swarmed toward another car.

Once inside the security gates of Ayera Village, she drove past the rich Filipino children with their *yayas*, children who were allowed outside to play each day only under cover of patio or garage, to go to the park only much later when the sun was low. *Ayera*—the word meant *Yesterday*, Yesterday Village—would recreate the estates and haciendas of the century before, the Marcos-supported industrialist who was developing the village, had proclaimed.

Slender glass panes framed the carved front door, letting cool blades of light into the long entrance hall; just inside, an antique cut-glass mirror hung over an altar table from a sacked parish in San Felipe. The nuns there had supported the New People's Army, and so General Ess had given orders that the parish be shut down, and he gave the antique provincial-style furnishings to his friends and compadres, including Raymonde de Varcegno. The mirror reflected her dark outline against the brilliant whiteness from the open door behind her.

Later, at dusk, she swam in the pool while geckos chirped their birdcalls, guarding their territories behind pictures on the wall, at the base of the aquarium, on the rafters. Once she'd found a gecko egg, the size of a dried pea, on a bookshelf. She left it. They were like neighbors. She watched them and discovered their homes and habits.

She came up for a breath, dove under.

We are all responsible for each other, her father often told her. When she was young he befriended a freakish new neighbor whose apple and pear orchards adjoined their own, a blind man whose arms ended at his elbows. The man had grown up on the place and gone off to war in Korea, and had now come home after several years of rehabilitation. She was afraid of him at first.

She would watch him read braille with his lips. When summer came they brought fruit to him. Her father peeled a St. David's pear, cutting it into sections. He showed Rue how, let her use the knife to cut the bite-sized pieces. When their neighbor ate he would put his lips down to the plate. When he was finished he wiped his mouth on his shoulder.

Her father taught her compassion by saying nothing, making no remarks.

Use your napkin, she could hear her grandmother scolding.

One day the neighbor let her taste his braille books with her lips like he did. He read every day, he said, it saved him, to join the world again on the page. Her father recommended some horticulture books he would read aloud to the man the next winter. They would make his place a working orchard again. It had become overgrown with red cedar and purple thistle.

She bent to the white book that was no more than an empty plate. She closed her eyes and felt the small seeds of letters with her lips, on the cool paper. But she couldn't make any words grow from them. So he read them aloud to her, with his mouth tracing the leaves of paper. He read the story of a monster, part man, part bull, in a deep cave. She imagined then their barn's limestone-framed entrance (where she would find her father a few years later). The story of a labyrinth, of a monster there in the dark center, waiting, and a young man holding on to a string to get in and get out.

The blind man said to her, "In all of us there are labyrinths and there are monsters, we go in with our piece of thread and find our way. My thread," he added, smiling at someone who seemed to be just behind her, "I hold with my mouth."

She loved his fortitude, his endurance.

But their friendship ended. The horticulture books were never read to him. She and her mother left the orchards, one season after a late-spring day when she opened the door to their limestone barn to find her father lying there. She remembered a wail had come from her then, so unearthly she could not believe it was her own lalling sound; she ran through the orchards with soggy skirt and socks, wetting her pants, a warm rushing, a big twelve-year-old how could you, her grandmother, his mother, would scold, until she knew, too.

He'd shot himself, his chest dark, head turned away. Startled pigeons flew up again at her sound, then settled along the eaves.

She dreamed that flowers grew higher than the steps to their back porch, that the sun shown through them, back-lighting their perfect forms, that when she dug into the earth purple iris were blooming below. She'd settled only for sureness, no risk, never bending her mouth to the white page to taste the world and feel it with her lips and tongue, never entering the labyrinth of her own heart.

Rue came up from underwater in her pool for a breath, and heard, like a distant gunshot, the first blast of fireworks as the city's celebrations echoed in the humid night air. The inauguration gala was beginning. In the city, glittering portraits of Sir and Madame lit up the sky around Malacañang Palace and then cooled to blues and purple and mauves and faded like apparitions.

In the city, in the almost empty plaza, squatters fought over the pieces of wood they took from the empty dais. Now the players were these ragged dark men, prying the wood from the scaffolding with their bare hands, taking what they could carry away with them. The rainy season was upon them and these would make good roofs.

The booming sounds brought Paco out to the pawn shop's back porch where Doming was reading. The night's celebration would be like New Year's. Already jeepney tires burned in piles, gunshots sounded. Specially commissioned firework portraits of Ferdie and Imelda, from the finest firm in Italy, illumined the sky and fell like glitter over the city.

Doming regarded the handsome boy with the bruised cheek.

Paco began to sing again, foolish but stout-hearted. He'd learned the "Bayan Ko" song of the opposition from his cousins in Negros and for the second time today repeated it.

"Hush, and don't tell any of your neighbors what happened this morning," Doming warned him. "There are spies even here. You have been foolish, done dangerous things," Doming scolded him.

Doming shuddered to think what would have happened if he hadn't arrived on the plaza when Paco sang.

"What possessed you this morning?" Doming asked him.

"But, Tító Doming, it was a *kalachuchi* tree. Your story, in a *kalachuchi* tree the boy was invisible, even the wind would blow through him," Paco said.

"You don't believe that anymore," Doming said, remembering making up that story, where a boy would seek to disappear from his stepfather's wrath with a book.

"It was just a song," Paco complained.

"Well, some songs make your thoughts visible, and that's dangerous."

We are a country of tyrants and servants, he thought. There is not much else in between. We learn never to say what we're really thinking; only the very young and the very old can sometimes get away with it.

BABY JESUS PAWN SHOP, the sign said in English at Abbe's shop, and below it, hand-lettered: *New ownership, fair rates.* Even God had to trade something.

The porch where he sat overlooked a canal that flowed into the Pasig River. He drank the next to last bottle of beer. It was from a supply Sonny had brought Abbe a few days before, as Abbe seemed to feel better.

Doming would deliver the timing devices late tonight. This would prove he was cooperating with Sonny's friends. But he and Abbe didn't speak of this in front of Paco and Linay.

He put down the book Sonny had given him. It had turned up in the pawn shop a few weeks ago and Sonny had grabbed it for him, the worn paperback book *The Pretenders*, by F. Sionil José, Sonny's favorite writer. Now in the light of a single bulb above the stoop, he opened the book to the page where an earlier reader marked this passage:

> *"But if you want to know what the price of a man is, or his services, you must be wise." Don Manuel brought his fore-finger to his right temple and gestured twice. "It's all a matter of understanding what a man wants most. If you can give him that, then he is yours to command. Don't expect that he will be eternally grateful . . . It's the truth. Everyone has a price. Christ had a price—the Cross and the salvation of mankind. I have a price—the future of the Villas and everyone in the family. You have a price—and don't feel that I'm insulting you. Your self-respect. I'm just stating a fact . . . I just ask that people like you be realistic enough to know that the world is a world of compromise."*

He rested the book on his legs. There is no integrity in compromise. It's always the rich, those in power, who ask those with little for compromises.

Linay came out, pushed the book away, and situated herself on his lap as the inauguration fireworks continued. The fireworks lit up the night; broken pieces reflected in the canal's water. The baby was inside with her mother, Angel. The infant was fussy; she was sleepy with the constant noise and already coughing up the sooted air.

It was almost 8:00 p.m.

His eyes ached. The foul-smelling canal made gurgling sounds as if someone was drowning. Then like a malevolent troll, out of the black smoke that hung around them, the barangay captain appeared on their porch. Abbe called to Angel to bring the man some drink, and Doming heard her purposely rattling things in her tiny kitchen.

Abbe's wife Angel was a young woman still, attractive, but canny-eyed. She had to be, Doming considered, to survive. She came from Smoky Mountain, in Tondo, the garbage heap of the city, and the little she and Abbe had saved and scavenged seemed like luxury to her. She would never give it up. She fussed at Abbe constantly to improve their fortune. To do more, have more. When the fireworks began she covered the bedclothes with old newspapers. Burning tires and local fireworks would make a sooty ash that would fall over everything in the city. She loved Abbe because he provided, and she loved him because she was certain he was smarter than she was, so she could feel safe with him. This was no small thing. She loved him with simple gratitude.

Angel brought the barangay captain, Mr. Ipis, the lychee juice.

"I was saving it for the children in the morning," she hissed to Abbe. She served *bibíngka*, a cake. Mr. Ipis called to Linay and the girl came forward to press her forehead to the hand he offered. The short man reeked of old garlic and sour metal that always hung on him. (And once near his house he'd called the girl and offered her two pesos to touch his privates.)

Now with the formalities over, Mr. Ipis began his cloying solicitations.

"We're collecting for the mayor, what will be your donation?" he said formally to them. "The mayor's birthday is tomorrow. So many robberies in this barangay recently, I've asked him for two more Metro-Com officers. So help us make a nice gift so he'll remember us."

Doming was certain the man was lying, but Abbe was the one who must get along here.

"Us? Who do you mean—*us*?" Abbe said, belligerent, looking around. The man would pocket part of whatever he got.

"The barangay," Mr. Ipis said.

"Sorry, *Pô*, you're too late, we've spent all our money today on the fireworks and cockfights," Abbe said.

"But you know I am a money lender, now?" Mr. Ipis said.

"You have the worst rates in the city," Doming said.

Abbe shook his head. "My shop, we're already in debt to the landlord," he said.

"Then a gift in kind, perhaps," said the barangay captain, his voice mocking. "Something from your shop." And he made his way through the back room and then into the front as if the place were his own. He looked around and picked up a valuable pair of *tari*—the metal spurs for fighting birds. Then he coughed delicately, into his sleeve, as if it were the air there in Abbe's shop that was bad, and not the sooty night around them, not the blackness of his own soul.

"These will do," he said, putting them into a deep pocket of the orange nylon jacket that fell halfway to his knees.

Then he took out his book and made a mark, bowed slightly and went to the front door of the shop. Abbe unlocked it and let him out, clenching his remaining hand.

"I am feeling my lost hand," Abbe said, maddened, shaking his forearm stump. Doming saw it was purplish—Abbe was no better. Doming would take him back to the clinic.

They sat down again on the back stoop, over the water.

"Careful, Linay," Abbe growled at the girl who climbed up and then balanced on the railing.

Of all of them, only Doming knew how to swim. Abbe could not save himself there if he fell in. The canal and its river were central to their survival. Angel would dump waste, garbage, vegetable scraps out into it. Occasionally something useful or valuable floated by. Doming had made Abbe a small raft from pieces of bamboo corded together. Abbe paddled and poled with a long strip of peeling plywood. He went out and hauled in anything promising.

"It's like the Smokey Mountain scavengers who live in Tondo, but instead of the garbage being piled up, it's floating by," Abbe said. He talked low to make sure Angel didn't hear him. She was ashamed of her past poverty.

"Here we are, a nation of islands," Doming said, "yet most of us turn our backs to the water. It's only the rich who go to their beach houses and swim. The fishermen take what they need from the water, now by dynamite or cyanide, and then turn their backs to the sea and go to the village where they live with houses facing away. Maybe because when the typhoons blow they bring walls of waves, or maybe it's because we turn our backs on getting anywhere.

"Why is it most Filipinos cannot swim, and have no desire to learn? It's as if the sea is our enemy—dangerous. If the fishermen get washed out of their boats, they can only hold on and hope that the sharks do not come."

"But the *banca* boat can take the highest waves and not tip, the two long outriggers, *batangs*, on either side like the hands of God," Abbe countered.

Linay stood on the railing, her hands out, her light blue plastic headband glowing in the darkness.

Doming saw a likeness of the Baby Jesus Santos from the shop window, balanced above the water. "Linay, climb down, be careful," he said.

"We may need money for more medicine for him tomorrow, Paco," Doming said, distracted, and tired from the trip. "I left much of what I had in Negros." He knew Abbe would have no money after the holiday. The poor spend, making a fiesta. And if they were ambitious like Doming and saved any sum, some family member would always need to borrow.

"I will see to it," Paco said, his voice deep with new responsibility.

Paco left, and walked the few blocks to the house of Mr. Ipis, the barangay captain. He knocked on the door. He would not tell. He knew the man used boys and paid them. He felt his penis growing damp and smaller.

He waited, feeling jittery.

Paco, come to me sometime, Mr. Ipis had whispered. The man had shown Paco and his friends pictures of grown women with boys, boys with boys. It was to him like looking at a dead cat floating in the canal—repugnant in his heart, but also deeper in his stomach and loins.

"Paco!" Doming yelled to him.

Paco turned from the door, caught.

Doming was running up the street. "What are you doing here?"

"To get money," Paco began.

"For what price, for your soul?"

Doming pushed him away from the door.

Captain Ipis opened it.

Doming grabbed hold of his orange collar. The nylon fabric slid away and he took the man by the back of his neck.

"Give me the money for the *tarì*," Doming demanded.

Captain Ipis smiled uncomprehending. No one challenged the barangay captain.

"Now—the money."

Ipis reached deep into his jacket and removed a wad of bills.

Doming gave the money to Paco.

He shoved the man's troll-like head hard against the wooden doorsill.

Doming and Paco left. Doming felt his heart pounding. He truly had felt the urge to kill the man. He balanced on the volcano's rim between violence and despair and he kept silent until he was calm.

Paco took his hand.

"Paco, you have an obligation to your father, but your first obligation is to your own soul," Doming said. "Do you understand?"

"Yes, Tító."

"He would fuck you, and not as a lover, do you know this?" Doming said, still angry. He decided he must use blunt words with the boy.

"I don't care. It would be over and I would have money."

"And what would you remember, the money or the old man's garlic breath on your neck?"

"But we'll be poor now, poor, my mother said."

"Not with Sonny and me, we wouldn't desert you," Doming said.

But what Doming thought, what had startled him, was how very good it had felt to lay hands on that man in anger.

He laughed, but unsmiling, heavy-hearted.

"What's funny, Tito?"

"I try to teach you goodness, yet I would kill for you," Doming said.

The holiday of Marcos' Inauguration celebration was over. A new era was beginning. In a few hours he had to be across the city, in Ayera, at her house.

Part III
Bayan Ko—My Country

Three months later

Eighty-one days after the Inauguration, in mid-September, Abbe died.

When Doming and Abbe had returned to the clinic a week after the inauguration to check the bandages, the doctors did not know why the wound healed so slowly. Soon Abbe tried to work. The Sparrows came back to the pawn shop. Everything would have gone right, eventually, if it was only a matter of time. But Abbe grew weaker. Finally, Doming took him to the Makati Hospital, three days' salary. They said there was nothing they could do, they would not admit him without ten thousand pesos cash. The doctor in the clinic that first night had neglected to order a tetanus shot.

It seemed incredible that however much evil existed in the world, the negligent actions of an educated man, a doctor, could bring about such ruin.

Even Paco might have thought to ask for a tetanus shot, Angel complained. You and your education, Doming.

Tetanus—a death worse than torture, some said, days and days of agony. Some claimed it was the most horrible way to die. Toward the end Abbe could not swallow, all his muscles contracting so tightly it seemed he turned to stone. The rigid muscles in his neck pulled his head back, and it was agony to Doming just to see him. Another doctor at the clinic prescribed muscle relaxant, that was all they could do, but it was never enough. Finally, after days of muscle spasms, he would drown in the fluids of his own mouth, unable to swallow. Doming blamed himself. He was supposed to be smarter. He'd driven the jeepney that night, not objecting to the foolishness of a man acting like a boy, he'd not been clear-headed at the clinic either.

He told himself, I should have known to ask them for the vaccine, I should have taken him to a hospital instead of that poor man's butcher shop. "What do you say, little brother?" Abbe would always ask, "you're the educated one." Doming remembered how he had to urge them to get the children's vaccines. They thought as long as the children were healthy they shouldn't waste time in the line, said the children were frightened of the needles. But then one of the neighbor's children got TB and they saw how expensive the medicine was and so they went to the clinic thinking they could get a vaccine for TB. The doctor laughed at them, told them no, there was no vaccine for that. Angel said, all medicine other than the *hilots'* was just some rich men's joke on them and didn't work.

Then she said she hated him, though he offered to support her.

But you won't marry me, she demanded.

Absolutely not, he said.

Why didn't you ask for the vaccine, Doming, why didn't you know? Angel moaned, again and again, turning on Doming in her fear when they found out why Abbe grew so ill. She had three children, no husband now.

Sometimes in the city the bodies of those who died a pauper's death, or who were unclaimed from the military salvagings—bodies dumped along roadsides—were collected, and sold as cadavers, their bones re-made into skeletons and sold overseas for medical purposes. That had haunted Abbe. He feared it, but it was also the humiliation of being sold if they couldn't pay to reclaim his body from a morgue or hospital. But Abbe wanted no money spent on a mass or burial. They needed it for the children.

"Put me in the canal when it's time, just near the river," he insisted to Doming, before the last days. "It's running so fast now I'll be in the bay and past Bataan by morning, on my way home to Negros."

"I cannot," Doming objected.

"No, husband, don't do this, I'll taste your flesh there— pineapple in the milkfish," Angel said. Abbe smiled. These private words of love—she claimed she could always taste on him the pineapples from the plantation of his boyhood.

Doming thought some might judge that she showed no loyalty toward Abbe in the end. Within a month of Abbe's illness, and the knowledge of the dreaded outcome, she found a military man who could help her with money, who was not jealous and asked only for her body, with one day's notice. Doming worried only that Abbe would sense it and the knowledge would kill him.

Angel would spend her money on bright print dresses in the market. Doming knew she told the man that the baby was hers, that Paco and Linay were her little brother and sister and would not be staying with her much longer. The military man would not want a woman who'd already borne three children. Doming decided he couldn't judge her. For half a life she'd lived in the garbage of Smoky Mountain; there is no cure for that, he reasoned. She agreed only that he should take Paco and Linay to their grandmother and cousins in Negros.

They could stay with me for a while, he'd offered.

Never, she said. I hate you. It's your fault Abbe will die.

She hated him because he would not marry her.

Abbe died on a Thursday morning after a night of suffering. That evening Angel alone sewed up the newly pur-
chased *abaca* mat around Abbe's body. She was alone, waiting
for Doming, when he got there after dark.

He was surprised that Sonny wasn't with her already.

"See, you two will desert the children now that Abbe's
gone," Angel complained.

"I'll find him later," Doming said. But he was surprised
and worried that Sonny hadn't appeared.

Without preliminaries, Doming carried the abaca mat
and its load down a few steps and put it on Abbe's makeshift
raft and rowed north along the canal to where it met the
Pasig River, flowing west toward the bay. He landed just
up from the Mendiola Bridge where the current was fairly
strong and pushed the raft in. The current grabbed it in its
swift flow toward the bay. He prayed for forgiveness.

He watched Abbe's progress on the raft as far as he could
see. It was a clear moonlit night and the wrapping shone
from the raft. In this river, Abbe had found lumber, lengths
of bamboo, a worker's bag with a few tools, pieces of plywood to add to his house, a large plastic basin to do the
wash, a half empty tank of kerosene he sold at the market,
rubber slippers, singly, but eventually two of about the same
size that fit one of the children.

Abbe's name could not even be listed as a death in the
newspaper. His mother in the Negros province would not
be told yet. The name *Abbe Villa Hermosa* was Sonny's name
now. Doming hadn't told Rue or Celia about Abbe. He was
ashamed and felt too much to blame.

He saw Abbe's body floating in the moonlight. Paco and
Linay hadn't seen Doming or Angel, but they heard the sounds
of preparation, the sound of splashing as Doming pushed off
into the canal's current, the sound of their mother's crazed

fear of being on the street, and her cruel words to Doming when he returned, blaming him for everything, turning on them all in her fear of going back to Tondo. Angel would do anything not to go back there. She already had.

Sonny was supposed to have met him at Angel's, but he hadn't turned up. Doming took a jeepney east through the city, to the hills overlooking Antipolo, back to Sonny's bar. Even when Doming was still outside the bar, he hesitated, already feeling that something had shifted.

A man they called Istak, The Drunk, sprawled on the curb, called, "You know him, you're his little brother, did you run away?" Istak was another former university student from the old days.

With sick foreboding, Doming understood he meant Sonny.

He followed Doming into the bar, saying, "Here's the one, his best friend."

But Doming said, "No, *hindî*, you're wrong. I don't know him so well."

The drunk shrieked with high demented laughter and Doming hated him.

"Diablo Crimebusters," Istak proclaimed, "Crimebusters, Crimebusters," he chanted the theme-song to an American movie. They were Marcos' new urban paramilitary, who offered bounties to those who turned in troublemakers.

Only a few patrons remained.

Doming noticed Sonny's glasses, the thin temple wires bent. Someone had put them on the counter, with his broken false teeth, the teeth that his father had paid for, too big for his mouth almost. His father had also paid a huge bribe to get Sonny out after months, the first time.

These few remaining customers helped themselves to the remains of fried *calamari*, to *sinigáng*, raw squid in bitter tamarind fruit juices, and other higher-priced delicacies. They looked at Doming like he'd come back from the dead. But no one said, the Diablos were after you too, Doming.

He shooed the last customers out. I am so sorry, each said in turn to Doming, as if they were departing from a wake. Until we meet again, they said, voices full of doubt.

Doming closed up the place for good. He locked it up and hid the key, but to what end, he wondered. He left a tape of Freddie Aguilar still playing and took a jeepney across the city to Sonny's rooms, which were near Abbe's shop, still hoping.

The door to Sonny's place stood wide open. He went in. The neighbor, an old woman, came in after him.

He learned from her that a boy, only fifteen but a new recruit of the *Barangay Kawal*, community soldiers, had spied on Sonny and turned in his name, told them where Sonny worked. The youth in poor areas were heavily recruited to be part of Marcos' community soldiers. Each barangay in the city and countryside had spies, urged by the New Society Party to be the eyes and ears of Marcos.

Doming gave her some money, offered some of Sonny's cigarettes they'd missed. He waited for her to say more. Neighbor against neighbor, he thought. She stood there before him wringing her hands.

"It was the captain, the captain," she said.

Under the New Society, barangay captains were appointed, along with officers, and these community soldiers ruled. Rumor-mongering became a capital crime, and under National Security Code provisions, criticism of the government was deemed a crime punishable by death, the sentence imposed by a military court. It was like the time of Rizal, when even being found in possession of his book, *Nóli me Tangere*, meant execution by the Spanish rulers.

"What did the boy find, what did he say to them?" Doming asked the woman, leading her.

"Your friend was reading a subversive book," the woman screeched. "He is with the National Democratic Front, their NPA."

"What did he read?" Doming said.

"The boy who turned Sonny in, he goes to school, almost every day, he learns English, he used his dictionary to translate the word he did not know."

It was her son, Doming knew it now. But she was frightened and ashamed.

"He is a new member of the *Kawal*, who watch the barrios and report to General Santan," she said.

"What was the book he found?" Doming said.

"He told them it is *How a Sparrow Kills*," she said, using the word for the gray bird that rides the shoulders of the carabao, cleaning its hide of nits. "Your compadre is teaching Sparrow recruits how to ambush the military," she announced.

The witch, he thought, the witch, the *mangkukulam*.

"There's no such book," he said.

"He found a book with a black cover, written in English," she said.

"Show it."

"A black book, I cannot read, it was there." She pointed at the table with her thin lips, drawing back as if she were repelled by such contraband.

He spotted the familiar paperback book that lay face down. *To Kill a Mockingbird*, a brittle-paged American book sent in a mission box, rejected by the Sisters, which Doming bought from them in Baclaran market for thirty centavos and gave Sonny as thanks for those Sonny had loaned him.

A dog howled mournfully. A train rumbled.

"You don't mean this one?" Doming cried, raising his voice over the sound of the engines. The walls shuddered as the engines passed. He heard the train's rhythmic *I am, I am,* banging words of the rails.

"Perhaps," she said, shrugging her shoulders. "Who knows? *Bahala na,* It's fate," she said. She snatched the book.

The air went out of him as if consumed by fire, he was so bewildered that in this place a harmless book could bring down such disaster.

"Look here, the gray bird like a sparrow, my son would not have translated the words if he'd not seen the picture, and now they have appointed him to be translator for the barangay captain, they will pay him." She pointed to the bird on the book's cover with her claw-like nail.

"How many times did Sonny ride your son on his back over these years?" he shouted at her. "How many days did he share his food with your family?"

He stared at her, recognizing the ignorance and fear, her eyes like those of a mongrel bitch, afraid of being eaten by her neighbors. She shrank back as if he might hit her.

"Get out of my sight," he said.

He gathered what he could. A picture of Sonny and Abbe and himself. He searched the room carefully, suspecting Sonny would have much to hide. Finally he found typed pages that had been rolled into a cylinder, hidden in the hollowed bamboo leg of the rough table. These were notes made by the journalist, Gold. He must have trusted Sonny with a copy.

Doming rolled them up, put the cylinder inside his shirt, and left. The dog still howled, the sound had become a low-pitched resignation.

Doming found a ride on a public jeepney, which traveled to Baclaran and then turned south, along the coastal road.

The Reluctant Participant, Doming remembered Sonny had called him.

But Sonny had been careful, too, his fierce dread of what they could make of him again matched only by his hatred and desire for revenge.

"It will not happen to me again, the horror, when I could no longer be moved by the screams of the others in the dark. When all that was alive in me was the fear of what was to come to me," Sonny would say, when he spoke of those days at all.

"This is also what Marcos took from us, the few of us who came back, we had to eat our hearts from the inside to survive," he said.

Doming had worried that Sonny remained very thin and stiff in his joints; his ill-fitting false teeth aggravated him, his jaw had healed crooked and so worked noisily when he chewed his *adobo*, his *siapao*. The man next to me, they put charcoals from their cooking in his mouth, Sonny said, so he was left with teeth but no tongue, no words. Then they fed him a dead rat.

"Cavite," the jeepney driver said. "The last stop."

Doming climbed down, shook his head to clear it. He would not let himself imagine Sonny being beaten with a rubber hose, or hear the punch into Sonny's delicate stomach that sounded like a mango that falls and hits fresh earth, or wonder whose names Sonny cried out right now, somewhere in this city.

A few nights later he waited on the street in Forbes Park. He'd driven Trace and Rue to a big party at Anne Larkin's house. He heard Filipino guitar music, laughter, and talk in many languages, and so he moved closer to the garden's high wall.

There was conversation between three men, one of them Trace Caldwell, just on the other side.

In a British accent—"The point is, this country is an after-thought to the U.S., unless the military bases are involved. You know, when Marcos declared martial law in seventy-two he knew he couldn't win or steal another election. And your ambassador then couldn't even get Nixon's attention on it. Fine, fine they said, just keep the military base negotiations going. Nixon was busy with Viet Nam, Kissinger had his Paris diplomacy, they all had the beginning of Watergate. The main thing was not to do anything to screw up the base agreement.

"It's always been like this; almost a hundred years ago your president McKinley sent a quarter of a million troops over here to fight a war that lasted a decade. Some moral responsibility to look after the Filipinos, the little brown brothers, spread knowledge and science and save them from themselves. A grisly war all for raw sugar."

Then he heard Trace—"It's always been about markets, about protecting what's yours."

"So history is repeating itself?"

The British man again—"No, think of what your great humorist said, the bitterest man in the world, finally, *History rarely repeats itself, but it often rhymes.*"

A pause.

"Mark Twain, of the anti–imperialist league."

The men laughed.

Doming sat with the door open and the overhead light on. He tried to read, but really he contemplated a mango tree nearby. Mango trees always had the red ants, the large ones with ferocious bites that protect the tree. That was why the young boys harvesting the mangos from the trees never climbed up them or leaned on their low branches. The boys used a short arc-shaped knife attached to a long pole, perhaps twenty-five feet. Under the knife hung a small scrotum-shaped sack of burlap. The boys would hold the knife high where the mango fruit grows, give a short chopping motion, the long pale green stem on which the mango hangs down is cut, and the ripe fruit falls the few inches into the sack.

He wanted to get a stick and cover it with angry red ants and toss it in the open window of a car nearby, the car of Doctor Deldrano.

When he'd seen Doctor Deldrano get out of his car earlier he'd recognized the man's pudgy Chinese eyes like dark sugar beans, and his voice as smooth as flan as he asked a few drivers to keep an eye on his car, the windows open in the night's hot air. He'd seen him walk in that oddly feminine way, on his toes.

This was the doctor who'd treated Abbe that first night.

He noticed Rue, coming toward the car, leaning on a man as they walked up the street. He disliked the man without knowing him, just seeing her lean on him slightly. A man well dressed, dark-haired and bearded, a somewhat heavy westerner. Then Doming recognized him as Sonny's friend, Daniel Gold. For the past two days he'd been searching for someone who might know about Sonny. He'd returned to the cockfighting pit in Los Baños, looking for Sonny's contacts there. The Sparrows who'd once stayed at Abbe's place claimed Sonny was at Fort Bonifacio.

He put the book on the seat, pages face down, to keep his place. It was F. Sionil José's novel, *WAYWAYA*.

He took off his glasses, small round wire frames that looked like they were World War Two surplus, put them away. He got out of the car when they reached it and opened the car's back door for her. She explained Trace would be leaving later, Doming didn't need to come back for him. Evidently Daniel Gold had insisted on walking her up the long driveway and to the car—she'd had too much to drink, perhaps.

She thanked Gold, leaned back on the seat, closed her eyes, dismissing him.

Before Doming could close the door, Gold said to him, "Wait, I want to talk to you."

Gold introduced himself to Doming, as if they had never met, speaking partly in Tagalog. Call me Daniel, he said. "I told Rue I wanted to meet you, that you and I are both friends of Sonny's."

With that, he had Doming's cautious attention.

Gold peered into the car's front seat.

"What are you reading there?" he said.

Reluctantly, Doming reached for it. He handed it over as if it were a weapon, palm up.

"A good man, this writer, he has a bookshop too. Do you know the place? You should go there. Sonny said once you have a gift for languages."

"I just borrow books," Doming said.

"I need some translating done, how about it?"

"Why me?"

"I think we're on the same side," Gold said. "I'm writing an article about illegal arms shipments coming through the country, payoffs to Marcos and Ess."

250

Doming purposely stared at Gold's shoes, at his watch, at his somewhat fleshy belly, and said, "I doubt that we're on the same side—Sir."

"I'll pay you well, very, very generously," he said.

"Why not a student?"

"They're afraid, plus, you know Sonny, I trust you. I'll pay a very good price."

"I don't take charity, Sir." Doming wondered if he even knew about Sonny.

"You know, in the other language I know well, Hebrew, there isn't a word for charity. The word means justice, you don't do charity, you live justly. If everyone lived justly, the word *charity* wouldn't be needed."

"And that's what you do, Sir?" Doming said, unconvinced.

"I'm trying—and please, don't keep Sirring me, *sige?*" Gold said.

"All right, *sige*," Doming said.

That seemed to satisfy Gold, as if the deal were done.

"I'm staying here at Anne's for a few days, and then I'm based at the Regent Hotel along Roxas. You can get a message to me there, anytime," Gold urged. He took a business card from his wallet and held it out.

Doming took the thick card and put it in his pocket without reading it.

Then Gold said, in a lower voice, "I know about Sonny, he's okay so far. His I.D. says his name is Abbe Villa Hermosa, so his files have gotten lost amid the hundreds of others they're holding."

"You've heard, he's alive, he's okay?" Doming said. His heart beat hard.

"Yes, he's okay," Gold said. "He's been moved to a re-education camp beyond Los Baños, near Calauan."

"How do you know this?" Doming said, not quite believing him.

"I've got a lot of friends here, I don't desert them, and Sonny's one."

"If he hadn't been working with you he might not have gotten picked up," Doming said. "You can just take your passport and fly out of here if things get difficult for you."

A car approached, headlights on them, slowed down. They both turned away from it.

Sonny had once said it was so bad, the torture, I forgot my name. Sonny's months in detention at Camp Crame years ago had made him weak, he couldn't stand it even when one of Abbe's children got hurt and bled. They all knew just the smell of the blood would make Sonny's false teeth hurt, his stomach heave, and that Sonny was ashamed that he was still so fragile.

He realized Rue was listening. The car door was open. He didn't care.

The two men stood under the streetlight, assessing each other.

"So, do we have an understanding, you'll do some work for me?" Gold asked, holding out his hand.

Doming did not take it. There is no deal, no deal, he told himself.

He drove. The black fingers of long-edged palms seemed to catch the sides of the car as he passed. It was as if he couldn't see what was in front of him. He turned the car headlamps to bright.

From the car, Rue watched the black-jungled gardens pass by. She saw the lit-up stucco facade of the San Antonio

Church, the bell tower and pillared tiers like a fabulous ornately frosted wedding cake. Here rich Filipinos from prominent families were christened and buried. Here Marcos and Imelda had married after an eleven-day courtship.

"Doming, have you heard of Boko Riccie?"

"Of course, the journalist, a friend of Ninoy's."

"Daniel was his friend, too. He's trying to finish Boko's work," she said.

She told him the story she'd heard from Gold. Boko Riccie, his best friend, was a Filipino journalist who'd blatently turned against Marcos and Imelda. Despite their warning, his writings got him picked up.

"When they got word, Boko was being held over there in Fort Bonifacio. Then the family heard nothing for about two months, nothing at all, but then a phone call came, and his son, their only child, took it. The caller said if you want to see your father, come to Fort Bonifacio right away, your father will meet you at the officer's club. And so the boy went. He was fourteen. He jumped on his bicycle and left before his mother and the driver came home, his *yaya* and the cook ran after him to stop him. He rode up this avenue, here, McKinley, past the golf course and through the American cemetery to the gates of Bonifacio to see his father.

"A few days later, his body was found, dumped along a road on the way to Subic. He'd been tortured, hands, feet, genitals, burned with battery fluids, while his father was forced to watch. They made the boy swallow a gold chain he wore, then cut it out of his stomach and placed it bloodied around his neck and dumped the body and burned it. The chain was the only way the mother could identify him. They let Boko out for two weeks after that, for the funeral, watched him, and when he began to write again they came for him, and that was it.

"They have his wife at the Sisters of Mercy asylum. When she began to appear on the street outside Fort Bonifacio every day, wearing black in silent protest, General Ess had his doctors declare her unstable. They keep her sedated now so she will stay off the streets."

All this Rue repeated, what Daniel Gold and Anne Larkin had told her tonight.

They sat in the car at the intersection for the main road at Pasay. He'd stopped driving to turn around and listen to her, face her. She held up her hands, open empty palms, *Walâ na*, no more.

He nodded and turned round to drive. "This story is repeated again and again here. Marcos knows we'll forget. Some other horror occurs and attention turns away. What bothers you most about this story?" he asked, in a neutral tone.

"That it happens every day, that we know only the names of those important enough that others tell their stories, that the father had to watch and the son had to see that his father couldn't save him, that *she*, she is there, waiting, alone," she said. "Being a survivor of something you don't think you could live through, to come out on the other side."

She pictured the Sisters of Mercy Home, along the Azapote Road just before the turn for Ayera, past the spreading bottle-green mango trees, then up the old drive to a former plantation house with broad verandas; she imagined dark-haired women in white cotton gowns sat in chairs of rattan, caged finches sang and wild birds flew to nests in the rafters above them, the women's souls as hard and small as the white dove-shaped bones that come out of broken sand-dollar shells.

He said nothing.

"I asked Daniel, why are you telling me this, and he said, *So you are not a fool*," she said. She looked at his eyes in the mirror but they were unfathomable.

The tall buildings of the financial district and five-star hotels of Makati were in front of them.

A little girl walked toward the car, leading an old blind woman by the hand. The woman's eyes were blue white in the streetlight. She worked that corner regularly, approaching cars snarled in the heavy traffic. Rue had seen her there with about a dozen other blind beggars, who'd flock to cars at red lights, led by children.

The woman tapped on the window next to Doming. An old dirty hand with yellow claw nails, her waxy eyes rolling back. They weren't really blind, Baby said, it was a scam, just another way they preyed on the rich Filipinos and foreigners, making them feel guilty. It's amazing how their sight miraculously returns when a bus is coming at them, Baby always said.

"Doming, give her some pesos from there next to the seat."

He rolled down the window and said something to the girl as he gave her a handful of change.

"*Salamat, salamat*, Ma'am," said the girl, looking past him at Rue. She handed him two of the *sampagita* necklaces she was selling, carried in a bunch on her forearm. Doming passed them back to Rue. She smelled the clove-sweet scent, felt the intricate weaving of honey-bee buds on a rope of garlands.

"Another charity for you," he said. His voice had its cynical tone, but underneath she felt the sadness, the way he also held himself in.

"Well, should I just ignore them all?" she asked.

"They just give it to the syndicate anyway," he said.

"Doming, what happened to Sonny? Daniel said he's missing," she said.

"Yes," he said.

"Are you in trouble, in some danger, too?" she asked.

He didn't answer.

They were already at the next stoplight at Pasay Road. An old man pushed a small bamboo cart with wooden wheels. He knocked on the passenger window, patiently, again and again, until Rue looked. He held up a basket of strawberries, a woven pine needle basket the size of a robin's nest.

She rolled the window down.

"How much," she said. "*Magkano?*"

"Thirty pesos only Ma'am. Just arrive here from the cool mountains of Baguio a few hours ago."

"*Itó ba ay matamís?*" she said. Are they sweet?

"Of course, Ma'am, they are so sweet," the man said.

She bought a basketful. Their woven basket smelled like the cool pine mountains of the north.

They turned south to leave the city. They passed the hovels along the rail tracks, soiled canvas flaps of vendors' stalls at the edge of the road, another broken-down jeepney. The driver sat without passengers, and a military jeep was parked facing it. They drove the ten miles down the dark highway, exited at Ayera, and passed through the market. They passed the turnoff for the asylum there in Muntinlupa. The Sisters of Mercy who lived there made beautiful embroidery, it was said. Their work is known everywhere, so delicate. They teach the mad women in their asylum, even some of the retarded, these stitches, so small, so carefully rendered, as to look like individual cells.

To her Doming also seemed behind some cell wall, confined. She felt her own carefully constructed solitude.

Its cell walls, the stark nucleus. A molecule of chlorophyll and a molecule of blood are almost identical. Where chlorophyll has a single atom of magnesium at the center of its molecule of hydrogen, carbon, oxygen, and nitrogen, blood has the same exact arrangement, but at its center is an atom not of magnesium but of iron. One red atom the only difference. We are all related, everything living. Blood has the same mineral content as seawater; our blood is swayed by the moon like the tidal waves. Even the sea is our common ancestor, she thought.

When they were almost at the turnoff for the compound she leaned forward and touched the back of Doming's neck, touched his hair.

With her fingertips she traced the outline of his face from his forehead, down his nose, his lips, his chin, his neck. She felt his measured breath, his heart beat. She felt comforted, she felt he must be a good man, made of goodness. She said his name. Doming.

Then she heard the whining sound of a high-pitched motorcycle gaining on the car.

Just before the turnoff, he'd noticed two motorcycles following the car, and then they disappeared. Then he felt her hand on his skin, his hair. She touched his face. He breathed into her hand. Then her hand on his chest. He wanted to touch her skin. He would drive past the turnoff for the house, stop the car. He would press her back against it. He wanted to put his mouth on every part of her.

Then he heard the high-pitched buzzing and the motorcycles converged again, one on each side of the car. He was still perhaps half a mile from the guarded Ayera gate.

"*Diyós,*" he called softly, under his breath. He saw white wings beating like a dove's prayer: it was the light-colored windbreaker of one rider flying out behind him.

She sat back against the seat.

"What is it?" she said.

He turned on the car's inside light. So they could see she was alone.

The two motorcycles pulled close alongside, too close. The one in front looked in at him, and at her, and then they sped away, in front of the car, zooming through the guarded Ayera gates without stopping, the rising drone of a high whining acceleration and exploding backfire like demented mocking laughter.

Perhaps it was someone the guards knew.

"Who were they?" she said, shaken.

"I'm not sure," he lied. His fear for her safety grew. If he warned Trace, Trace would report it to the embassy, and Doming might be picked up. But they were only after Raymonde or General Ess, so far. This was their warning to Doming to help them.

All the more reason for him to leave? He should leave the job for good. But they'd still follow their prey, Raymonde, they'd watch Trace's movements with him and she could be with the men when they struck. There was no way to protect her by leaving—unless he told her everything.

He slowed down and drove into the guarded village, over the speed bumps to the gates, into the walled acres, and down perfect streets where private security guards sat smoking or playing cards in front of the gated houses. They drove past the dark grounds of the Ayera Polo Club, the flat black clouds of acacia trees overhead. He thought of driving farther, but the motorcycles were somewhere in the walled village.

He stopped in front of the house to let her out, before he pulled the car along the side gate and into the drive.

"Please don't hate us," she said to him.

She got out.

"Not you," he said. She'd touched him, he'd not responded, and now his silence passed for scorn. He'd lost his chance. She walked in front of the car lights and he watched her. The silky pale green of her dress gleamed like sea-water. The iron gate clanged shut behind her.

They had avoided each other for weeks and weeks now, had not been alone together until tonight. He would not look at her again. He felt a black despair. He hated whoever had interrupted them just now—despite his good sense, fortitude, rational thought. The three legs he strode upon. He'd reasoned their intentional indifference to each other was born of fear and desire.

He parked the car in the side driveway and got out, his legs weak. She'd left the *sampagita* necklaces on the back seat. He wadded them together and flung them away as hard as he could.

A mangy cat ran from the garbage. Orion hunkered down overhead. At the west end of the drive, a thin, hooked moon seemed to wait for him there.

"Where are you going now, where is Sir?" Celia called from the open garage door behind where he stood.

"I'm going home, *Pô*," he said, using the Filipino word of respect.

"Have a bite, or let me send something with you," Celia said. "They've given you a long day."

He followed her.

They went in the garage door. She had some leftover fried rice there in the maids' kitchen, and she mixed it with some greens.

"Why are you up so late?" he said.

"I never sleep until *she* gets home," Celia said.

"Are you so dutiful, *Pô?*" he said.

No reply.

In the almost dark, she brushed a broom across the floor. Then she took a plate down, a plate from a new set Rue had bought for the "maids' kitchen" after she'd eaten with Celia and noticed the old mismatched ones of Baby's. Celia put the plate on the high counter in front of where he sat down.

"You like her," he said, after a while, accusing.

"I do," she said. She put a large spoonful of rice and a filet of *tanguigui* on the plate for him.

He started to object.

"I had all I wanted already," Celia said.

"*Salamat*," he thanked her. He ate, silent, hungry.

He heard the frogs calling louder, one beginning a night of chorusing, and then more and more. In several minutes they became one loud thrumming, a green engine.

"Rich or poor, people suffer," Celia said, nodding her head toward the doorway that led up six wide *narra* steps to the grander part of the house. She had to raise her voice to be heard over the sound of potential lovers' wooing croaks.

"Don't you know that for some, being kind to servants is just a different kind of control?" he said.

"Pah, let kindness be kindness for once," she said.

Celia was a most generous soul, he thought. She gave her service and good food with no expectation of reward, Doming considered, just a home. She had always served people she was better than.

"But perhaps you're too kind to them, *Pô*," he said, testing her. He wanted to be sure of her. "And surely you don't believe that the rich really suffer. Even the best of them, they ponder the meaning of life while they're indifferent to those around them, while the poor just look to survive while holding on to some remnant of their own humanity," Doming added, tasting the bitterness of the words with the sharp rice vinegar she'd used to flavor the delicate white-fleshed *tanguigi*.

"Humanity, my boy? Surely you know the poor are not all humane either. What of the security guard who throws his weight around like some *cabo* when I show my I.D. after I've gone out of the Ayera compound? There is only one by one, loving or hating or indifference—where is humanity, can you point to it, feed it, love it?" she said.

He so rarely tried out the ideas he chewed on like stale bread, unused words in his mouth. Without Sonny there would be no one to talk to about these thoughts.

"What's on your mind? Where does this come from? Not *my* cooking," she said, sitting down on the high stool across the counter from him in the dark room. She looked like some ancient wooden statue carved there. He needed someone to tell.

So he told her about Abbe, dying from a doctor's stupidity, from what Doming felt was his own stupidity, of Angel wanting him to marry her, he told her about Sonny, adding as if he were in a confessional that he would have been picked up with Sonny that night, and Celia uttered noises of comfort, no words, in all this like a wise grandmother. But he didn't tell her about the threats to Raymonde and General Ess. He didn't tell her that Rue was in his thoughts constantly.

She asked no questions at all, she only listened, and that somehow was a relief to him.

"Tell me about Raymonde," he said to her, finally, his voice going flat.

"About *him*? But really, why Raymonde, he is so below us, he is not worth your breath, don't even think about him," Celia urged.

"Then anything good you do know about him," Doming said. That would keep someone from arranging his death, he was thinking.

Celia took her time considering. Doming heard the thump of a mango falling from the tree in back of the house, hitting the wash shed below it.

Then she said, "Well, this is all the good I'll say— Raymonde's *yaya* loved him the way I did Baby, and he still goes to see her at their place in Pampanga. He is loyal and dear to her, a boy that way. And when she asks him if he has been to confession, and he says no, she can make him go. And when she asks him if he has had his medicines, and he says no, she can fuss at him until he goes to the doctor. And in her eyes, and hers only, he can do no wrong. He has the proper respect and affection for her now that she is grown old as the *pandan* tree. Somehow I never taught that to Baby, I never taught her how to love me. That one upstairs? She loves me more, much more."

Doming understood for the first time that she did not view herself as just a servant, uneducated, but as someone who could see right into those around her and know their hearts, shining or leaden, crooked or grainy or splintered, lumbering or as light as a bird. She was like a small bird who loved the whole sky.

"Thank you, *Manang*," he said, and took her hand and put his forehead to it.

When Doming left the house was dark.

At home, back in Cavite, he found a note. Hintayín mo kamí. Mag-abáng. *Wait for us. Watch*, it said. *We are friends of*

Sonny's. We will arrange a compromise for his safety. Do your duty. We have been patient—you know who we ask for.

Doming usually didn't dream. But this night he dreamed that he put his hands under a water faucet and heard it gurgling and was pleased to find it working for once. Then the large red ants found on mango trees came pouring out, and their jaws bit into his open palms.

Celia was annoyed and grouchy by early the next morning. It was six a.m., had been light out for an hour. She put on her uniform and a clean white apron. The rice would not come to a boil, a bad sign. Nothing was right. She felt she should have spoken up with more vigor to Doming the night before, about what a dangerous man Raymonde was, her fears for Doming. But Celia told herself, it's just an old woman's worry and imagination running over like this *caldero*, boiling pot.

This morning Celia couldn't even get her favorite radio show to keep her mind from chewing on this, because Ferdinand and Imelda Marcos were on all the radio stations. They were on their first state visit to the U.S. since 1965, to visit their friend, President Reagan. No other U.S. president had been willing to receive them in the past seventeen years, but now it seemed the whole world had stopped to watch them. For the last several days the constant live radio coverage of their trip disrupted Celia's morning radio soap operas. Each evening's event in the States was covered live the next morning in Manila. This was hard for her to grasp. Last night was done, over, and here was Imelda in the midst of it again, singing at a reception, "We Are the World."

Celia had not slept well. She'd tossed and turned like a pinned *talangkâ*, small crab, in the market, and then her bowels seized up. When she'd finally drifted off to sleep just before daylight, around five o'clock, Lleoni had appeared. Celia had heard the bell for the front gate ringing, insistent, as if the caller were mistress of the house. Celia scuttled there, thinking it was Trace finally come home. Then she saw Lleoni and was ready to scold her, but Lleoni simply indicated her big bag and walked in the front door.

"So, you're not in Germany or Australia?" Celia said.

No, she'd gone on a trial honeymoon in Baguio for one month and then been thrown out when she talked back and now Celia guessed she was pregnant by her blotchy darkening face. Lleoni asked her to get a sanitary pad.

"You are bleeding?"

Lleoni nodded.

Celia guessed that within a week she would lose the baby. Lleoni confided she'd asked him for money too soon, but she was desperate. Her brother was missing, and the rumor was he'd been taken from his province of Quezon by the military. His wife, fearful, had run away, and now Lleoni was responsible for her two nephews.

The boys had moved in with Lleoni's mother in the squatter area near Ayera market, along the railroad tracks.

Now, at six-thirty in the morning, Lleoni was settled in the *sala*, her feet propped up on the good table. She ate green mango—a sure sign, Celia thought. Lleoni had turned on the Caldwell's television like she was the lady of the house. She'd been spoiled, in that hotel room, Celia thought. Room service, people waiting on her.

But Celia didn't have the heart to scold Lleoni now. She brought Lleoni *tutóng*, the burnt rice from the bottom of the pot. That was Lleoni's craving. It was what you would give a favorite child.

The television announcer told how President Reagan welcomed Marcos and Imelda to Washington with open arms. Sir and Madam had traveled in an entourage of three Boeing 747s, Philippine Airlines, with seven hundred in their official party, not counting bodyguards and intelligence experts. One plane carried only their luggage, eight hundred pieces for Sir and Madam alone. After all, they were staying ten entire days.

But she'd overheard Trace and Carter while she served them dinner on the lanai, and their talk about the Beirut massacre, Lebanon, Jerusalem, refugee camps. From their talk she learned the grand Marcos state visit was only a circus sideshow.

Her radio had told how in San Francisco Filipinos from Ilocos Norte, Marcos supporters, were at the airport to greet them, waving banners that said in English and Tagalog, *WE LOVE MARCOS.* Everyone knows they're paid to be there, she thought, although of course the clannish Ilocanos northerners would never disavow him. After all, he'd helped those loyal to him get a hand in everything.

ONE COUNTRY, ONE THOUGHT, the *Daily Express Newspaper,* the voice of Marcos, had announced as the official theme of Marcos' state visit to the U.S. Yesterday's newspapers showed a picture of the four of them standing in front of the White House—Imelda with soft limpid eyes, high crevassed cleavage presented as if on a platter, Nancy with tight red ruffles high around her neck (some American women need more flesh on their bones or they look like the poor, she thought), Marcos looking slightly right and up, his good side, chin lifted, and Reagan, looking straight out at us, she thought, like a cowboy in the American movies, jaw jutted out.

So she watched Lleoni and Lleoni watched the television. The three government-owned channels carried the official State dinner, *LIVE—FROM WASHINGTON*.

Celia heard her favorite radio soap star, Tristi Rimarim, who'd accompanied the entourage, report that one thousand Filipinos were bused in from Norfolk to be at the Andrews Air Base when Marcos' planes landed. There was free food, hotels, entertainment, and t-shirts saying *I AM A FILIPINO*.

Then she saw Benedicto, the sugar baron from Negros, with Marcos on the television screen, as "Yankee Doodle" played and the Defense Secretary of the United States gave Marcos replicas of the awards Marcos always says he won from the U.S. after World War II.

Then Tristi Rimarim interviewed George Hamilton about Imelda.

Celia pursed her lips, wrinkled her nose as if discerning the freshness of fish from her vendor in the Ayera market. Everyone knew that Marcos' father, Mariano, executed for war crimes, had worked for the Japanese. When Filipino guerillas had questioned Mariano, he confessed. Name others, they said, and he said, spare me, it is my son Ferdinand, he was the one who recommended my services to the Kempeitei, the Japanese, at the start of the war. *Ferdinand was first a houseboy for the Japanese*, he said. *My Ferdinand made his money by buying and selling plenty on the black market during the war.*

And the Filipinos tied Mariano to four carabaos that tore him limb from limb, and they hung the pieces in a tree.

Now only Radio Veritas reported that the bill for the roses alone in the Marcos townhouse in New York City was forty thousand dollars, charged to the Philippine Embassy in Washington. What stink is Imelda trying to cover up, Celia wondered.

The end of Marcos will be the smell of rotting fish, her priest had proclaimed. Celia's priest in the chapel along Lake Laguna had read the morning clouds a few weeks before and made this prediction—when the Marcos reign is almost over, the sign will be that live fish fall from the sky. From this Celia now took comfort.

Just then she heard the front door open. She'd left it unbolted, the front gate unlocked when Lleoni came in. Before she could move, Trace appeared in the *sala* doorway. They were caught. Celia was ashamed and embarrassed.

But he only said, "Is Rue up yet?"

"No, Sir," Celia said. She was annoyed at him as well.

He headed for the guest room.

She went to the front door and looked out. She already heard the knife-sharpener there, crying his *Ha-saán*, Sharpen. He was too early, he was coming too often, watching the house too long.

"Did he give you a ride from the Ayera gate on his bicycle, Lleoni?" Celia said sharply. The man was after something, and it wasn't Lleoni.

"What if he did? My child will need a father," she said.

Celia went to the guest room door. Trace was changing clothes, getting ready for a shower.

"Sir," she said, not looking at his half-nakedness, "I don't like the knife-sharpener, the *hasaán*-man. I think he's watching the house," she said.

Trace stood as if she'd struck him.

"I'll tell the Ayera security, they'll pull his I.D., his entry card," he finally said.

She had an uneasy feeling the man meant them some harm. But she felt no joy at her keenness in discerning this. Her intuition had perhaps just cost him his livelihood.

By mid-morning, Lleoni was in the kitchen, working away, grinding the dried coconut palms from Palm Sunday that had hung tucked into a crucifix over her bed for six months. She would use it for medicine. Her brother had been killed by clashing paramilitary and NPA guerillas one hundred miles south of Manila. His sons Balthazar and Juvenal were with her mother. His young wife, frightened, had run off. That is what the mother-in-law said about her. But Lleoni suspected the girl had been raped by the military and was ashamed, or dead. There was no one to support these boys but her. Lleoni poured the finely ground dust onto a page of newspaper. Then she rolled the newspaper into a cone and poured it into a yellow plastic butter dish she'd saved from the trash. She wadded the newspaper, stepped on the pedal of the plastic trash can to open the lid, and tossed it in.

She had the distracted look of someone on whose livelihood more mouths depend than can be served, that whatever she does to save them will not be enough. Celia told her, Ask for a raise, our Ma'am will give it.

She'd cut her hair, had a curly permanent put in at the Baguio Hyatt Beauty Salon, trying already to look like a Westerner. She was butchered, Celia mourned. But she would not tell the vain girl this.

The next morning, a Saturday, Doming on impulse took a jeepney to the Los Baños re-education camp, Camp September Twenty-First Movement.

Now he was without the two compadres, the two older brothers, who mattered most to him of any men in the world.

The camp was in Los Baños near the Rice Institute. He stood outside the camp gates. He asked two female cooks who were about to go in, do you ever see a man in here, a very thin man who looks older than the students, with no front teeth? Not newly smashed out and broken, but instead missing false teeth.

They had seen him.

Doming wrote a note. *Abbe,* he began, using the name Sonny was being held under, *Abbe, tell them, I will do anything. I will follow their instructions.*

"Will you smuggle in a note to Abbe Villa Hermosa?" he asked the cooks.

"It is very dangerous for us."

He slipped a fifty peso note into an outstretched hand. A day's salary.

The re-education camp in Los Baños was the place where prisoners were held by the Japanese during their occupation. The ground was soaked with suffering. Doming heard the sound of running, in formation. Through the high wire he saw what he thought was Sonny's tall thin frame, collapsing over. He heard them parrot back commands. A re-education camp, its euphemism, where beliefs and causes were leached out of you, like blood. Your will broken, like bones. Sonny could not survive this a second time.

Doming owed Sonny the debt of his own life. He would act. *I will put the plan in motion, but your friends must guarantee your safety.* The smuggled note ended. *Keep hold, Kuya. Kumapit kang mabuti.*

Later, at the gate of the Rice Institute, he told the guards he was Rue's driver, the American woman scientist, he said.

They knew right away, there was only one white woman who went into the fields and screen houses. She worked on Saturdays, like they did.

He found her. "I'll drive you home at the end of the day," he offered.

"Perhaps," she answered.

She showed him her screen houses, the lab. The laborers clearly respected her. She would do any work they did.

"Trace has never come to see it," she said.

In one of the screen houses she pointed out for him the signs that the newly hatched generation of stem borer larvae were expecting a change in the weather.

"When too many newly hatched larvae are on one plant, too late in the season, some will cut a tiny piece of the green sheaf around them and make what amounts to a little raft for themselves. It drops them safely into the water and floats them to another rice plant. They are cunning," she said, letting him examine it.

"They're made for survival in the excesses of nature, too much rain or too little. They can even plan for the beings they'll become—when the full grown larvae have pupated for the last time in the stem, they will cut larger exit holes through which the emerging moths, that they will soon become, can escape," she said, pointing out an example among the rice stems and glowing water.

Miraculous, that they sense what they will become, unlike us, he thought.

"The larvae are already clever spinners, they make translucent silk covers over the hole they've prepared, so the cocoon's place of transformation is totally waterproof in case the paddies flood," she explained.

"Wise creatures, if they can plan for the difficulties of nature, of life, better than the squatter in his shack," he said.

They examined some tillers carefully. She showed him some holes the larvae bored there, tightly sealed over with silk. Then she had him look at this under the microscope. Their escape.

"Where are you going now?" she asked him.

"Nowhere—home," he said. "Sit down with me."

They sat on the wall overlooking the field. They talked. To her questions, he told her his story, how he came to Manila and got a new name with Sonny's help. He thought he talked like a blabbing parrot with her, but she said, go on, tell me the rest.

"I was studying to take the entrance exams for the university in Dumaguete, he said. Marcos and his labor minister Blas Ople declared labor unions in the sugar industry illegal, under their new martial law. I helped Father Rex organize strikes, and at the same time, the sugar market collapsed, as if our efforts had been the cause. It was said the sugar crony held one thousand tons of sugar in warehouses, waiting for the prices to go up, and his sugar turned as solid as stone, worthless, and so he claimed he couldn't pay the laborers who'd cut and hauled it. Can you understand any of this?— to make just one ton of sugar takes more than nine tons of cut cane.

"Under Ess they began taking labor leaders at night, accusing them of being New People's Army sympathizers."

She was very still. She listened well, unlike most foreigners.

"Now, I may ask you the questions," he declared.

She looked terrified.

"Why did you give those birds away to Anne Larkin, the two cockatiels?" He'd reserved this question for months, until the time was full.

"I don't know—they were almost dead when I found them, I just wanted to save them," she said.

"They loved you. Didn't you think you deserved that from them?"

"They're birds, they don't know."

"You were like a goddess to them, and one day, you disappeared. If you will not let your heart be open, even to a living being that loves you, if you simply give it up, what does that make you?" he asked.

"What are you saying? They don't have feelings."

"Nor do you, perhaps. And perhaps you think I don't either."

"I don't want to talk about this anymore."

"You did not want them to love. You are afraid."

"Perhaps. Leave it alone."

The sun climbed high. On the stone wall, under the shade of the tamarind branches, they were unobserved.

Monday, two days later, Doming drove for Trace.

"We have a strange errand today, Doming," Trace said.

He'd driven Trace and Carter toward an old part of the city, north along the Bay, past Intermuros and Fort Santiago, over the Pasig River and along Recto Avenue, to near the Church of Santo Seng Kong, where the Chinese priest used icons in geomantic divining. Now the priest's claim to divine power was his assistance to Madame Marcos in choosing the site of the Marcos Museum and Basilica overlooking the Taal Volcano basin.

Doming hadn't been to this part of the city in years. The place was like a cauldron, flies, algae-covered waters, and soot. People everywhere, people like human waste, overflowing, spewing out of buses and jeepneys.

272

He'd dropped them off at a big house, and now waited up the street with the car.

A dog nearby barked and barked. He thought, it will be dead by morning. In this part of the city dogs were eaten by the Chinese-Filipinos, and the dog's fresh blood used for medicine.

After a while, Trace called to him—come into the house.

"We need a translator, the words in Tagalog are too obscure for us. The witch talks in circles," Trace said.

She would not speak English to them.

"Why not wait and get Raymonde to help us?" Carter said, when Doming came in.

"We don't want Raymonde involved in this. He could double-cross us," Trace said.

Doming saw it was a fine house for this part of the city. Water flowed in a little fountain near the front door.

"Why no English? *Walang Inglés? Marunong ba kayó ng Inglés?*" Don't you know English?" Doming said to the woman. He stayed just inside the door.

"Bad luck. The words do not relinquish themselves to that language," she said formally.

She was smart, he saw, and after that exchange she taunted the two American men then by speaking only to Doming, but in heavily accented English.

"Bad luck, bad luck," she said, pointing her chin at the two.

She wore an old-style Maria Clara dress with a piece of stiff embroidery that stood up around her thin neck. She had a creamy lace mantilla-like scarf over her head, as if she'd just come in from the hot sun. Heavy gold earrings shaped like flat-winged dragonflies hung from her long earlobes.

The room felt stifling to Doming, but when she touched his arm her hand was cool. Her skin was light, her teeth her own, and her eyes clear. Seeing her at morning mass one would assume she was well educated and from a rich family.

Doming explained what the men had come for, repeating a few lines at a time. They told him, and he repeated it as if she hadn't heard it. They were offering her a visa, a green card to the U.S., if she would pass on a certain prediction to the First Lady. Make it sound real. They'd heard she was very good, that the First Lady relied on her.

They'd give her a green card, a visa, the coin of the realm, Trace called it, for her services.

The coin of the realm, of the kingdom, he translated this into Tagalog for her. She was interested. A new word, another, for bribe; now there would be a dozen meanings for *bribe* in Tagalog.

"The Embassy wants, through your good graces, to suggest to Imelda that Ninoy Aquino's return would mean the end of the Marcos reign forever," Doming said.

In addition, they were offering her an amount of good faith money now, up front, for her discreet services.

She counted the stack of pesos, two thousand, in one-hundred notes.

When she was satisfied she put the money back in the nylon pouch it had come in. Carter handed her a piece of thick paper on which the lines were typed, what she should deliver or say to the First Lady.

Doming watched some strange history being made, this transaction. Was this also a form of commerce? Imelda must be convinced Ninoy's return would mean the end of Marcos, and so the end of her own chances. Then she'd make sure forces loyal to her wouldn't let him through immigration and he couldn't sneak back into the country. Exile, permanently. What harm could he do in Boston? And once he understood the inevitability of disaster should he return, he wouldn't be foolish enough to risk it.

Doming read the paper looking over her shoulder.

The harpy finished reading. Then she smiled up at Doming.

"Sometimes," she said, holding her scrawny head to one side like a coy girl, "Sometimes I sit in my window here, watch the people go down the street, smoke my pipe and work my beads. If I see a face that interests me, sometimes I have a moment's view of some connection with a bigger event, some premonition. I send my houseboy out into the street after that face. You have a face I like," she said, reaching out to touch his jaw.

He saw her sunken downy cheek, her plump belly. He drew back, still careful of her intentions—it was said that some bad *hilots* have the power to take energy, goodness, out of another, put it in their belly. Evil was real, something he believed in.

Doming heard the street sounds outside. Vendors called out the names of their snacks for sale, but they would also sell *shabu-shabu*, the poor man's drug. Another way to see the future.

She smiled to herself. "I will do it," she said to Doming.

"I'll tell Imelda—I know what these men want, I knew it was coming. But I want three green cards for the U.S., tell them three," she insisted.

He repeated this to Carter and Trace. They nodded, impatient. She had a peculiar accent Doming couldn't place.

"I also want one of the fat beef cattle that they raise in Zamboanga, that is my home, for my *despidida*, the going-away party, the cattle fattened with bananas," she said. Zamboanga, on the island of Mindinao. The bananas there were raised by Marcos' banana crony. If they were not perfect for shipping to the Japanese market, they were fed to cattle to sweeten their meat, and the Zamboanga beef was renowned for its sweetness and tenderness. It was said that when the crony began to complain of far too many bruised bananas because of the bumpy overland shipments, Marcos had a new road, as smooth as *leche flan*, built from the plantation to the sea.

"Yes, we can get that. The meat might have to be frozen, tell her," Trace said.

"Now, finally, as to the method, this is not the way to the First Lady," she said, holding up the paper Carter had given her. "These words the Americans bring me are too clear, too rational, for the First Lady—she would see right through it."

"You write it for me yourself," she said to Doming. He felt her poking her bony finger into his gut as if testing a sweet cake.

She offered Trace and Carter soft drinks. They accepted at once, to move business along. It was brown soda in bottles with loosely fitting lids that came off with only slight pressure. Trace looked at the bottle top, sniffed at it. Not smooth enough manners, Doming observed.

"Never mind," the woman said. She called sharply, "Chica!" From what must have been a kitchen, a dark room toward the back of the house, a lovely girl still in a nightgown, with a broad face and delicate nose and lips still full from sleep, came out and after a few words she went out to the street and brought in two icy bottles of San Miguel.

She gave them to Trace and Carter, who stared at her. She brought out sugared nuts, and motioned for the two men to sit down across the room in bamboo lounge chairs. Trace seemed to relax. Perhaps he was now assured that things were finally progressing. Until you have been offered some refreshment in a Filipino home and refused it politely, and then accepted only when it's urged, you have not acted out your part in the ritual of hospitality. She didn't know foreigners, Doming thought, and treated the men as she would treat bumpkins.

Next the woman had Doming sit down at a round Chinese-style ebony table and begin, marking out what was typed there and writing beneath that. Carter got up as if to help Doming with the writing. She motioned to the two men to keep their distance, making a shooing motion with her hand. Doming felt her breath on his neck as she looked over him.

"This paper will not do either," she said to Doming. "We must use Chinese rice paper. Get some from the desk," she commanded.

He did so and sat down again.

"Then, after it is written, the paper must rest for one night near the altar at Baclaran. I will deliver it there myself, *gratis*, no extra charge," she said.

Many fortunetellers relied on letting the rice paper rest, hidden in a church. When he cleaned the sanctuary for Father Rex he would find strange scraps of paper with indecipherable words written on them. The superstitious would make their own amulets, not even going to the fortuneteller. They believed that just leaving the paper there on the altar would give it power. Of course the priests frowned on this, but the wooden altar that had come two hundred years before with the Spanish friars had cracks in it, and often the papers with curses written or drawn would be wedged in these cracks, hidden there overnight. Sometimes the words meant nothing, and he didn't know if it was a symbol, or just some gibberish by those who believed that their thoughts, their curses, nonetheless, would get through to God by the scratches that they left there for Him.

"Put something about the meteors, he will come sometime after the time of the Perseids, another star in white falling from the sky," the woman said.

He felt sick with foreboding. This was real, too real. He turned on her.

"Who is pretending to predict the future here—You? Or these two twisted brothers with their errand?" Doming accused, keeping his voice low.

He glimpsed the future. Raymonde had people watching Ninoy's every move in Boston, and these Americans didn't want to protect Ninoy either. Can two fates conspire? He was weary of it all. Of trying to protect anyone—Sonny, Abbe and his family, Rue, himself. And who was he to intervene in any of it—a man who didn't even have his own name? But he glimpsed for a moment something to come, a great gathering of Filipino people like a mighty river, resisting threats of force and violence, each person buoyed up with hope and song.

"Each one of us sometimes senses what is coming and thinks this means we can control it. But time has just been waiting for this gap. Ask these two if they want their own fortunes told, gratis. They are setting in motion only what is already," she said.

"This isn't such a good idea, Sir, for you to be here doing this," Doming said. The woman had some powers.

"Do it, and let's get the hell out of here," Trace said.

The woman said, "You must, you see it has already begun without you. Do your best and you can make the iron stars pound out some blessing," she pleaded. He looked at her, she was wild-eyed, he realized, here in the face of her enemies, Trace and Carter, and the powers behind them. What Doming wrote would be not for them but for Abbe and Sonny and his own stepfather, his sister, Father Rex, and all the children born and buried this day on the edge of a sugar cane field.

And so he was the one to write the words, the *tsismis* that would fly around the city, through the streets of Manila, that everyone came to know. They are just words he told himself. *Just* words, he thought.

> *To Imelda, Queen of the Islands,*
> *A man in white will come here from the sky, preceded by the night of meteors when the sky weeps hot white tears, this as certain as each night the Seven Sisters proceed before Orion.*
> *A man in white will come back. When his foot touches the ground, your days will be done—*
> *The Pasig will bear you and your children away.*
> *Justice will roll down like water,*
> *And one million will gather,*
> *A mighty stream to breach your crumbling bridge of stone.*

He thought this would echo the well-known prediction of the Mendiola Bridge, the promise that when the students again crossed over the bridge, the Marcos reign would be over. It had been barricaded since martial law. Imelda would believe in a bridge. Even the billion-peso San Juanico Bridge in her home province was rumored to be the source of her skin turning scaly, her other curse.

He heard a whisper of hope, repeated in the sounds of the *shabu-shabu* vendors outside, and boys selling cigarettes one by one, and in the voices of the sooty-colored pigeons on the roof above, a low plaintive murmuring, as if a crowd were already rising up.

"Ah, very good," the fortuneteller said, reading the paper over his shoulder. "This will be sufficient for the First Lady. You have made an elegant way with threatening words for her.

"Take heart, they may kill the one who comes but he will rise up again in the people," she said.

"It's done," the fortuneteller said, turning now to Trace and Carter, who fanned themselves in the murky heat.

"I'm curious to see how Madame will respond," she said obliquely.

Doming left to get the car and Carter followed him. Doming wanted to be alone for a few minutes, to calm down. He saw these Americans as angling like a wedge against the future of his own people.

When Trace came out a little while later, he was frowning. He tossed his jacket in the front seat, and got in the backseat with Carter. The temperature gauge on the car's dash read one hundred and ten degrees.

Doming turned the car around in seconds on the narrow street.

"Like a trip to hell," Trace said. Doming pushed the air conditioner to high and set the vents toward them.

"There's one word she kept repeating to me just now, so insolently," Trace said.

"Maybe she was telling your fortune," Carter said.

"When I didn't understand, she acted out slapping the table with her palm, saying *Uód, uód,* then she held up her thumb and forefinger just slightly apart as if measuring, and laughed."

"*Ulól,* is that it, *fool?*" Carter said.

"No, of course that's not it. Doming?" Trace said.

He turned the car onto a main street, south toward the embassy. He'd understood immediately.

"Yes, Sir."

"Well what?" Trace demanded.

But then something in the mirror caught his attention. A motorcycle pulled up close behind them, then dropped back. This could always be the beginning of an ambush, the driver with his face covered, and a rider who sat behind him.

Doming glanced toward the oncoming traffic, scanning for another motorcycle that might pull out to slow them down, so the pair behind could easily overtake them, and the rider would turn and shoot.

"Doming!" Trace shouted, wanting an answer.

"It's a kind of very small worm, Sir," Doming said.

"What?"

Trace is foolish, in over his head, Doming thought, to mess with the woman's magic. He forgets that here cunning is better than confrontation. The woman had vexed him. Doming had been humiliated in his task of betrayal for Trace, of plotting these games of hocus-pocus with a woman who truly might have powers. He wanted to stop the car and just get out and walk away. But Rue held him like a planet fixed in orbit.

"*Uód*—from flies, the worms that eat the dead," Doming said, provoked.

"The damned witch," Trace said.

But Doming heard with some satisfaction the alarmed sound in Trace's voice, as if he believed the woman. He'd asked for this.

The motorcycle jerked forward, pulling next to them. A passenger rode behind the driver, not a good sign. The driver's head was wrapped in dark blue cloth, masking all but his eyes. Some on motorcycles did this to keep out the dust. The driver looked straight ahead, seeming to disregard them. Doming stared; it seemed he saw each woven fiber in the cloth wrapping. But the one who rode behind glanced over at Doming, began to take his hand from out of his open jacket.

Doming slammed his foot onto the brakes and turned the car sharply into the driveway of Chinaman Bank. The tires squealed, the car jerked to a stop, throwing the passengers to the side.

"What's going on?" Trace said.

Doming saw they were crouching into the back seat, the way the embassy security classes had instructed.

"I thought they were setting us up," Doming said, lifting his chin to point at the motorcycle now weaving away, disappearing in traffic.

"Just drive, Doming, don't think, and then scare the shit out of us," Carter said.

But Carter still crouched, looking up toward the back window. Sometimes kids on motorcycles followed closely and buzzed around a car just for sport, but they risked being shot at. A driver for a Filipino or Chinese would have already pulled out his own gun and used it.

"Let it go," Trace said to Carter. "He's usually right, he's been at this a long time, he has a sense of these things."

"That damn witch," Trace said, and he let his breath out in a long low whistling Doming had rarely heard him use.

Carter sat up, still looking out the back window.

"It's getting out of control here," he said.

"The NPA will have to turn recruits away if Marcos dies and Imelda and Ess take over," Trace said. "We need a military man, a real one."

Soon the two men began to talk about work, to construct again the anthill of an ordinary day, in their relief at having an unsavory job done, in their relief in being alive, not threatened. They could forget he was there with them.

The Beirut Massacre—news of it screamed from the *Stars and Stripes*, the *International Herald Tribune*, the BBC. They talked of the irony of how the Marcos' private two-hour visit with Reagan, planned by the earnest State Department underlings and congressional committee hacks to cover human rights issues in private, had quickly turned into an exchange of stories about assassination attempts— the attempt on Reagan's life six months before, in the spring. Nancy was still spooked. Imelda told Nancy her own story of the attempt on her life, many years before. My bra-zeeer, eeet was full of blood, she always began. She'd told it many times in public in Manila, to each American ambassador, to the Pope. Marcos told Nancy of the various plots and coup attempts uncovered, how he always wore an *anting-anting* for protection. Imelda told of the woman she relied on in Manila's Chinatown, a fortuneteller. Mrs. Reagan had been very interested, asked many questions. NSC aides had listened to the tape of the conversation, decided that Imelda's woman in Manila could be useful to them in manipulating Imelda. They'd put Carter McCall on track to follow up, and this morning they'd found her.

Doming pulled up to the embassy's massive gates. Manila Bay flashed in sunlight behind the shaded building—the water seemed on fire, the massive acacia trees on embassy grounds glowing in the noonday's penetrating light. The Marine guards opened the car's trunk, used their mirrors to check under the car, then signaled him to drive in.

Doming imagined cutting down all the trees on the embassy grounds, like they did in Mindanao. Cutting down and selling all the grand trees at the Ayera Polo Club and the Forbes Park Club. Why did they think only the poor could live without trees?

He waited there all afternoon.

By the time he drove Trace home that evening, there was total darkness in the city.

Say it was because that very day the harpy fortune-teller did as they'd asked her and flew to Malacañang and delivered to the First Lady a strange new warning. Say this was the day that some sea-change in the country's history began.

All the electric lights in the city had suddenly gone out, but the sky glowed with an eerie green light. At the embassy, the flat-branched acacias were outlined against a western sky that bled long streaks of deep violet. These flat branches looked like open hands, palms lifted up. Even a fist was once an open hand, Father Rex had often said to him.

They passed through a military checkpoint along Edsa Boulevard, and then turned onto the highway. The car radio said that General Ess ordered the military on red alert, some rebellion of dissatisfied troops, some infiltration by the NPA was rumored. The NPA had sabotaged a power station north of the city—this was the reason the city now sat in darkness, the government radio station proclaimed as Trace listened. Doming was skeptical, the rumor among the drivers who waited at the embassy was that Marcos himself secretly ordered the cuts in power—causing brownouts—to keep all sides off balance: the ambassadors who must explain to their governments, the foreign companies who complained to their ambassadors, Marcos's own cabinet ministers who could never be certain when one would be out of favor, and also his generals whom he played one against the other.

But also, Doming had learned news from another embassy driver. An American, a JUSMAG officer, in Manila on assignment to help update military equipment, had been ambushed this morning in the Manila suburb of Quezon City by a group claiming to be NPA. The local papers this afternoon already had gruesome front-page pictures. Although the JUSMAG officer's driver knew how to drive anywhere, onto sidewalks in the heaviest traffic, ways to avoid being jammed in, how to do a one hundred and eighty degree turn in traffic, small motor scooters had crept up on each side of the car, and the riders opened fire into the car at very close range, killing the officer and driver.

The NPA threatened there would be more ambushes on the military and its supporters, in reprisal for Marcos' latest crackdown and the military murders of students and labor organizers. A local beauty queen, a student from north of Manila who'd spoken against the government, was found naked, trussed like a pig, arms and legs bound to a pole. Her photo was in every magazine being hawked on the streets that day. Trace had bought the magazine and a newspaper from a roadside vendor at the checkpoint, and now peered at it in the near dark. He left the reading lamp in the back seat of the car turned off, so as not to spotlight himself.

"What do you think about this morning?" Trace asked him.

"You mean the fortuneteller, Sir?" he asked.

"No, the motorcycle."

He chose his next words carefully, turning them over in his mind like *sampolac* in the market.

"I think, from what I'm hearing, that anywhere in public now with the generals is dangerous, perhaps even with Raymonde," he said.

"And it's a good idea you have, to leave the inside car light off for a while," he added, wanting to keep the man safe, but also wanting to keep Trace's suspicions of him in check as long as possible.

"Thank you," Trace said.

It would be so easy, Doming thought, to set up Raymonde and Trace, as easy as it was for Trace and Carter to convince Imelda to be like the cat who envies the flight—but is intent upon the kill—of a bird, a white bird that flies down from the sky.

Mid-October. A tropical depression was parked just north of the country. A huge typhoon was predicted. The barometric pressure was falling to the lowest on record.

The next afternoon it began to rain. Typhoon Evangelista stalled up north off the coast, over the island of Batanes, and for five days it rained iron bars over Luzon. Trace's leather shoes in the closet began to turn green with mold, and the electricity went out, which meant there was no water, since it was pumped by electric generators.

The Rice Institute paddies flooded. The road into the institute flooded. The larvae sealed their new holes with silk and waited. Along the seawall in Manila, the squatters left their homes.

For five days it rained. Because they had no running water, Rue used water stored up by Celia and Lleoni in plastic garbage cans in the shower stall, cold, greasy-feeling water. She used a dipper to pour it over herself.

Then the winds came south and toppled the papaya trees that grew along the north wall of the garden, outside the kitchen. The leaves of the banana trees beat against the east windows of her bedroom; all but the newest leaves became green tattered fringes, like old flags. They knocked against the back wall of the house at night, keeping her awake. The lanai filled with the palmetto cockroach that flew in for cover and with every other crawling thing seeking shelter. Tree frogs and lizards took refuge on the beams that crossed the lanai's high ceiling.

Doming couldn't get over the river in Cavite to come to work. The roads were flooded. Jeepneys weren't running. It was a holiday. Trace stayed in the city.

She paced.

Late in the afternoon Rue went to the storage room built under the stairs in the garage, the darkest coolest place in the house where Trace kept the best French wines. She wanted a modest one she could drink alone. When the light from the bulb came on, cockroaches ran.

The rollicking cockroaches were chewing the glued labels off the wine bottles in the wine cellar. That was the only insect she couldn't tolerate, that she in fact loathed. They were too bold, too predatory.

Wine bottles with the labels half-eaten or completely gone lay on their sides. She saw the damage they'd done, eating the paper labels for the sweet glue.

A tiger mosquito flew up, landed near the light switch. They were everywhere in this breeding closet with a half-inch of water covering the floor. The tiger mosquito, about an eighth of an inch long, brightly marked by a white stripe running down the middle of the back, white bands on the legs, and white markings on the thorax and abdomen, like a striped tiger. Specimens were valued by collectors for their unique markings.

She felt the bites on her legs.

Just as the rains were ending, Celia learned that her sister Mary had died. A PLDT telegram, which would only bring bad news, arrived at the house in the mid-afternoon, while Celia was having her *merienda*—coffee and *buko* pie. It said Celia's sister had died two days before. Baby had already scheduled a mass for tonight.

Celia ran upstairs to Rue, who was in bed, not feeling well. She sat down on the edge of the bed and wailed aloud, her dark face a thousand wrinkles, her head back. Rue held both her hands. That helped. Celia needed some touch, some comfort.

"She died without me, with no one, no one to hold her hand," she cried. From the time they were young girls, Mary had made sure Celia lacked for nothing, had taught her even to share the bounties of Baby's father's house with the less fortunate. She'd seen to it that Celia got a sixth-grade education, that she knew her catechism.

Celia was relieved when Rue finally reached Baby by phone. "How could you be so unfeeling?" Celia heard Rue say.

"She wants to talk to you," Rue said to her.

Celia took the phone. She'd never talked to Baby on the phone, Mary always answered.

"Ma'am?" Celia said.

"Now, Celia, I'm sorry but I've done nothing for two days but arrange this funeral. Because of the rains the phone lines were out all this week," Baby shouted over hissings in the line. Baby had even called Raymonde's doctor, Dr. Deldrano, to see about Mary.

"It was Ray who said we must go ahead with arrangements. I tried to send a telegram that Mary was failing, but the metro is swamped by them right now and they said it would not be delivered for two days. I sent Raymonde's driver to get you but the roads in Ayera were flooded. He would not risk the new Mercedes there, Ray would be so angry. The morgue wouldn't hold the body any longer."

Celia grieved bitterly. Baby kept repeating to her, don't cry, don't worry Celia, I'll pay for the funeral myself.

That evening, Trace and Rue took her to the chapel of the de Varcegno's parish in Forbes Park.

Celia rushed in to view the body alone. She saw a coffin in a dark side room. So, it was real. She forced her legs to move. There lay her sister, who'd always looked out for her. Celia felt her legs sinking, her knees give way. She was not ready for this. They'd promised each other they would reach their ninth decades together, as their grandmother had, but Mary's old heart had given out, her lungs congested and filled with fluid.

Celia was upset to find Mary dressed for burial in a gold-colored gown Baby had worn once a few years before to the Manila Polo Club Christmas Ball. Baby never liked the way the sewing girl made it, said it made her look too flat, and of course Baby still worried when Peaches Gonzales was around, flirting with Raymonde. The old flame had grown stout and blowzy, but she carried a too-full chest that he always looked at, Baby complained. So the once-worn fancy dress was now Mary's.

289

The young priest came in to the side-chapel with Baby. Baby exclaimed to them how nice Mary looked—she'd never looked better in her life, Baby said.

Celia was angry, she grieved, but she was the only relative and she kept her dignity in front of Baby and Raymonde.

It was an expensive undertaking, Baby protested, though no one had criticized the box she'd ordered, a box made from plywood treated to look like solid *narra*, Philippine mahogany. No order had been made to use preserving fluid and the body had begun to deteriorate.

The next morning, Mary's body was put into the crypt next to their father, who'd worked for Baby's father in his hemp factory for many years. The crypt was at the old cemetery in Pila, beyond Los Baños at the south end of Laguna de Bay, about fifteen kilometers from the Rice Institute.

Doming and Trace accompanied Celia there. Baby and Raymonde did not come, they sent the driver Delgado to drive the youngest parish priest with Mary's coffin in the back of a jeepney, to finish what he'd begun the evening before. His high-voiced perfunctory manner grated on Celia's nerves. She wanted to cry out to him, Stop your noise. She wanted to be alone with Mary, whose box would now be slipped into the cool white-stuccoed vault, built above ground since the land here near the lake's edge was soggy. Doming, Trace, Delgado, and the priest together lifted the box as if it were light as a word.

"I'll make sure you get back here for All Saints' evening, *Manang*," Doming said to her, when to her relief the high droning was finished. All Saints' celebration was only a few weeks away. Then, she thought, she would have true comfort and consolation. A whole night in which she could tell stories of her family, and of the old days with Mary.

Rue had not been able to come to the interment. She was ill with fever. Celia suspected it was dengue, remembered Rue's hands had felt warm, holding Celia's own hands at home and in the car. Celia felt torn between wanting to stay longer at the cemetery with Mary, and wanting to go home where she was needed.

That evening, at the Ayera house, she stood at her bedroom window and gazed north toward Manila. Celia thought about Mary's life, their life together.

Celia and Mary had spent those first years in Manila on a street called Calle Solano, in San Juan near the Cardinal's residence, the Villa San Miguel. It was 1932 when Baby's father had rescued Celia and Mary from his hemp factory, where their widowed father, who was the caretaker, couldn't care for them. They'd joined his fine household as maids. In a garage down the street from them in 1938, when Celia was sixteen, a poor seven-year-old girl watched over her younger brothers and sisters. The girl had come begging to them several times and Mary always fed her. Celia and Mary often sent food home with her. They seemed to have so much there in Baby's father's house compared to this poor oldest child. This girl was known then as Imelda Romuldez. It was she who became Madame Marcos. Celia and Baby's mother had died when they were young girls—so had Imelda's. When Mary learned that they had this in common, Mary mothered her, too. The girl has spunk, Mary would say. But during the war Baby's father moved his family and servants to Batangas. It was rumored he collaborated, supplied hemp, to the Japanese enemy. This was when they lost track of the girl.

In later years Mary would say that their lives had intertwined with Imelda's, and it was Imelda who had chosen the wrong fate, followed the braid of twisted hemp rope to hard-heartedness and treachery.

Who would have known that girl would be Imelda? Who would have imagined the grief the girl would bring to the whole country? Mary had helped that young girl, good Mary who sent scraps from Baby's father's dinner home with the girl. Mary, now buried in a cast-off dress, always said, Celia, we have so much more, we will share our hospitality with that wretched being.

Celia imagined that tonight, around Malacañang Palace, the buzzards circled. She'd heard the *tsismis* that Imelda was convinced someone regularly set the birds loose nearby and then bribed one of the many servants to put raw meat on the palace roof. Now they were camped on the eaves and made terrible cries. She imagined Imelda alone in her own room. Imelda heard the boats hooting forlornly on the Pasig River below her balcony.

Over the years Celia and Mary had finally agreed that perhaps Imelda was what any woman might become, if suddenly you could have any possession, anything, and you couldn't find the one thing that could hold or swallow the hollowness inside you. So you hoarded your own soul and everything else you could find, shoes, bags, houses, yachts, jewels, umbrellas, mountains, and it was as if you did not see all these things, but only what you did not have, and you couldn't name what was lacking and didn't know if you would recognize it. For a brief joyful moment you thought it was the babies of your own, those sweet ones, here was salvation, and yet soon they were with *yayas*, preferring *yayas*, who were always carefree and so patient, who knew how to mother and would teach the children how to share, and you knew only that you were still a seven-year-old and had four little ones who must not fall into the waters churning around the ferry that carried you back to Tacloban, little ones who would eat and eat so much and there would not be enough, there never would *be* enough, for you.

Celia's own priest always claimed that those souls whom Imelda and Marcos condemned to torture in the palace's Black Room and those she cheated knew her secret, even those who swept her streets knew, they knew the one secret that even Madame Imelda's fortuneteller would never declare to Madame, would not name for fear of her own life: It would have been so much better for Imelda if she'd grown up to become a street sweeper in Tacloban with a fine vegetable garden and an honest husband who was a fisherman—this had been revealed to the seer as Madame's bypassed fortune.

Compared to her, it seemed to Celia that she and Mary had lived very good and fruitful lives indeed.

Celia thought she heard her sister calling.

"Mary?" Celia called back, looking out the window. She could swear she heard Mary's voice calling her name. Celia went to her vanity. She took out a necklace, made of white mother of pearl carved into the shape of a dove, with grain-sized beads of pink abalone shell and turquoise-blue coral. This had been Mary's. Celia worked the beads like a rosary.

Then she realized it was Rue, calling her again from her room. Rue had never called out to Celia, summoned her like this. Celia rushed down the long hall to her. The embassy doctor Trace had called had already said sometimes the fever medicine for dengue was no use at all. You had to ride it out.

Celia saw Rue wrapped, from her tossing, in the white mosquito net that had fallen down around her. The veil fit her like a pupae, like a shroud, and Celia was very afraid of this sign. That Rue could die. If not of dengue, then of solitude.

During the evening mass for Mary, Rue had disregarded her own fevered unsteadiness, thinking it must be the sharp chemical smell of preserved plywood and the attar of *sampagita* garlands that a contrite Baby had covered Mary's plain box with, to Raymonde's displeasure.

On this first morning ill in bed, she heard military recruits run by in step, singing a chantlike song that matched their stride, the footsteps in unison, pounding the ground like her dusty heartbeat. She raised up on her elbow to look out the bank of bedroom windows to the east, and through the banana trees' green flags she saw it was only the polo horses from the stables of the Ayera club, taken out for morning exercise.

On the second morning she heard Taal Volcano rumble. There were black crows there, someone said. Come away from the edge, the crows said to her. Then they hobbled by in formation, their footsteps in unison, too.

On the third morning Lleoni came into the room and brought her thin rice—Rue saw an old woman so bent over from planting she could not stand straight, her bones fused.

This was dengue hemorrhagic fever, Breakbone fever. Her bones ached when she noticed them, as if they would break and tear off. She became like Taal, burning off some part of herself, some distrust of joy or promise or great gladness, a re-opening of marrow. No one gets such a fever for

294

so many days and emerges unchanged, she heard the embassy's doctor say to Celia and her husband. But it must bring its own course to bear, he added.

On the fourth morning, she fever-dreamed of days when she was learning to skate on the backwater bays of the Mississippi. Her father wears his blue-plaid wool jacket and laces up her skates and now he skates backwards in front of her until there it is, she becomes a swooping wild bird leaving him behind, skating away. The catch of metal blade to ice, the push, the slight shift of balance and then a glide, long and low.

Mabuhay, he says, as she skates away, *Mabuhay*, Live. Life to you abundant. Or does a man's voice—Doming's?—call that into her room, from the doorway.

But then her father lies down to sleep on the ice, and she understands she can no longer save him. She never could. I must go, she says. But she finds the whole world is frozen when he goes to sleep. The oceans freeze in mid-wave and are the color of light green jade.

She skates joyously up and down over the hills of waves, effortlessly skimming over this frozen sea. Seabirds and long-legged cranes, in gray and white formal jackets, watch her progress, nod at her beneficently.

Then she is falling through the ice, afraid she is freezing like her father. She is shaking and wet when she wakes up, but the fever is breaking.

She is saved. She is alone in her room.

For the next three days Rue could not eat. She had trouble swallowing even liquids. Celia worried aloud that her bones were being ground to dust. It will be a long recovery, the embassy doctor counseled.

Celia wanted to take Rue to a healer. She felt uneasy, sensed some trouble coming, and by the next afternoon she'd enlisted Doming to help her.

The healer, *hilot*, was one who practiced medicine without tools, only with his hands. Rue lay on a wooden cot looking up at a circle of chicken feathers above her. The *hilot* was saying the *Our Father*, she recognized the rhythm in the Tagalog words. She'd unbuttoned her white blouse, he said she could leave on her bra. He had her open her mouth and he pushed at her tongue, then his hand rested on her wrist. He put his ear to her stomach, then to her breastbone, the hard plate over her heart, and she listened with him to the creaking bone.

The only window was open and unscreened, and pink bougainvillea vines grew in old coffee cans placed on the sill. She heard the noise of traffic like a constant river. A rooster crowed. There were squatter shacks nearby. The low drone of a jet landing—the place was not far from the airport. She smelled the sewer, the bowels of the city, in the deep curbs along the street outside, mixed with the smell of *sampagita* flower necklaces hung near the bedside.

The healer washed her neck and shoulder blades with water and a sponge. The man's hands kneaded and worked the flesh of her neck, pushing hard into her skin, hand upon hand. She willed herself to stay put, to stay calm. In the hollow of her neck, at the base of her throat, he pushed with his three middle fingers.

"There is a blockage, here, your throat," the *hilot* said.

He placed a number of flat stones on her chest and breastbone and held his hands over her. Her heart beat like wings in her throat. She felt his hands push again into the hollow of her neck, and she struggled.

"You must let yourself—have faith, have courage," the man urged her.

To bend, to trust. She was on the edge.

"Don't be afraid," Doming said. He'd knelt and now took her hand in both of his, and it was over.

She sat up. She felt tired, unsteady. She'd done this for Celia, trusting her, and Celia had done it thinking to save her. This was a kind of love. But she had felt Doming's love as well, like a blessing upon her.

Doming watched Celia help Rue fasten the top buttons of her blouse. Her shoulders were slender and as pale as day-old rice. When she saw him watching, he looked away. He moved from her cot to stand at the window. More who sought the healer's services waited outside on a bench. It was not a secret. Yet he'd never believed. He was startled when the *hilot* spoke of her throat—in the beginning Hebrew he'd learned from Father Rex, *throat* was another translation of *soul*. The way a word could be for him a path, his way through the roots to some insight.

"She will be able to eat now," the healer said to Celia. "Give her goat's milk, each day, though most don't like it," he added.

The man came to the open window and threw the contents of the bowl out.

"What was wrong with her?" Doming asked, in a low voice.

"She carried some very old injury," the healer said.

"So what does it take for her to be cured, only faith?"

"Not faith. More like a dance. Hope is being able to hear the melody, but trust is the dancing," the hilot said. "I only saw her soul did not dance."

"You could do this if you wanted," he added. "I can see it in you, you are strong *here, dini.*"

The *hilot* tapped his own old drum chest with his fist, twice.

Then he drummed two times on Doming's breastbone, and Doming felt the knocking, and some part of his heart saying, Come in.

"Come back, I will teach you how," the *hilot* said.

"I'll think about it," Doming said, which they both understood meant no.

The *hilot* sat down. "I've made this offer to only a few, I'm curious why you hesitate," he said.

"They say you get these cures from a sleight of hand," Doming said.

"Believe what you want. It is the intellect, the eye that wants proof, more than the soul. I sense what logic needs to see. But if one is looking for tricks, he won't be cured.

"The healing part, the sense of what is lacking, the imagination to see the whole, you have that manner. No one can put it in you, but when it's there, I can help you use it," the man said, wiping his hands.

He took a pencil and wrote on a card.

"Here," he said, giving it to Doming. "I live in the hills above Los Baños, near Mount Makiling. Come visit me, when the time comes."

Doming read it. Not an address but cryptic directions and a rough map.

They stopped on the way home at an outdoor stand. For *bibingkas*, sweet cakes of coconut and rice flour, for her.

Baby had offered to let Rue use her family's ramshackle beach house as soon as she was well. Stay there for one night, breathe sea air, this is what will fully restore you, Baby urged. The only way there was by boat; she and Baby had taken a *banca* when she'd visited before.

Rue felt an urgency to go. She'd liked the place when she went with Baby. The little house seemed a refuge to her.

She had returned to work. She was rescuing what rice-plant samples she could from the still-flooded paddies.

The morning's newspapers spread on the table on the lanai reported that fifty thousand squatters who lived along the sea, in the reclaimed land, were homeless. Only those who had scurried to high ground, with their pieces of packing boxes and metal, could rebuild.

She read, over Trace's shoulder, a copy of a cable he was absorbed in. He sat with his coffee at the lanai table, writing:

> *Right wing political organizations directly controlled by Ess' intelligence apparatus, private militias and paramilitary are mercenaries for hire . . . One billion dollars in ten years in exchange for the military bases . . . future guarantees? Urge consideration of establishing new U.S. base in Mindanao, away from general population and protesters.*

Celia brought her milk.

"Drink this," she commanded.

Rue tasted warm goat's milk. Celia had located a supply from a local farmer near Ayera who delivered it each morning.

"This is a very bad idea, Ma'am, to go to the beach house just because Baby gave you the key; you don't even have your full strength back to go to work," Celia said. "And what if the one who takes you on the *banca* boat does not know how to find the place?"

Rue wanted to ignore her. She'd been cooped up in the house, first because of the rain and floods, then because of her illness. She was ready to fly away.

"I can take care of myself, Celia. You need more to think about than just worry about me," Rue said ungratefully. She despised the thick taste of the half-warm milk.

"You must know by now you can't tell Celia anything, once she has it in her head," Trace said. He'd made it clear he was provoked with Celia, that she had superstitiously taken Rue to the healer.

Rue saw Celia pucker her mouth in concern. Celia grieved for Mary and had no one left to worry about and that also frightened her and they both knew it. Celia was without relations now.

"This is a very bad idea, Ma'am."

"Nonsense, Celia," Rue said, but she felt badly because Celia's feelings were hurt.

Then Celia raised her voice, almost wailing—"I can sense trouble, something bad will come of it, and when I say that you all laugh at me, but I am warning you, Ma'am!"

Rue had never once heard her raise her voice.

Then Celia burst into tears. Perhaps she didn't know what to do next.

"I'm sorry, Celia, I didn't mean to forget you're still missing Mary," Rue said. To placate her Rue agreed she would take Celia's advice about traveling alone to Baby's place.

Celia turned on her heel with the tray, victorious. She went to the car in the garage nearby where Doming waited.

She made Doming swear that he would take a jeepney to the Rice Institute, wait for Rue, then be the one to drive Rue to the harbor in Nasugbu himself. He would be the one to make sure the *banca* boat owner knew how to cross the inlet to the house, that the waves were not too high for the little boat, and finally that the boat itself was safe, and that the man who would carry her there in the boat was not a bandit.

But what if the boat gets lost on the water, Trace said to Celia, kidding. Perhaps you should go along with her yourself, Celia.

No one took her seriously, Celia complained. But she pressed on.

So this was why Doming was waiting for Rue when she finished her work in the late afternoon. He would drive her car the sixty kilometers east from the Rice Institute in Los Baños, up along the edge of Taal, then down the hills to the harbor in Nasugbu.

This was the day when everything began to shift slightly. Everything was on a slight slope, not so noticeable to anyone. Not until they were almost at the edge of a vast crater, like Taal's, and suddenly the entire landscape changed.

"You don't look well, yet," Doming said, at the harbor. "What if you feel ill there?"

"I'm fine," she said.

"Your skin is as sallow as day-old cooked rice," he said.

Her luminous skin was her pride.

"The place may not be safe," he said.

"I'm only afraid of the military, and they won't be there."

She willed him to reach over and touch her but he did not. Neither could say the words.

He hired a *banca* boat to take her. "It's a fine evening, you'll be safe on the water," he began, as the boy took her cloth bags, one with a few clothes and one with food and bottled water, into the boat. The west sun was sending every color into the clouds.

She rode in the *banca* toward the beach house. The jagged hills around the harbor in Nasugbu came down almost to the water. They were the cooled lava that had flowed from the Taal volcano ages before. The land dropped into the water, only a narrow strip of fine-ground charcoal-colored sand and rock in places. The hills were deep green, jungle-like, with a rocky promontory between the harbor in Nasugbu and the point of land that curved out toward the South China Sea where the beach house was.

She was alone in a safe *banca* with the boy who steered, the boat a double outrigger with long bamboo stabilizers at the ends of arched rattan supports, like wings, that kept it from capsizing in the rolling waves of coastal waters. The *banca* was about twelve feet from stem to stern, with a small motor.

They came around the promontory from Nasugbu, from the southeast. The house stood in the secluded hillside, hidden from view. The place was marked by two almost identical barrel-palm trees that dipped out over the water at a sharp angle as the ground beneath them was torn away each year by tides. The boy pointed the boat in that direction.

The water was very still, the sun already setting as they came close to shore, and through clear water she saw the shallow bottom in the remaining light. Bright blue starfish, Pacific blues, the size and shape of children's hands. The clear water's refraction made it impossible to judge its depth. It seemed as deep as the sky. For a moment the earth and sky had traded places and she was looking down into the universe.

They passed over coral that grew near the beach, then suddenly there was an empty place of only dust and dry white skeletal remains.

"Dynamite," the boy said, over the loud motor. "Some of the new fishermen explode it in the coral, so the fish just float up to the surface. And some say the de Varcegnos had this done so a big boat can get closer to their place."

At the shore, the faint line of black beach was almost covered by the high tide. She waded through the water carrying the bags. The path up to the house was made of sand from the beach, edged by pieces of broken shells, the steps from round trunks of coconut palm. When she'd been there another time with Baby, Baby had the caretaker place oil torches along the path up to the low cottage. The torches had burned with an orange flame and sooty smoke. When she and Baby had approached the house by boat at night, the burning torches looked like some newly struck constellation in the low sky. Now the place was dark.

The long covered veranda faced the sea. A double door led inside from the center of the porch, and on each side of it were floor-length windows, their old-style shutters made of pearl-colored flat capiz shells set into latticed frames. The open windows would make the small rooms inside seem just an extension of the veranda. There were four rooms—a half-kitchen and dining room and two small bedrooms with windows that faced the sea.

The running water was brown, a small burner used bottled fuel, the electricity came from a noisy generator that Rue would do without. She and the boy unlocked the heavy door, found the oil torches and lit two, one on each side of the porch steps.

"I can send a girl to be here tomorrow to cook something for you, to clean it up a bit, Ma'am," the boy said, looking around. "She comes when the de Varcegnos are here, when they don't bring their maids."

"No, thanks, *salamat*, but I don't think I'll need her. Is there anyone else who is staying around here?" she said.

"No, Ma'am, the nearest house is between here and Nasugbu. The families that own them come from Manila on some weekends."

"When do I come back for you?" he said.

"Tomorrow morning, very early, *sige?*"

He nodded and went out. She heard his footsteps on the path, crunching the bits of shell a storm had brought up, and then heard the motor start, the sound of it carrying back across the water. She watched him from the door. The lantern he hung on the *banca* moved in the darkness across the water like a slowly falling star, a comet in slow motion.

She opened all the windows leading to the porch. She felt rooted somehow, calm. She could take a breath that someone else had not just breathed.

She walked barefoot, feeling the smooth bits of shell on the path she took back down to the sea. The dry sand at the water's edge was still warm on the soles of her feet, as if Taal's overflowing rock and lava, cremated bone and coral, were still cooling. The breeze seemed full of moisture, lush, ripe, coming from Ceylon and Borneo, Mindanao. It was like being touched. She left the clothes she took off, like a husk, on the black sand. The water was warmer than the air. She was careful of the sharp rocks and splintered coral near the shore. She felt her way blindly with her feet. Once farther out, she swam. The water was the temperature of her skin. She felt lifted up, weightless.

She could see up through the trees, the two yellow-orange kerosene torches marking the porch.

Doming was standing in the light between them.

She was glad. It was as if she had wished it. She was glad above the stars and out through the bottom of the sea. Waves that shone with bits of broken moon brushed against her. The water tasted salty and warm, green, blue, *matamís*. It was as if she were expecting him, but hadn't admitted her hope.

She raised up slightly so her shoulders were out of the water. She called out to him, not his name, but a low bird cry that carries over the water, a cry like the loons that she heard when they migrated from Minnesota and over their orchards when she was a child. When he reached the edge of the water, he stood for a long time.

He put his clothes next to hers, there on the black sand. Then he swam out to her.

He'd walked the several kilometers from the road near the harbor, the almost impassable road to the place.

It was difficult to explain even to himself why he was hurrying there, what he expected.

He didn't know the way to woo a woman. Despite his doubts, he felt she would not be afraid of him, though there was a friction between them that grated when their eyes met.

He composed his story; he told himself he would just check on her, see if she beckoned him. He left a way out for disappointment.

He wanted to move his hands up her bare legs, underneath her skirt, put his hand there, his mouth, then skin to perfect skin.

The smell of the mango here, or was it her perfume, the sound far away of dogs barking, the taste of salt still in their mouths, mixed with sweetness of a river. Faultless, smooth curve of thigh. Her hipbones where they jutted out left smooth hollows. They became like starving people given bread.

Later, they were several meters away from the shore, the tide coming in, the water only to their shoulders.

Tiny fish thin as centavos, shining like new silver, schooled around them—the hooked barbs of some stuck to her hair, caught against their skin, making tiny cuts like sharp barbwire.

They dove underwater and opened their eyes and even in the dark could see they were in the middle of millions of silver fish, a galaxy of silver, glittering, converging like mercury, like a flowing silver river of stars moving past as they traveled somewhere south on their journey. He wished he and Rue could simply go with them.

They swam among them, scooping up handfulls of silver life.

They went into the house, put out the oil lamp. He put his mouth on her breasts and then her mouth and breathed her in. He pressed her smooth as a dark moon.

The unshuttered window, the sea, the wind moving the mosquito net around them. To hear her say his name. Ikáw, ikáw, you, you.

"Tell me your real name," she said, later.

He would not, but he thought surely the words would fly out against his will, into her hair, her ear, onto her lips. And to what end?

His throat tightened around the words he would not say, his name. Until Abbe died, he'd trusted his own cunning, his intelligence, his will to survive, to live, more than anything else in the world. Now he trusted her as well. Even if this was a foolish thing.

"What if I look for you someday, and can't find you. Tell me at least the name of the place in Negros you come from," she urged.

"It doesn't matter," he said. "The people there are so abundant, so many, names don't matter."

"Your name does."

He considered. "The people there—when all else is gone, when the sun is cooling, when time itself is collapsing into gravity—they will endure. A name is nothing."

"If we trusted each other enough, you would tell me," she insisted.

For a while, he didn't answer.

He swallowed like stones the words he would not say.

"What is your *real* name, anyone's?" he asked finally. "I'd give you a new name. One that doesn't mean regret, but to turn the earth, to turn the galaxies, the center of the wheel, *Rueda*."

They slept, and he woke suddenly.

A lizard cried above them, where it hunted in the rafters, waking him up. It let out a shriek like some ancient prehistoric bird. Later he'd think it was a warning to them, to leave.

When he awoke it was about two o'clock. He was not certain he should leave her alone in the house. He touched her face, that face of light.

He lit the lamp and boiled water for coffee. He took the cup and sat on the porch and ate a few *pan de sal* rolls, a mango. At three o'clock he decided to leave while it was still dark. He walked back up the hill to the rough road and began the long walk to the place he'd left the car.

After a while he heard the sound of a motor, cursed to himself, and he waited behind a tree.

Within a minute an army jeep came around the rocky corner of the road that clung to the hills there. A jeep with the driver Delgado and Raymonde in the front seat and a young woman in the back. The motor gunned loudly up the steep hill ahead of them, leading only to the beach house, where she slept.

She woke up alone in darkness, to the sound of a motor whining. For a moment she imagined she was being carried through the sky in the *banca*, Doming the guide pointing out new planets, the Milky Way falling mist-like upon them. Doming was gone.

She remembered him leaving.

The engine noise came closer, she came fully awake.

He told her he'd wait for her in Nasugbu, to be cautious, taking no chances. Now she was afraid. She got dressed quickly, stepped out onto the porch through the long open window at the foot of the bed. She ran down the path toward the beach and stood hidden behind a squatty barrel-palm tree. She saw lights of a jeep that stopped on the old road above the house. One man carried a lantern with a purplish fluorescent light that threw ugly shadows. The torch lights had gone out, but in the kitchen the kerosene lantern burned.

She was careful not to touch the tree, because red ants sometimes lived in its flowers, but one found her anyway and she pulled at the thing behind her knee while hot pain seared.

"But someone is already here," Raymonde's voice slurred. "Let's hope it's not my wife," he said, mocking, and kicked the door open.

Rue heard the girl with him laugh softly, dove-like.

"Look around," Raymonde said to Delgado, who'd already sat down in a bamboo lounge chair.

She decided she must not wait any longer. She came up the path, willing her legs not to tremble.

"I was sitting on the dock," she said. She came into the harsh purple light. "Baby gave me the key for one night, I'm leaving in just a few hours."

Raymonde appraised her, frowning.

He put his arm around the girl's shoulders, pulling her toward him. She wore shorts, her stomach showing under a haltered top like the bar-girls. He looked mean, bleary eyed.

"Baby must have forgotten to tell me you were here," he said, "but this is our niece who has just arrived from the provinces, and Baby will be here later today."

Rue nodded. Any excuse would do, to save face, and it would not be mentioned again.

"Let me just get my things," she said. In the bedroom she grabbed the cloth bag, pulled off the sheets.

"I see you've already had breakfast," he said to her as she passed him in the main room. He was looking at the two cups on the table, the lantern burning low.

"Yes, I couldn't sleep."

"Afraid here all alone?" he said, a cross-tempered cunning. The purple lamplight swayed in his hand as he moved closer to her.

She didn't answer. She knew he was angry to be caught there. And it seemed he could smell her fear, and by instinct he would take advantage of this, feed upon it.

She backed up, toward the door, and he followed her step by step until he was too close, within a foot of her.

"Answer me!" he said. He grabbed her arm. She felt what Baby must feel, the black-hole force of a brutal man.

Doming followed the jeep on foot. He ran back up the hills. He was afraid for Rue to be there alone with two men, Delgado and another. He wasn't sure if the other was Raymonde. He used a stone and broke the lock of the large garage, a storage building on the hill above the house, thinking to find a tool or piece of board he could use as a weapon. What he saw in the half-light were large wooden boxes on pallets, floor to ceiling, *PROPERTY OF U.S. GOVERNMENT* stamped on the sides. *M-16 ARMALITES.* There would be thousands. He left them— he heard Raymonde shouting.

The driver Delgado noticed him just off the porch but said nothing.

He saw her dark eyes were black, with fright and anger. Raymonde shoved her, enjoying her fear, intimidating her so that she would not tell Baby she'd seen him at something.

He stepped onto the porch, into the fluorescent light.

"Leave her alone," he said. His first concern was that Raymonde not realize he'd been here with Rue.

Raymonde turned—pure hate flowed from him.

"What are you doing here? Who sent you to follow me?" Raymonde demanded.

"Only your drunken imagination—*langó guniguní*—follows you," he said. He gestured with a lift of his chin, as if legions stood just beyond the porch, coming from the garage carrying those M-16s.

Raymonde jerked round and looked.

"You're stalking me, for your employer, for who else," Raymonde concluded.

"Perhaps I am," Doming said.

"What do they want from me?"

Raymonde was suspicious always, paranoid when drunk. For good reason—many hated him. Doming had seen him almost schizoid in his paranoia for his own fiefdom and possessions.

But perhaps the driver Delgado sensed the truth, about Rue.

Delgado nodded at Doming, a smirky grin.

"I'll protect you, Sir," Delgado said.

"Shut the fuck up," Raymonde said, bleary-eyed.

"Who knows about the boxes stacked in the garage? How long have they been here?" Doming asked.

Raymonde recoiled. "You know they're for Ess, to be trans-shipped out of here tomorrow—and your employer knows all about it. That's why I'm here. Is that why he sent you? To see if I'll keep my word? Get into this deal and you're a dead man."

But the young woman with Raymonde, who'd been quiet all along, perhaps fearful now of trouble, wanting to make sure the night ended with her being well rewarded rather than in a brawl, began to pull at his shirt, where it tucked into his pants, whispering coaxing urgent words. Raymonde turned to her, distracted.

Doming turned to Rue. "Do you need a ride to leave here, Ma'am?"

"A boy from Nasugbu is coming with his *banca* just after daylight," she said, matching her tone to his.

"I'm going to the beach to wait, Raymonde, let me just get my things, I'll be out of your way," Rue said to him. "Baby just wanted me to rest here, I won't say I saw you, that's between the two of you," she added.

"He may have had too much drink to remember," Delgado whispered to them.

The girl guided Raymonde into the house.

Doming left. He felt Delgado watching him as he climbed up the steep path behind the house. He would sit on the hill above the house the next few hours, waiting until she left.

He'd thought they were taking no chances. Foolish. To leave her, to stay away from her in the future, would be an act of will, some perdition.

While he waited, Doming considered whether to tell the knife-sharpener that Raymonde could be ambushed at this house later that day. Here was his chance. Raymonde would be vulnerable, sleeping off his drunken night. This was the opportunity Sonny's friends were hoping for. Raymonde could be surprised; they could spare the girl. He would tell them to spare the driver Delgado. He would not tell them of the weapons.

But the idea of setting up Raymonde seemed too cowardly. It would not absolve him. He could not bring himself to simply arrange another's death.

He remembered the old saying—*He is very, very hungry, though he is carrying rice on his head*. He has what he needs and doesn't even realize it, Doming thought, and he looks in vain for deliverance.

He couldn't foist the act upon another—if it's to be done at all, Raymonde's death, I must be the one. But not yet, not yet.

He knew that Trace and Rue would be vulnerable to the same sort of ambush he contemplated now for Raymonde. But first he needed to make sure Paco and Linay were safe, out of the city. If anything happened to him they would have no one to look after them, to support them. So he had reason to wait, to hesitate. This was not the opportune time. Both sides claimed him.

He heard the sound of the *banca's* small engine from across the water, saw it pointed toward the dock below him, where she waited.

He thought he could not stop himself with her now. It was a kind of knowing, like working fresh earth and tasting it with hands and tongue and skin, but to what end.

"I'd do anything for you," she'd said earlier that night, "let me help you somehow."

He was amazed, glad.

"What would you want?" she said. "You could go to school, study, be anything."

But, he thought now, she just doesn't understand that there are no jobs for even college graduates. Doesn't she know about all the diploma mills in Manila turning out useless chaff, pieces of paper good for nothing, unless your family has connections. But she already gave her thoughts and prejudices away—that one must be an educated man. Without that, and without a name to begin with, he is nothing.

★ ★ ★

313

People can get lost, in a city of ten million where three million squatters have no fixed addresses. Doming worried that Angel would just disappear with the children, and he would not be able to find them.

A few days later he got word from Daniel Gold to meet him at the Regent Hotel on Wednesday night. Paco went with him. The note had come to the pawn shop, which was unexpected. He didn't know how Gold would know of the place, unless Sonny had told him.

Urgent. I am traveling to Negros. See me before I leave. I will carry the package for you.

The message didn't make sense to Doming. He didn't know about a package.

On nights when Imelda wasn't here at the Regent Hotel, young *baklas*, gays, in Manila would dress up like Imelda for Imelda Dress-up Nights. He and Paco went in. Tonight the Regent hotel was in full swing. In the lobby the Imelda impersonators shrieked with delight as each sashayed in, heeled, gowned, makeup subtle and hair piled high, each with a scarf worn over one shoulder, as a fortuneteller had once advised the First Lady.

Doming got out the card Daniel Gold had given him. Room 1004, Gold had written. Inside the elevator, Paco pushed several buttons on the panel. It would be Paco's first time in one. Doming saw him brace himself against the rising, bend his knees, go up on his toes.

From the elevator's glass sides, they looked across the street, across Roxas Boulevard toward the bay. There on sixteen acres of land that Imelda had reclaimed from the bay for her next building project, sixty-four thousand squatters had settled, a mass of brown shanties, mud and dust. He saw a long line, like ants; it would be women and children in line for a single water spigot.

"How old are you?" Gold said to Paco.

"Twelve years, Sir, and my sister Linay is six and our baby girl is almost one," Paco said. He stood up straighter.

"Here you are, Paco," Gold said. He turned on the luxurious room's television to a government station, a talent show. "Sit tight for a few minutes."

Paco plopped down on a dark leather couch.

Doming stood at the window that overlooked the coconut palms lining Roxas Boulevard. Ship lights on the bay glimmered. He'd never seen the city and bay from such a height. It was almost beautiful.

"What is this about a package?" Doming asked.

"It will be here in a few minutes," Gold said.

"I have a favor to ask of you in the meantime—in exchange for some information I can give you," Doming said.

Gold opened his hands. "You don't owe for any favor I'll do."

"*Sige*, never mind then," Doming began.

"It's something good, isn't it? Tell me," Gold said.

"Raymonde is storing arms, U.S.-supplied, cases and cases, at his beach house, passing them through the country. I think a private boat brings them in. They've cleared away coral. Ess and Marcos get some kickback, perhaps. He said Trace knows all about it."

"That does help me, it may confirm part of Boko Riccie's Iran story, the one that finally got him killed," Gold said. He gazed off, fingering the black chain around his neck.

Doming looked again toward the horizon. With the sun already set he could see now from this height the great curve of the earth, a line of pale fire the only boundary between earth and sky.

"So now, what can I do for you?" Gold asked.

"It's a big favor—the boy's mother, Angel, has told her boyfriend that the two older ones are her own brother and sister, that they'll be returning to the provinces soon. I've told her I'll help get them there, if that's what she wants. This is the only way he'll continue to support her, she believes. She's no longer so young, cannot be as young as she's claimed to him, if these are her children.

"If you're going to Negros, you can help get them out of here. Otherwise, the barrio captain has offered Angel money, for Paco and his sister, saying he would support them," Doming said.

Gold looked at Doming, raised one eyebrow. He understood. The children would be used in the sex trade, even if Angel was too naive to believe it. That's why Doming wanted to get them away.

"I know, you think I should be the one to go with them, but I tell you, they're no longer safe with me, I could be picked up at any time," Doming said.

Doming waited. He saw Paco was trying to listen, was ignoring the television.

"Why can't they just live with you?" Gold said to Doming, in a lower voice.

"I can send money for their school, but I can't have them alone at my place. I may be caught between General Ess and Raymonde de Varcegno on the one hand and the Sparrows who know I work for an American."

"Perhaps you should come along with us, and stay there as well," Gold said.

Doming shook his head. "I can't leave here, not yet."

"Is there anything I can do to help you?"

"Just get them safely to their grandmother's in Negros," Doming said. "You said, you're traveling there to take a package?"

Gold smiled.

He went to a side-door in his room that led to an adjoining room. He knocked, twice.

"Come in, *Pasukin*," a voice called.

The door opened, and there was Sonny.

Doming was overcome.

But Paco ran to him and held him round the waist, weeping for joy. His father Abbe had been dead for five weeks. The boy had not cried much until now.

Sonny said, "I know, I'm sorry, boy, that it isn't your father given back to you, but he saved me, he gave me his I.D., forged a picture in it. His smart thinking and generosity saved me," Sonny said.

So Sonny himself was the package Gold was delivering, Doming realized.

Gold agreed the children could travel with him and Sonny. They made their plans.

"I'm here only because you agreed to trade my safety for you cooperating with friends of Alejo, in the message you sent in," Sonny said.

He showed Doming the desk where his work was spread. He was translating documents for Gold. "I can be a new person—Abbe Villa Hermosa—and I'll get Paco and Linay settled with their grandmother, for you, we'll see to their schooling, then it's back here to fight on," Sonny said.

But Doming noticed Paco said nothing.

Sonny had new teeth. His head had been shaved, and now his hair was very short. He wore a white barong like Gold's. He wore rimmed glasses. All cleaned up, he looked again like one of the class he'd come from, the well-to-do. Yet, he was thin as a *balete* leaf and moved with stiff joints. His fingernails were purple-streaked to the base. He looked older than Celia now.

"In the future, you and even Paco can work with me, with my friends," Sonny said.

"Keep Paco out of this, Sonny. If I'm to do it, Paco and Linay must be out of the city. Angel wants them with their *lola*, and I have to know they're safe," Doming urged.

"Give me your word they'll be safe, traveling with you," Doming said, turning to Gold.

"I give you my word, I promise," Gold said.

Doming nodded.

"We'll leave within a week; bring them both to me in a few days, to the hotel, they'll stay with us in these rooms until we leave, no one would look here for Sonny," Gold said.

He took off the heavy black chain he always wore.

"Doming, under the black it's solid gold. It belonged to my godson, Boko's son. I want you to have it, *sige?*"

"I'd be honored," Doming said.

This is a good man, he decided. And our fates have entwined in each other's like a climbing helix-vine. He put out his hand, Gold grasped and shook it.

The only light in the room was from the disco lights from the top floors above them, reflecting outside, and the television Paco stared at.

Doming and Paco took the fire-escape stairs down the ten floors, walked through the grand lobby, and went out into the night. They would walk a few blocks south toward Baclaran Church, to catch the jeepney there.

Paco stopped. "*Tító*, you should help them kill those bad men who hurt Sonny—before they hurt us. I'll help you."

Doming wondered exactly what Paco had heard or understood.

"You must be very careful what you say," Doming said. Paco—ready to strike back, just a boy, and already wants to kill, he longs for revenge.

He looked around. He saw the guard at the entrance to the Regent watching them closely.

"Keep walking, Paco," Doming said sternly.

"No," the boy said.

Why did he choose now to be defiant?

"Were you listening up there?" Doming said.

"I already know. *Tító*, I'll be lonely, even with my grand-mother. Don't leave us there without you," Paco pleaded.

"Is there anywhere you'd feel safe?" Doming said, wanting to give him that.

"Only if Linay and I were with you," he said. "Keep us," he pleaded.

Paco had started out boldly but was overcome at the end of his statement and began to cry.

Doming put his arm around the boy and they walked together.

He was surprised at his distress for Paco, and in his own doubt at what must be done. We disappoint our children at every turn, he thought, they suffer because of our foolish-ness or urge to nobleness, even as we try to protect them from every danger.

Say he could find a way to keep Paco and Linay with him. Maybe Celia would help him. But even this impulse to just take Paco and Linay and have them live with him, even here, he hesitated. What could he promise these children?

319

He himself was hunted already. Sonny had warned him—Doming, I learned your name is on that list, you must begin again, with a different name.

Doming took Paco home. Angel was not there.

"She is not here so much, now, she works and stays at the *povlerone* factory, and when she is here she does not leave her bed," Paco said. "She fights with her boyfriend."

"Tell your mother we almost have things worked out; you'll go to the Regent Hotel in a week, and meet Gold there. Sonny will also travel with you, Paco, he loves you like your father did. Your mother will—"

He stopped. He didn't know. What would Angel do. Since Abbe's death she had half-lost her mind. She acted on impulse only.

He knelt and held Paco to him, feeling the boy's strong heartbeat that seemed to exactly match his own.

"I know it's the best place for Linay," Paco said, when he was calm.

"You're a good brother, Paco," Doming said.

He'd felt infuriated at his hesitation to simply rid the world of Raymonde and Ess. It would be a just act to cut off even a few legs of a thousand-tentacled octopus with the head of Marcos. Even Gold would not disagree.

At Paco's house, he tucked the boy into bed, checked on Linay already asleep in her mother's bed, alone. The baby was not there. He went to the front of the house, into the pawn shop, and took the Baby Jesus Santos from the front window. He would deliver it to Daniel Gold, who could sell it to a collector and use the money for the children. It was worth something. Abbe had never told Angel it had value.

She had no idea a thing that was chipped and worn could be worth much more than the new and shiny.

Doming found a white dishtowel to wrap around the almost life-sized figure. In his grip its pose looked less all-knowing and serene, with helpless hands outstretched, creases on the wooden forehead. He carefully rolled the dishtowel around the bundle and tied it with twine.

He left the pawn shop and returned to the Regent Hotel. A half-dozen young prostitutes were lined up outside on the steps. Several gestured to him, calling *Pogi, Pogi, Handsome*. It was almost midnight.

Gold was waiting for him just inside the lobby, as they'd agreed. Doming placed the cloth bundle into Gold's arms. "The hands are delicate, be careful," he said.

Gold cradled it on one arm as if it were a newborn.

"I'll keep this for them. You're doing the right thing for those kids," Gold said. "Bring them here next week, I'll buy their ferry tickets myself."

The next day Doming left word for the knife-sharpener that he was ready. They met in the Ayera night-market. The night air was cooler, now in late October. They sat in a booth where the knife-sharpener sometimes conducted his trade.

"If you don't accomplish this against de Varcegno, then you can be certain that your employer, and his wife, will be our targets some night soon, along with Raymonde," the knife-sharpener said.

Doming watched scorpions in a deep ceramic bowl in the next booth, delicacies to Chinese-Filipinos who'd cook them in oil and tamarind pulp. The bowl sat under a yellow light bulb. The curved spiders crawled over and over each other, in fruitless attempts to climb the sides and escape.

A few nights later Rue was with Trace and Carter after work, in the Embassy's Seafront Club along Roxas Boulevard. The club had originally been a rest and relaxation post for officers during the Viet Nam War. Now it served the embassy—a pool, tennis courts, a softball field, and a fine restaurant that served American food to Americans.

Music began. The night's show was a well-staged traveling cultural show, like those done in the big hotels in Manila with brass *kamalan* drums, a wooden xylophone, Spanish guitar, the bamboo dancers.

She watched a dance while the men talked, this dance left over from the Spaniards, three beautiful girls dancing with small goblets of oil in which a yellow flame burned. Each girl balanced the flames, one in each of her cupped palms and one on her head.

Then another dance, the *Binasuan*, where a glass of wine is balanced. Finally, the Bamboo Dance, *Tinikling*, the Philippine National Dance where they always look for volunteers.

She liked the compelling rhythm. She had tried the dance before—a driving five-beat rhythm made by the long bamboo poles held near the floor, pounded hard on it and then together. The dancers stepped between them.

Between the beats, she heard an American man behind her, talking loudly.

"These girls are gentle, quiet, respectful," he said, "all the stuff the Western women have given up. The men here are all show, no substance. Like little brown roosters. Have you ever seen a cockfight?" he asked the men with him. "Same thing. Give these guys some sharp blades, and they go at it like the other one is just another skinny neck and a bunch of feathers, until one is flopping around in the dust. But in the end, the owner takes the winning bird home with a string tied around its leg, and it's nothing but a chicken with a busy prick." They laughed, drank.

He was military, retired, from Clarke Air Base.

"I'll live here till the day I die," he said. "No taxes, still can get everything American at the PX. The Filipinos who think they can get rid of us, who think we're going to pack up Clarke and Subic and go home, they have monkey brains."

The bamboo dancing, the *Tinikling*, continued—each set of long bamboo poles was "played" by two experts who kneeled on the floor, facing each other, clapping the poles. Barefoot women and couples step-danced between them, jumping in and out as the pace quickened. Three sets were going at once, in unison. She was captivated by the hollow pounding. It was a dance of endurance. Some said it had begun as a punishment by the Spanish, for workers who moved too slowly in the fields.

After their demonstration the cultural dancers asked for volunteers to try it. A young woman came to her and Trace. He waved her off.

But Rue followed her to the spotlighted dance floor and took a place alone between the bamboo poles, waiting for the beat, self-conscious. What induced me, she wondered. They began slowly.

Soon it was a frantic sort of abandonment, trance-like, faster and faster, like time speeding up. The dancing would not end for her until a foot was caught. She concentrated and found the cadence, was light on her feet, and lasted the longest of the amateurs. Faster and faster and finally, she was caught. She heard some spectators clapping, some calling out bravo.

She was laughing when she looked up and saw Doming. He stood in the entrance hall.

He'd come in only to buy a newspaper, but he was entranced with her movement. He watched her gracefully stoop down and pick up her shoes and walk in her bare feet across the glowing wooden floor, as if walking on fire. He thought of the fire-walkers in Batangas, how they would dance across flames and not get burned.

He went out. He smelled smoke like burning electricity. Smoke hung over the softball field and the tennis court next to the parking lot like a black cloud, a cooking pot. There were no stars. He heard sirens.

There is a fire at the Regent Hotel, the Filipino guards at the Seafront Club gates told him. Doming ran the few blocks south along Roxas to the hotel. Flames were coming out near the top floors; he tried to guess which room was Gold's and which was Sonny's. He felt sick with despair. He searched the crowds of people looking for them, but he recognized only Raymonde and General Ess. They sat in Raymonde's open jeep. The driver Delgado was examining the Santos, Abbe's Santos of the infant Jesus. He tossed it to the ground.

Hate rose higher in Doming, like the leaping flames.

Imelda had built this luxury hotel, and her Cultural Center, and the Film Palace, all on reclaimed land along

Manila Bay. She calls it reclaimed, people said, but how do you reclaim something that was never yours, how do you reclaim the sea?

This hotel would not be missed. There were too many five stars competing. In the past few years cronies and military men had built these luxury hotels, using loaned money from the government—fourteen new ones, months of frenzied construction, getting ready for the World Bank Conference, rubbing their hands at the thought of six thousand international bankers and their wives. Fifty thousand workers around the clock, ten thousand alone on Imelda's own Regent and Plaza. Imelda had sixty thousand families removed, their shanties pulled down, and the families taken by garbage trucks under police guard to somewhere south of Manila, in Cavite. Finally she'd brought in eight thousand military to finish the job, but only half of the expected bankers showed up. Robert McNamara called for an end to world poverty, although he refused to meet with any families in the world's greatest slum, Tondo. In one week, in these hotels, bankers consumed more food in the dining rooms than the quarter million stomachs in Tondo had in a month.

But although the hotels were five-star, the top of luxury, they were poorly constructed, dirt and coal cinders had been mixed with cement by the contractors, and this hotel burned ferociously.

He ran the few blocks back to the Embassy club. They were waiting for him at the car.

When she came outside, the air was already hazy and Rue could smell sharp smoke. She, Trace, and Carter got in the car, and Doming drove out of the restricted American compound. Traffic outside the spacious grounds was backed up. Sirens blared, but fire trucks sat screaming, stuck in traffic.

Almost every floor of the Regent Hotel was on fire. She followed Trace and Carter, after they got out and began walking a half-block south along the boulevard. Men were shouting, gathering around the base of the hotel.

"What floor is the fire on?" Trace asked a man.

"It started on the upper floors, Sir. You stay here?"

"No," he said.

The sprinkler systems were run by pumps, and the electricity went out before the fire started. They were trying to pump water from the hotel pool.

"Some of the employees who were in the lobby say they were warned to disappear," the man added.

She heard the sound of glass shattering, high above. A few fire trucks that had reached the fire didn't have ladders high enough for even the fourth floor.

She saw Trace and Carter at an open jeep where Raymonde sat, parked off the boulevard under the coconut palms that bordered the bay. An orange sodium streetlight illuminated them. She saw General Ess get into an armored limo and drive away. Raymonde followed him.

How strange they both would be here.

Carter and Trace stayed there under the palms. They seemed to be arguing. Carter threw down his cigarette and stomped on it like a mad dance. Trace put his arm on the younger man's shoulder.

She walked up the street, back to the car.

"Did you see Ess and Raymonde over there?" Doming demanded. He'd waited there, standing outside the car.

"What do you mean?" she asked.

"Did Trace talk to them?" Doming demanded. "Did he know this was going to happen?"

"Of course not," she said.

"Sonny was hiding in that hotel, staying with Daniel Gold, on the tenth floor. I've heard people saying the fire started on that floor," Doming said.

She looked up. Glass exploded.

"They are murdering butchers," he said.

"Trace couldn't have been involved," she said.

Then Trace and Carter were in the headlights. She saw with shock that Carter was crying, wiping his eyes.

Raymonde and General Ess had something to do with the fire. She knew it. But she would not ask.

They would go home now.

When Doming left them in Ayera that night, he waited for a jeepney along Azapote Road.

He'd had a chance to set Raymonde up and he'd hesitated, sparing the man, and it had cost Sonny and Gold their lives, and cut off the chance for Paco and Linay to leave with them. He was thankful at least that he hadn't taken the children to them yet.

And what about the rest?—a monstrous act to destroy so many, to get at one, or two.

He took a jeepney to find Paco and Linay. He would deliver them to the ferry himself, buy a ticket, and pay someone to look after them. He touched the blackened chain at his neck. He would use this. But their house was closed up. Bed-clothes and food were scattered. The neighbor said that when Angel learned of the fire, she'd panicked, crying that it was the place where Sonny was staying, where Paco and Linay were to be taken. She'd fled with them in fear.

Late that night he went to find the knife-sharpener in his usual place in the night-market, outside Ayera compound, even though it was late. The man sat with his sharpening stone, his bicycle wheel turning a belt.

"Raymonde and perhaps General Ess will be in Los Baños two nights from now, at the cockfight arena," Doming said, without preliminaries. He'd overheard some discussion between Trace and Carter, about going to the cockfights Sunday night in Los Baños. Raymonde had told the men that he and the general were just passing by the hotel after an illegal private round of cockfight-betting in nearby Baclaran. That is why he was not pleased to see them. He had lost so badly. He would make it up in a few nights.

So it would be there in Los Baños that the two of them, Doming and the knife-sharpener, would strike.

"I'll back you up, I'll have a motor-scooter so we can escape."

Doming's gaze was fixed on the kerosene lamp.

"Where do you come from, where is your home?" Doming asked the knife-sharpener.

The man sat on his bicycle, sharpening a knife for one of the guards. Sparks flew out.

The man looked at him, suspiciously. "Don't ask for any answer that they could pound out of you, if they catch us," he warned.

"You're too suspicious of me," Doming said. "I just want to know who I'm entering into this deed with; if we're to support each other, I want to know who you are. Sonny told you about me, you have the advantage."

"We are not wooing here, there is no need for mutual exchange of confidences, though it is good you do not trust too easily. Perhaps you think I work for the other side?" the knife-sharpener said.

Doming said nothing. But he felt the hairs on his neck kindle in quick heat.

The man smiled, a cunning amused face.

"I was not always a knife-sharpener. I was in the Constabulary, and I became one of Ninoy's keepers; for five of the last years he was held in solitary, I was one of his guards.

"I'm from Ilocos Norte, Ess' province. I joined the military as a young man, for the power I'd have in the barrio, for safety for my own family. When they sent me to fight in the south, to Mindanao, I told myself these were not my own people in this place. We slaughtered them like pigs, left them to bloat in the sun. It was wrong.

"But then I was assigned to Fort Bonifacio and after a time I became one of Ninoy's guards. I was the one who watched him when he was alone, heard him reading aloud, praying. I was there when he proclaimed a hunger strike in 1975, and accompanied him when they rushed him to the hospital; he'd dropped seventy pounds. He—plump Ninoy—weighed one-hundred-twenty. He told us, the guards—the only ones he could talk to—the long fast of his hunger strike changed everything for him. He began to speak out, even from prison. He would run for office from there.

"Marcos sensed this. Ninoy, an honest man still unafraid. So he had Ninoy charged with being involved in some government official's ambush and the sentence was death. No one knew what day it would be, but I was one of those who escorted him to Malacañang when Marcos announced he would be executed the next morning, shot by a firing squad at dawn. I was one of those who guarded him through the night, only to have day after day of waiting for a sentence that was never carried out. Finally, the date was set— November the twenty-fifth, of 1977. It's not so long ago."

"But they didn't kill him," Doming said.

"You don't remember this, Ninoy's death sentence? President Carter's ambassador threatened Marcos, his funding," the knife-sharpener said, glancing up at him from his work.

Doming shook his head.

"You see, that is what those in power would like to have, our memories. I am memory.

"And all this time he was alone, held in solitary, seven years and seven months, except for his guards. Finally, Marcos let his family visit. To watch this man day by day, who thought each day would be his last, each time to see his family for what might be his last, to see how he would not relent, would hold on for our people. It changed my heart.

"When he is our leader, the Filipino people will come together. Those in power sense this, his patient hope," the knife-sharpener concluded. He took the blade from the stone, wet it again, wiped it. Felt its sharpness with his tongue.

"But he has said many times that the Filipino people are worth dying for, not *killing* for," Doming said. He couldn't resist the argument. "They say his years in solitary chastened him, changed him. Ninoy would not want you to kill on his behalf, killing is never right."

"He must be given a chance, this time. Marcos stole that from him. So we must clear the way for when he comes, by doing away now with those who would use any means to stop him from coming home, whether Ninoy wishes it or not," the man said.

"You sound like John the Baptist—and you know what happened to him? His head was delivered to the wife of the emperor on a platter," Doming said.

"What would you have us do?" the knife-sharpener asked him. He worked at the blade more furiously, spinning the wheel.

Doming spoke over the harsh sound of metal on stone.

"The most dangerous words to a tyrant are those that make people laugh at him, to see his banality, to take away the mystery of his evil," Doming said. "Our own complicity is in not speaking up like Ninoy does."

"Ninoy would die to save us, would you?" the man spat at him. "Will words save us?" the knife-sharpener asked. "I warn you, they did not save your friend Sonny, the people in the hotel; they won't save your employer—or his wife," he said.

They agreed they would meet in two nights, at the cockfight arena in Los Baños. That would be the night of All Saints' Day.

"If you don't see me, look for the one who wears a wrap like this one." He pointed to the black and white woven hand-loomed cloth he always wore wrapped around his head, so that he could pull one portion down over his mouth and nose, leaving a gap for his eyes. "This will be a sign that all is ready, from your partner," the knife-sharpener said.

"And if I don't do this?" Doming asked.

"We'll follow Caldwell's car each night this coming week to each stop, until Raymonde is with them. He won't have his bodyguards like he does when he's alone. And whoever is in the car will be done for."

He handed the sharpened knife with a sheath to Doming. "Carry this, it's for you," he said.

Doming would not remember how long he walked, along Azapote Road, on the way home. He wanted to savor these last two days.

Early the next morning, Celia had the local papers spread out at Rue's place on the bamboo table on the lanai. Rue read each one. They reported that even as the fire raged on, some volunteer rescuers at the scene removed valuables, rings, watches, wallets from the bodies. The wife of the chef's assistant, in the basement restaurant, whose body was brought out unmarked, having succumbed early on to smoke inhalation, stated that even by then his wedding ring was gone.

She read a story on each of the three foreigners who died, including Daniel Gold, the journalist for the *Christian Science Monitor*, the article ending with the fact that twenty Filipinos were believed to have perished, including ten staff.

The papers reported that the wine cellar was emptied that night, and the hotel vault, while there were still people alive in upstairs rooms. The papers carried quotes from the local mayor in that section of the city, Cuneta, the same mayor who refused to approve a new street scheduled to be built through his vast property so that fire trucks wouldn't sit backed up by traffic.

The mayor said, "What else do you expect from these firemen? They make two hundred pesos only each month from the government. Even if many do their duty, can they live on that amount? Of course not. This disaster is a bonanza for them. They may have picked up more in saleables than their salary for the entire year. With their pay, that's how they live."

The papers reported that the fire trucks sent from Makati, the ones that carried hook and ladders that would reach at least to the fifth floor, had been stuck in traffic. They're trained only for the back streets of Cubao or Paranaque, a hose fire, the idea is to put enough water on a fire to keep it from spreading to every house in the neighborhood. If one family loses a house, the neighbors and relatives will help provide. There is pressure on the family not to speak up and report missing valuables, or the next time the police or firemen may not come at all when they are called.

"It isn't that easy a thing just to phone for help," a Filipina woman was quoted. "You know how many busy signals you get, how many wrong numbers, and crossed lines, people telling you to hang up, they're already talking on that line. Often we just send a young boy running, it's quicker, and then he rides back with them, pointing the way. Even if it's a squatter area there's the chance of some booty."

Within weeks squatter families and their goats would be living in shanties built on the steps and in the burned-out lobby of the hotel's shell.

By noon the same day, the last phone call came for Trace. The defense attaché reported that Daniel Gold had been found tied up, handcuffed to a bathroom sink, on the hotel floor where the fire started, when he died. She knew Doming's friend Sonny had been there as well. No one mentioned another man.

Phone calls had come to Trace all night and throughout the morning. She listened. He made no effort to keep it from her. The official police reports stated that Gold had been engaged in some sexual encounter, reportedly tied in some way by a teen-aged boy who'd apparently become angry, set the fire, and run from the hotel. The police had him. He had confessed.

That afternoon Carter McCall came to the house. He brought the ambassador, Ed Lange, for a private meeting. Daniel Gold's wife had been calling the embassy from Hong Kong all night, with wild accusations.

Rue brought drinks to the men who met on the lanai, and she sat down with them and listened. Trace and Carter agreed that with the military running all the courts, the lawsuits could take forever, there would likely never be blame assigned, that a commission might be set up for an inquiry, but by the time it had issued any findings, witnesses that had turned up would likely have disappeared or been paid off, official files lost or misplaced.

"Why can't you do something for Gold's wife?" Rue asked.

Trace explained that the first word among the legal attachés and their inside group at the State Department was that they must remember that the Embassy's presence, their presence, in the country was political, not personal. They needed to think about the contacts to maintain, and also the frailty or the loss of face, they might appear to have to their Filipino counterparts if they reacted to this woman's pleas emotionally.

"It's a private matter, not a political or international one," Trace said.

This was the ambassador's bottom line, he said.

"Besides, Gold had excellent life insurance, inquiries were made, his family will be well-provided for," the ambassador continued.

This enraged her, she wanted to slap the man. She hated his voice, the cultivated prissy tone that Trace emulated. The bottom line, he explained, was that no one can afford to go out on a limb on this, no one wants to risk it. The embassy might find a way to arrange some settlement with the widow, a payoff, Trace and Carter and the ambassador explained to her.

"It's blood money," she said to them.

"This doesn't even concern you, Rue. How well *did* you know him, you're over-reacting," Trace said. His face was dead to her. The ambassador examined his college ring.

"What does the autopsy show?" Ambassador Lange asked vaguely.

"Multiple stab wounds," Carter said. "Torture, then asphyxiation by smoke."

"He was murdered, and what about all the others who were there?" she cried.

The three men left in the ambassador's car, for the embassy.

Late in the day, Doming came to the house. He sat in the maid's kitchen looking at newspapers. Rue found him there.

"What have you heard about the fire, what does it have to do with Sonny and Daniel Gold, or you?" she asked. The official headlines screamed in bold print about the American found tied up, a hint of scandal. That story sold the papers. The story of the fire was secondary. She wiped off the ink that smeared like soft soot from the pulpy newspapers onto her fingertips.

335

"There are as many rumors as there are people to invent them, each thinks that it relates to their own interests. So it's difficult to look at it objectively," he said.

"What do you think?" She wondered if he would tell her the truth.

"Some are saying it is because the hotel's Filipino ownership interest is held by a former crony of Marcos who had a falling-out when the First Lady's hand reached into his pocket too deeply.

"The barrio captain says it is because the local mayor received an offer for the land around the hotel. He said the mayor's son was paying off some families' survivors already, for their silence.

"The official newspaper says the NPA wants to endanger the tourist trade, keep the country on the edge of bankruptcy just as Marcos says we're beginning to make some recovery.

"A woman in the Cavite market says it is well known that the First Lady was offended by a snub from the wife of the owner, having been kept waiting at the entrance to the disco one night with her entourage, and vowed revenge.

"The jeepney driver says it's almost the Christmas season and there haven't been any big fires this year and so the fire chief and his superiors saw this as a way to get some booty and to pay off their men, since there are too many five-star hotels in the city anyway.

"The priest at mass says it is because there is corruption everywhere and this hotel owner was a good man who refused to pay off the inspectors and tax authorities, the local mayor and the police, so they made an example of him to other businesses in the city.

"One who is not a fool says it is because Gold was about to finish a news story linking Marcos and the U.S. to smuggled weapons, passing through this country."

She nodded.

"And your friend Sonny?" she asked.

"He must have been in there, he was staying with Gold. But he died like all the others, murdered to get at one. Sonny was just chaff to them, kindling. Did you see in the paper that it gave the names of the three foreigners killed, and added, *and more than 30 Filipinos*? They were the maids and busboys and laundry girls, invisible, or nameless, like Sonny. His death doesn't matter to anyone but me."

She saw his rage over Sonny, but had no words. He waited for her to speak.

She'd never seen such anguish. She was afraid of it.

"Did you see Ess' black limousine parked along the other side of the street from the hotel, pulled onto the side-walk under the palms there?

"Didn't you see that the window was rolled down a bit so the sounds of dying could be heard, so the futile efforts of a few would-be rescuers mocked?" he said, his voice rising sarcastically.

"Doming, there's nothing you could have done, you're not responsible."

"See, you're stupid, stupid—we're all responsible. And you don't know what I could have done, you could be in danger and you wouldn't even see it," he lashed out at her.

"Don't you pay attention to what's around you when you leave this safe place in Ayera? You must, from now on.

"It was Ess, he loves to see his victims afterwards. Raymonde was with him. They're murdering bastards, and they should be made to pay for this," he said.

They stood outside the garage now. She looked off at the southern horizon, the empty space Taal Volcano had once occupied.

"Don't go near Raymonde or his house, he's a marked man, now, we'll be after him."

She felt a surge of terror for Doming. He would risk his own life, she thought, to get at Raymonde and Ess. He would leave her for that. It made her hate him.

She said, "You're becoming just like they are."

"Just saying that shows how foolish you are," he said, still angry. "It's getting late, I'll go home."

He started to leave her. "I'll have to leave in a few days."

Her fear flared up in anger at him. "Doming, don't do this, stay in Manila, don't go away—if you're not afraid," she said, purposely misunderstanding. She knew he was not, she was the one afraid, of losing him. She was afraid she was not as important to him as other obligations he had, as important to him as he was to her. Perhaps this was selfish, she thought, and she regretted the words as soon as she said them.

"Is that what you think, that I'm afraid so I'm running home to the provinces?" he said, indignant, choking out the words. "Do you think me capable of that?" he said. "Of running away, just to save *myself* like I did when I was a boy?"

"No." She'd hurt him.

He took her shoulders, turned her to look at him.

"I'm caught in the middle, I have to choose, I'm trying to protect you."

"I don't need that—you're becoming just like Raymonde and Ess and Trace, you're just as bad. You're all dying inside, from violence and hate," she said.

He tried to continue. "It's not that I'm afraid for myself, but for you, if you're with him, they—"

He couldn't say the words. "And you're the one who's like those with power over another—righteous, naive innocents, using power like a child with a cleaver," he continued.

He seemed already far away from her.

She touched his face, his jaw.

"I feel half crazy," he said.

He turned away, began walking back and forth, pacing. He picked up a rock and heaved it toward the field beyond the house, a sound of effort like a groan.

He stopped.

There was more he wasn't telling her. They were running out of time.

"Where can we go?" she said. She didn't know if she meant for the moment, or for a lifetime. Why can't we just be each other's country, she wanted to say.

"Come to my house tomorrow, late in the day, you must."

She agreed. She saw Celia was gathering up her things in the kitchen, coming toward them.

He told her how to find his place.

"Don't carry a bag or anything, so beggars don't follow you to the door. You'll pass," he said. He left her.

Mid-afternoon the next day, Sunday, Rue drove her old car west along Azapote Road just past the pottery vendors. Large ceramic pots lined the road, pots fired cobalt blue and jade-green, with dragons etched into them, each dragon's tail circling the pot, as if eating itself. The pottery vendor was the place where Doming had told her to turn toward Cavite.

She parked in the lot of a restaurant where large families with their grandparents and cousins sat on a covered porch, families of twelve or twenty. Chunky Chinese-looking children ate as juice ran down their fat chins. Darker, thinner children hovered just beyond the canvas and vine-covered porch. They would grab the leftovers when the family departed. They watched the diners without expectation of hand-outs.

She walked through the market to blasts of American music. The voices of the few competing vendors rose up harshly. One old woman's hair looked hacked off with dull shears. Flies struck down by the heat rested on the algae in the still canal, like thick brocade.

She followed the directions, crossed a deep-set river on a high slatted bridge, over the steep-sided chasm filled with green, with vines hanging from trees like curtains. On the other side, beyond a wall, she saw the factory-houses built of mud bricks with second-hand tile roofs, each two sharing a common wall. The narrow lane between them was rutted. In the heat of a Sunday mid-afternoon, no one stirred.

Look for a wooden gate, paint peeling from dry gray wood that used to be turquoise, now the gray-green the color of the sea. It's the only gate that color, he said, that's how you'll know. They're not numbered.

She entered a small courtyard with a bamboo chair and *kalamansi* bushes growing in old tires. In front of her black pots were stacked in an open shed. This area would be where the cooking was done, outdoors to be cooler, shared with the people next door. To her left a small window with wooden slats set in, a few missing, and an open door. It was dark inside against the glare around her. She couldn't see anything inside but she wanted to get in the shade. She called his name, surprised he wasn't there. Perhaps some strangers would come home and find her in their house. Perhaps he'd already gone away.

A wooden table stood in the center of the room with two rattan chairs and a metal folding chair. A swallow startled and flew out. On the table a tea pot and a cup with clear tea still in it. Cracks in the tile roof let bits of light in. A bird cheeped. Straw from a nest hung down near the window.

She explored the house. On one shelf cans of condensed milk, a bag of rice, tins of coffee and tea, a dark jar that held sugar, eggs in a chipped porcelain bowl. Along the window a basket with fruit, mango, banana, durian. Three plates and two spoons, two cups, a glass, all in a plastic drainer on the shelf. A tin of crackers, a kerosene lantern in a corner.

No running water, no fan, not even a light bulb hanging bare from the ceiling.

She'd asked him once why he didn't use illegal hookups to run a fan like the other squatters did, when he said he didn't sleep well because of the heat. He said sleeping in the heat was better than worrying about a possible fire from the wiring.

She went in the back room. A few shirts hung over a hemp rope line. A round face-sized mirror with the backing peeling off, a tin wash basin with a gecko on the damp wood next to it. A bookshelf held four rows of books, some with paper covers torn off so the yellowed spines showed.

But what dominated both rooms, propped against the walls, were large wooden-framed and stretched canvases in various stages of white. Some had drawings, patterns of turtles, lizards, and fish surrounded by designs that looked like *ikat*-cloth shapes of tribal animals. The names of colors were neatly written in: *black, ocher, scarlet, copper, white.* Samples of the patterns he'd copied from pictures were propped against them. In a work corner the floor was dusted with a chalky white substance and bits of dried colors. Brushes in glass jars, the smell of rice flour and turpentine.

She looked around, trying to get some sense of why he was leaving, why he had nothing packed to take along. She wanted to memorize everything.

On the bottom shelf of books in the back room she saw a familiar brown rough weave, folded over into a square. She reached for the brown cassock and shook it open. She recognized the robe she'd once seen him wear. She held it up.

"What are you doing?" Doming asked.

She startled.

He'd come back. He carried bottled water and a San Miguel. "I thought you'd be thirsty," he said, more kindly, setting the bottles down on the table. He opened the water, held up the glass to the light, wiped it, poured the water and held it out to her, gestured for her to sit at the table.

He was quiet, watched her look around.

Their angry words of the day before were still between them.

"I've never had a woman come here before," he said. "I know you must think it's very rough, but, you know, it's better than what many have."

"I see that, I don't care, why—"

"Let's just have some time together, *sige?*" he said.

He was restless, nervous. He took a sharp pick, sat on the low stool and began to pick out hardened grainy-looking paste from a small plastic tub.

"What is that?" She said. It looked like children's cereal, cooked and hardened there.

"It's the base for the canvas, like priming it, before someone paints on it. See, I put six or eight coats on the linen to get the canvas ready."

"Did you just leave that there to harden?"

"Yes, I was interrupted, I couldn't work."

He finished hacking at it, poured the pieces out. Then he poured the dry white rice flour and put the red plastic pan on the floor in front of him, rubbing his thumb over his fingertips to smooth out the lumps. He added some water. It became a thin paste.

She watched him, thinking, what have I come for.

He was on edge, she thought, not wanting her, doing something with his hands so he wouldn't have to touch her.

She didn't realize he was spending what might be his last few days as a free man with her. She didn't know that if he put his hands on her skin again he was afraid he would never be able to take them off her.

"You must think I'm very primitive," he said with false humility, "squatting here like a peasant at my work." She realized he was doing this on purpose. He had read her mind. She was wondering how he could sit like that, and then she thought he was doing it to make himself look worse, awkward.

But she said, "I'm wondering, do you discern a drawing in there, its lines in a stew, as you're working it?"

"As I paint the layers of white on, I imagine the rich Filipino in his *sala* on Sunday afternoon with his paint-by-number kit, being creative, painting in gold-color where I told him to put copper. The next week he has it framed and has his maid hang it in the *sala* and calls it all own work," he said dismissively.

"How did you learn this?"

"To stretch and prepare the base of a white canvas? Father Rex. He could draw and did paintings of the landscape, smaller ones, that he rolled up into tubes and sent home. He worked with small Chinese brushes, some only a few hairs. He called it his only vice. I built the frames for the canvases, I could always work with wood. He had books the missionary women had sent, religious art and some other paintings. When he looked at that book, I knew he was homesick for civilization."

"The drawing is good," she said. She felt he purposely kept her at a distance, and she felt desperate.

"It's just copying," he said. It was as if he were testing her.

"I like it here, it's quiet," she said after a while.

"Not at night, everyone's napping now in the heat of the day. But at night, children crying, neighbors fighting, drinking, singing. Many drink cheap gin, cough syrup even, just to knock themselves out enough to sleep through the night despite the noise, the heat, their worries. That's what it would be like to live here, to live with me, for you."

Two children came running in. A boy and girl burst through the door. The girl glared at her and then talked excitedly to Doming in Tagalog. He gave them money, a few pesos in change from his pocket.

She heard him say the word *manang* to them, gesturing toward her, a word of respect for older women. Then they smiled, nodded at her, and dashed out. Doming followed them to the wooden gate and locked it.

"Did you call me *manang* to them, old woman?" she asked, indignant, when he came back in.

"Do you want them to tell their parents that I have a beautiful woman here with me? If I say *manang* they won't know the difference, that's what they'll say. Don't you know they can't tell one foreigner from another, that you all look alike to them?" he asked, laughing.

"I told them you're ordering some canvases," he said.

A bird flew in and out, intent on building a nest on the perch just above the window. She couldn't bear to just sit and watch him.

"I'm not sure if I'll come back here one day or not," he began.

"I want to go wherever you go," she said.

Without a pause he took hold of her ankle, her foot propped on the stool next to him, where her frayed light jeans ended, took her dusty sandals off her feet, his hands wet with the rice paste.

His hand around her ankle like a heavy bracelet.

"It's—" she began, pulling away.

"What? Too dirty, too messy, too poor for you?" His voice was impatient, agonized.

"No, only too public," she said.

He got up, closed the door, locked it, pulled one of the largest white canvases in front of the west window, another over the window to the courtyard.

He was talking to her as they stood there, against the center wooden post, then his mouth deep on her mouth, his hand on the back of her neck. The cool cement on her feet, the cool stucco against her back.

The late afternoon sun sent its own color through the canvas. The room glowed like the inside of a sweet ripe papaya. He breathed in her breath. The sound of water running in the river and children playing in it became muffled. The high squeak of wheels from a fruit vendor's cart came from just on the other side of the wall. Now the room was dark as dusk, western light shining through the cracked tiles and the canvas glowing with the last canted light.

He dressed. She walked around the rooms once more, as if learning them. On the shelf in the back room she noticed a pair of earrings, the patina on them old and fine.

"Whose are these?" she said, suddenly pained with jealousy.

He smiled. Did he feel delight in her quick misery?

"They were my mother's, her mother's before that. They're from the *Tiboli*, try them on."

He showed her how to pry open the soft gold metal, like a tiny clam shell. She put the earring on, bending her neck, adjusting the brass, gently squeezing it together again, then took up the matching one. From the gold hung ornate carved discs made of nacre, mother-of-pearl. He watched her try to peer at herself in the dark mirror, satisfied.

He pressed against her back and hips, the back of her neck, where her hair was damp with sweat. If they could just stay like this, stop time.

"Keep them, I want you to have them," he said, without hesitation, pleased to offer her the most beautiful object he had to give. And it was timely—he would leave this house and take little with him.

He told her about the *Tiboli* country, the hills and lakes in Southwest Cotobato on Mindanao. How he remembered leaving the place in Mindanao when he was about three years old. Often riding on a man's back, accompanied by a colossal dog. The rocking of the ferry. His mother's music.

How even in Negros his mother still played the *hagalong*, a long slender spindle-shaped wooden guitar with only two strings, one giving the melody and the other, called the drone, playing a single note, like a chant.

He told Rue how in her hands the instrument could make the sounds of a husband and wife fighting, of lovers wooing, of a woodpecker, not only with the strings' melody but her thumb tapping another rhythm against the body, she could make the sound of a man's hoeing.

What became of her music, she asked him.

He didn't know.

"The same that will happen to her people in Mindanao, their hills and lakes?" he said. Between the military and claims by mining and forestry interests, the beauty would be lost. The people would be scattered remnants.

He noticed that the colors of dried paints and white rice powder from the floor now decorated her feet and legs. He got some water, added *kalamansi* to it, and helped her wash off the colors.

"We must leave here now," he said. He wouldn't stay here tonight. He'd sleep in a jeepney parked in the market and come back early in the morning. In a day or so he'd leave everything behind.

"You're going, you're doing this because of me," she said.

She looked around.

"Keep this with you," she said. She picked up the brown cassock and handed it to him.

The next afternoon there was a memorial service for Daniel Gold, organized by friends from the university and other journalists. Because Gold was an American who had died in their host country, some from the embassy's diplomatic corps would attend as well.

Rue and Trace took their reserved seats in the tiny balcony of the church. It was built of timber and stone, an Episcopal parish just off McKinley Road. Gold was Jewish, but this was all his friends could arrange. A few in the foreign diplomatic corps had reserved the small balcony for themselves because it was safer, less exposed. The Canadian ambassador's driver guarded the stairs.

Gold's widow, a Filipina, walked into the service alone. She would not allow her children back into the country from Hong Kong, even for a memorial. She sat alone, straight-backed, looking ahead, her face hidden under a black lace mantilla.

Doming had driven Trace and Rue there. On the way to the service Doming had heard the pop of a motorcycle backfiring. He registered, more than saw, Trace's involuntary flinching. Doming watched everywhere for Sparrows, listened for the sputtering of their small scooter motorcycles. He drove them into the city and up to Forbes Park for the funeral. He wore his best white barong and stood in the back for the service. In his mind, this memorial was for Sonny as well as Gold. Gold would have a Jewish service in Hong Kong, but this was all Sonny would have.

The service began. The foreigners did not speak to each other or visit during the service, unlike the Filipinos. He'd never been to a foreigner's funeral or wedding. They were such a stiff people.

May Michael the Standard-Bearer lead them into the Holy Light, he prayed, for Sonny and Gold.

In the middle of the readings, a sharp splat echoed in the arched stone vault—a black prayer book, lobbed like a grenade from the balcony, smacked to the floor of the center aisle. The women gasped in unison. The men ducked their heads, raised their shoulders, involuntarily shielding themselves from the sound.

Then he heard her voice above him, clear and unfaltering, ring through the small vaulted chamber.

"It's just like he said about us all, so careful, careful to say nothing, to do nothing that might offend, take no responsibility for lives that are buried or cut short by force—we are fools," she said. Her voice was cool water on parched stone.

Rue.

Someone up there shushed her, a low voice.

But she would not relent. "We're all responsible for this, if we simply keep quiet," she persisted, raising her voice over those around her trying to make her sit down.

Doming walked forward along the side aisle to get a view upstairs. He saw Trace stand up to walk out. She had shamed him, Doming saw, named him. She had broken out of some self-exile. Doming glanced outside through the deep-set window next to him. Trace would leave by himself.

But then Madeline Valenzuela Gold turned around. She lifted the lace edging of her head covering and looked up at the balcony to see the shadow still standing in front of a rose-colored stained glass window. Doming saw her face— proud, fearsome, vindicated. It only took the voice of one, unwilling to connive, to strengthen her.

We are not excused, Doming thought.

"Would anyone else like to speak, in remembrance of the deceased?" the Filipino Episcopal priest asked. Of course, the priest hadn't known Daniel, but it was clear that this could turn into a political event and perhaps offend some of his well-heeled parishioners.

Doming decided, he came forward. He stood at the lectern, faced the fifty people gathered. In the back of the church, four bulky men in white barong, military monitors who carried sidearms, came alert. He saw Raymonde, who'd come in late, take a seat.

He swallowed. His mouth felt hot, the heat of all those words not yet spoken.

"I will simply read this quote," he began, and took a folded piece of paper from his pocket. He'd found it as he went through Sonny's things a few weeks before.

He read aloud:

> "The Filipino has lost his soul and courage. Our people have come to the point of despair. Justice and security are myths. Our government is gripped in the iron hand of venality, its treasury barren. Its resources are wasted, its civil service slothful and indifferent. Not one hero alone do I ask, but many."

He folded the paper. He looked up at the people there. He took a breath.

"Sonny Mercado was one hero, Daniel Gold was another. They worked together and died together. We can no longer be silent, we are not excused," he said. A few of Gold's friends from the university clapped.

"The writer criticizes the government, in violation of the Subversives Act—who is he?" one of the men in the back shouted out.

"A dead man's words cannot be used against him, so this man is responsible as well," Raymonde added, assuming the writer was Gold.

The men in the back moved forward as if ordered.

"But the writer is not dead yet," Doming began.

"Then who wrote this?" Raymonde demanded.

The spectators, for that is what they'd become, it seemed to Doming, sat hushed.

Doming held up the folded clipping. "It's an excerpt from Marcos' 1966 Inaugural speech," he said. Sonny had clipped the quote from an old college history book.

"Where did you find it?"

"Is it not in Marcos' newly written history books?" Doming answered, making his voice one of naive surprise.

Even the military monitors could not disguise their confusion.

Light seemed to break in through the dark leaded windows. People began to snicker, then gave way to laughter. It was as if the words had opened up their ears, cleared their heads, made the dust fall from their eyes.

Raymonde's mouth was open. He looked like one of the open-mouthed gargoyles along the stone church's roof whose mouths disgorge rain from the gutters. *Gurgulio*, gargoyle in Latin, Doming thought, throat, windpipe. And you are dry and empty-mouthed, Raymonde, against the truth.

The priest signaled the organist.

She began to play a dirge-like melody.

"In your hymn books, number two-forty-three," he intoned.

Doming went out through a side-door, into the churchyard.

Two of the men in white barongs met him there. In the daylight he saw they were younger than he, barely of shaving age, but thickly built.

"Identification," one demanded.

Doming showed it.

The man looked at it, then put it in his pants pocket.

"Who are you?" Doming asked. He would not ask him to return it.

They were from Fort Bonifacio, just up McKinley Road.

"You're charged with using subversive speech."

"I swear to you, it's Marcos' own," Doming said.

351

"It doesn't matter. Anything critical of the government is prohibited, is grounds for arrest for subversion."

But the more intelligent looking of the two hesitated. Doming saw his chance.

"If they are from pre-martial law years and are Marcos' own words, can he use his own words against himself?" Doming asked. Marcos, brilliant in his command of legalese, would use just such a circular argument.

"You will be in great trouble if you bring his words to light under a worthless statute, shaming him," Doming added.

Doming watched the young men consult, their low tones like the plaintive buzzing of flies. Then, the people began coming out. The service had ended.

"Get out of here," one began. "We'll have you inside Bonifacio within the week."

The service had ended. Rue and a handful of foreigners walked down the stone steps into the courtyard. He shook his head slightly, saying no to Rue's questioning look. Don't come near me.

Her friend Anne drove her home.

November 1, 1982, All Saints' Day

In the late morning, on All Saints' Day, Celia witnessed an unsettling event. She sat at her upstairs window, which faced northeast. The winds were stirring. It had been a hot morning, very still, but now she noticed clouds gathering over Laguna, and then they spun and one dropped a tail down into the water, like a funnel cloud, and a brown water spout simply rose up, out of the water. It moved toward the shore, spiraling gray and muddy water, bigger and bigger, monstrous. Then the water spout must have traveled across the water to the fish pens where freshwater fish were raised. Finally, it seemed to be over land, coming up the rise toward Ayera. She could not leave the window. She could not even look away.

But once the waterspout moved only a kilometer over the land, it lost its fuel and stood still and then the fish it carried fell out. This happened over the main highway. Lleoni was on a bus on her way home to Ayera from a morning off. Fish came down on the bus like rain, every size, she said. Of course the cars and buses stopped, and we all began to gather them up.

Celia marveled.

Lleoni brought home these very fresh fish. People gathered them up in baskets, like a miracle, like manna in the wilderness, she said to Celia. Freshwater fish in the market were so expensive. But then those who raised fish in the pens of Laguna de Bay came running up the hill from the lake and complaining, Lleoni said. What do you want with dead fish, the people asked them, and how will you claim which fish is your own?

There would be nothing allowed in the newspapers about it even though hundreds of people witnessed it.

Celia realized it was just as her priest had predicted. This was a sign of the approaching end of Marcos' ten-thousand year rule—fish will fall from the skies.

My priest says if you look at prophecy, it is just a matter of seeing present times differently, of looking at the loom instead of the warp and weave, Celia said to Lleoni.

By early afternoon Celia saw Rue coming home. This pleased her. Rue could drive her in the old car to the cemetery if Doming didn't appear soon. For November 1, All Saints' Day, Doming had promised to go to the cemetery late that afternoon, but he hadn't shown up. Maybe Trace wouldn't let him go, she worried. This was the most important holiday of the year for her now.

By dusk at the cemeteries on All Saints' Day, the graves or crypts will have been swept and washed clean, the inscriptions repainted. The people spend the day and night there preparing, then eating and drinking at graveside picnics. They have long mahjong sessions. The click of played white bone echoes. They play bingo and cards, make music, sing the old songs, like a fiesta. Celia, having no family to share the bounty of her cooking with or to pass the time with, and because it was unacceptable to go to the place unaccompanied, had asked Rue to be her guest.

Celia spent the rest of the afternoon cooking. She hummed happily in her little kitchen, as if the food she made would be shared with Mary.

So in the little cemetery where her father and now her sister rested, in the town of Pila, near the Laguna de Bay, at dusk, the people sang and played guitar, sang the songs Celia and the others asked for. To Celia it seemed the old sisters Mount Makiling and Mount Banihaw watched over them.

Several old men brought their instruments—harmonica, guitar, wooden flute—and sang together. Neighbors at the crypts nearby, who often saw each other only that one day a year, year after year, were deferential to Celia. She'd suffered the most recent bereavement, and this was her first time at her sister's tomb.

They feasted. Celia shared her food, *babingka, adobo, pancit noodles, lumpia,* fresh grilled fish. Later they heard the sound of gunshots and the children whimpered. It's just fireworks, the women told each other, don't worry. She saw Doming arrive late. He sat down to play cards with the old men.

As the evening grew dark, the cemetery glowed with the candles placed on each crypt and with the holiday faces.

Then someone began the "Bayan Ko," My Country. To sing it was to risk arrest or worse.

The voices so full, half-sorrowful joy and half-drunkenness. Even Celia drank one San Miguel and became almost tipsy.

"I'd like to sing a song that my grandmother taught us," she announced, formally.

"It is a song in English," she said. "My grandmother lived to be an old woman. When we were young, she would sing this for Mary and me. She told us how the American soldiers taught her this song. They were here after the war with the Spanish. I sing this for my beloved American guest."

"A song by Mister Stephen Foster," Rue heard Celia say. Rue saw her lift her chin proudly, like Baby would have. Celia sang, alone, in a clear trembling voice in the yellow-candled light. She rocked slightly back and forth, in a lullaby-like rhythm—

> *Beautiful dreamer, wake unto me,*
> *Starlight and dewdrops are waiting for thee;*
> *Sounds of the rude world heard in the day,*
> *Lull'd by the moon-light have all pass'd away.*
>
> *Beautiful dreamer, queen of my song,*
> *List while I woo thee with soft melody;*
> *Gone are the cares of life's busy throng,*
> *Beautiful dreamer, awake unto me.*

Some began to play guitars to accompany her, picking up her tune with tremulous echoes.

Doming approached Rue. He seemed remote, preoccupied, already gone from her, their tender words of a few days ago almost painful. Their actions at the memorial service seemed to have exiled them from others. She would not think of the memorial service.

But now he came to her and they danced, waltzed, one two three, one two three, wake two three, me two three. Under a massive tamarind tree, they danced, slowly at first, lifting their feet over the cords of tree roots as if stepping between the clapping poles of the bamboo *tinikling*, then faster, among the tombs, down the path, turning into the night, into the fog along the ground.

Where did you learn, she began to ask, and then she remembered. The fat lady at the Polo Club, some good has come of it.

She felt as if they would always dance, that they could just go on and on, two three, two three, that this moment would last and last. She marveled at the change within her. To just be the song, the dance, the rhythm.

The music ended. They stopped dancing.

Some people began to pack up their things to leave.

"I want to stay with her, Ma'am, a little longer," Celia said to Rue. To Celia, Mary was as real as Rue and Doming on this night.

"I can get a ride with the neighbors," Celia suggested.

"No, I'll wait," Rue said.

Celia gathered up her empty dishes of food and plates.

"We must pray for those who have gone before us," someone said, beginning a Hail Mary.

"And who will pray for Marcos when he is gone," someone shouted from the darkness.

"Marcos has a solid gold baby Jesus in Malacañang. He pays in advance for his masses, many, many. Already the bribes are in place," a drunk voice answered.

"Imelda will buy her way directly into heaven," a voice called.

"Then she will tear down heaven's palace and have it remodeled and rebuilt within a week," Doming said. "She'll bribe the landlord."

"But does God take bribes?" another voice called.

"Why not, isn't he a landowner?" Doming said.

"Will a billion pesos buy her way in?"

Doming said, "I'll tell you how it will be." Some settled in to listen. Stories were the best part of this night.

"Imagine our blind God," Doming began. "He can conceive all, but sees nothing here on earth. His eyes are as covered as a newborn kitten's. So he won't know who they are when they arrive, Marcos and Imelda. Imelda will have pulled her hair down like a peasant woman. She'll wear an old house-dress and slippers. Marcos will be wearing his medals."

"And God will say, an old war hero and his wife have arrived—Saint Pedro, let them pass."

"I am here to see the cockfights, Sir, Marcos will say."

"Good morning, Sir, says Imelda. At first we were so poor on earth we had to build our house out of coconuts. But we used the talents you gave us Sir, multiplied them, helped the poor, brought them Bliss."

First Doming did the Ilocos Norte accent of Marcos, then the high voice of Imelda, and now the resonant voice of God.

"But God will say, I know only what I hear from my priests and bishops and cardinals."

"Don't believe everything you hear from that fat Chinese, Cardinal Sin, Imelda says then."

"But Marcos, always calmer, of course, always ready to make a deal and to charm, says, Sir, if you need real eyes, to see as we do on earth, I think I can get you some."

"And God says, How is that?"

"And Marcos answers, In the hospitals my lady has built, people sell their kidneys, they are willing to part with one, to help others. If we did it right, Sir, we could find two brown eyes. Two peasant farmers could each give up one, the rice harvests are not so good this year."

"Why not three? God interrupts him."

"I'm sure we could, Sir. Marcos feels he almost has him."

"And one blue, I want one blue eye, God demands."

"That would be more difficult, Sir, Marcos says, hedging."

"Is there no one who sells blue eyes, then?"

"There are no blue-eyed Filipinos, Sir."

"And why are they the only ones who sell?"

"Because, because, Sir,—and here Marcos thinks frantically."

"Because we are the most generous people in the world, Imelda says quickly."

"Then I shall have yours, says God."

"And he plucks out an eye of Marcos and an eye of Imelda, and they stumble away, holding onto each other, one looking left and one right."

"Marcos is upset."

"Hush, Imelda scolds him, we'll buy more. And she reaches into her plump bosom for the gold that is hidden there."

Doming paused. Rue saw more people had gathered around to listen.

"Where does the third eye come from," someone asked, "the blue eye?"

"To get the blue eye, Marcos snatches one eye out of the albino carabao who wanders in the fields of heaven that Imelda has already begun clearing for her new projects," Doming concluded. He made a playful snatch at the boy who sat nearest him. The boy jumped, then smiled sheepishly. The ones who'd listened, sitting on the lantern-decorated crypts around him, applauded.

Celia made her *sssst* sound, her crackly brown face drawn up. She took Doming's chin in her hand as if he were a boy and shook it.

"This is a terrible story you tell about God," she said, laughing. "Yet somehow I could believe it, I could see it," she said.

"And what did you think?" he asked Rue.

"I'd listen to your stories forever."

"What if they run out one day?" he said.

"Pah," Celia interrupted. "The world will never run out of stories for you. You give us hope. Look at them, what fineness you have wrought, crafting your words like fine iron."

The faces of the people leaving the cemetery looked satisfied, jubilant, determined. Doming thought of Rizal, whose execution by the Spanish changed nothing and yet changed everything. Rizal had celebrated his people's endurance, their will and laughter that not even three hundred years of Spanish tyranny could tamp out. Nourished by stories and songs and poetry, their hearts would always spring green, like young rice shoots.

He felt freer than at any time since he was a young boy with Father Rex when everything seemed possible for him, for his people, for the earth itself. Wild-rice seeds of endurance, newly sprung.

Father Rex had spoken of living as if, *parang*, my boy, live *as if* you are above tyranny. Resist the inclination to strike back or give up in resignation. Then you are already free, the dragon has no power over you. Do not let evil dictate your terms—both acceptance and counter-violence are evil. We must name the jawed dragon, its fear of goodness and its hatred of those who speak truth in its face.

Yes, Doming thought. If I mirror the evil in their hearts with my own inclination to violence and revenge—that worm that gnaws us all—it will eat away at my soul. But if I name it, then I am made whole. So I can not keep silent against the dragon's violence, no matter how bloodied I become. Call it by name in story and song and imagination. And laughter. That, too, is a form of resistance, Father Rex had said.

How close he'd come to entering that gyre of violence. He had agreed to meet the knife-sharpener very late tonight, at the cockfights. He'd learned Raymonde and Ess would be there on this holiday. But if he became like Sonny, taking on Sonny's desire for retribution, or like the knife-sharpener, accepting the justifications of violence to gain peace, he would only feed the dragon's voraciousness. Never had violence ever brought healing; never did striking out in revenge, or believing the angels were on your own side, ever bring anything other than more violence.

"What is it?" Rue asked.

He would not kill, one death would not protect her, this beloved companion of his mind. Just say it, he thought. Tell her the truth and leave.

He felt a settling into his own body.

"You were once what I despised most, and it was like despising myself, and now I love you.

Her face filled with light.

The party-makers were dispersing to their own family graves and night of watch.

"I have to go away," Doming said to her, when they were alone.

The words pierced her. "But you'll come back again?" she said. The sky had grown dark. It seemed to her that ghosts still hovered among the treetops. Stars glowed like embers over a ruin-strewn land. She did not have one regret.

"I will not," he said.

"Let me go with you."

"You can't be there, but—just know Raymonde will be hunted until he dies. Swear to me you'll stay away from him, warn Trace."

"Only if you promise you'll meet me later. Go to the mango grove in the hills above the Rice Institute, go there tonight no matter what. Promise," she insisted. "I'll wait for you tomorrow."

His heart leaped at her word. Promise. *Promitterre*, to let go, to send forth.

"I promise." He smiled. The mango grove was in the lava foothills below Mount Makiling. Where the healer lived, the one he'd been to see with her when she was sick.

"You are my own grace," he said. He held her face in his hands like one who, as he leaves a beloved place, takes in one last time the fix of light and contours of landscape.

Doming got his pack from near the gate of the cemetery, an abaca mat in which he'd wrapped a few things from home, including the cassock. Then he walked along an open road toward the cockfight arena. He cut through a vast pineapple field with soft soil. He thought of Abbe, how Angel said he always smelled of pineapple. He had no plan, except to find the knife-sharpener, call it off. He walked like a carabao in a mud paddy, onward.

When he drew near the arena he hid his pack under a stand of banana trees. He passed through the parking area at the edge of the field. It was filled with jeepneys, pedi-cabs, and a few fine cars. He heard the crowd's shouts rise up. At the entrance he paid five pesos and passed through the wooden stile, feeling his hips trapped for a few moments between its turnings. He heard the noise of the finish followed by silence. Then he felt the quake of stamping feet, the crowd's spewing chant, *itó na, itó na.* He walked through an opening between the stands into the heat. He spotted Raymonde in the packed stands, sitting alone near the front row. He was brushing dust off his lap with a pure white handkerchief that could have been a signal of surrender.

Raymonde glanced up and looked at him with the cooly appraising eyes of an assassin. Then he smiled and held up his brown beer bottle, gesturing for Doming to join him. Doming nodded in acknowledgment but went out-side, troubled, wary.

Delgado, Raymonde's driver, approached him.

"Why is Raymonde friendly to me tonight, what's he planning?" Doming asked.

"What do you give me if I tell you?"

"A chain of solid gold," Doming said. He yanked the blackened chain Daniel Gold had given him from around his neck.

Delgado examined it, taking his time.

"He plans to kill you next, now that Gold is done," Delgado said. "You caught him in his business for Ess, that night at the beach-house."

Doming nodded.

"Be careful, he carries a blade tonight, a *tarì* razor. He had to give up his gun to me so he would be admitted into the arena," Delgado said. This was the rule in case some did not lose gracefully.

"Why isn't Ess with him tonight?" he asked.

"He's being *entertained* in the owner's private *sala* in the house across the field." Delgado said, delicately. "I'm waiting for them."

"Delgado, Raymonde is a marked man tonight, you could be in the middle. He'll kill you, too, eventually, for all the things you know. Leave now, save yourself," Doming urged.

Delgado examined the chain, pouring it fluidly from hand to hand.

Delgado turned to go, then swung back. "What would you say if I told you he wanted me to be the one to get rid of you, on his behalf?"

"How much would he pay you?"

"Less than the value of this gold," Delgado said.

They heard the chant, *Itó na, itó na*, It is, It is. A match played out.

Delgado left. Doming watched him dodge between parked cars and jeepneys. Then, to his astonishment, Sonny emerged from behind one of the cars, walking out as if from a dark grave. He'd wrapped a black and white cloth around his forehead like the knife-sharpener. Sonny put his hand to his mouth, signaling Doming not to call out to him. So Sonny was the other Sparrow tonight. The knowledge came to Doming like an arrow, a fishhook caught in his chest. If one Sparrow misses, the other does not.

"Delgado, Delgado!" Raymonde came out through the turnstile, calling for his bodyguard.

Doming rushed to him. "Get down," he said, pushing Raymonde's shoulders. "Watch out, now, Delgado's finished with you."

They squatted next to some hens' brooding boxes.

"Nonsense, Delgado watches over me like a dog watches his house," Raymonde said. But he didn't get up.

A Babel-like cacophony came from inside the arena. Bets shouted out to the Kristos for the new match drowned out the first of Doming's low-voiced warnings.

"Do it, do it!" Sonny was calling, urging Doming on from a distance.

Raymonde also heard, and recognized the trap.

"Doming, have pity, I have a new son."

Raymonde began to sweat from fear. It was clear that Delgado would not protect him.

"A new son? Aren't all Filipinos each other's sons or brothers?" Doming said.

"We can change everything between us," Raymonde began. He would work his way out of a trap like the *babuy-ramo*, wild boar.

"What, what could change between us, Raymonde?"

"We can help each other now—spare me—and for you, a new house, a business. I'll set you up. It's my promise, that's my final word."

"Raymonde, your kind no longer has the final word."

"*Itó na, itó na!*" The crowds' crying came to them. A match ended.

Raymonde gazed at him, not understanding.

Then Sonny stood over them, a curved *bolo* knife in his raised hand. He swung the knife toward Raymonde's neck as if he were threshing a harvest.

"Sonny, wait, let's take him to the field," Doming said. He would buy some time.

Sonny held the knife to Raymonde's back as they guided him. If Raymonde cried out, the blade would slip into his spine and kidney.

"Have pity," Raymonde pleaded.

"Do you wet yourself already? Just wait, it will grow worse; when you die your bowels release. I saw it often," Sonny said.

Doming led them to the pineapple field beyond the parking area. The sound of frayed leaves of banana trees made *shhh* noises in the night wind. Chirps and chants of frogs and lizards: four calls, a pause, then four more. Thousands of stars, bright enough to give off some milky light, became visible.

The three men stood in the field, not far from the house where General Ess relaxed. Only one window there was bright.

"I feel like some music, what about you?" Doming said. "Let's have a song, Raymonde."

Sonny smiled. It was not uncommon for those with a vocation for torture, like Ess, to put their victims to some tests.

Raymonde began to bleat a popular song, the first words of "Pamuwilanen," a love song Marcos often requested.

"Sing the 'Bayan Ko,'" Doming said.

Raymonde hesitated.

"You want pity? Sing, Brother!" Doming demanded.

"We will die together," Raymonde moaned. The song was banned. Ess would fire into the darkness at the song, without hesitation.

"Like brothers," Sonny said.

Raymonde began weakly. The tune carried up into the night.

"Louder," Doming said.

Raymonde sang in slow measures:

> *Philippines, My Heart's sole burning fire,*
> *Cradle of my tears, my misery,*
> *All that I desire—*
> *To see you rise forever, free!*

On the third line, the door of the house flew open.

By the fourth line, the crowd that had gathered round the edge of the field, watching the shadows, perhaps hoping to see a knife fight, began laughing. Even the stars and shadowed mountains seemed to laugh.

"Who mocks me?" General Ess called out.

"*Pô*, it's me," Raymonde called.

"It's me, it's me, it's me," some in the crowd called.

"*Itó na, itó na*," It is, it is. The sound of voices betting on one certain death.

A rooster crowed, then again.

"Sing on," Sonny said. He pushed into Raymonde's back with his sharp knife, commanding him.

A spot of blood appeared on Raymonde's light blue barong. Sonny recoiled. Good, Doming thought. Even the sight of his enemy's blood is repugnant to him. Perhaps Sonny has extracted sufficient vengeance.

Raymonde sang again.

A few onlookers on the edge of the field joined in with him.

366

"Who began this?" Ess called, belligerent, trying to take charge.

No one pointed toward Raymonde.

Ess took unsteady aim with his pistol and shot several times into the air, reasserting his authority.

The people sang.

"It's just words, Sir," someone called out to Ess.

The singing became louder.

"See, Marcos and Ess and you who serve them will not have the final word," Doming said.

Raymonde's voice broke. His energy seemed to drain out of him.

All the people joined in on the chorus:

> *Birds that freely claim the skies to fly*
> *When imprisoned mourn, protest and cry!*
> *How much deeper will a land most fair*
> *Yearn to break the chains of sad despair . . .*

Raymonde wept, from fear or shame. The words of the song came out of Raymonde in jagged breaths. Where had he learned them? Then Doming guessed—it was said Ess forced some victims to sing their opposition song when they were tortured, then he would cut their tongues and make them swallow. Raymonde had been a part of this as well. His singing was a lament.

The people sang, the vendors and children who could not afford the price of admission for the cockfights, and the drivers who waited for those inside. This is what Marcos feared, thought Doming, the breaking of silence. Ninoy sang in his chains, like Paul in prison. Their voices grew joyful and defiant. Singing to bring the future about, singing as if.

Inside the cockfight arena, the Kristos took their bets.

The song ended.

The singers gathered at the edge of the field laughed and cheered.

Ess realized he was alone, undefended. His guards had left him. His host, the house's owner, had mingled with the crowd. Ess backed into the house like a crab scuttling into its hole and slammed the door. He would abandon Raymonde to them in order to save himself.

Doming heard a motorcycle's putter start up.

"Heto, heto, Here he is," Sonny cried to someone beyond the perimeter of starlight.

Raymonde took his chance and leaped at Sonny, knocking him over so that his head thumped the ground like a ripe fruit. He drew out the *tarì* razor and put it to Sonny's throat.

Doming pulled Raymonde off. They were eye to eye.

"Do it," groaned Sonny. Raymonde struck.

Doming felt the *tarì*-blade sink deep into his right shoulder. He grabbed the hand that held the blade, cutting cleanly into his own hand. He gasped and twisted the blade into Raymonde's forearm like a fishhook.

Raymonde cursed in pain. "Assassin!"

As if summoned by Raymonde's word, the motorcycle pulled up. The knife-sharpener. Sonny stumbled to his feet and climbed onto the seat behind him.

"I'll do it," the knife-sharpener said, balancing on his seat.

"Move," he commanded Doming.

Doming stood between him and Raymonde. He would not move.

Raymonde began to run.

Itó na, Itó na.

Doming heard a single shot sound and at the same instant Raymonde cried out and jerked like a fish caught on a line. His legs wobbled and went limp beneath him.

The spectators, who'd been expecting a knife fight, scattered at the sound of the shot.

The motorcycle revved to a high pitch and in moments the two men on it were gone.

"Save me," Raymonde called out. No one came to him.

Doming ran through the field to get his pack and be gone. The smell of pineapple filled his nostrils. He felt the bleeding, then smelled the blood like the inside of a rusty iron cooking pot. Blood soaked through his white t-shirt, where his shoulder met his chest. When he reached his pack, he tore the shirt off, wrapped it around his arm and over his shoulder, and pulled out Father Rex's cassock. As he walked, he slipped the long sleeves down over his hands and pulled the brown hood over his head, down to his eyes. He knotted the roped belt low.

He walked deliberately, the slow stately walk of a priest with all the time in eternity, to where Raymonde lay. Only a few had gathered near Raymonde. No one acted to aid him. He was known and despised.

Raymonde's eyes were closed. He lay on his side, legs twisted.

"A priest, a priest is here," someone said.

Doming knelt down on one knee beside him.

"Save me, save me, Father, I cannot feel my legs," Raymonde said. His skin looked sallow. He'd suddenly grown old.

Doming kneeled closer to him, inches from his face, recited a few words of prayer, the quick cadence and tone of Father Rex. He put out his hand and realized it was bloodied, from the *tari* blade Raymonde had carried.

Raymonde saw it and drew back his head in alarm, to look into Doming's face. "Assassin," he called. But no person moved to help him.

"Will no one help you?" Doming asked.

"You would finish me now?" Raymonde said.

"I won't be your executioner," Doming said.

Itó na, itó na. The call came to him across the field's soft-soiled ground like a petition, imploring that this be so.

"Get him a car, get him on his way, his pockets are full of cash for the one who aids him," Doming said. A few onlookers scurried to obey orders.

He felt light-headed when he stood up.

No one stopped him. He passed under some *acacia* trees along the road, walking calmly. He smelled smoke. The house where General Ess was hiding was in flames.

Sonny and the knife-sharpener sped by him on the road. Ess would die by the fire they started. "Join us, we'll hide you in our place near Magdalena," they urged.

He said no.

Ess would not come out of the house. Like children hectoring a crab from its hiding place, the people gathered.

Sonny and the knife-sharpener had poured gasoline around the outside. In moments flames were consuming the framed house. The *nipa* thatched roof became a burning torch. Lizards who lived in the thatch shed half-melted tails and shimmied down the posts to the ground. Sparrows who nested there flew up, the last with feathers aflame.

No trace of the general was ever found. Some would claim that like a crab, he'd retreated deeper and deeper into the house's underground rice-storage cellar, that he'd emerged unscathed two days later and fled. Others were certain that they saw his dark shadow among the flames, twisting like a *gagamba*, a spider, when you hold a match to it.

Doming walked toward the mountains beyond the Rice Institute. His shoulder bled afresh when he tried to run. He thought the *tarì*-blade must have tipped a lung because he had trouble breathing. In a few hours he reached the grove of mango trees.

He spread the *abaca* mat on the grass and laid down on it to wait for her. He felt the wind toss the grass around him like waves. He rested there as if floating on a boat at sea. In a few hours it would be light.

He woke to the sound of the low muffled rumble of a jeep engine, men's voices shouting. Summoning his will, he began walking up into the jungles of Mount Makiling, toward the faith healer's place. When he reached their place, high up in the hills, he could see down the stone-lava slopes and out into the vast dark bowl of Taal. He lay down and closed his eyes.

Now it's all coming true, he thought.

She arrived before dawn to look for him. She felt he must be nearby. She wandered the field and found the abaca mat, bloody. She lay on it as if it were a raft at sea, willing it to carry her to him. She looked up and saw the departing stars of Orion.

Soon she heard the noises and saw the lights from the nearest barrio. She hurried there through stands of coconut and banana trees. The people looked up as if she were a ghost.

"I'm looking for a man who was hurt nearby, a few hours ago," she said.

No one moved, no one seemed to understand her. Then one of the women went to get her son, a young man, brought him out of their house almost sleepwalking. The woman nodded at Rue, lifting her chin, indicating she should explain what she wanted.

"Just tell them I'm looking for a man, he's bleeding. Ask them, has anyone seen him?"

He told the people solemnly what she'd come for.

Some shook their heads, others just continued to stare at her as if she were a madwoman come out of the mango forest, a bad omen.

"They have seen nothing, I think, Ma'am," the boy finally said.

"Is there a clinic nearby?" she asked. Perhaps someone had found him and taken him there.

The boy smiled. "Nowhere near here. The closest is in Los Baños. But if you need someone there is a healer, he lives off by himself up high." The boy pointed toward the place she'd come from, beyond it, the jagged, cooling magma hills.

"I want to borrow a light," she said, using their words, "I want some people to search, he might be nearby, hurt."

The boy told them and the people looked at her doubtfully. They began to leave.

"I'll pay," she said, clinging to him. "I'll pay each person fifty, one hundred pesos."

This was understood, there was interest, there was a scramble for some wood from the fires, to be used like torches burning. They went with her. They walked through the grass following her back to the place. Perhaps it was not so much the money. They couldn't have believed she carried so much money. They just saw that she was desperate.

"He was here, see the mat is here," she said.

They looked at the tall grass which was pushed flat in places, looked at her, saw her wild eyes.

"Now just go in different directions and call his name, Doming Aquinaldo, and find him, look everywhere."

The boy translated. The light of their torches reflected in their solemn faces as if they were in a holy place. She stood there in the night and looked across the sky at Orion, the straight line of stars, receding. She saw the torches moving in the distance, forming patterns and then reshaping, like new constellations with their new stories. The voices of the young men and old women go out into the night, calling, not too loudly, Doming, Doming Aquinaldo.

Manila, August 21, 1983

It is early Sunday afternoon, August 21, 1983, nine months later.

At the Manila International Airport, a noble man in white barong and white trousers, purposely wearing the same clothes he'd worn when he left in exile three years and three months before, but now with a bullet-proof vest under his barong, is arriving on a China Air flight from Taipei. His forged passport says he is Marcial Bonifacio. Any airline that will transport him to the country will have its landing rights permanently denied, the government has announced. He has become that most difficult of men, an honest man who is unafraid. But when he calls his children in Boston, before the flight from Taipei, he cries when he hangs up. During descent, he grows quiet, ceases joking with the journalists who accompany him, and takes out a rosary. At 1:15 p.m.

ten thousand supporters have assembled here to welcome him. One thousand soldiers from the Metro-Command are in position around the airport and on the tarmac. The plane comes to a stop far away from the terminal and a set of stairs is brought to a side door. The door is opened. Several soldiers come into the plane and take him out into the piercing light of home.

Dead before his feet reach the tarmac. Within a few days a procession of millions from Santo Dominico Church in Manila will form along the road to his home in Tarlac to mourn him. The government newspapers will not mention his name, nor will any television station. Only Radio Veritas. Truth will always overcome the lie.

At the same moment, in the south of the country, rights for gold mining on ancient *Tiboli* lands in Mindanao are being bargained away during a game of golf on a private course near General Santos City. The buyer is an Australian mining company, the silent partner is the new general there.

In the northern Cordilleras, two villages, as old as the rice terraces around them, are burning. The Sixth Battalion claims this is where the New People's Army hides.

In Manila, at Malacañang Palace, Marcos is ill with kidney failure. They are looking for a match for another try at what will be a successful transplant that buys him a few more years. Imelda has rushed back to the palace from a six-course luncheon at a Chinese restaurant at one of her five-star hotels, in high spirits. Marcos throws his lunch tray of bland food at her, cursing.

Just south of Manila a future president is betting on a cockfight at the new air-conditioned pit in Batangas.

Near the Rice Institute, Sok and his son reap the first harvest of wild rice from old lines of seed Rue gave them, an heirloom rice variety his grandparents grew at the time of Rizal. His neighbors help. They will store these seeds of ancient lineage in clay pots left from the old times.

At the U.S. embassy, phone calls and cables go back and forth. A certainty there that it is possible to control the future, to set history spinning by doing nothing today, by not stopping what has been set in motion.

Trace has moved into an apartment in the city before moving on to work with Admiral Poindexter in Washington. Weapons are passing through the Philippines on their way to other countries. Marcos takes his kickbacks and a new general signs end-user certificates that satisfy the U.S. Congress for now.

Evil is always a kind of absence of action or words. There is no way that some people in the embassy do not know that Ninoy is flying into Manila this day. There is no way they do not understand that protection for him will arise from just some word from them. Do they consider allowing—insisting—that the plane land at Clarke Air Base? Perhaps the air tracking tower at Clarke is even shut down for the afternoon, so no pilot can radio to them for permission to land safely there.

They do nothing, nothing. Ninoy might close the U.S. bases. He might let Mindanao go back to the Muslims and up-country tribals. He would be soft on the NPA communists. This is not in the U.S.'s interests. It is more expedient not to act.

But north of Manila, a six-hundred-year-old dormant volcano overlooking Clarke Air Base, a volcano so old that no one even remembers its name, is again beginning to gather molten rock, deep under the earth. Pinatubo broods with ambition and anger. Taal, to the south, wills his brother his energy, his unfettered outrage.

Rue looked for Doming. She even hired a private investigator who looked for Doming Aquinaldo, but he was gone. There was no such name, there never had been, not in Negros or in the National Registry. The area in Cavite where he lived was bulldozed, a new factory going in as part of the new Free Trade Zone.

Once, she dreamed he came out of the water, he walked toward her and embraced her. He wore his jeans and a light shirt with the sleeves rolled up, as if he'd just arrived for a visit, bits of water weed hanging from his clothes.

Now in Makati Hospital, Metro Manila, in a dank room on the fifth floor, Celia, who has sat with Rue these last twelve hours, holds out her hands to catch the black-haired child. She calls to the doctor that the baby is coming, is coming.

A baby shining like a stone under clear lake water, mewing its first bewildered cry, is coming with the rush of water.

Two and a half years later, for three days in February, after Marcos tries and fails to steal the Snap Election, the people resurrect their country. They are reborn. Ninoy is their prince of peace. Soldiers are met with food and drink, given flowers, prayed over. Tanks are confronted by those who kneel in prayer. They become one. Men who didn't think they had any nobleness of spirit, possess it for those three days. Intrepid women take to the front lines and will not back down to threats of overwhelming force. For three days, one's birth status, province, economic standing, no longer matter. Young and old, *mestizas* and maids, nuns and priests from the provinces, pour into the city carrying banners of yellow, to be one of the millions forging a bridge across a chasm of evil.

The pictures the world sees are of a people who show how to resist violence, who use prayers and songs, story and hospitality, offering food from their pantries and flowers from their gardens to men who put down their weapons, crawl out of their tanks, and leave their planes.

Their leader for these three days is Ninoy. He lives there in spirit, the man in white, who said he believed in the great goodness of his people, that the Filipino people were worth dying for, that one day they would be an inspiration to the world.

Baby and Celia bring *pancit* noodles and even fried *lumpia* to the lines to share. They make a table from chicken crates and sit together. They stand on the front lines, arm in arm. They sleep curled round each other on *abaca* mats with their new neighbors on Edsa Boulevard.

You do forgive me, don't you, Celia? Baby asked, on the first night, when they heard the drone of gunship helicopters flying over the city. They held each other and wondered with the crowd if they would be alive in the morning.

Yes, Ma'am, don't you know that? She took Baby's hand, like when she was little.

Yes, I know you always love me, Baby said. Thank you, Celia. *Salamat, Pô*. Baby used the word of respect for an elder, *pô*, with Celia for the first time in thirty-five years.

Celia called Baby my daughter, *anák, my child*.

Celia and Baby and one million others prevailed over absolute evil, for those three days.

It seemed to Celia that after such a miraculous accomplishment the Filipino people together could do anything. If Baby's heart could swell up like this, with hope and reborn spirit, then anyone's could.

Epilogue

Eight years after Ninoy's assassination, on August 21, 1991, Rue received a letter from Celia, a letter mailed to the U.S. six weeks earlier in Manila—

> *Dear Ma'am, how is your boy? Give him eighth birthday greetings from his old godmother. A few days ago, Mt. Pinatubo burst open like an over-ripe fruit. All of Manila is covered with dust. It is the last of my priest's predictions. It is like snow, they say. But I believe it is the opposite, this ash, it glitters and bites, but this dusty ash is the weight of the ages falling on us. And they say only the highest roofs of the Clarke Base now show, like they are underwater. On that day, I thought I saw Doming, Ma'am, he was driving a jeepney named Glory round and round the church tower in Baclaran. Or perhaps I dreamed this.*

Celia's letter continued, *Ma'am, thank you for all the money, and I will say six Novenas for you and the boy in Baclaran. And Ma'am, I won't fly to the States yet for a visit. I don't believe in planes yet, that way.*

And Doming? He has found the shape of his own calling.

Imagine, like Rue does, that when he sings the mass, it is the song of Father Rex. When he plays with the children at his mission in the hills of the southwest coast of Mindanao, he hears the soft sounds of his mother's songs in the *Tiboli* language. When he brings them lunch, he smells the welcome rice like Celia used to make. Sometimes he takes them on the *banca* boat to fish, baiting the hook carefully with his one good hand, and when he sees down through the glassy water that turns clear as night turns to morning, before the sun begins to glare, he sees the blue starfish.

He looks up and sees the white trail of a jet's soundless passing, a white line reaching down in the blue, like his fishing line reaching into the blue water. Only once he reached up as if to grab on and climb up that white rope, hand over hand, back to her. Don't leave us, Father Doming, the children of the missing in Mindanao called out, and he felt his feet re-settle upon the blood-red earth.

He sees the great miracle of life. Their landscapes are growing back. Lush stretches abound on the southern and western coasts of Mindanao, once a moonscape. Even now in the gray lava earth of northern Luzon, in new ground five meters above Clarke Air Base, green tendrils wrap up from the ground, curling gracefully around the rusting top of a light pole.

One woman sent him forth to discern his own goodness, his name, and his calling. For that he is grateful. He is in the place of his birth and his vocation, serving and teaching. This is sufficient abundance.

Hope, more than evil, is the wonder, is what endures. Life *is* a grace, a greening gyre, and you were my conversation and grace. Look around, look, Rue, and I am here. Blessings upon you, *Rueda*. Center of my center.

And you? Say you arrive in Manila tonight, at Ninoy Aquino International Airport. The sky is aluminum gray, the orange sodium lights flare. The lush sweet smell is of fruit, quick decay, and green smoke.

Mindanao is burning. Mindanao is thrumming again with the beat of U.S. military helicopters, training drills, military aid–money and well–booted feet running the jungles, clearing the old tarmacs.

In Mindanao, the war drums beat again.

Does no one remember? Does history keep repeating itself in a rhyme? The average age of the population is fifteen years old now. There is no memory but your own. You are present. You are the witness. You hear the beat, smell the green fires burning.

Here, just outside the airport, you see the aged woman selling gray lottery tickets. She could be Angel.

Your taxi driver in the old yellow Toyota from Japan, reading a paperback book while he waits. He could be Paco.

The sullen woman you pass, who beckons, who stands on the corner waiting? She could be Paco's younger sister Linay.

She is Linay and her child is hungry. She will trade.